Enthrall Her

Enthrall Sessions

A Novel

Vanessa Fewings

FBI Anti-Piracy Warning: The unauthorized reproduction or distribution of a copyrighted work is illegal. Criminal copyright infringement, including infringement without monetary gain, is investigated by the FBI and is punishable by up to five years in federal prison and a fine of $250,000.

Advertencia Antipirateria del FBI: La reproducción o distribución no autorizada de una obra protegida por derechos de autor es ilegal. La infracción criminal de los derechos de autor, incluyendo la infracción sin lucro monetario, es investigada por el FBI y es castigable con pena de hasta cinco años en prisión federal y una multa de $250,000.

Enthrall Her
Copyright © 2014 Vanessa Fewings
All rights reserved. No part of this book may be used or reproduced in any manner whatsoever, including Internet usage, without written permission from the author.

This story is a work of fiction. References to real people, events, establishments, organizations, or locales are intended only to provide a sense of authenticity and are used fictitiously. All other characters, and all incidents and dialogue are drawn from the author's imagination and are not to be construed as real.

ISBN-10: 0-9912046-1-1
ISBN-13: 978-0-9912046-1-8

Cover design by VMK
Cover photo is from Shutterstock - Photographer rangizzz

Book formatted and edited by Louise Bohmer

For Anne Rice

Pioneer. Teacher. Advocate.

"Until you make the unconscious conscious, it will direct your life and you will call it fate."
                                         Carl Jung

v

CHAPTER 1

GIVING MY WRIST another pull, I tried to escape this handcuff securing me to the headboard of the four-poster. I'd been lying here for the last ten minutes, feeling a heavy mixture of arousal and frustration. Being restrained was doing crazy things to my body. My toes curled in anticipation.

Cameron Cole's signature style was all dark wooden furniture with understated elegant pieces like this bed, that corner high-back chair, that mahogany dresser over there, and a flat screen TV halfway up the wall.

Breaking my stare from the fine silver chain dangling above, taking in deep calming breaths, I returned my attention to the décor, replaying the words I'd practiced before I left Malibu. Words that would change my life forever. The kind that meant there'd be no going back.

This wasn't about securing your girlfriend to the bed as a precursor to a night of lovemaking. No, this was secure your best friend's girlfriend to the bed and hope she tells you what the hell she's doing here, dressed provocatively in a corset, high-top stockings, and a thong. My blonde locks were tussled to perfection and my makeup hid the fact I was only twenty-one. I'd gone for sex on a stick.

It was hard to tell from Cameron's expression if it was working. Casually, he leaned against the doorjamb, his tuxedo rounding out his usual look of perfection, tieless and with an open collar, hinting he might relax that fierce demeanor.

He sipped from a glass of dark amber liquor.

"Can you unlock this?" I said.

He shook his head.

These were his handcuffs and this was one of his many bedrooms in his million dollar Beverly Hills mansion. I trusted Cameron, really I did. How could I not? He was a respected psychiatrist and he'd also been the one to get me the job as secretary at Enthrall, L.A.'s elite S & M club. A place where the rich played out their darkest fantasies. Becoming Enthrall's secretary had seen financial freedom for me as well as placing me on a fast track to maturity.

I needed to know that look on Cameron's face wasn't fury.

Not that I wasn't used to that expression, and coming from one of the most handsome faces I'd ever seen it had the expected effect of stunning me into silence. It didn't help that his genius outshone his beauty.

Short black inky hair framed that intelligent face. A chestnut gaze saw beyond what you willingly shared. As the director of Enthrall, Cameron could hire and fire at will and he'd plucked me out of obscurity, only it wasn't my admin skills he'd been interested in but my innocence.

He'd used me to entice his best friend Richard Booth away from his obsessive thrill seeking. Richard thought nothing of swimming with sharks as a way to get his adrenaline fix. He faced off with danger and then gave it the finger.

Still, I adored my beautiful Richard. I hadn't known love until I'd met him. It was that love that had driven me here tonight. The willingness to do anything to save the most important relationship I'd ever had.

"Dr. Cole," I tried again, "you told me I could talk with you anytime."

"It's Cameron." He strolled on in, exuding dominance.

This was the kind of man you could tell anything to. Though I'd never want to disappoint him. Cameron set the bar so high that those around him could never reach it.

That familiar slow and steady walk, that ability to rule a room without speaking a word. It was impossible to drag my gaze away. This man left both men and women alike spinning. His laser-sharp perception ensured any outcome he desired. Yet his kindness, his ability to always know what to say and when, put you at ease and balanced out his intensity.

I wondered what it might be like to get inside Cameron's head. Turn the tables on him for a change. That ability of his to see the truth beneath the surface of avoidance was admirable. Cameron was a mystery. Surrounded by the city's most beautiful women, yet even after the several months I'd known him I'd never seen him with a lover. I'd merely witnessed swarms of ever hopeful submissives encircling him at parties. The lure of an impossible conquest.

Cameron perched on the edge of the bed and it dipped slightly. He was close. Too close. Close enough for me to get a whiff of his cologne that sparked every cell in my body.

He knew he was affecting me. I gave the handcuff another tug and it clanked its disapproval.

His lips curled in amusement. "Mia, if you ever enter any one of my properties uninvited again I will not be held responsible for my actions. Understand?"

I slid down the bed frame.

"Interesting response."

Focus, Mia, I warned myself. *Ask him. Say it. Go through with why you're here.*

A thrill tingled between my thighs as my imagination ran off with thoughts of what I might experience if I dared to go through with this. The dominatrixes at Enthrall, the ones I affectionately called the 'girls,' had told me Cameron could make a woman pass out from pleasure. I believed it. He was making me lightheaded with merely his presence.

With Cameron's laser-sharp perception, I didn't stand a chance. He was intoxicating. Any woman would be hard-pressed to refuse his advances if she were lucky enough to get his attention. He oozed raw sexuality. The get under your skin kind. The stun you into silence kind. Even the way he set his glass down on the side table reeked of control.

Light glinted off his onyx handcuffs.

"Next time, Mia," his tone was deep, cultured, "choose somewhere else to turn up in the middle of the night. Like Bailey's. That's what best friends are for."

"Bailey's out with Tara," I said. "It's her mom's birthday."

He picked up his drink and ice clinked. "Want a sip?"

I rested my lips against the glass where his had been and he tipped the tumbler. Bitterness burned my throat, sending a shiver through me. He reached in and removed a cube of ice and popped it into my mouth. I resisted the urge to nip at his fingers, grateful for the melting ice soothing this burn.

Cameron acted as though all this sensual tension was business as usual while placing the glass down squarely on the coaster, taking his time.

"Say what's on your mind," he said.

"Richard refuses to talk about it."

"It?"

"Me becoming his submissive."

Cameron narrowed his eyes. "He has mentioned his concerns."

Of course he had. Richard and Cameron were best friends. They told each other everything. Life had been going along perfectly well, my relationship blossoming, my trust solidifying, our intimacy progressing. It had been decided that I would become Richard's submissive. Days later my dream had been shattered.

Everything I'd known had been turned upside down when a family secret had reared its ugliness and caused my entire world to implode. A revelation so dark that it had sent me into a tailspin.

And Richard had changed his mind.

If there was one thing I knew how to do well it was survive. Though my ability to cope was apparently freaking out Richard. He'd expected something different, a crumbling victim of her circumstances. Richard didn't believe I could get over something so quick. Move on. You'd have thought I'd have received a standing ovation for my strength in leaving family trauma behind me, but no. Instead, Richard treated me like I was made of china.

These men were infamous for helping victims deal with their pasts. Using pain to banish pain. Not with me apparently. I was too broken even for them.

"Share your thoughts, Mia," said Cameron, shaking me from my daydreaming.

I didn't want to talk about any of that now. Didn't want my father's betrayal to encroach on this moment. Not after the courage I'd rallied to be here. I was alone in a room with the most incredible man I'd ever met, other than Richard of course, and Cameron was the one man who could save my relationship.

I needed to focus.

Not only was Cameron a master of conversation, he'd also conquered the art of silence. I wanted him to speak the words I couldn't say.

"How long have you lived here?" I said, slicing through the tension.

"I've owned this property awhile. I entertain here. My family's coming into town, so I need to prepare the house."

"To impress them?"

"They don't need impressing."

"The Venice Beach house is too small?"

"It's the location. Too many tourists."

"What about Chrysalis?" I cursed myself for sounding so stupid.

Cameron looked amused. "I can't have a naked gimp appear from nowhere and scare the hell out of my Great Aunt Rose, now can I?"

"That would not be good."

"That would be very bad." He flashed a mega-watt smile. "Very bad indeed."

Chrysalis was a fetish manor extraordinaire, visited from all over the world by rich clients who wanted to live out their fantasies. A place where L.A.'s finest partied to the extreme, with Cameron Cole as the grand master.

Maybe I really did need therapy. I wasn't going to let him into my mind, though. That was the promise I'd made to myself before stepping foot over the threshold of the grandest foyer I'd ever seen.

"Do you live here alone?"

"Let's talk about you—"

"Will your dad be coming too?" I sounded casual. "That will be nice."

"Why are you here, Mia? Straight to the point, please. It's late."

I could do this. I was ready. So I braced for the words I'd practiced to say.

"Mia," he coaxed.
"I want…"
"I'm listening."
I couldn't say it.
"Ah," he said darkly. "You want me to teach you how to become a good submissive."

CHAPTER 2

CAMERON GAVE A subtle shake of his head.

He shrugged out of his jacket and threw it over the high-backed chair and strolled around to the other side of the bed. Climbing on it, he lay beside me, resting his head on a fluffed up pillow and stretching his long legs out.

He texted away on his BlackBerry. I assumed he was letting Richard know I was here.

"You're angry?" I said softly.

"I'm not angry." He followed it with a smile.

It was as though we'd never even shared a kiss. That first physical contact I'd had with him in Enthrall's dungeon. That intimate moment wasn't meant for us. He'd merely seduced me for the sole purpose of giving me over to Richard.

At first I'd found Cameron's ways a little scary, unconventional even, though as I'd gotten to know him his matchmaking skills took on an endearing quality. It was only when days, or weeks, had passed that truth spilled like rain on a stormy day, clearing the view and allowing for retrospect. Cameron had flirted with me in hope of stirring Richard's interest. It had never been about what Cameron wanted. He'd shown no real interest in me other than that. I was merely a plaything. Which made it all the safer to fantasize about him. Not only was this man out of my league, he was in his own words a connoisseur of the dark arts, and known as the ultimate master of BDSM.

As the heady thrill of adventure settled, there came relief

he'd turned me down. What the hell had I been thinking?

Cameron tucked his phone away in a pocket. "Get under the covers." He squeezed his eyes shut. "Get some sleep."

I'd not realized how cold I'd gotten as I pulled the comforter over me. My chilled flesh welcomed the warmth. Cameron leaned over and tucked me in. That small gesture made me feel safe.

"Promise not to wonder off?" he asked.

"I promise."

He reached over, freeing my wrist from the cuff. He caressed where the metal had chafed my wrist, his fingertips massaging the redness and easing the soreness. I snuggled down in the bed and the sensation of his strokes helped me drift asleep.

Those nightmares didn't find me here.

Gentle fingers trailing through my hair woke me. I blinked awake to see Richard sitting beside me on the edge of the bed.

"Hey," he said.

His golden blond locks were disheveled. That handsome tanned face showed the tension that had risen between us. Doubt etched in those ocean blue eyes had become the norm. His ripped designer jeans and T-shirt hinted he'd come here in a hurry.

Cameron was still here. He sat with his back up against the headboard, looking back at Richard.

I braced myself for the argument.

"Maybe I'll take a leaf out of Cameron's book and start cuffing you to the bed."

"How was the drive over?" asked Cameron.

"No traffic." Richard took in my corset and then shot a concerned look at Cameron.

Judging from Cameron's arched brow, he and Richard were sharing a thought, that silent way of communicating I'd come to know.

Richard eased the covers down and trailed his fingertips over the bust of my corset. "You wore this the first time I took you into the dungeon."

"I remember." I blushed, wishing he hadn't mentioned it in front of Cameron.

"I like it on you."

"That was the last time…"

"We had an agreement," said Richard. "You broke it."

"You promised you'd resume my training." I raised my chin defiantly. "You went back on your promise."

"Your training's on hold," he snapped.

"Why?" I snapped back.

"We're on your second therapist. And you refuse to talk to this one too."

"I'm not discussing this now."

"No, Mia, we are talking about it," said Richard.

"It's boring," I said. "Anyway, the therapists do all the talking."

"Talk to us now," said Richard.

I was sure he'd regret those words. "You waited three days to tell me. Three days after you found out my dad was alive."

"Before that day, you were so happy," said Richard. "I was reluctant to shatter your world—"

"You had no right to wait."

"I know I fucked up."

I pushed myself up the headboard. "You knew all that time."

"You're right. I have no real defense other than my need for you to be happy."

"If Scarlet hadn't given me that file, the one where you spied on my past, none of this would have come out."

Cameron rolled onto his side to face us and rested his head on his palm. "It's called a background check, Mia. My investigator followed a lead. That's what I pay him for. There was nothing sinister about the process—"

"No, the only sinister aspect is my father."

"It's good we're talking about Napa," said Richard.

"They have great vineyards." I glanced at Cameron. "That's about it."

"I was selfish not telling you as soon as I found out," admitted Richard. "I knew it would change the dynamics between us."

His words were a blow to my heart.

"You're both tired," said Cameron. "You're both welcome to stay here."

I pulled the comforter over me. "I don't need therapy."

"Let's talk about that," said Cameron.

"Let's not," I countered.

Cameron sat up, looking all business, poised to take back control. "Firstly, you are a remarkably well adjusted, mentally stable young woman. The only reason we believe therapy may help is because of the signs of stress you've exhibited lately."

"Baby, you've lost weight," said Richard. "You're not eating properly."

"My appetite has been a little off. But that's happiness."

"You're argumentative," said Richard.

I shrugged. "I have my opinion. I like to share it."

"How can your father's betrayal not affect you?" said Richard.

"I'm over it."

Richard looked over at Cameron.

"Dr. Lucy Raul is a great therapist," said Cameron. "Now, if you're not connecting with her either—"

"Why can't you be my therapist?" I said. "You're Richard's, and you're his friend."

"Unique circumstances," said Cameron.

"Mia, you've been unsettled since Napa," said Richard. "Since you saw your father—"

"My dad's dead. At least he wants us to believe that."

"Well he now knows you know that he's very much alive," said Cameron. "Perhaps I could set up a meeting?"

"Don't you dare."

Richard looked shocked.

"Sorry," I said.

Cameron's laser focus zeroed in on me. "You're doing well. Keep talking."

"He might as well be dead. He faked his death so he could start a new life with a new wife." I pulled my hand out of Richard's grasp. "I'm fine. Therapy is like muddying the water. It's a luxury for the rich."

"You're so disagreeable," said Richard.

"Why stir all that crap up?"

"It's more about clearing the air," said Cameron.

"Richard, it's not you I'm upset with," I said. "It's me for trusting you."

Richard looked hurt, and I felt terrible and wanted to take it back.

"Immersing yourself in our specific lifestyle centers around trust," said Cameron quietly.

"Richard, that first session made me feel so close to you," I said.

"You merely got your feet wet," said Richard. "Other than trespassing into Chrysalis, you've never truly been exposed to what it is we practice."

"What about the dungeon? You took me through a session there."

Richard looked sympathetic. "Light spanking."

Cameron gave a nod. "What we're trying to establish is your understanding of the psychological aspect of BDSM, which is intense. We're talking about establishing trust before one becomes a submissive."

"I'm stable. You just confirmed it."

"Yes, you are, but you don't trust us," said Richard. "You said it yourself."

"You have to earn trust," I muttered.

"I should have told you immediately about your father," said Richard. "I was trying to protect you. I love and care about you. What more do I have to do to earn your trust back?"

"Make me part of your lifestyle."

Richard glanced over at Cameron. "We could use drastic measures?"

"What measures?" I said.

Richard ignored me and kept his focus on Cameron. "A master's expertise."

My toes curled in anticipation.

"You've got this," whispered Cameron to him. "I think it's only fair to give her what she's asking for. Start slow."

Richard turned back to me. "Mia, first I need you to open up to me."

I folded my arms across my chest.

"So that's a no then? That's your answer?"

"Richard tells me you're having nightmares?" said Cameron.

I tried to push my latest night terror from my mind, a foggy memory of me on a boat, drifting out to sea and away from Richard, away from Cameron. The only two men who had ever taken the time to know me. *Love me.*

Other than Bailey, I'd never felt such a connection. A feeling of belonging.

"We should explore your dreams," said Cameron. "Mention them to Dr.—"

"You banned me from Chrysalis." I shot him an accusatory stare.

"I fucking hate chaos," snapped Richard.

Cameron gestured to calm him. "Let's get back to your father, Mia. Richard has a point. We need to establish you're in recovery from this event before—"

"It's like there's a tidal wave behind my words," I said. "What if I start crying and never stop? I don't want my past to have that kind of power over me."

"It's best to open up and get it behind you, baby," said Richard. "You'll feel better for it."

"Does my pain scare you that much?" I said.

He looked away. "I want what's best for you."

"You're what's best for me." I took his hand and squeezed it. "You're scared you might break me even more, is that it?"

"How could I live with myself?" he whispered.

"You think I'm like Emily? You think I'm not strong enough."

Richard dragged his fingers through his hair. He looked tired, worn down, as though this battle raging within was winning.

I swallowed hard. "Richard?"

"Yes," he said quietly. "Like Emily."

Bringing up his dead ex-fiancé was a low blow, but no crueler than refusing to give me the healing I needed. Emily, his lost love who he had lived with in New York. Emily, the elegant socialite who had slit her wrists when Richard's father's financial scandal had touched her family.

Cameron slid off the bed and stretched. "It's time you two had a real talk. You both have to trust each other with your feelings. Push fear aside and share your concerns. It's time you moved forward together."

Richard stared down at his hands, his brow furrowed.

He still loves her.

"Stay here tonight," said Cameron. "Get some sleep. Things are always easier to cope with in the morning."

He closed the door behind him.

Richard unbuttoned his shirt, taking his time to undress. His eyes averted from mine. I rolled onto my side, not wanting to see the memory of Emily in his eyes.

Not wanting to see we weren't going to make it.

CHAPTER 3

THE SOUND OF running water stirred me awake.

Sitting on the edge of the mattress, I took in Cameron's bedroom again. His jacket was still lying across the back of that high-backed chair.

Red rose petals lay at my feel and trailed off towards the bathroom. I climbed out of bed and padded across the hardwood floor, following them.

The bath was full of water and foamy bubbles frothed. A few rose petals had been scattered upon the soap suds. Several candles were lit, their flames throwing shadows on dark green walls. With the blinds still drawn, it would be easy to forget it was dawn.

Richard sat below the window with his back pressed against the wall. "Good morning."

I knelt at his feet and leaned into him, wrapping my arms around his neck and nuzzling close.

"I ran a bath for you." He rose and pulled me up with him. He twirled his finger for me to turn around and tugged at the strings of the corset to free me. "Who helped you into this?"

"I tightened it and turned it around," I said.

"Sounds like a neat party trick." He loosened the corset enough for him to ease it up and over my head. It didn't take him long to remove my stockings and panties too.

"Did you bring a change of clothes?" he asked.

"Yes, they're in my car." I turned around and took in his beautiful face that looked so worn. "Did you sleep?"

"A little." His hand swept through my hair. "God you're beautiful. You've been so knocked about by life it really has blinded you to how hauntingly gorgeous you are."

Stepping forward, I buried my face against his chest, wooed by his words and wanting to believe them. "I came here to ask Cameron—"

"I understand."

"No, listen." I looked up at him. "I wanted Cameron to reassure you I am ready to be your sub."

"Dressed like that?"

"I thought it would get his attention."

"Oh, you got his attention."

"I wanted him to show me how to please you."

"You do please me. It's not about that." He gestured to the bath. "Get in. I'll bathe you and we'll talk."

"Nothing happened."

"I know," he said gently. "It's my fault you're here. I know you felt you had no choice."

"You've just been hard to talk to lately."

"I admit it." He gestured to the tub again. "I've been working through something."

"You once told me we couldn't be together if the dynamics of our relationship wasn't me as your sub."

"I was an arrogant ass." He nudged me forward. "In."

Dipping my foot into the hot water felt good, so welcoming.

He took hold of my forearm and guided me in and I sunk into the water. Stretching my legs out, my body disappeared beneath white bubbles frothing around me.

Richard eased my long hair away from my neck, pulling it over the back of the tub so it wouldn't get wet. His fingers running through it made my scalp tingle, and it soothed me.

He reached for a bottle of soap and squirted a musky scented liquid onto a golden sponge and brought it up and across my throat, trailing it down and around my breasts. I let out the softest sigh. The dark, luring scent filled my nostrils and made me feel heady, along with the pleasure of being bathed. It wasn't just where that sponge might migrate that was turning me on. The aroma was dreamy.

"I've been thinking," Richard said softly. "About my

lifestyle and what it means to us."

"I so want to be part of it," I said. "I like it."

"Hear me out, Mia." His frown deepened. "I know we shouldn't talk about past loves, but for this purpose we need to."

Cameron's bathroom was luxurious. White tiles and gold covered faucets. The room was almost as big as my old studio apartment.

"Mia?"

Reluctantly, I snapped back to him.

"Emily wasn't into it. She hated the idea of any kind of pain connected to sex."

"Even though it's cathartic?"

He shot me a look of sympathy, as though sensing I wasn't getting where he was coming from. This seemed hard for him too, and the sooner it was out the better it would be for both of us.

He swept the sponge across my belly, moving in circles. "I loved her completely. So much so that I was willing to change. Be anything she wanted me to be."

"What did she want you to be?"

"Normal."

I too had asked Richard to pull back on his involvement with *the* scene. I'd even gone as far as asking him not to take part in his regular duties as one of Chrysalis's senior dominants. I regretted that now.

"I turned vanilla for her." Richard squirted more soap onto the sponge.

I gripped his forearm, hoping he'd read from me the words I wasn't ready to say. The need for me to be taken, dominated, mastered, enslaved. Richard had awoken within me a need so deep that I marveled I had never known that part existed until he'd roused it that evening in Enthrall. That night he'd taken me into the depths of the club and brought more pleasure then I had ever known.

"I love you," said Richard, shaking me from my daydreaming. "You've already been through too much to endure any more mishandling."

"What are you saying?"

"Mia, you came to work for us at Enthrall. We took

advantage of your innocence and brought you into our world when you probably would never have considered living this scene."

"I'm glad I found it."

Or had the scene found me?

Either way, I found it exciting and had grown to desire it completely. The enthralling intimacy shared between master and sub had an addictive intensity. And there was still the lure of Chrysalis. That sprawling manor nestled amongst the hills of Bel Air.

"What are you thinking?" asked Richard.

"Nothing."

He peered beneath blond lashes. "You never had the chance to explore a real relationship with a man who is gentle and loving—"

"You're gentle and loving."

"Yes, but I also have an inclination to do very bad things to you."

I swooned with the thought. "I want that."

"No, Mia. Look, we've swept you up into our world and quite frankly you don't belong."

"What are you saying?" I reached for his arm.

"It's my job to protect you. Even if it means protecting you from me."

"But Richard—"

"I've given this a great deal of thought."

My head spun into a panic. "But I—"

"I'm going to give it up."

Or was it the room spinning? It was hard to tell. Richard threatening to deny his natural urges went beyond his promise to protect me. He'd be living a lie.

"My love for you goes so deep," he said. "You're my oxygen, Mia. If I ever hurt you, I would never forgive myself."

Sinking lower, water whooshed around me and bubbles spilled as I recalled the day he'd taken me to Hsi Lai Temple. We'd sat opposite each other sipping tea in the small corner café and he'd shared the story of how his father had betrayed the family in a crooked financial scheme. The incident had brought shame. The fallout forced Richard into hiding and he had dropped his last name, Sheppard.

We'd both been dealt a cruel hand. Only Richard had survived his, guided through the healing process by Cameron. A remarkable feat by a talented therapist. Though Cameron's unusual techniques were never discussed. Nor would they ever be, apparently.

The very reason I'd come here.

This misunderstanding was forcing a fracture in a perfect relationship. The trust we once shared was an illusion.

"I like it when you spank me," I whispered.

"Spanking leads to darker exploits." He brushed a strand of hair out of my eyes. "It triggers something in me."

"Which I want to explore."

"No, Mia. It's best it remains dormant." He swept the sponge between my thighs and I arched my back, pushing my breasts out of the water, my nipples hardening.

"I can still fuck you hard, baby."

But it's not enough.

It will never be enough. Not now. Not after he's shown me what ecstasy is.

"But you need it," I said. "You find solace in it."

"I find solace in you."

He moved the sponge languidly between my thighs. Widening my legs, I moaned my pleasure. Gripping the edge of the bath, I lost my will to speak.

"I'll do anything to protect you," he said. "Keep you from danger."

My head fell back and I stared up at the ceiling. The truth seemed to seep out of those dark green walls as I realized he feared I was as vulnerable as Emily. His lost love he'd been destined to marry. Emily, who bled out from her wrists after slicing through them with a razorblade. Emily, who he'd found dead in the bath—

I scrambled to get out, knocking his hand away then staggering from the bath.

"Mia?" Richard reached for me.

My feet slipped on the tile. Righting myself, I stumbled forward, reaching for the door handle. Naked and still covered in soap suds, I burst into the bedroom.

And jolted to a stop—

Cameron stood inside the door.

His gaze rose from the screen of his phone and locked on me. "Breakfast?" he said calmly.

I wrapped my arms around myself in a futile attempt to cover up.

The warmth of a towel enveloped me.

"Mia, what's wrong?" said Richard, pulling me back towards him. "Did I say something to upset you?"

"Mia?" said Cameron, his tone deep.

I gestured to the bathroom, but I couldn't say her name.

Cameron took in the scattered petals. "Looks romantic."

"I fucked up," said Richard.

"I don't see how," said Cameron.

"I'm such an idiot."

Cameron tucked his phone into his pants pocket. "Well, Mia?"

I swallowed hard, feeling the terrible awkwardness, and said timidly, "Emily died in the bath."

Cameron frowned. "Richard had nothing to do with that."

"No, but—"

"Then apologize," said Cameron.

"She doesn't need to apologize," said Richard. "It's my fault."

"Sorry," I said. "My mind kind of ran off."

"It's my fault." Richard gave a nod. "I wanted to create a new memory. I thought it would help push out the old one."

"Marvelous idea," said Cameron. "Maybe next time share the plan. Look, I have to go into work. I have a patient waiting for me in the ER. He's had a psychotic break, according to the resident." He arched a brow. "Looks like a current theme."

"We're fine." Richard gestured this was all some big misunderstanding.

"Mia?" asked Cameron. "You okay?"

I gave a shrug. "I overreacted."

"I agree. Get back in the bath," he said.

I stepped back, but he quickly closed the gap between us.

"This moment is evidently not for you," said Cameron. "Richard is working through something. Be patient with him.

Give him what he needs."

Despite Cameron being set on using this moment to help his best friend, my uncertainty grew. I glared at Cameron for his misplaced encouragement. "I'd rather take a shower," I said.

"Of course," said Richard.

"Richard says he's giving up the lifestyle," I burst out.

Cameron gave a nod. "Whatever makes him happy."

"You won't change my mind," said Richard.

"Your happiness has always been of the highest importance to me," said Cameron. "You know that."

"I have your support then?"

"Are you giving it up for you or her?" asked Cameron.

"She's so fragile."

"I disagree." Cameron leaned towards me and reached for my towel. He grabbed a corner and pulled it off.

Naked again, I relaxed and dropped my arms to my side. A sense of freedom flooded me. No more hiding.

"Cole," said Richard. "That's meant to serve as your support?"

My nipples hardened in response to the sudden chill.

Cameron's eyes remained on mine. "I agree she's defiant. Nothing you can't handle."

Richard's passionate glare swept over me as though fighting his primal need. His inner struggle caused his jaw muscles to flex.

"What are your thoughts when you look at her?" asked Cameron softly. "At her naked flesh. Flesh that needs the hand of a master. She goes right into subspace. The sign of the perfect sub."

"Maybe you're reading her wrong," whispered Richard.

Cameron looked stone-faced. "Arms by your side, Mia."

My arms settled at my sides, leaving me vulnerable, trembling. *Aroused.*

"She needs to be nurtured," said Cameron. "A firm hand. She needs to learn to trust again."

"Exactly," said Richard. "Upon that we agree. But is our way the right way?"

"For her it is." Cameron folded his arms. "This conversation should not be happening in front of your sub."

Richard ran his fingers through his hair.

"You desire amongst all things to worship her," said Cameron.

"Of course."

"Control her."

"Always. But I've made my decision."

"Richard, how else are you are going to shed your burden of selfhood?" said Cameron. "The one true therapy."

I snapped out of my self-consciousness and tuned into Cameron's words.

He frowned at me. "I won't ask you again, Mia."

My arms had once more wrapped around my chest to cover my breasts. I dropped them to my side, feeling the chill of nakedness. The scent of expensive body wash rose off my wet skin. The scent of Cameron, and it was doing crazy things to my senses.

Standing there in that dark tailored suit, white shirt open, tie hanging lose, Cameron was too much. It was all I could do not to fall at his feet. Dare to be in his presence. He oozed the kind of power that debilitated.

He was intoxicating.

Richard was meant to be my master, yet I couldn't take my eyes off Cameron. My betrayal felt dreadful. A familiar angst welled within once more. Staring at the floor, I feared either one of them might catch me pining after this man who ruled the room with intensity.

He'll ruin you, warned my muse. *Consume you.*

"Relax, Mia," cooed Cameron. "That's better."

I shot him a look to warn him he was having no effect.

He saw through my lie. "Eye contact represents defiance. You're not defying me, are you?"

"No, Sir," I said.

"She's too fragile for this," whispered Richard.

"I disagree," said Cameron. "Mia needs firm handling. Anything less would be an injustice. On your knees, Mia."

I dropped before him with my head bowed low and waited eagerly for my next command. This throbbing between my legs intensified, this subspace promised freedom.

"You're intimidating her," whispered Richard.

I raised my head, ready to pronounce he wasn't. "I need—"

"Silence," said Cameron. "I know what you need."

"What if you're wrong?" said Richard. "What if we take her too far?"

"I'm more concerned you're not willing to take her far enough," said Cameron. He sunk to his knees beside me and ran his fingers through my hair. "Every part of her is yearning for this."

Eyes closed, I leaned into Cameron's chest and snuggled against him, his firmness. The sensation of his fingertips tracing along my scalp caused me to swoon.

"Can't you see it in her?" Cameron rested his hand on my lower spine and his palm pressed against my skin. "She's ready to blossom. We must ensure she flourishes. Reaches her potential." Cameron lifted my chin. "Ease her into it."

"I want this," I said. "I need this."

"Did I give you permission to speak?" asked Cameron.

I bowed my head again. Just the tone of Cameron's voice sent me reeling.

Cameron rose to his feet and pointed at Richard. "Make a decision."

I tried to wrap my head around what was being insinuated. My heart thundered.

Richard stepped back. "She has no idea about what happens at Chrysalis."

"She saw it when she trespassed into the place. She witnessed Ruth's ceremony."

All I'd seen was some pretty girl with a mask on being taken by two men on a table. A public fucking in the Harrington Suite. I wondered if I'd get the chance to meet Ruth and talk to her about that night and ask her whether she'd enjoyed being watched by so many people as much as she'd seemed to.

"Well, Cole, what do you suggest?" Richard sounded defeated.

"It's fine to take her to Chrysalis. She's ready now that she's had several sessions with you. Her innocence will be a boon to the other members."

Richard swept his hand through his golden locks.

Cameron shook his head in frustration. "Richard, you're the

one who came up with half the entertainment ideas at Chrysalis." Cameron smiled his insistence. "She doesn't need to be penetrated."

It was like he was talking about a fricken racehorse and not the girl subjugated at his feet.

"I've never taken anyone I've loved to Chrysalis," said Richard. "She's different."

"That's why I gave her to you."

My eyes widened at that.

"Mia," said Cameron. "Up."

I turned to Richard for approval.

"Now," snapped Cameron.

I pushed myself to my feet as elegantly as possible.

"Get back in the bath," he said. "Richard, get in with her."

I tried to read Richard's reaction.

"Get back in the bath, Mia," said Richard through gritted teeth.

After a flutter of excitement, I swooned at his fierceness. The old Richard was back and taking the lead. A reward of pleasure awaited on the other side of that austerity. Cameron had finally gotten through.

"Can I be assured you will continue to lead her with a firm hand?" said Cameron.

Richard looked away.

Goose bumps rose on my body. I was chilled from standing naked too long. Half in a daze, I brought my arms up to cover myself again. Cameron caught it and reacted with a glare.

A threat of the punishment I need.

Delirious from his dominance, I relaxed a little, feeling safe as I gave the softest sigh. I grew lightheaded from this rush.

Richard's words went unspoken and the corners of his eyes wrinkled in confusion. He didn't want me. That's what I read from his ocean blue gaze. Richard wanted a primed submissive. Someone knowledgeable of what would please him.

All I saw was disapproval.

Shame found me in this space that I had no right to be in and disillusionment soaked deep into my bones, causing me to tremble.

I will never be good enough.

"Richard?" Cameron gestured to get his attention.

Richard shrugged.

"I'm taking a fucking shower." Scurrying back into the bathroom, I slammed the door.

I pulled the plug in the bath.

"I told you she's not ready." Richard's voice carried.

"She's never been more ready," Cameron raised his voice so I could hear. "Now get your sub under control before I do."

I stepped into the shower and turned on the faucet. Pressing my cheek against the glass door, I reeled from Cameron's fingers caressing my scalp, which still tingled. He'd sent a shiver of anticipation up my spine. A shiver of foreboding.

CHAPTER 4

HOLDING MY HEAD under the enormous shower faucet, I left the world outside and Cameron and Richard in the other room.

Lashing out at two testosterone fueled alpha-males wasn't one of my better decisions. But then again over these last few weeks I hadn't exactly been clear headed. The revelation about my dad had left me spiraling, and it was only now, after seeing the reflection of my pain in Richard's eyes, that I admitted it was affecting me. My appetite had gone and my self-worth had taken a nose dive.

The only saving grace was Enthrall. The one place where judgment was left at the door and the pathway to forgetting waited inside.

Despite pretending not to notice, I could see Richard through the veil of steam. He gathered the strewn rose petals from the floor and picked out the rest from the tub and discarded them unceremoniously in the trash. He ambled over towards the shower door and splayed his hands on the glass.

Resting his head against his arm, he looked like the ultimate Adonis, a suntanned statue, eyelids heavy, his expression intense, his thoughts all-consuming.

Massaging my scalp with shampoo, I ignored him. The stuff smelled heavenly. Smelled like *him*.

"You not talking to me could be considered a benefit," Richard called through the glass. "Am I still your fucked up bastard?"

"Yes."

He beamed at me. "Cameron told me to grow a pair. That was a first."

"You've been very out of character lately," I said. "You're an adrenaline junkie famous for chasing danger."

"True again. Looks like you're on a roll." His lip curled seductively.

"I'm rather proud of how well I've handled all life has thrown my way. I only wish you could see it."

"Can I get in there with you?"

"No, because you'll render me speechless with your carnal tricks and we're talking right now. This is a good thing."

"So mature for one so young." He snapped his fingers. "Don't even think of a witty reply."

"How did you know I was going to say anything?"

"You have that mischievous look." He pulled his shirt over his head and hopped out of his pants.

His erection rose out of blond curls. Merely the sight of my soaped up nakedness had spurred him into action.

"Has Cameron gone?" I said.

"Yes, so you can relax."

"Did you talk about why I came here?"

"Let's take a rain check on this." He opened the door.

I slammed it shut in his face. "What are you afraid of?"

"Hey, I may be delaying your training, but don't think I won't punish you for insolence."

I stepped back, allowing him to join me. "Isn't that the same thing?"

"No." He shoved open the door and stepped in, raising his face to the cascading water. It poured over his head and down his body, shimmering off him. My hand found its way to his chest and I ran my fingers over lean muscle.

God he is gorgeous.

Trying to maintain eye contact was a struggle, and by his grin he knew it too. That hefty erection was vying for my attention and promising all kinds of bliss. My nipples hardened with the thought of it.

He massaged soap into my scalp, the heavenly sensation relaxing me. Again that smile, that bite of his lower lip, as his hand left my head and reached between my thighs, running along my cleft. "Baby, you are so ready for me."

I moaned my answer.

He caught my wrists and held them above my head. "I want to hide you away. Keep you all to myself." He raised my arms higher and pressed my wrists against the glass with his left hand and with his right caressed my breasts, running his palm over pointed nipples, tweaking and punishing, and they responded to his touch.

"I've been waiting hours for this." He shifted closer and reached around to grab hold of my buttocks. With one swift movement, he lifted me up and forced me against the glass. I wrapped my legs around his waist. With one shove he was inside, stretching me wide, his girth causing ripples of tight pleasure.

"See, I know what you need," he soothed.

Holding my breath, I took these few seconds of stillness to get used to this position. Gripping onto him, I relaxed my inner muscles, allowing him to push deeper.

"Mia, you're not ready for anything more. Say it."

"I'm not ready," I relented.

He swirled his hips. "Looks like we finally agree on something."

I dug my fingernails farther into his back, my sex throbbing from his slow, steady thrusts, and as though hearing my silent wish he increased his pace, pounding me against the glass.

"I need you," I said.

"I'll always be here for you," he said hoarsely. "Always."

"I need more."

He pulled back to look at me, his eyes ablaze. "Then take all of me."

Richard pushed deeper, grinding mercilessly.

It was hard to argue with a man who was on the verge of making me come. Resting my head on his shoulder, I gave in to this well earned pummeling. His pelvis slammed against mine and forced gasps from me as my thighs clung tight around his waist, shuddering with tension.

Richard whispered, "It's vanilla or nothing, baby." His grip tightened.

"But I—"

"One more word about this and I will fire you from Enthrall."

My orgasm tore a scream from me. I dragged my nails along his back and it fired his passion, driving him on, and I feared the glass might shatter. Flesh slapped against flesh as my butt whacked the panel again and again.

I bit into his shoulder, hard.

"I can still give you what you need," he said.

Never had he ridden me so violently. But it wasn't enough. I needed more. I yearned to have Richard rip out this torment from within me.

Know me.

Heal me.

Save me.

Richard was right there yet he still couldn't get to it. Couldn't see it. This unnamed agony that had made a home for itself. A well burrowed misery from my past. My hero was turning away, thinking he was doing the right thing, yet all I felt was abandoned.

Richard stilled and his warmth filled me, sending me over the edge again. Shuddering, I was speared too completely to move.

All power was lost.

CHAPTER 5

THE CARP POND reflected Enthrall's serenity.

This private and very exclusive BDSM club was tucked away on a hill in Pacific Palisades.

Enthrall's well-tended garden behind the property was my frequent sanctuary. I liked to visit here during my lunch break and sometimes after work too. Today, I shared this calm corner of L.A. with Juan the gardener.

He balanced on a tall ladder that he'd leaned against one of the palm trees at the end of the garden. Juan was pruning the dried up fronds by hand. I'd brought him down a bottle of water and then took my usual seat on the bench overlooking the pond.

Sipping my morning coffee, my attention fell on the carp. They'd settled back to swimming now after all gathering at the edge, seemingly happy to see me, all pretending that Juan hadn't just fed them.

I took advantage of the quiet to process last night's visit to Cameron's home, and this morning's lovemaking with Richard in the shower. After he had firmly shut down any further discussion, he'd spent the rest of our time under the water lavishing me with affection, massaging conditioner into my hair and washing off all evidence of our lust filled tryst. Kiss after kiss let me know he really wanted the best for me. We returned to Malibu and had quickly gotten ready for our day. We'd driven to work together, stopping off at Diane's Coffee Shop for breakfast.

Honoring Richard's wish, I'd not mentioned last night, and

he'd acted like it had never happened. The irony was not lost on me that the assistant director of Enthrall was giving up the scene. For me, no less. And for all the wrong reasons. He'd made it quite clear that should I broach the subject again I'd be out of a job. Considering we now lived together, that would be an interesting scenario. If Richard didn't change his mind there was no doubt my failure to live up to what he wanted in a girlfriend would be a deathblow to our relationship.

A chill caused goose bumps to rise on my arms.

Feeling Richard's stare on my back, I turned slightly and peered up at his office window. With a curl of his index finger, he summoned me to his office.

Enthrall was one of the most high end club's in the world. Having never been in any other, I took the word of the dominatrixes on that. This luxury interior hosted two floors. On the lower level were the artfully designed dungeons and the upper floor hosted the grandly decorated offices, a well decked out coffee room, and even a full-service spa. Clients were only allowed in there with their dom's permission. My spot was an elegant desk at the end of the long entryway where I welcomed guests and served as the executive assistant. The salary still blew my mind. I wasn't only being rewarded for my clerical skills but my discretion too. Enthrall's clients were the high end kind.

Richard, my beautiful and consistently bossy boss, had the biggest and best office. I loved nothing more than stealing a few minutes to lounge with him on his long leather couch. Him giving me a foot rub was a fricken awesome way to start my day. I loved my job.

"What were you thinking about down there?" He arched a brow.

"Just like watching the carp," I said, throwing my head back. "It's relaxing. So is this." He'd lulled me, worked out the tension, his fingers pressing into the ball of my left foot. "Shouldn't I be massaging you?"

"Good point." He looked astonished. "Seems like my little minx has put a spell on me."

"It worked!" I beamed back at him.

"What's in that box in the front office?" he said.

"A surprise."

"I hate surprises."

"You'll like this one." My eyelids became heavy. Seriously, I could get used to this, but something told me a foot rub was his way of making sure everything was still good between us. He really did have a gentle way about him.

"Who discovered massage?" I said. "The Chinese?"

He looked thoughtful. "Apparently the earliest evidence of massage was found in The Tomb of the Physician in Egypt in BC2330."

"Well, what else would they be doing?" I said. "Apart from building pyramids."

"Mummifying their pesky girlfriends."

"Very funny. How do you know all this stuff?"

"Because unlike you I don't consider Facebook the equivalent of reading a book."

"That's mean."

"And yet true." He gave a nod. "That Kindle of yours won't work unless you take it out of the box and charge it."

The only reason I'd not opened it was because being given gifts made me uncomfortable. I'd had to work my butt off just to survive and kindness made me suspicious. I wasn't going to share that though.

"Talking of Facebook," I said. "Did you hack my account?"

"Your password is next to the computer."

"Still, you deleted photos of us. Why?"

"Please don't post photos of us together, Mia. You know how serious I am about privacy."

I tried to read from his face if that was the truth or perhaps I embarrassed him. "You had no right."

"I have every right to take down photos that put you in danger. You know my father's dubious history puts me at risk, and that in turn—"

"My page is set to private."

"Trust me, nothing is private," he said. "It would take seconds to access your account if someone wanted to."

"What's the point in having a code?"

He looked towards the door. "Next!" he mimicked, summoning someone else to deliver a foot rub to.

"Hey," I said in mock surprise.

Richard laughed. "Your annual foot rub is over."

"You do realize this could be considered sexual harassment?"

"Really?" He sat up and leaned forwards and planted a kiss on my cheek. "Then what I wonder could this be considered?" He cupped my chin. "Or this?" He pressed his lips to mine and gave me a long, leisurely kiss, his tongue languidly lavishing affection.

Richard peeled my hands off his butt.

"Yeah, that's going to have to wait. I have work to do."

"I suppose that's what they mean by a perk," I said.

"Some employees get thousands of dollars in way of a bonus. You get a foot rub."

"Along with free coffee."

"Did you just compare my kiss to free coffee?"

"Never." I tried to wriggle free from his tickling attack. "I have to get back to my desk." Giggling, I managed to escape his grip. "My boss is a real stickler." I turned to look at him. "And well known for bestowing the worst punishments."

Richard rose off the sofa. "Don't, Mia."

"It was a joke. I meant it as a joke."

He shooed me away and rounded his desk chair, all business as usual. His demeanor brought a chill to the room. I'd gone and ruined the mood. Luckily for me Richard wasn't the sulking type.

Back at my desk, I ran through my usual routine of checking emails and answering a few, mostly scheduling appointments. For those requesting more information on sessions I forwarded their contact information onto Mistress Scarlet. Her office was down the hall.

Grabbing the box from underneath my desk, I peeled it open and pulled out the roll of blue tinsel I'd bought over the weekend from Macy's. I knew only the best Christmas decorations would be good enough for here. Starting with my desk, I roped it along the front, excited that the holidays were looming. This would be my first Christmas with a boyfriend, and Richard was throwing a party at his house. I liked the thought of hosting an event with him. Despite all that had happened between us, I looked forward to this show of solidarity in front of his friends. By now they might have gathered we were just another conventional couple. I hoped they'd realize this was his decision and not mine. Richard had told me not to worry about what other people thought of us and that it was none of their business. I wondered how long it would be before I had that kind of confidence.

I paused when the elevator dinged.

Cameron strolled out with his head bowed, as though deep in thought. He threw me a wave. I could have sworn he was ignoring me. Not that I minded. It was kind of nice to admire the director and Enthrall's ultimate eye candy from the safety of behind my desk. He swept his fingers through his dark locks and frowned all the way towards the staff hall door.

"Good morning," I said.

His hand snapped back from the door handle. "What is that?"

"This?" I pointed to the blue strand. "Tinsel."

Cameron looked horrified. "Get rid of it."

"But it's pretty."

"Christmas is over two and a half weeks away."

"The shopping malls have their decorations up."

"That's because they're manipulating shoppers."

I held back on a frown.

"Firstly, Ms. Lauren," he said, "it's too soon to celebrate a pagan holiday that was high jacked by the Catholic Church. Secondly, instead of celebrating winter we're celebrating Santa." He shook his head. "An atrocity."

"Why would you want to celebrate winter?"

"The return of the sun. Darkness to light?" He made it sound like I really should know this.

I moved towards him. "You think Santa Clause is an atrocity?"

"I may have understated." He gestured insistently to the tinsel.

"But I bought it from Macy's."

"Mia, I don't care if the Pope personally delivered it."

"That's very Scrooge-like," I whispered.

Being dragged though the doorway and down the hall by Cameron Cole was both thrilling and equally terrifying. He really did seem offended by the shiny strip of tinsel.

Talk about Jekyll and Hyde. This guy hadn't flinched when I'd accidently backed my Mini into his Porsche and left a dent.

"I'm sorry," I said. "I'll take them down."

"Them? Please tell me you haven't decorated the dungeon?"

"Of course not. I'm not that insensitive."

"The jury is still out." Cameron threw Richard's door open. "Richard." He burst into his office and dragged me along with him. "What the hell is going on?"

Jeez, thank goodness I'd not put out the baby Jesus.

"Will you get your fucking sub under control," said Cameron.

Oh, that got my attention.

And Richard's too from the way he rounded his desk. "Please, Cole, let go of my girlfriend."

Cameron's grip tightened. "Mia's placing shiny Christmas decorations everywhere."

"Only the foyer." I cringed when Cameron's glare shot to me.

Richard's eyebrows went up in surprise. "That's what was in the box?"

"Maybe."

Richard did a double take at my answer. "We'll get rid of them. Don't panic. None of our client's have been subjected to copious amounts of happiness yet."

"The day is saved," said Cameron dryly. "Aren't you a Buddhist now? How can you not be offended?"

"I'm more surprised that the good Catholic boy in you isn't drawn to the spirit of Christmas," said Richard.

"Your sub," said Cameron. "Has subjected me to a sensory assault of gaudiness."

"I'd only put one strand out."

Cameron looked defiant. "Punish her."

Covering my face with my hands to hide my blush, I took a step back. He really was going to do this.

"We've talked about this," said Richard. "Mia and I have a different dynamic now."

"She needs reigning in."

"Mia, go make us some coffee," said Richard.

Cameron folded his arms. "Black. No sugar."

Scurrying out of there, I headed straight into the coffee room. My cheeks were ablaze. The thought of having to face Cameron again sent me spinning. How did he know I longed for this? How could Richard not?

With a shaking hand, I flicked a switch and brown liquid poured through a filter and into the pot. The delicious scent of the finest brew filled the room.

I tried to suppress this unfaithful crush on Cameron.

To listen in on their private conversation was wrong on every level, yet Cameron possessed the only access to Richard's true thoughts, and this felt like the only way I'd get access. Reassuring myself this would be a good thing, I headed back out into the hall, glancing left and right to make sure the way was clear. Despite this guilt over invading Richard's personal space, I pressed my ear to his door.

"You're crossing the line, Cole."

"Richard, you and I have never had a line."

"Maybe it's time we did?"

Silence lingered and it even made me feel uncomfortable.

"I'm sorry," said Richard.

"It's okay," said Cameron. "I get it."

"I could never have survived Emily's death without you."

"I'm not going anywhere. Neither is Mia. Emily would want you to be happy."

"Mia is everything I want. Everything I need, and if anything happens to her."

"I'll oversee her training. That's always been my promise."

"I have enough issues of my own to deal with."

"Richard, Mia is screaming out to be dominated."

"Loved, Cameron. She needs love. You've only been in love once and it was so long ago you've forgotten what it feels like."

Again that silence as Richard's emotional punch hit its mark. I'd have given anything to have seen Cameron's face. Read from him how hurt he was by Richard's words. Maybe a broken heart was why he was always so intense.

"I'm sorry," said Richard.

"No harm done."

"She's terrified of losing us."

"I'm concerned we'll lose her," said Cameron. "If we don't

give her what she needs, she'll go elsewhere. Navigating our scene is tricky for someone so inexperienced."

How could Cameron have known my rambling thoughts had leaned toward visiting another L.A. club?

"You're reading her wrong," said Cameron. "You must be strong for her. She needs to be handled with a surety."

"This is what she wants."

I wanted to burst through the door and yell it wasn't.

"This situation started off with my concern for you," said Cameron. "Right now, I'm devastated for Mia."

"During a session, she pushes back too fiercely," said Richard.

"That's her way of begging to be pushed beyond what she believes she's capable of. Purge her pain."

"I never thought I'd say this, but she's too feisty."

"I brought her into this world," said Cameron. "I'm responsible for her."

"Mia's happy with my decision."

"Let's visit Tiffany's," said Cameron. "Buy Mia a beautiful collar."

"Cole."

"You're halfway into subspace, Richard. I can see it. This is what we are. This is what we do."

"We both know Mia needs to be hot housed to reach our level of expertise. And we also know who the best person is to get her there."

"You have what it takes to see this through."

"You heard what Laura suggested. There's something deeper going on."

"Mia does appear to have a shadow complex, yes," said Cameron.

What the hell is a shadow complex?

Pressing my ear against the door, my intrigue rose.

"Look, I came here to talk about Pendulum," said Cameron. "I'm not comfortable with you going—"

"It's set."

"You know how I feel about that place."

Oh no.

Mistress Scarlet glared at me from the end of the hallway. It didn't help that she was wearing a tight latex bodice that showed off her curves and a leather skirt. Laced up six inch thigh-high boots rounded out her killer outfit.

She turned and walked into her office.

Reluctantly, I followed her. Richard had made his thoughts very clear. I tried to suppress this ache and hoped to salvage my self-respect. Despite my nerves, I reassured myself that Mistress Scarlet was more open-minded than most. She'd gifted me my first vibrator weeks ago and asked me to return to her office after I'd used it to discuss my tryst with the toy.

During the time I'd worked here, I'd gotten to see beyond Scarlet's sternness. Still, this school mistress stance she was holding right now was intimidating. The way her long black locks curled over one shoulder was so elegant, so sensual, and her rouged lips, high cheekbones, and stunning deep blue irises caught her prey off guard.

She folded her arms across her chest. "What was that about?"

"I'm not sure," I said. "Something about hot housing."

"I wasn't talking about their conversation. It was the fact you were listening to it."

"It was about me."

"Never listen to a private conversation. At least not here. Understand?"

"I'm sorry. Please don't tell Cameron."

"What were they saying?"

"Richard's concerned for me."

Her expression changed subtly. "I see."

"What's hot housing?"

Scarlet looked thoughtful. "It's where a plant is grown in a warm and nurturing environment. Ideal for rapid growth."

"Do they hot house at Chrysalis?" I said. "With people?"

She came closer. "Everyone has your best interests at heart. Do you believe that?"

"Yes." I focused on the spanking bench and I felt myself drifting.

"Why is Cameron angry with you?" asked Scarlet. "It takes a lot to rile him up."

"I put out a Christmas decoration."

She smirked. "That's a first for here. My advice is unchanged, Mia. Stay out of his way."

"I know. I try."

"Time with Cameron and his special brand of skills would change you irrevocably. We love you the way you are." She gave a nod. "From what I gather, Richard senses what is best for you."

"I feel very safe with him."

"Safe isn't always fulfilling though, is it?" she said.

My eyes widened. She'd sensed what I needed, and though no words were spoken she'd comforted me.

"What's Pendulum?" I asked.

"It doesn't exist. Do yourself a favor and never mention that name again."

Trying to suppress my fired up intrigue, I looked over at the spanking bench. "Is it uncomfortable?"

"It's designed for comfort." She strolled over to it. "See how this ridge is curved so your pelvic bone rests on it? A slap to the buttocks resonates right into your g-spot."

Scarlet was easily one of L.A.'s most sought after dominatrixes. She had an hypnotic aura. Even her voice exuded a fierce confidence and her understated elegance was timeless.

"My door is always open."

"Thank you, Mistress Scarlet."

Her phone buzzed and she grabbed it, gesturing that she had to take this call. She stepped out into the hall and shut the door behind her.

Running my hand over the soft leather of the bench, I wondered if it was just a showpiece. Straddling it felt divine. Being naughty caused my head to spin and a thrill to shoot between my thighs. Scooting up, I aligned my pubic bone perfectly with the raised ridge and lay flat out. This position sent a thrill down below and I understood the appeal. The promise of being taken from behind, a vulnerable feeling, a divine tingle.

Squeezing my eyes shut, I imagined a slap. My pussy flinched with expectation and I wondered if it was possible to come from a spanking. My fingers curled around the upper curve of the leather and I sniffed its fresh lemony scent of furniture polish. With my pelvis tilted just so, it was easy to trance out.

"I was wondering where my coffee was." Cameron came in

and closed the door behind him.

I scrambled off the bench and yanked my skirt down, blushing wildly. He came in farther, tucking his hands into his pockets in that casual way of his. His dark stare scrutinized.

"Aren't people meant to knock around here?" I said breathlessly.

"Then I would have missed this joyous vision," he said.

"Mistress Scarlet had to make a call."

"Ah."

"Sorry about the tinsel."

He shrugged. "I tried."

Oh, it really wasn't about the tinsel.

"How was your patient?" My rapid fire speech continued unabated.

"Patient?"

"Yesterday, you mentioned you had to visit the ER?"

"I'm afraid I had to issue a 5150." And on my confused stare, Cameron added, "I had my patient admitted to a psych unit. Against his wishes."

"That's horrible."

"To protect him from himself."

"Was he scared?"

"Yes."

"I would hate it."

"I sedated him."

A wave of nausea hit my stomach.

"Such a thing will never happen to you." He smiled. "And I should know."

"Do you like your job?"

"Of course. It's emotionally challenging at times, but I like the thought I'm soothing my patient's mind."

"How do you know you're reading someone right?"

"Reading?" he said. "Those are Richard's words. Did you eavesdrop?"

"No."

"Did you eavesdrop?"

"Yes."

"What did you ascertain from our conversation?"

"I'm sorry. It was wrong of me."

"I didn't ask for an apology. I asked for you to express what you learned."

I gave a shrug, not willing to go there.

"Mia?"

"I have to get back to my desk."

Cameron arched a brow, unaffected by my stubbornness, and his stare drifted over to the spanking bench. I hung my head in embarrassment. Not only had I given my snooping away, I now looked like a wanton hussy.

"You like the bench?"

"No," I lied. "It's very uncomfortable."

"It's me, Mia." His tone softened. "You don't have to be embarrassed."

I nibbled on a fingernail, needing him to break through these walls that arose every time my sexuality came into play.

"We must respect Richard's wishes," he said. "*I* must respect Richard's wishes."

"Richard's wrong," I whispered.

Cameron went to speak and then seemed to think better of it. His eyes locked onto something outside the window.

I let out a long sigh.

"Mia, share that thought with me," he said, that steely focus back on me.

Cameron, there's something about you.

"Have you not learned by now you can tell me anything?" he said. "That nothing shocks or offends me?"

"As far as I'm concerned you're all going to hell," I snapped.

He laughed. "Where did that come from?"

I glanced over at the spanking bench and then back at him.

"As much as you want me to spank you for that, it's not going to happen." He looked sympathetic. "Mia, it's not a *no*. It's a *not right now*."

"I failed you."

"Why do you say that?"

"You needed me to help you save Richard. All I've done is hinder his recovery."

"Richard's doing great. Because of you. Now it's our turn to be there for you."

"How did you know?" I said. "When you first found me. How did you know I would be drawn to this lifestyle?"

"A hunch. The only way to know for sure was to get you in front of three of the world's most distinguished dominatrixes."

"During my interview?"

"Lady Penny is not only my secretary, she's also a qualified psychologist."

"They knew when they interviewed me?"

"I validated their findings when I met you." He glanced at his watch. "I have to go. I have a clinic starting in an hour."

Surely sailing around the world on a yacht or hanging out at a gentleman's club would be less stressful than being a doctor? Cameron really was interesting. And so damned handsome. Part of his allure was the kindness in his smile. The same one he held for me now.

"Aren't you volunteering at the soup kitchen tonight?" he said. "Leo will pick you up at five."

"I can drive myself."

"He'll drive you."

I shrugged my reluctance and glanced over at the spanking bench, the only therapy that felt like it would work.

"Finish up on your sessions with Dr. Raul," said Cameron, "and maybe Richard will come round."

I headed towards the door.

"Goodbye then."

I ignored him.

"No goodbye, Mia?"

I grabbed the handle, wondering how he'd react when I slammed the door.

"Mia," he said softly. "Come here."

Slowly, I turned to face him and forced myself not to roll my eyes.

"Now, please."

I couldn't look away, couldn't turn away. "What?"

Cameron rested a finger beneath my chin and raised it. *His* gaze, his touch, his attention, caused a shudder.

My nipples hardened, pushing through my blouse and giving away my secret crush.

"We need to shatter that barrier," he said.

A frisson tingled and spiraled, and invisible fireworks burst out of my chest as though in testimony to our forbidden chemistry.

Scarlet's words came back to me. *"His special brand of skills will change you irrevocably."*

"Mia," he said.

A wave of lightheadedness. "Yes."

"After much thought…"

I blinked up at him.

"Make mine an Earl Grey."

I scurried out.

Being around him was making my heart ache. And I had no idea why.

CHAPTER 6

CAMERON ARRANGED THIS for me.

Despite my initial reservation of volunteering at Charlie's Soup Kitchen in Santa Monica, I soon learned what a joy it was to serve nutritious hot meals to the homeless. Dr. Laura had been right about concentrating on other people's needs and I'd come to realize I was pretty lucky.

After settling in and getting to know everybody and where everything was, I felt like I belonged here. The modest kitchen was staffed by two chefs, Andre and Jose, and they worked here full time serving the dining room, which sat just over fifty at a time.

Charlie's was run by Luke and Rebecca, a young married couple, and they made me feel welcome. This was my third week and I was being treated like a respected member of the team. After finishing off my errands that included stock taking in the kitchen, as well as wiping down the tables in the front after closing, I waved goodbye to Rebecca and Luke who were getting ready to lock up.

I grabbed my purse and made my way outside.

Leo had gone for the car. His constant presence made me wonder if he also served as my bodyguard. Throughout my shift, he'd sat at a corner table while watching customers come and go and only occasionally took his eyes off me to check his phone. His towering height, classic square jaw, and flawless suit and tie, hinted of his military background that Cameron had mentioned. Leo had apparently been a marine and had even seen action.

Those dark eyes might have been kind but they also hid an interesting past.

I waited for him on the corner, a little way down from Charlie's. I didn't want to be seen climbing into a top of the line Rover Land Cruiser.

"Mia!"

My gut wrenched when I saw Lorraine, my step-mother. There was no sign of the Rover, so there was no chance of hopping in and making my escape. Lorraine crossed the street. That wrangle with breast cancer had left her painfully thin, but at least her hair was growing back. Dressed in low hung jeans and a T-shirt, she actually looked better than she had in years. Her remission had given her a new lease on life it seemed. The lightness in her step had made its way back.

"Mia, please," she said. "We have to talk."

"Did Bailey tell you I work here?" I was unable to suppress my annoyance.

"You won't return any of my calls."

"Lorraine," I said. "I've already told you I need more time. What you did to me was unforgiveable."

"I'm here to explain."

"You knew my dad was alive and you let me believe he wasn't. Have you any idea how cruel that was?"

"I was trying to protect you. It was hard to tell you. He rejected me too, Mia. He started a new life without us." She looked frustrated. "I only found out he was still alive days before you did."

"That's a lie," I said. "And you know it. You got rid of all his stuff in a fit of rage and you had me help. You told me we needed the money."

"It wasn't easy taking you on, Mia."

"I'm not ready for this," I said wearily.

The Rover pulled curbside and Lorraine gave it a passing glance. "Where are you living now?"

"With a friend."

She had no right to know about Richard.

Leo leaped out of the driver's side, his dark eyes trying to get a read on Lorraine. He opened the rear passenger door and gestured for me to get in.

"Do you know this man?" asked Lorraine.

"Yes, of course. Bailey tells me you're in remission. I'm happy for you. Really I am."

She looked guilty. "Look, I know this is a bad time…"

I swallowed hard, reaching into my handbag and pulling out the rest of my cash. "Sorry, it's all I have on me."

She took the thirty dollars and shoved it away in her bag, throwing a self-conscious glance at Leo. "You're a good daughter."

"I'm sorry, but us meeting is too soon," I said.

"Who are you?" she snapped at Leo.

"He's a friend," I said. "He's taking me home."

She looked harried. "Bailey tells me you're working for some wealthy men. They're not taking advantage of you are they?"

Bailey had no right to share anything about my new life. I'd have to warn her to keep her big mouth shut. "Lorraine, you lost the right to know anything about my life when you betrayed my trust."

"Mia, please."

"It's best we don't see each other for a while. I'm working through everything and this isn't healthy for me. My therapist—"

"Therapist?" she said. "How can you afford that?"

"I'm not paying for it," I said, hating where this was going. "I'm sorry, I have to go."

"Who does this car belong to?"

"My boss."

"I'm worried about you," she said, gesturing towards Leo. "Is he your boss?"

"No." I climbed into the back of the car and Leo shut the door behind me.

Sinking into the luxury leather and feeling guilty for leaving her behind, I burst into tears, unable to stop the torrent of emotion that had merely lay beneath the surface. Lorraine had betrayed me but she still needed me too. I didn't feel strong enough for either of us right now. Seeing her again dragged it all back. That terrible day when I'd discovered my father was still alive and had abandoned me. Lorraine had kept the truth from me. My father had not only left a bad marriage with his second wife, Lorraine, he'd also struck a deal with the devil and left me behind too.

Forgiveness seemed out of reach for either of them.

Leo didn't question me about Lorraine. He merely played track after track of loud music, blasting it through hidden speakers as though knowing I needed this distraction. He took the side streets to get me home as quickly as possible. The music lulled me, though barely touched the surface of this self-hate.

I'd brought this all on myself. All of it.

Refusing to let Richard see me like this, I made my way inside the house and went straight for our bedroom. Splashing water on my face, I shoved down the pain. A shift in my mood always unsettled Richard. Since moving in with him three weeks ago, I'd learned to suppress my angst. He had enough of his own demons to contend with.

This Mediterranean Malibu beach house was Richard's home, despite him insisting this was our place now. With its spacious rooms, including five bedrooms, it was tastefully decorated with immaculate furniture as well as those impressive far eastern pieces he'd collected from his world travels. There was also the usual suspect of his bachelor past, a den full of New York Giants memorabilia. Whenever he was in there, I left him alone. I was more than happy to swim in the sparkling pool or take a walk down the pathway at the end of the garden. It led onto a beach. That ocean still awed me, even now.

It was hard to feel I belonged amongst all this luxury.

Within minutes I'd changed into my little black dress that would be perfect for tonight's event at Pendulum. The place that didn't exist. The place that Richard was taking me tonight. Despite Cameron expressing his reservations, I knew Richard wouldn't take me anywhere I wasn't ready for.

After putting the finishing touches on my makeup, I slid into my strappy high-heels. A fluff of my hair and I was ready.

Richard was in the kitchen. He was feeding Winston, his British Bulldog.

"I didn't hear you come in?" he said. "You didn't come find me."

He looked swanky in black pants and a white shirt. His hair was newly washed and I wanted to bury my nose in it.

Enthrall Her

His pale blue eyes took in my dress. "Are you wearing that to see Dr. Laura?"

My sense of unease persisted. "My appointment's cancelled."

"Did she cancel it?"

"You didn't ask me about Charlie's."

He shook his head as though shaking off a thought. "How did it go?"

"Great. I like it there. I'd love for you to do a shift with me."

"Sure." He didn't sound convincing. "Just tell me Leo doesn't take his eyes off you?"

"Everyone is super nice. It's very safe."

He rolled his eyes. "Until it's not."

"Cameron's seems fine with me being there. He agrees with Dr. Laura—"

"Have you been crying?"

"Seasonal allergies. Do you have any Benadryl?"

"I have Claritin. Benadryl will make you drowsy. Sure you're okay?"

"Never better," I said sheepishly.

"Why are you dressed up?"

"For tonight."

Richard opened another cabinet door. "Not this one, baby. It's a private event. Members only. Sorry. This one's been on the books awhile."

"Where are you going?"

"Manhattan Beach." But he didn't say Pendulum. He merely moved on to another cabinet. "That's weird."

"What are you looking for?"

"I could have sworn we had a full jar of peanut butter." He scratched his head and stared into the cupboard as though expecting it to reappear.

I bent down to pat Winston.

"I was going to make myself a peanut butter and jelly sandwich," he said.

"Why can't I come with you?"

He turned to look at me. "It's a boy's night."

I tried to keep the disappointment out of my voice. "Is Cameron going?"

"No, he's still at the office." Richard pulled out his cell. "There's lasagna in the fridge. Or you can order in. Did you cancel your appointment because you thought you were coming with me?"

I feigned I was helping look for that jar of peanut butter, opening the cabinets one by one.

Richard stared at his BlackBerry. "Cameron's asking why you cancelled the car."

"How does he know?"

Jeez, that guy didn't miss anything.

Richard came towards me and cupped my chin. "You've told me these sessions with Dr. Raul help you. They are helping, aren't they? You're not just telling me what you think I want to hear?"

"They are helping." I broke away from him.

Instead of an intriguing evening at a secret location, I was going to trawl through painful memories so a doctor could get paid. The entire process was a waste of time.

"You know you can tell me anything, Mia, right?"

"Yes."

"Then tell me why you were crying?"

I wanted to tell him not to go out tonight, but I didn't want to be that kind of girlfriend.

I headed back into the bedroom.

"Why won't you open up to me?" he said.

"I'm fine," I called back. "I wish you'd leave me alone."

"I'm telling Cameron you're seeing Dr. Raul." Richard followed me down the hallway. "And please, this time open up to her. She costs a small fortune."

"I thought Cameron was the best therapist?"

"You need gentle handling. A female therapist—"

"Isn't that reversed sexism?"

He followed me into the bedroom. "Can I say this, Mia?"

Defiantly, I rested my hands on my hips.

"We have a bright future together. I love you. I want you to be happy. It makes me sad to see you sad."

I fell into his arms and hugged him tight.

"See? Everything's fine," he said, rubbing my back.

He was right. I'd been so guarded lately, so full of mistrust.

It was time to find my center, just as Dr. Laura had suggested.

It was time to trust again.

Richard kissed my forehead. "Besides, there's no fucking around in Cameron's chair." He laughed. "He wouldn't put up with your attitude."

I thumped Richard playfully. "And look how you turned out."

"Exactly. Cameron's mad experiments turned me into a psychological Frankenstein."

I stared up at him.

"I'm joking," he said. "Despite my reluctance to admit it, Cameron's a genius."

"My loveable Frankenstein,' I said, laughing. "Let's go find you something to eat before you go out."

"Ten girlfriend points. Looks like you made it back to even."

I thumped him again and together we made our way back towards the kitchen.

CHAPTER 7

RICHARD HAD FORGOTTEN his BlackBerry. I grabbed it and flew out the front door.

His Mercedes sped out the driveway, passing the black Land Cruiser pulling in. My ride was here. Leo threw me a wave to let me know he'd seen me. I ran back inside and grabbed my purse, dropping Richard's BlackBerry inside it. I set the alarm on the way out.

Thanking Leo for holding the rear passenger door open for me, I climbed in and settled into the backseat, sinking into the soft leather.

"Small detour," I told Leo. "Manhattan Beach. Richard's forgotten his phone and he'll be lost without it."

"Well be cutting it tight, Ms. Lauren."

"It's okay," I said. "Can you follow Richard's car?"

Leo glanced at me in the rearview. "The Mercedes? Sure."

"Thank you."

It felt good to be bailing Richard out, and I was glad Leo offered no resistance. He did, after all, have Cameron to answer to, but he'd understand.

We left Malibu along the Pacific Coast Highway, keeping Richard's car in our sights, heading towards Manhattan Beach.

The ride was smooth, and despite some traffic slowing us down we followed the sunset along, all the way to Pine Avenue.

As we pulled up, I saw Richard parked in front of a sprawling white house. All modern glass windows and soft lighting coming from inside. I'd not expected him to be visiting a private residence. He leaned against his Mercedes, his arms folded.

I was so happy to have come through for him. He might even change his mind now and let me join him.

"Leo," I said. "Can you pull round there."

He drove around the corner so we were out of sight and pulled up to the curb.

"Give me a few minutes." I stepped out.

Richard might be a little annoyed to see me at first, but once I'd handed over his phone he'd be relieved and I'd earn more girlfriend points. It made me happy.

I slunk back behind a palm tree.

Richard had approached a cab that had pulled up behind his car. He opened the rear door and a tall, leggy blonde climbed out. She looked about thirty, and if you'd have told me she modeled for Victoria's Secret I'd have believed it.

Her sparkly silver dress was way too short and showed off her stocking tops. Bright red lipstick marked a stunning face, flowing locks, and unlike me she was busty. She oozed sex appeal. And she was wearing a black collar around her perfect slim neck.

The mark of a submissive.

A lump lodged in my throat and tears stung my eyes when I saw Richard wrapping his arms around her in a hug.

No, please God, no.

Tectonic plates shifted beneath my feet, causing my balance to fail, and I reached out and gripped the tree. From my discreet vantage point, I watched Richard guide the woman into the house. From the way they shared a private joke, they knew each other well. The way she smiled at him spoke volumes. Richard shared a few words with the man who answered the door and they were in.

Having no memory of getting back in the car, I merely sat for a few seconds, trying to still my beating heart that was doing its best to shatter my rib cage.

My life was a lie.

Leo was focused on his phone. "Ms. Lauren, was he pleased?"

"I missed him," I said weakly. "He'd already gone in by the

time I got there."

I didn't want him to know what I'd witnessed and certainly didn't want him to see me cry. My fingers trembled, loosening the top button of my blouse.

"Can you put the air on," I said.

The speed with which Leo drove us away from there shot me back in my seat. Something told me he'd deliver me to Dr. Laura right on time. Caressing my chest, I wondered if this ache in my heart would ever go away. Richard had questioned my ability to trust, all the while betraying it.

It's not what you think.
It is. You know it is.

The drive to Beverly Hills was a blur.

With a wave, I headed on into Cedars Sinai east wing and watched Leo drive away. With him out of sight, I made my way back out onto the street and walked briskly along San Vincente.

Replaying all my interactions with Richard over the last few weeks, I tried to see what I'd missed. My mind circled, trying to fathom why Richard had lied to me. Thoughts of unworthiness rattled my brain. I was no match for the waif-like beauty who he'd escorted into that house.

Peering through Stella McCartney's shop window, I tried to focus on the dresses and not the searing pain in my chest. Mannequins were lined up and all of them wore expensive outfits. The kind I'd never worn until I'd met Richard. My relationship had never been about money, or this decadent lifestyle that I'd never pursued. My love for him had come from a pure place, the last remnants of goodness within me.

And now that too was shattered to smithereens.

I kept walking, trying to think.

Trying not to think.

Trying to remember that I was a survivor. How could I find any of this surprising? Abandonment was my calling card and this pattern really proved that the blame lay squarely on my shoulders.

The glass front signage of Beverly Hill's Ink reflected this was an upscale tattoo parlor. I headed on in and viewed the wall art. There really was an endless display of choices.

I was met by a short, pretty brunette, twenty-ish, covered in tattoos and with the face piercings of someone who didn't give a fuck. I liked her. Her name was Tammy. She made some joke about mine and said she'd read a dystopian novel with my namesake. She liked to read and wanted to know if I did too.

She soon sensed I was in no mood for conversation or any of the usual social pleasantries. I just wanted a fucking tattoo. I didn't feel like talking.

I wanted pain.

Within minutes of choosing my design, I'd settled in a leather seat and Tammy took her place next to me, pulling her tray of instruments close.

I'd chosen the smallest hummingbird. I liked the idea of being able to fly away and disappear. Strange how the needle pricks helped take my mind off the agony wedged in my heart.

Tammy focused in on the design, punishing me with small stings, and gradually the tiny drawing of a delicate bird in flight took shape. Those greens and blues brought the small, delicate creature alive on my ankle. It was going to be beautiful.

She worked away quietly, as though recognizing her own pain in me. She even shared her thoughts on how being marked would give me the strength I needed right now.

She really did get it.

All air was sucked from the room—

Cameron stood a few feet away.

I wondered how long he'd been there.

Tammy swapped a wary glance with me and whispered, "Boyfriend?"

"No," I said. "My boss."

She frowned and did a double take at Cameron.

He burned a look through me as he closed in on us. "Are you done?" he asked Tammy.

"I am now." She finished taping a dressing to my ankle. "Leave it on for at least two hours."

"Mia, time to go." Cameron reached into his wallet. "This should take care of it." He handed Tammy his credit card. "You sterilize your needles?"

"Of course," snapped Tammy. "That will put you back a C note." She flipped over his card, seemingly unsure. "What is this?"

"American Express," said Cameron. "Run it, please."

She left the room.

"Where's Richard?" asked Cameron.

"He went out for the night." I studied his face, hoping to read more. Read the truth.

"That's right," he said. "He had an appointment."

With a ho, I mused, sneaking a peek at my tattoo.

"I'll meet you outside." Cameron turned and left.

I joined Tammy at the reception desk and thanked her for her fine work, along with apologizing for my friend's interruption. She handed me back Cameron's card.

"Thank you," I said. "I love it."

"He's a little scary," she said. "Are you safe to go with him?"

"Yes, he's actually very nice when you get to know him."

"If you say so."

I hurried to join Cameron outside and returned his card. He tucked it back into his wallet and led me towards his parked BMW.

"I'll pay you back," I said.

Cameron opened the passenger door and gestured for me to get in. He made his way around to the driver's seat and climbed in.

I pulled my seatbelt on. "I'll tell Richard."

Cameron punched a dial on the front panel and then raised a finger to silence me. "Hey Brian," he said. "I'm running late. I'll be there in about half an hour." He went on to say something about looking forward to seeing Brian's new drawings.

I kicked off my shoes and rested my feet on the dashboard. My pink toes would perfectly match my hummingbird. I couldn't wait to take off my dressing and reveal Tammy's masterpiece. It really was pretty and delicate and everything I could have asked for in a tattoo. I hated it being covered up.

Cameron ended his call.

He ran his thumb over his key fob, stamped with the initials C R C. "You never made it to your appointment with Dr. Raul?"

"No." I glance at the backseat.

There was a lone Journal of Clinical Psychiatry and a spare sweater. Other than that there were no other clues to this man.

"What does the R stand for?" I pointed to his key ring.

"Raife." He placed his key in the ignition, turned it, and pulled the car away from the curb.

"What kind of name is Raife?"

"I was named after my grandfather." He glanced over at me. "What happened with your appointment?"

"Something came up."

"What came up?"

"Did Dr. Raul call you?"

"Yes."

I stared out of the window. None of this was any of his business. Yes, he was my boss, but really this kind of thing was personal. "So you called Leo and asked him to come find me?"

"Leo dropped you off at Dr. Raul's office. You can imagine my concern when Laura told me you weren't at your appointment."

"Is nothing private?"

"You gave your permission for me to consult on your case, Mia." He tilted his head. "So nothing is private."

"So what's your conclusion Dr. Cole?" I scowled at him. "I'd love to know your grand deduction."

"You don't talk during a session. It's hard to deduce from silence."

"People get over shit," I said. "They move on."

All that crap was lodged somewhere inside and talking about it was essentially stirring monstrous emotions from slumber.

You can all fuck off.

I let out a frustrated sigh. "Leo followed me to the tattoo parlor? Then he called you?"

"Leo's job is to get you to your destination safely," said Cameron.

"He's not in trouble, is he?"

"No."

Seriously, I might be dating his best friend, but neither of them owned me. This was my body and I could do what I wanted to it. They had no right to dictate what I did or when.

I looked over at him. "I know what you think of me."

"Mind reading?" said Cameron. "We have a new skill to add to your resume."

Verbally sparing with him was ill advised yet I found myself wanting to push his buttons, mainly because I always seemed to have his full attention that way.

"Anything you tell me is confidential," he said.

"Dr. Raul has given me some coping techniques to get over a lot of stuff."

"Yet you still refuse to talk during the session?"

"You obviously talk about me after them."

He gave me a sideways glance. "What does your tattoo represent?"

"Haven't decided."

"Hummingbird's can fly backwards, did you know that?" On my confused glance, he added, "I saw the drawing. It may be a conduit to your thoughts."

"How?"

"Your subconscious is talking to us."

"It's just a tattoo."

"An indelible mark that symbolizes a significant meaning to your heart. An immortalized whisper from your soul. It's not just a tattoo, Mia."

Even his words were hypnotic.

We drove in silence with Cameron navigating the heavy traffic with ease, taking side streets to avoid the drudgery of the commute. Up Beverly Glen we drove, and it was lovely to peer out at the passing scenery, a mishmash of houses, all of them different, some crowned with palm trees and lush shrubbery. We arched the highest peak of Mulholland Drive. Off in the distance, I saw those funny looking homes built upon the hill with a quarter of their structure balanced on stilts.

"What about earthquakes?" I said, pointing. "Don't those people freak out?"

"They must pass building codes," said Cameron, as he pulled the car onto a dimly lit gravel pathway. "You'd never catch me in one though."

He killed the engine.

I peered into the darkness of the private driveway. "Why are we stopping here?"

"I have to drop off an item."

"Who lives here?"

"One of my patients." He pointed up the pathway.

"A client of Enthrall?"

"No, my private practice." He shifted in his seat to face me and leaned his chin on his hand. "You're a perfect match for Richard. You're as spontaneous as each other."

"I think that too."

"How are things between you?"

"Good."

"I sense doubt?" he said.

"Can I ask you a question?"

"Of course."

I studied Cameron's face. "You think Richard might be seeing someone else?"

He blinked at me. "If Richard wants to date another woman he ends the relationship he's in. What made you ask that?"

That grungy feeling returned.

"He would never have asked you to move in with him if he wasn't serious about you," he said. "What made you bring that up?"

I gave a shrug.

"I promise you can trust him."

My shoulders lowered and the tension they'd been carrying lightened a little. Still, believing in his words was a lure of the naive. "How do you think he'll react when he sees this?" I gestured to my ankle.

"He'll be ecstatic."

"He'll hate it, won't he?"

"I don't think he'll hate it, no. Perhaps talking with him first would have been wise."

"Well, I like it."

"Good for you," he said. "What inspired you to get a hummingbird?"

I chewed my lip. "It made me feel good about myself."

"Dr. Raul shared an interesting finding with me."

"Oh?"

"She believes you're holding back on sharing a significant event that happened before your mother died."

"Like what?"

"Like what?" he whispered.

"That morning?"

"Yes," he said softly. "That morning."

Pressing my hands to my mouth, I weighed up what was safe to share. Nothing came to mind.

"What happened, Mia?"

I swallowed hard, refusing to make eye contact with him.

"I want to help," he said.

"I'm over it."

He arched a brow. "How would you like the opportunity to ask me any question? I'm always poking around your noggin. It only seems fair."

"What kind of question?"

"The kind that will let you in."

"I can ask you anything?"

"Yes."

A jolt of excitement slithered up my spine.

"But first, answer me this." He seemed to weigh his words carefully. "Who hurt you? Was it your mom?"

"You're not my psychiatrist." I shook my head. "My mom took good care of me. She was there when my dad left. She made sure I got to school on time and she helped me with my homework and she may not have been perfect but she was a good person. She loved me."

Again that shocking silence.

"Now you get to ask me a question," he said calmly.

"Why are you into pain?"

"Well—"

"And why do you get turned on by inflicting pain on others?" I added fiercely.

The silence made me regret the question. Unlike Richard, Cameron didn't blare music from the speakers to suppress the awkwardness.

"I'm a sexual sadist," he said.

The fine hairs pricked on my forearms.

"It's the way I'm made."

"Do you want to change?"

"Never," he said. "You do realize you've asked more than one question? Our agreement was one each."

"You're very controlling."

"Without a doubt. There are times in my therapeutic endeavors that control is extremely useful."

"How?"

"Trade secret." Cameron's focus drifted to my ankle.

"A masochist and a sadist are a great fit then." I laughed. "As long as they don't kill each other in the process. Death by fucking."

"You're extra feisty tonight, Mia. What's brought this on?"

"It's rare for us to be alone. I'm making the most of it."

"You have a rude mouth, but a beautiful one nonetheless."

"You noticed then?"

Cameron leaned towards me and my heart missed a beat. He reached into the glove compartment and removed a white paper bag. A prescription label stuck to the front. He put it on his lap and drove the rest of the way up the pathway. There, appearing before us, was a standalone townhouse with an east coast styled porch and a swing with a rose patterned pillow seat.

"What's that?" I gestured to the bag.

"Wait here." Cameron turned off the engine. He flung open his door and strolled on up towards the house.

After knocking several times, he waited. A twenty-something man wearing pajamas answered. His hair needed a comb. Cameron must have noticed it too because he seemed to mention it. The man raked his hands through his locks, trying to smooth his wayward hair.

Cameron handed over the paper bag and words were exchanged. They stood there for a few more minutes chatting away, the man showing him something in a magazine and Cameron nodding his approval. They talked about it for some time. Cameron seemed to like what he was being shown.

Within a few minutes, he returned to the car.

"Was that Brian?" I said.

"Yes."

"That was his prescription?"

"I like to check in on him."

"How often do you do that?"

"Every week."

"Bet that's expensive."

"My practice doesn't just treat patients who can afford us,

Mia."

"Pro bono?" I said.

"Exactly. Brian's living with his sister. He's a comic book artist. Very sweet."

"That's what he was showing you?" I said.

"His latest drawings. He's extraordinarily talented. Very sensitive, as artists often are." Cameron navigated the car back down the pathway.

We drove the way we'd come, down Beverly Glen and gliding around twisty roads while avoiding the cars driving on the other side of the road and coming too fast our way.

It was hard to take my eyes off this man. His handsome face, the way his eyes flitted toward the rearview mirror, the way he smiled and threw glances my way.

My cheeks blushed when I recalled what he'd done to me in Richard's office to help me get my job back. Playing with me in front of Richard to prove I was ready to work at a place like Enthrall. Just the thought of those artful fingers touching me down there made me squirm. Seeing Richard with another woman softened the guilt of fantasizing about Cameron. A forbidden saving grace.

We drove the rest of the way in that awe inspiring silence.

Cameron parked outside Richard's home and he followed me in.

Sir Winston's paws padded along the hardwood floors and he skidded around the corner to greet us. If he was disappointed it was Cameron and I and not Richard he didn't show it. He merely rubbed his body against my leg, probably excited about the snack he knew was coming.

After giving him a treat and sending him out the back door to take his last pee of the night, I headed back into the kitchen to fill his water bowl.

After giving my hands a good wash, I peeled off the dressing on my ankle and threw it in the trash. The redness around my tattoo was lessening. After taking a few moments to admire it again, I joined Cameron in the sitting room.

He stared out through the double glass doorway. "Did you hang those lights, Mia?"

"I put them up yesterday," I said.

"They look fantastic."

"Do you want to see them on?" I slid open the glass door and made my way over to the wall switch and flicked it. The garden was transformed into a wonderland of dramatically trailing Christmas lights strung from one end of the garden to the other, making the blue sparkling pool the central showpiece. It looked magical.

Cameron nodded his approval.

"We'll have caterers tomorrow night," I called over to him. "So I won't have to worry about everyone getting what they need."

He looked amused. "How very decadent."

"You're used to all this." I gestured to the garden. "This is my first time hosting a party."

This would not only be the first party I co-hosted with Richard but probably our last. Disappointment replaced this short lived excitement.

"You'll be a wonderful host," said Cameron, as though sensing my angst.

I'd been so happy spiraling those lights across the garden, with no idea that soon my life would also be spiraling out of control. Where the hell was I going to live now?

I made my way back in. "Will you stay awhile?"

"Sure."

"Can I get you a drink?"

"No, thank you," he said. "Mia, why didn't you talk with Richard first?"

I broke his dark gaze.

"What was the driving force in getting a tattoo?" he said.

My boyfriend walking hand in hand with another woman. And the impending truth that we're over.

I kicked off my shoes and made my way over to the couch and dragged my feet up. Lying down on my side, I rested my head on the armrest. This day had been grueling and all I wanted to do was cry into my pillow.

Scream into my pillow.

Wail away this agony until I'd rid myself of this rock lodged in my chest.

Cameron sat opposite in that big leather chair, staring at me intently. Even if he was a rascal, like Richard, I so loved having him near. Cameron made me feel safe. I knew he made everyone feel that way, but it was nice to believe he was fond of me.

He came over and pulled a chenille throw on top of me. "I'll give Richard a call on the way home." He returned to his seat.

"Thank you," I said. "He listens to you." Rubbing the tiredness out of my eyes, I tried to fall asleep.

"Mia."

I pried my sleepy eyes open.

"You don't have to go back to Dr. Raul."

I blinked at him. "Really?"

"You've completed enough sessions with her."

"Did she say I'm fine?"

"She knows you'll be fine. Try to get some sleep. I'll see you tomorrow night."

I no longer looked forward to it. I squeezed my eyes shut to prevent tears from escaping.

This once happiness was over.

CHAPTER 8

MORNING BROUGHT WITH it the memory of being picked up from the couch by strong, capable hands and carried to bed.

Richard had undressed me and then tucked me in. His attentiveness made me feel so loved, so nurtured, right up until the point that memory of seeing him with another woman screeched into my brain.

This wave of sorrow threatened to drown me.

Stretching, I looked over at his side of the bed. It was empty. Noises carried from the kitchen. He was in there feeding Winston breakfast. I shoved myself up the headboard and mulled over how to discuss with him what I'd seen. Talking about last night would put our relationship on the fast track to being over. The argument leading to the kind of tension Richard refused to tolerate.

I'd given up my Malibu beach house to be Richard's live-in girlfriend and lost my independence. Though I never felt suffocated in our relationship, Richard really was a bossy bastard. But he was my bossy bastard and the thought of losing him was heart wrenching.

I reached over to my bedside table, rummaged inside it, and withdrew my birth control pills. I popped one in my mouth.

The bedroom door flew open and it made me jump. Richard carried a tray in with pancakes stacked high on a plate and a coffee mug.

"Breakfast in bed?" He beamed and laid the tray next to me.

"What's this for?" I wiped the sleepiness from my eyes, the

confusion.

A guilt laden offering?

He sat on the edge of the mattress. "This is my way of thanking you. Love the lights."

"I had fun putting them up."

Richard handed me the mug. "There you go."

"Did you have fun last night?" I watched his face.

"I didn't stay long," he said. "Apparently you tried to bring me my phone?"

I took a sip of coffee. "I missed you."

"Phones are forbidden." He ran his fingers through his blond locks, leaving it disheveled.

Or maybe he just didn't want to be disturbed. Didn't want his girlfriend ruining his fun.

"Why not leave it in your car?" I said.

"It's actually nice to take a break from technology." He picked up the fork and handed it to me. "Eat."

I rested the fork back down. "I did something too last night."

"I saw it when I put you to bed."

"Cameron told you?" I said, pulling back the sheet and lifting my ankle.

"We had drinks last night." Richard took my ankle in his hands. His thumb stroked the outline of the hummingbird and his eyelids fluttered, but other than that there was no reaction. "You have to rub in antibacterial ointment for the first few days."

"I know," I said. "Well?"

"I already find you fuckable. You didn't need to get this."

"Very funny."

"Why get it now, baby?"

I gave a shrug.

"Where did you get it?"

"Beverly Hills."

"I'd rather you talk with me first before making this kind of decision."

"It was spontaneous."

"I'm the spontaneous one, remember?" Richard stood up. "Cameron and I talked last night, Mia. We talked for a while about you."

"What did he say?"

"We threw around some ideas."

"Sounds ominous," I said. "Did he meet you at Pendulum?"

Richard looked horrified. "How do you know about Pen?" He flung his arms up. "Never mention that name again. Understand?"

"Okay, why?"

"Because it doesn't exist."

I gave him the look that deserved.

"What do you know about it?" he said. "Who told you about it?"

His reaction stunned me.

Richard moved closer to the bed. "Tell me."

I hesitated, searching for the right words. "I know exactly what goes on in there."

"Impossible." His tone was somber, cautious even. "You're bluffing."

I shrugged. "Maybe I overheard someone talking about it."

He scraped his fingers through his hair. Wow, I'd not expected this.

If the place is that bad, why the hell was he there? And what was he doing with that girl inside?

"Eat your breakfast. Let's not mention that place again." He headed towards the door and paused. "Mia, whenever you're ready to talk, I'm here from you."

"Do you still love me?"

"A tattoo is not that big of a deal." He frowned. "But why you got it is."

"I'm fine."

"No, you're not. I'd do anything for you. Anything. Surely you know that by now? Have I done anything to make you doubt how much I love you?"

Say it, my brain screamed at me. *Get it out before this devours you.*

"You've been nothing but wonderful to me."

He strolled back on over and kissed my forehead. "You're my everything, Mia Lauren, and don't ever forget that." He pointed to my plate. "Eat, before it gets cold and ends up tasting like your cooking."

"Hey." I reached for a pillow and threw it at him.

Richard bolted out the door, laughing as he went. My pillow missed him.

I sank back against the headboard. Our Pendulum conversation was never going to happen. My mind drifted to what kind of place Pendulum was. If it topped Enthrall and Chrysalis, no doubt there was illegal activity going on in there.

And Richard was into it.

Whatever *it* was.

CHAPTER 9

THE PULSE OF the party matched my mood: vibrant.

Having pushed these feelings of betrayal out of my mind, I wanted, no needed, to give Richard the benefit of the doubt. It sat well with me. It felt like I'd been granted a second chance.

I'd chosen to wear my new Elie Tahari Reilla dress. The white eyelet cotton was perfect for this warm, fall evening and I'd matched it with comfy flat pumps. My hair was spiraled into delicate curls and my makeup was a perfect blend of emboldened dark eye shadow and soft pink lips. Tiny diamond studs were my only jewelry.

Rock music played in the background to this, our bustling party, the air bristling with excitement. Most of our guests mingled in the garden. Many of them seemed to know each other well from the way they embraced. Others moved from group to group, shaking hands, the formalities soon falling away and their laughter carrying.

This crowd was not only beautiful, they were rich, all dressed in classy casual clothes and carrying themselves with the air of the privileged. At the far end of the garden, just to the left of the pool, sat a long table draped in a white cloth and laden with the finest hors d'oeuvres. Small bites, like the Bruschetta, I'd gone back for seconds of, and that delicious Smoked Salmon Crostini.

Drinks were carried upon silver trays by waitresses, all donning the same black and white uniforms, all scurrying around to make sure the guests had what they needed.

Richard fed me Beluga caviar topped on miniature pancakes. His attention, along with a second glass of champagne, made me giddy with happiness. He led me off across the garden to greet his newly arrived guests and introduced me as his girlfriend. My confidence soared and my sense of belonging was at an all time high. These were some of the most interesting men and women I'd ever met, and I spent most of my time listening in awe as Richard traversed conversations ranging from politics to foreign issues and proving he was impressively well informed on current affairs. I leaned against him, admiring the ease with which he transitioned from one subject to another, easily matching the intellects of those around him.

Richard led me into the kitchen. "I want to introduce you to someone very special."

"Who?" I said.

"Los Angeles's finest D.A."

"As in District Attorney?"

Richard smiled. "Mia, you'd be surprised who half our guests are." He tugged me after him.

There, in the kitchen, taking a bite out of an hors d'oeuvre, was Cameron, dressed in jeans and a black shirt. He chatted away to a handsome forty something, his deep frown lines hinting at stress. He too held a small plate of food.

Cameron threw us a wave when he saw us.

"Ethan," said Richard. "Good to see you. This is Mia." He gestured to his friend. "Mia, this is Ethan Neilson."

"It's a pleasure to meet you, Mia," he said, with a Georgia lilt. "Thank you for the invite."

I beamed at him. "Thank you for being here."

"It's uncanny." Ethan turned toward Cameron. "She looks just like her."

"Who?" I said.

"My wife," he said.

"Is she here?" I looked back into the garden, waiting for him to point.

"I'm afraid Sarah passed away, Mia," said Cameron.

"I'm so sorry," I said.

"I saw a photo of you in the hallway," said Ethan, by way of explaining. "It kind of stopped me in my tracks."

"I'm so glad you could make it," said Richard, softening the moment. "It means the world to us to have you here. I see Cameron's taking good care of you. Can I get you anything else? Something stronger to drink perhaps?"

"Maybe later," said Ethan.

"The garden looks fabulous," said Cameron. "Mia put all this together," he told Ethan.

Again that drawn out stare, and the reason for it now known.

"I kind of had help," I said. "Richard hired a party planner."

Richard reached toward Cameron's plate and picked a stray tortilla chip off it. He dipped it into the guacamole beside it and shoved it into his mouth with a grin.

Cameron rolled his eyes, amused.

"Did I see Andrew Harvey here?" said Ethan, sounding impressed.

"Shall I introduce you?" asked Cameron.

"I'd love that," said Ethan.

"Come on," said Cameron. "I also want to show you the view. It's one of the best in Malibu."

He led Ethan away.

"Who is Andrew Harvey?" I said.

"A newscaster," said Richard. "His public image is Republican, family man, charity supporter. Impressive resume actually."

"And his kink?" I said.

Richard leaned into my ear and whispered, "Pony play."

"Really?"

"That's confidential." He raised his finger in a warning. "I'm going to check on the valets. I'll be right back."

I watched him go and then opened the fridge for a bottle of Perrier.

Shouting came from the south hallway.

"Fuck you too," yelled a male, in an English accent.

Leaving my Perrier on the countertop, I headed off in that direction to investigate. Halfway down, I saw a man gripping the shoulders of another younger man in what looked like an aggressive embrace.

Nearing them, I took in the tall, dashing thirty something attacker, ready to swipe him away from the other guy.

"Excuse me," I said. "What's going on?"

"This is private," he said. "Do us both a favor and piss off."

"I will not. I live here."

The tall guy let go of his victim. "I'll meet you by the food table," he told him. "Stay away from the fucking bar."

His victim scrambled away, not even making eye contact with me.

"What just happened there?" I said, vaguely recognizing him as a member of a rock band but forgetting the name.

"Trust me, you don't want to know," he said. "Are you Richard's girlfriend?"

"I am."

He held out his hand. "I'm Karl."

"And I don't care."

He turned away from me and knocked on Richard's office door.

"That's private," I said.

"That's why I'm knocking. Jeez, lighten up will you?"

I followed him in, ready to snap his head off.

He took in the office. "We can talk privately in here."

Richard's wallet was on his desk, and from the way he arched a brow Karl had seen it too.

"Don't worry," he said. "I'm not going to steal anything."

Resting my fists on my hips I glared, throwing daggers. "What was that about then?"

"He's my lead singer."

"Oh?"

"Sorry you had to see that." He looked frustrated. "He just got out of rehab."

"Maybe you should be a little kinder to him then."

"Look, I just took a Bud Light out of his hand." He shook his head as though clearing a thought. "Bud Light today turns into crack tomorrow. I've been through hell and back, and quite frankly I'm not willing to go through it again."

My shoulders dropped their tension. "Oh, sorry."

"I imagine it looked bad." He shrugged. "He's got the willpower of a girl."

I glared at him.

He burst out laughing. "Sorry. Didn't mean to offend."

"Then maybe you shouldn't open your mouth anymore."
"You said you're Richard's girlfriend?"
"Yes."
"How long have you been dating?"
Like it's any business of yours. "A while."
"How come I've never seen you at Chrysalis?"
"We'll..."
"Are you his submissive?"
I went to speak, but the words didn't come out.
"You don't look too sure," he said.
A ping on Richard's phone drew my attention. "Excuse me. I have to get this."

Karl didn't need to know this wasn't my cell. I walked around the desk. A tilt of my head indicated this conversation was over and after a few more seconds he took the hint and left. With the English guy gone, I opened the desk side drawer and dropped Richard's wallet into it and made a mental note to tell him where I'd hidden it. I went to hide his phone there too when a new text lit up the screen.

Jasmine: Hey, Rick,

Rick? He hated being called Rick?

Jasmine: Ha! Have sneaked a text out. I'm freaking out. Am so in trouble. This is a complete mind-fuck. In a good way. LOL! Thursday night was fantastic. Everything is amazing. I'm in for a real punishment for sending this! Thank you for being here and helping my transition go smidle.

What the hell was smidle?

Jasmine: F*Auto-correct. Helping my transition go *smoothly*. Miss you. Can't wait to see you again. Love you, babes!

Bile rose in my throat.
Thursday night? That was the evening I saw him with that pretty blonde. Pain laced my hand as I dug my teeth into it. I had

a name to go with the face. That pretty supermodel face that right now I wanted to punch a hole through. Bitch.

Richard had removed photos of us from Facebook. Was this why? So Jasmine didn't see them?

I threw the phone into the drawer. Slammed it shut.

Richard was staring at me from the doorway. "Are you giving our guests a hard time?"

My hands were trembling.

Richard came in. "Karl just gave me an earful about my unruly submissive."

"I caught Karl beating up his friend," I said, finding my voice.

"Bret's going through a hard time coming off drugs. Karl is sticking with him. Very honorable. Not sure I would."

Throw Richard's phone at him, my muse screamed at me, *and then the fucking chair.*

"He was very complimentary about you," said Richard.

"He asked if I was your submissive."

Richard came towards me, his expression tense. "I've been giving that a lot of thought."

"Oh?"

"I can't wait for everyone to go so you and I can talk privately."

My mouth went dry. "Talk?"

A break up talk?

"You look incredible tonight." He reached out and grabbed my waist, pulling me towards him. "You've just stepped into a five hour hug."

Overwhelmed, I softened against him, spacing out and trying to make sense of that text. "You shouldn't leave your wallet out," I muttered. "Anyone could just wander in and steal it."

Or read your private texts.

"Everyone here is very honest," he said, kissing my forehead. "They don't need the money."

I went rigid against him. "It makes me nervous." *You make me nervous.*

"If they want my stuff they can have it."

I broke away. "If they got hold of your cards you'd be in trouble."

"Are you pre-menstrual?"

I gawped at him.

"That was dangerous." He laughed. "Looks like my death wish is back." His eyes widened in wonder and he beamed a drop dead smile. The kind that always had me weakening. Bastard.

Ask him about Jasmine. Go on, face your fear. Face the pain. Get it over with.

"Baby, you look a little pale," he said.

Jasmine had called him baby. Did that mean he called her that too?

"You okay? Karl wasn't rude to you was he?" His accent was now flawlessly English. "I'll punch his lights out if he was."

"No. I'm starving, that's all," I said. "I'm going to grab myself a bite to eat."

"I just fed you a ton of Beluga. Still, your appetite is back. That's reassuring."

And the Oscar for most convincing happy person goes to…moi.

"I'll catch up with you," he said.

Relieved to put some distance between us, I made my way into the kitchen and headed into the pantry. Running my fingers along the full wine rack, I took my time selecting something special. Something mind numbing.

Just give me a few more hours with him, my heart begged. *The chance to savor these last few moments of us. Soon you'll be heading back to your old life and living in a studio apartment once again and eating noodles. A far cry from champagne, salmon thingys, and caviar.*

There really was no rush to get back to that life. No, no rush at all.

I found it. That bottle of Domain Leroy Clos de Bougeot from France, the one Richard had been saving for a special occasion. Reverently, I carried it out of the pantry and placed it on the kitchen counter and sat it beneath the Brookstone bottle opener and uncorked the sucker.

Hell yes, if I was going to be replaced by Ms. Victoria's Slutsville I was going to seek revenge first. And this overly expensive wine was the way to go. There'd be no casualties and Richard wouldn't realize it until I was long gone.

Pain was heading my way like a hundred foot tsunami. Sucking back tears, I poured a large glass of the deep red liquor and tasted it. Its sharp tanginess stung my taste buds. Several gulps later, I sensed someone's eyes on me.

Cameron walked passed me, frowning. "Steady on, Mia." He caught sight of the label. "Have you any idea how much that costs?"

"Tastes the same as any other. Looks like Richard was ripped off."

"Maybe if you'd given it time to breathe." Cameron pointed at me. "Cork it and put it back where you found it."

"Okay then."

He ambled off around the corner. I poked my tongue out at him. Childish, I know, but the rebellion felt fantastic. I looked around to make sure no one caught it.

"Put it back, Mia," Cameron shouted from the hallway.

After pouring my second glass and taking another sip, I realized there was something to be said for leaving it uncorked for a while. It was tasty. My thoughts drifted and I wondered how long before this ache in my heart would be soothed by the impending buzz. Champagne and red wine were a potent mix.

Now was a good time to speak with Cameron privately. If one person had an inkling of Richard's plan for me, it would be him. Perhaps he would help me convince Richard to keep me on at Enthrall, even if we weren't dating.

I charged around the corner and bumped right into Cameron, tipping my glass of wine against his chest and drenching his shirt red.

I slapped my hand over my mouth to hide my horror.

Cameron peered down and tugged the clinging material away from his torso. "Please tell me that wasn't the Domain Leroy."

"I'm so sorry." I blushed. "I'll get some napkins."

Cameron's glare rose to meet mine and he blinked at me several times before turning sharp on his heels and heading back the way he'd come, down and along the hallway.

Mortified, I followed, cringing all the way down. He headed into Richard's bedroom and disappeared inside the walk-in wardrobe.

He reappeared with a fresh shirt on a hanger. "One of mine," he said, making his way into the bathroom en suite.

Why the hell did he keep one of his shirts in Richard's wardrobe?

Joining him inside the bathroom, I feigned interest in the floor tile when he unbuttoned his shirt. He pulled it off, revealing well defined shoulders, that sculptured torso, his black pants hanging low and revealing a hint of a perfectly formed V.

I snapped my gaping mouth shut.

I'd seen Cameron naked once before from the waist up, that time I'd gone to his home in Venice Beach, but he'd wrapped a towel around himself, concealing the true beauty of his body. If Cameron knew I was dumbstruck he didn't act like it.

He threw the shirt onto the counter. "I'll get it dry-cleaned." His mirrored reflection offered reassurance as he dabbed his chest with a wet cloth. "Don't want to smell like a wino."

A tuft of dark hair teased and that six-pack rippled as the washcloth swept over his torso. "Best hide the Domain Leroy before Richard sees it." He arched a brow. "We'll get another bottle to replace it."

I tore my gaze away from his perfection and tried to concentrate on his face. "Why do you have a spare shirt here?"

"I sleep over sometimes."

I wasn't sure I was ready to hear anymore.

Cameron looked amused. "If there's a late game on and we drink too much. No drinking and driving. Very responsible, wouldn't you say?"

"What about Leo?" I said. "He could take you home."

"Having him wait around always feels selfish. He has a family with two young boys. Besides, I like crashing here. And it's easier to head straight to the office and avoid morning traffic. Since you moved in I've been giving you both the space you deserve. New romance and all that."

"Where do you sleep?" There, I said it.

"In the spare bedroom." He turned to face me. "Mia, Richard and I have never had sex. Not together, anyway. Of course I've had the pleasure of watching him have sex, as he has me." He looked amused. "Hope I cleared that up."

Oh yeah, thanks for that.

Of course I suspected this. After all, these two were the grand gods of sex, the dark lords of Chrysalis, but hearing it confirmed was something else. My mind turned cartwheels trying to imagine just what they'd gotten up to. A thrill shot between my thighs as wild images came to mind of these two and some lucky girl caught in their fuck-web.

He was turning me on.

Grrrr.

Cameron always did this. Seducing me with merely the arch of a brow, making me tingle deliciously down there. This highly charged sexual chemistry might be fun for him but it was a real curse, threatening to soak my panties. My brain warned me to leave, like right now, this second, only my legs and the warm fuzzy feeling down there wasn't getting the message.

He reached for a towel and dabbed his chest dry. "You're forgiven."

At least he'd removed this nagging doubt about just how close these guys really were. Still, now I knew Cameron liked to watch Richard doing it, and I had a brand new doubt to replace the last. Who had the girl been that he'd watched Richard doing? His last submissive? Jasmine, the texting whore?

"Don't be upset." Cameron shrugged. "I bumped into you."

I brushed a strand of hair out of my eyes. My scorching cheeks burned less.

Cameron buttoned his fresh shirt and tucked it into his pants. "Let's see if anyone mentions it. You'd be surprised how something so obvious goes unnoticed."

"If you have a moment," I said, "I wanted to talk to you about Richard."

"I'd rather he were here."

"Well, it's kind of about him and me."

"Of all the women in Richard's life, you mean the most to him," said Cameron from out of nowhere.

Had he just confirmed my fear? I wrapped my arms around myself.

Cameron turned around to face me and leaned back against the counter top, his hands resting on the edge, all perfect styled hair and dashing smile. "Do you want to talk about anything else?"

"No. Why?"

He scrutinized me. "I love that dress on you. Very pretty."

"Thank you."

"I'm here for you anytime you want to talk."

"Thank you."

"Let's grab Richard later and have that chat you need?"

"Sure."

Cameron went for the exit. I stepped aside and watched him leave. The waft of his cologne was the only evidence he'd been here. That, and his soiled shirt sitting on the bathroom counter.

Feeling guilty over the wine spilling saga, I made my way over to the sink and reached for it. If I ran it under cold water it would get most of the wine out. I flicked the collar and stole a glance at the Dolce and Gabbana label. It was definitely worth a try. The material was soft, proving along with the label it was expensive.

I hoped I'd never get used to all this wealth. I'd promised myself I'd keep this sense of value and not become spoiled and wasteful. Last week, Richard had bought me several hundred dollar T-shirts from a Rodeo Drive store and the cost had made my toes curl. Not that I wasn't grateful. One of them was a gorgeous royal blue Gucci top, the price hiked because of the label that no one would see.

After spilling five hundred dollars worth of wine on this shirt, I really needed to reel in my judgment of the wealthy and their irreverent waste.

Having spent my entire life living in poverty, I was still getting used to being around two millionaires. Though, according to Richard, Cameron was a billionaire, set to inherit the entire Cole Tea Industries estate. Cameron never talked about it. And he certainly never acted superior. I suppose he didn't have anything to prove.

Lifting his shirt to my nose, I inhaled the essence of Cameron, burying my face in the material and swooning at his soft cologne mixed with his sexy scent. It sent a shiver through me. Eyes closed, I found comfort in knowing this man was in my life. The most exciting friend a girl could have. Other than Richard of course. Cameron always knew what to say and when to put me at ease. He knew how to handle Richard. He could handle anything.

Scrunching up the material, I let my senses fill with him. Every part of me tingled and my heart fluttered. Cameron was so desirable. So irresistible. I loved Richard with every part of my being, though Cameron was a mystery I couldn't help but obsess over. I may not have been cheating on Richard, like he was on me, but I was as sure as hell betraying him with these thoughts.

I shoved them away. Or tried to.

The material felt smooth against my lips, soft, sensual even, and I closed my eyes and breathed him in again.

Oh no—

Cameron stood in the doorway and he was staring at me, his expression unreadable. Had I not learned my lesson from that day at Enthrall when he'd caught me on Scarlet's spanking bench? From the way he was staring, all steely and unfazed, it was an easy no. The floor beneath my feet became unsteady and I hoped this imaginary earthquake would crack open the ground and swallow me.

Cameron said nothing. He merely dragged out this torturous embarrassment as though measuring his words. "Mia." His tone was deep, seductive.

"Yes."

This was the first time I'd seen him speechless.

The door bumped Cameron forward.

It was Richard. "Am I invited to this party?"

He'd sunburned his forehead earlier, despite applying sunblock. That flushed skin would soon turn golden, enhancing those deep ocean blue eyes.

"I was washing it out." I looked to Cameron for confirmation.

Cameron arched a brow.

"Someone opened my bottle of Domain Leroy," said Richard.

I sprang into action and turned the cold tap on, preferring to stare at running water than continue to be held in this line of fire by the all-seeing Richard. Or Cameron.

"What am I missing?" said Richard.

Damn, how did they always see beyond what was right in front of them?

Shooting Cameron a warning glance, I said, "It was my fault. I bumped into him and accidentally spilled my drink over his shirt. I can save it though."

"I can get it dry cleaned," said Cameron. "I told you that."

Scrubbing the material together, I was grateful for the distraction. The water went from a deep red to a pinkish hue. "It's almost out." I held it up. "See?"

"Mia," said Cameron with sincerity, "has something she wants to talk to you about, Richard."

I flashed a confused glance his way. "No I don't."

Cameron arched a questioning brow.

I held up the shirt. "I kind of did you a favor."

"Oh really?"

Oh shit, I'd awoken the beast that was Cameron Cole.

Richard laughed. "Please don't tell me that's my all time favorite saved for a special day bottle of wine."

Unable to look at him, I scrubbed away like an old washer woman.

Richard shook his head in surprise. "And to add insult to injury Cole, that's your favorite shirt isn't it?"

"All time favorite," said Cameron. "Weaved by monks atop the Himalayas. My trek up there to find it was legendary. Grueling too. Took six months. Lost good men along the way."

"Very funny," I said.

"Mia," said Cameron. "I'll buy another. Please don't worry about it."

"The wine's replaceable," said Richard.

"I'm so clumsy," I said. "I should drink white." Staring down at the sopping material, I kept my focus away from them.

"What do you think of Mia's tattoo?" asked Richard.

I'd forgotten about that. My hummingbird itched feeling their scrutiny.

"I rather like it," said Cameron. "It perfectly represents her."

"What an interesting observation," said Richard, his right hand reaching out into the ether before him. "Mia's exactly like a hummingbird. Hovering right in front of you, yet you can't quite ever capture a hummingbird." He closed his fingers into a fist. "No matter how much you want to. And then of course there's the fear that if you do, you'll somehow—"

"Mia," said Cameron. "Next time you make a big decision like this you'll talk to us about it."

"I promise." I stared at Richard, trying to see if he was hurt.

"What are you thinking, Booth?" said Cameron.

"Any suggestions?" said Richard.

"A public spanking might teach her some respect," said Cameron.

"As if." I turned off the tap.

Cameron gave Richard a pat on his back before heading out to leave us to cope with the fallout.

Richard also knew a thing or two about silence. He stood there watching me, waiting for goodness knows what. I'd been so excited about hosting this party with him and now all I felt was awkward. Betrayed. Out of control. My lack of social graces raised their ugly head yet again.

Richard pried the shirt out of my grip and threw it into the linen basket. He replaced the lid to hide the evidence.

"He's wants to get it dry cleaned," I said.

"I'll take care of it."

Leaning into him, I rested my head against his chest.

Tell me she's nothing to you.

His grip tightened. "Baby, it's just a shirt."

"I'm sorry about the wine."

"Anything of mine is yours. I've told you that." He gripped my shoulders and pushed me back to better see my face. "What's going on with you?"

I looked up at him. "Am I good enough for you?"

"Too good." He kissed the end of my nose. "I'm more at risk of losing you. I've seen the way you drool over Enthrall's gardener."

I giggled. "Juan's fifty."

"Juan? First name terms?" He gave a crooked smile. "You're not exactly helping your case, Mia."

"Silly."

"I'm sure our Mediterranean, tanned and studly gardener is much younger than that," he said. "Must be all the sun."

"Are we even talking about the same person?"

He feigned mock horror. "There's more than one?"

I poked his chest. "Juan doesn't speak a word of English."

"Sounds perfect to me. Less chance of arguments."

I threw my head back in a laugh. He really was my funny Richard. And I was about to lose him. I pressed my face against his chest.

He hugged me back. "Mia, I love you more than life itself and nothing you say or do will ever change that."

Richard's words rendered me useless and I nuzzled in. His scent of a fresh ocean was soothing and safe.

"Cameron took a shirt out of your wardrobe," I said.

"I have stuff at his place too." He shrugged. "We're not bashful around each other. We're best buddies."

"I know."

"We've been through a lot together. Cameron and I trust each other completely. As I trust you." Richard held me at arm's length. "Everything between you and me is good too, baby, okay."

I was lost in his ocean blue eyes, that heart-stopping face.

"Trust me," he said. "Talk to me."

"There's nothing to talk about."

"Remember the first time I took you to <u>Hsi Lai Temple</u> and I opened up to you?"

"It's so peaceful there."

That serene Buddhist temple nested in Hacienda Heights. A slice of nirvana where guilt lost its way. Except for me. Guilt was so deeply part of my DNA it would never leave. I pushed these dreadful, creeping thoughts away.

Richard ran his hands up and down my arms. "After I told you about my past and shared those experiences with you there I felt cleansed. It was cathartic."

"That makes me so happy."

"Then open up to me now," he said. "Right now. Tell me what's been bothering you these last few months."

"There's nothing else to say."

"I'm not talking about that dreadful situation with your father."

"Have I disappointed you?"

"Never."

"But?"

"You're not going to talk to me are you?" he said.

I threw my hands up in frustration. "Why do you all assume there's something I need to talk about?"

"Your behavior."

"Because I got a tattoo?"

"Because something is hurting you and it's eating you alive." He clenched his fists. "I want it to come out naturally."

"As opposed to what?" I snapped.

"Mia?"

I wasn't there for my mom. I let her down. I let her die. I did something so terrible that, if shared, my future will crumble beneath my feet.

"I don't have the skill to get to the root cause, Mia." He looked sympathetic. "You have to open up to me."

My throat tightened, gasping air. "I wish you'd all leave me the fuck alone."

Richard stepped back and stared at me.

"What?" I snapped.

"Nothing, Mia. It's just as you say. Everything's fine."

My reflection stared back and she was glaring, wanting to congratulate me on ruining what had started out as a perfectly wonderful day.

"There's a small detail we need to take care of." He looked stern. "Before we proceed."

I raised my head to better look at him. "Proceed?"

"Deal with your indiscretion," he said. "You marked your body without my permission. A cardinal sin for a submissive."

My mouth went dry.

"Details need to be finalized." He shrugged. "First, we must deal with your indiscretion."

"How?"

"You will present yourself to me in the garden."

"Present myself?"

"For your spanking." Richard's demeanor changed from lover to master.

"That's not funny."

He strolled towards the door. "I never joke about punishing my submissive."

A thrill of excitement shot up my spine, matched only by this fear of humiliation that stomped on into my mind with all its tremulous glory. "But—"

He raised his hand in way of an order. "Remove your panties before leaving this room."

I was left standing alone in the bathroom, stock-still, staring at my stunned expression in the mirror.

Richard had just called me *his* submissive.

CHAPTER 10

I WANTED TO follow through on my master's order and remove my panties, but I wasn't quite ready to be displayed in public during any kind of punishment, and certainly not in front of this crowd. There was a D.A. here, for goodness sake.

With that decision firmly lodged in my brain, I headed back out into the garden—

And almost tripped over a young woman crawling on all fours, held on a long silver chain dangling from the choker around her neck. Like a dog on a leash.

Taking in the crowd, it seemed no one else was as shocked as me at this ultimate scene of dominance.

The girl's master was holding the leash up and almost choking her with it. I jolted in terror when I recognized Senator DeLuca, Enthrall's VIP client who Cameron had taken me to dinner with a month back in that swanky restaurant. The same man who'd insisted to Cameron that he wanted the chance to train me. Luckily for me Cameron had declined the offer on my behalf. I was really happy about that, not least because of the way DeLuca was treating his submissive. The woman was struggling to keep up. She looked about my age and was dressed in a bodice and thong. She showed no resistance.

"Mia," said Senator DeLuca. "It is Mia, isn't it?"

"Yes," I said, wondering if introducing myself to the girl was bad form. I tried to read from her face if she was enjoying this.

"How have you been?" asked DeLuca.

"Fine thanks, and you?"

"Just wonderful," he said, giving the leash a tug.

I looked around for Richard, hoping he'd come to my rescue. He was deep in conversation with Scarlet and had failed to notice his old friend DeLuca arrive with his plaything on a chain.

"Fascinating. Richard boring of you so easily," said DeLuca. "I'm surprised that you couldn't keep his attention?"

I glared at him. Was he purposefully trying to rile me up? Richard protected me. Something this man would never understand.

"You have potential, Mia." DeLuca cocked his head. "With the correct training, you'd surpass our expectations, I'm sure."

Fuck off was on the tip of my tongue.

I pointed to the girl. "Looks like you've already got your hands full."

"This is Sierra." He knelt beside her and ran his finger through her hair. "Isn't she exquisite?"

Her eyes flitted shut and she pouted her approval like she was in subspace, but then again he was tweaking her nipples now, tugging one and then the other right here in front of everyone.

DeLuca rose to his full height. "Why have you never visited Chrysalis?" He reached out for a glass of champagne offered up by a passing waitress and lifted it off the tray. He rested the glass against his lips.

A wave of uncertainty washed over me. "I've been busy," I said, summoning the courage to tell him what I really thought of him. Somewhere in that glorious monologue were the words *bastard* and *fuckwit*.

"Senator," said Cameron, appearing out of nowhere. "Glad you could make it." Cameron shooed me away. "Run along now, Mia."

"We haven't finished talking," I said.

"Yes, you have." Cameron pointed toward Richard. "Go on."

I folded my arms, remaining where I was and not ready to let DeLuca off so easily. "So when are you going back to Sicily?" I said. "Any time soon?"

"Now," demanded Cameron.

I made my way over to Richard, rounding the pool and strolling through the crowd, not willing to have any of these people see my butt exposed during my impending spanking that in no way was going to happen.

Richard smiled when he saw me. "Ready?"

"Actually, no." I glanced over at the senator and Cameron.

There were a few waitresses in the garden and strangers who may or may not have been members of Enthrall. Cameron and DeLuca were chatting away with that girl at their feet like this was a normal garden party.

"Look." I gestured toward Sierra and her master.

"What am I meant to be looking at?" said Richard.

"Go and help her?" I said. "He's embarrassing her."

"Mia, she's enjoying it."

I glared at him.

"Sierra's into subjugation."

"You know her?"

"We trained her at Enthrall."

"How did she end up with him?" I glared at DeLuca.

"We gave her to him."

"What? When?"

"During a session at Chrysalis. They matched up perfectly."

My head was reeling. "That's wrong on so many levels."

"Excuse me?"

"Oh nothing."

"What did you just say?"

"I was expressing my concern," I said. "For my fellow female kind."

"Do you still have your panties on?" he said.

I stole another glance at Sierra.

Scarlet peered into her glass of wine. Seriously, now would be a good time to get some girlfriend support.

Richard straightened in his chair. "Mia, are you defying me?"

I opened my eyes wide, sending a silent message of insistence. "Can we talk about this inside?"

"Then it wouldn't be a public punishment."

Fisting my hands on my hips. "Not in front of the guests."

Enthrall Her

He looked furious, his blue eyes icy.

I melted in the wake of his sternness. It wasn't lost on me that I'd been begging Richard for over two months to take me on as his submissive. Seeing Sierra pulled around by the senator like that had thrown me. Made me question what might be in store for me.

"Take off your panties," demanded Richard.

"Can't you spank me in the house?" I whispered.

"Do I really have to ask you again?"

I took in the many faces, the other guests all happy and relaxed, all of them enjoying this evening and none of them would probably be shocked by what might unfold during a garden party hosted by Richard Booth.

I turned and glared at Cameron for coming up with this idea. He was now standing in the far left corner of the garden, deep in conversation with Ethan Neilson. The D. A. was taking a long drag off of a cigarette. Smoke billowed around them. Maybe Cameron was lecturing Neilson on the hazards of smoking, but it didn't look like that.

Was Richard really going to do this in front of a District Attorney?

"You'd rather have Ethan spank you?" asked Richard.

Scarlet gave me the kindest smile and in her eyes I saw the truth. I'd wanted this. Told her as much. I'd done everything in my power to be here. Belong to Richard in this way.

Damn it.

Sucking in the deepest, most daring breath while flushing wildly, I hoisted up my sundress and eased off my panties, throwing a glance at those around us.

"Good girl," said Richard.

I handed my underwear over and he tucked them into his pants pocket. Biting my lip hard, I leaned forward over Richard's lap as elegantly as possible, squeezing my eyes shut and praying for it to be over quick. My heart thundered in my chest, my ears ringing, my fingers gripping the edge of the chair.

I was going to find that shirt and rip it into a million pieces. And then finish off that bottle of wine. And though Sierra would never know it, I'd be doing it for her too.

Richard shifted beneath me, dragging this out as he got

comfortable, re-positioning me on his lap. He eased up my dress to fully expose my butt. His hand came down hard and I flinched forward. I pressed my hand over my mouth and bit into it. My butt cheeks stung with each strike. Again and again, Richard spanked me and the only way to endure it was to bury my teeth in my right hand.

In-between slaps, Richard caressed my flesh, pinching, stroking, and massaging my red, swollen cheeks, though doing little to soothe this sting. The throb between my legs matched the slaps. My sex betrayed me and swelled with pleasure, my thighs shaking from the throbbing between my legs. Richard's erection dug into my abdomen, proving he was just as turned on by my punishment. The slaps surely made me the center of attention.

The lapping of the pool, the sounds of a hand striking flesh, the quieting of conversations proved everyone had ceased talking to better observe.

"Please stop," I begged.

He ignored me, striking again and again, punishing without ceasing. Forcing back tears, I willed myself not to scream and embarrass myself anymore. Oh no, the waitresses would be seeing this too. I'd have to avoid looking them in the eyes for the rest of the evening.

"Apologize," said Richard.

"What for?" I burst out.

"Cameron's shirt."

Despite this delectable throbbing vibrating between my thighs, I wanted to run and hide. I'd been so caught up with needing this I'd not thought it through properly. I'd not realized these moments would always be on Richard's terms.

He eased me back onto my feet and handed me back my panties. Trembling, my butt cheeks burning, I couldn't speak, couldn't move, couldn't cry.

"Go and tell Cameron how sorry you are," said Richard sternly.

"But I already did."

"Do you take pleasure from defying me?"

I scrunched my panties into a ball and hugged them into my chest, turning sharply and making a bee-line for Cameron at the back of the garden. If the guests had found this amusing, they were hiding it well. Refusing to make eye contact with anyone, I scurried across the lawn, head down, both my face and ass burning like fire.

Cameron offered a welcome nod as I approached, but it did nothing to ease my angst. Ignoring Ethan Neilson, I stared up at Cameron.

"Are those for me?" He held out his hand.

My head felt foggy. "Excuse me?"

Cameron's stare lingered on my panties and I handed them over to him. He tucked them into his pocket. "Thank you, Mia." He gestured to Ethan. "You've already had the pleasure of meeting Mr. Neilson."

"Hello, Sir," I said, half distracted as I took in Ethan's kind face that was hard to interpret.

Ethan blew out a long plume of smoke and it spiraled into nothingness.

"Will there be anything else, Mia?" asked Cameron.

Ethan offered me a patient smile.

"Do you need anything else?" Cameron repeated sternly.

With a shake of my head, I turned to go and a wave of anger welled in my gut as I remembered the way he'd shooed me away in front of DeLuca. And not only was my ass sore because of him, my humiliation was at an all time high.

"There is actually just one more thing," I said. "Now that I come to think of it."

"Oh?" said Cameron.

I stared right at him. "I hate you."

Cameron's eyebrows shot up, though other than that he was expressionless.

I strolled away, edging around the sparkling pool and through the sliding glass doorway, stomping through the kitchen and into Richard's bedroom. I plopped down onto the end of the bed and flinched when my butt met the comforter. I wished I'd never given up my Malibu sanctuary where I could have gathered my thoughts and seriously considered my future.

I'd been degraded in front of all those people and even if some part of me had enjoyed it, needed it, craved it even, I was annoyed that I'd just handed myself over for their twisted pleasure.

My twisted pleasure, my muse taunted me. I scorned myself, *if it was so bad why are you so turned on?*

Richard had humiliated me in front of all those people and I'd almost climaxed in the process. I buried my face in my hands. A frisson fluttered in my chest and my cheeks reddened further.

Shameful.

The door flew open and Cameron strolled on in then closed it behind him. He made his way across the room without acknowledging me, approaching Richard's chest of drawers. He slid open the top drawer and removed a black tie. He gave it a tug to test its strength.

I watched with a mixture of fear and fascination as Cameron neared me.

He leaned over my left shoulder. "Wrists behind your back," he said. "Bring them together. Good." He tied my wrists securely with the tie and tugged it tight.

My breasts were pushed forward and my pert nipples showed through my dress. My breath stilted when he knelt before me, his stare boring into me as he placed his hands on my knees.

Oh hell.

As if that spanking hadn't been enough.

Here was Mr. Intensity to deliver my berating, my punishment for speaking disrespectfully to him in front of the D.A., and anyone else who might have overheard. I braced for Cameron's scolding, the reprimand that would be delivered with such scholarly astuteness I'd end up tied in even more knots.

I raised my chin defiantly.

Cameron eased my thighs apart and only then did I remember I wasn't wearing any panties. They were still in his pocket. The ones I needed back right now. Slowly, he slid the hem of my dress up my thighs and hitched it around my waist, taking his time to completely expose me. My thoughts raced with the words this moment deserved, my voice failing along with my ability to exhale.

He rested his hands on my knees and eased my thighs farther apart, ensuring my pussy was on full show. Cameron's gaze left mine and focused in on my most sacred place. My face scorched bright red. A minute passed, or maybe it was an hour, or maybe a lifetime.

Cameron leaned in between my thighs and I jolted when his tongue met my clitoris with stunning precision, teasing with quick flicks and sending shockwaves of bliss.

My jaw gaped and I ceased to breathe…

Oh. My. God.

His mouth was firm, intense, his tongue masterful, languishing, spearing, forcing me toward coming and then planting kisses to my inner thigh in a tease, bringing me down, only to return to my clit again and reward it with blinding pleasure.

With my hands bound behind me, I was powerless to nudge him away, my legs too weak to close. Not that I wanted to. I never wanted it to end. I needed him, needed *this* with every cell of my being, and by the way he controlled every nuance, every one of my responses, he knew it too.

Only now did I understand time standing still. Nothing mattered but this moment. His kisses to my thighs were cruel punishments of denial until he relented to my cries and his mouth found my clit again and he resumed relentlessly bringing more and more pleasure. The only sounds were that of my sighs and that of his lapping.

Being bound felt divine, liberating even, the irony of freedom beyond my comprehension. He'd captured me and I was *his* to do whatever he wanted.

"Can I come?" My voice sounded strained.

He didn't answer.

I needed him to answer.

"Please," I begged.

The world could have threatened to end but I wouldn't have cared. The room could have filled with people wanting to witness our dark soiree but I wouldn't have given them a second thought.

All I knew was Cameron.

Cameron.

His punishment of denial was over as his mouth fixed firmly once again to my sex, his tongue worshiping me with blinding bliss. Moaning my climax, I sucked in short bursts of air that he'd stolen from the room, from the house, the universe. His tongue led me on again, strumming so fast, flicking and licking with such passion, such expertise, I was close to losing consciousness.

Cameron slid two fingers inside me, crooking his fingertips and pressing against my upper vaginal wall, answering my silent prayer to be entered as his tongue danced on my clitoris, alighting more spasms of ecstasy. His fingers worked me, reaching my g-spot and making me shudder. I widened my thighs farther and lurched my pelvis towards him, needing this never to end as my head lolled to the side. My channel tightened around his expert fingers, bringing another rippling orgasm.

I moaned for him and it felt like he'd unlocked something primal, this once deeply buried part of my psyche permitting him to do whatever he wanted as long as it pleased him.

Anything.

He took his time bringing me back down to earth with gentle licks and kisses, his hair tickling between my thighs, his firm grip relentless.

I fell back—

Cameron caught me and sat me upright, grasping either side of my head with an ironclad hold and pressing his lips against mine, kissing me furiously, his tongue fucking my mouth now, owning me again as he shared my taste with him, that sweetness, that proof of my arousal gifted by him. Another moan escaped me and entered his mouth. His grip tightened in a flash of power that sent me reeling, tingles spiraling in my chest as passion exploded like fireworks from my center.

Making me feel so feminine. So beautiful. More alive than I ever had.

Our kiss was spellbinding, causing the spasming in my pussy to rise to fever pitch. Rippling in anticipation, I wanted, needed, his cock inside me, and opening my mouth more I begged him silently to take me. My clit still throbbed for him, yearning for his touch to return. His mouth continued possessing mine, owning me, and I came again. Hard.

Shudders wracked my body, leaving me trembling, beholden. I was coming merely from his kiss.

Quiet filled the room.

I blinked rapidly as I opened my eyes.

Cameron pulled back, his lips glistening. "Still hate me?"

I shook my head *no.*

Enthrall Her

"Didn't think so." He reached around my back to free me from the tie, tugging me loose. He threw it down.

And held his hand out to me.

With my hand in his, I pushed to my feet unsteadily, my skirt once more covering my shaking thighs. He led me into the bathroom and, in a daze, I watched him as though seeing him for the first time. I had no idea how long we'd been gone from the party. Cameron had even reigned time. Everything before fell away and that which lay ahead had no meaning.

From the shower, he retrieved a sponge and wet it under the tap, gesturing for me to lift my dress.

"Open your legs a little," he said.

Caressing between my thighs with the sponge, he used soft, gentle strokes to clean me, almost bringing me over again, continuing this intimacy I never wanted to end. I rested my forehead against his firm bicep, lulled by him. Cameron dabbed me with a towel, drying me down there. My fingers tightened around the material of my dress hitched above my waist and I watched his deliberate strokes between my thighs as he patted me dry.

"Oh please," I murmured.

A waft of his cologne hit me and I let out a long, wanton sigh, tranced out all over again.

"Mia." Cameron threw the towel on top of his shirt in the linen basket. "You will bring the D.A. and I two bourbons. Chilled. Carry our drinks to us upon a silver tray. Understand?"

"Yes."

"Yes, what?"

"Yes, Sir."

He gave a nod of approval.

As I watched Cameron leave, I hoped I'd be able to remember his drink order, because right now I couldn't remember my own fricken name.

CHAPTER 11

HANDS SHAKING, I poured bourbon into a tumbler.

The aroma of liquor filled my nostrils. I took a large gulp, hoping to calm my nerves. My throat burned like it was on fire. This stuff was strong.

What the hell had just happened?

I'd willingly succumbed to Cameron Cole's masterful handling and now understood what all the fuss about. Cameron had proven he really was the ultimate sex god. My pussy still thrummed from his touch and, swooning still, the memory threatened to render me useless for the rest of the evening.

He's just a man. *Not just any man*, my muse barged on in with the obvious. He's the most beautiful man on the planet and he just made you come. Hard.

Something told me that had merely been a glimpse into what Cameron was capable of. No matter how hard I tried not to think about him, all thoughts led back to him. How was I ever going to face him again without blushing?

Despite this residual ache low in my belly from those mind-blowing orgasms, my heart squeezed tight, having betrayed Richard in the worst kind of way. I'd allowed another man to touch me. And not just any man but Richard's best friend. I had decimated everything, ruined what could have been and broken our trust.

My life threatened to tear into tatters all because of my ridiculous crush on Cameron that I'd been unable to shake. A sob wedged in my throat and I held back tears of regret. No one could see me like this. Questions would be asked and there was no way I could share this with anyone.

Strong arms wrapped around my waist. "Hey," said Richard.

Turning around, I hugged him, wondering if this was the last time he'd ever let me get this close. I savored his ocean scent, his firm chest, the arms I'd come to know as home.

"Mia?" He looked concerned, yet something in his eyes sparked intrigue. "Something happened?"

I glanced over at his bottle of wine. It was empty now. Someone had found it and finished it off. I hoped it was Richard.

"Want to talk about it?" he said, giving nothing away, merely brushing my hair behind my shoulders and running his fingers through it. "Nothing is as bad as we first think it is."

I dreaded he'd read from me what had just happened, seen the cruelest betrayal. A lover and a best friend's deceit. Self hate welled within and I sucked in a sob, loathing myself.

Richard took my hand and led me through the kitchen and we turned a sharp left down the hallway and into his study. His hand was as firm as Cameron's, who'd led me in the opposite direction not fifteen minutes ago.

Richard shut the door and strolled over to his desk, leaning back against it, his hands gripping the edge on either side of him, his left ankle crossed over his right, poised for serious conversation.

"Sierra has complex needs," he said. "I'll go get her and she can tell you this herself." He shook his head. "DeLuca's sensitive to her predilections. He really does treat her well."

"That's not necessary," I said. "I mean, I believe you."

"Please, tell me what just happened?"

I hated lying to him, hated holding back on the truth that he deserved to hear.

"Your frown has never looked so frowny," he said.

I refused to shatter his world, put him through any more pain and ruin everything we'd so lovingly constructed. The foundation to our existence had formed fissures and I'd been the one to weaken it. I'd silently accused him of cheating when I'd gone and done worse. I had no idea what happened when he'd disappeared inside Pendulum. It had been merely my imagination that had taken the ride all the way to betrayal.

"You liked your spanking?" he asked.

"Yes," I admitted.

"You like being watched?"

"Yes."

"Good." He looked so sweet, so endearing, and so persuasive.

I ran my fingertips over my lips, remembering Cameron's kiss, his domination, his mastery. His tongue fucking me down there. His tongue fucking my mouth.

Oh, help me now.

I needed to sit and turned toward the chair.

"Stay right there," commanded Richard.

My legs trembled and I steadied myself.

"You have something to tell me?" he said.

"Please, you need to know I love you more than anything."

"I know that."

I broke his gaze.

"Let me help you out," he said. "You're feeling guilt over Cameron's kiss?"

My hand slapped over my mouth in shock.

"I'm glad you were going to tell me," he said. "That's testament to the trust we have."

Trust I've shattered.

I swallowed my fear, knowing full well nothing could be hidden from Richard's all seeing eyes. Cameron wasn't the only perceptive one around here. Surely Cameron would never have shared with Richard what had just happened between us?

"The party's going well, don't you think?" He eased his cell out of his pocket and glared at the screen. "I was so right."

"What?" I stifled tears.

"The Dow Jones just took a dive. Luckily I dumped those crappy shares last week." He gave a nod. "I always did have a knack for reading the market." His eyes shot up to mine.

I deserved that. I hadn't exactly pushed Cameron away, refused his advances, told him *no*. Cameron had probably told Richard this too. Shouldn't Richard be equally angry with his best friend?

I glanced past him and out onto the patio. "Looks like we're low on chips. I'll take care of it."

"We have staff to do that."

Scraping my teeth across my bottom lip, I searched for the best words that would get me out of here and away from Richard's impending fury.

"Share what happened," he said.

"I told Cameron... I hated him," I said. "He found me in your bedroom. He wanted to talk to me."

"Our bedroom," he said.

Guilt wedged in my throat and silenced me.

"What did he say to you? You're very flushed."

Oh.

Richard gave a shrug. "The term you're looking for is cunnilingus, I believe."

Fucking hell.

I braced myself for an onslaught of anger.

"Did you like it?" Richard looked relaxed, as though he was asking if I'd enjoyed dessert. "I mean, I know you like your pussy being played with Mia, but did you enjoy Cameron being the one to play with it?"

Turning away, I refused to be drawn into this unknown territory of fucked-up fuckery. I feared his voice would carry and our guests would overhear. Our couple's argument loomed, ready to ruin the mood of the party that up until a few minutes ago had been going so well. Humiliation really had befriended me today and wasn't letting go until it too had had its way with me.

"Did. You. Like it?" said Richard.

"What?"

"From your blush, that's a definitive yes."

"I didn't know he'd follow me in."

"He made you come hard, I take it?"

"Please, Richard—"

"Answer."

I gave a slow, uncomfortable nod.

"With words."

"He made me come." Closing my eyes, I willed this moment to go away, the questions to end, my hands to cease their shaking.

If this was my punishment, so be it. I was his willing victim to subjugate. Richard's girlfriend to berate.

"How many times did he make you come?" he said.

"We didn't have sex."

"Oral sex *is* sex. How many times?"

"Can't remember."

"Apparently it was four."

Biting my lip, I cursed Cameron.

Richard's eyes closed, as though losing his ability to hold back. Teeth clenched, he whispered, "I wish I could have been there."

To stop it, right? He'd have stopped it…

"Establishing your feelings for Cameron is part of this process," said Richard.

"Process?"

"I have something for you." Richard reached back for a manila envelope. He handed it to me.

"What is it?"

My confidence shattered all over again. A roller coaster of emotions headed into a tailspin. As he handed the envelope to me, so many possibilities came to mind and all of them bad. This was probably my official dismissal from Enthrall. I was being fired, though this time it was on paper. I deserved it, having betrayed Richard in the worst kind of way.

This imminent yelling held at bay.

"Forgive me," I said.

"Always."

"I love you."

"I'm glad to hear it."

"It will never happen again."

His frown lifted. "Life is about taking chances. Risks. Grabbing opportunities."

Yes, but him leaping out of a plane with a parachute was a far cry from what I'd just done. "I messed up. I hate myself."

"Interesting perspective. You need to work on that." He gave a nod. "*We* need to work on that."

I'd never forgive myself if I'd compromised a friendship that went way back. Their charming bromance was a result of going through hell together and surviving. Would they survive me? I felt like an evil infiltrator wreaking havoc.

"Mia, everything is fine," said Richard. "Please, read it."

I pulled out the document. "A contract?" My mouth went dry, my mind addled as I studied the first page of the master and submissive written agreement. It crossed my mind he was about to tell me this paper was now redundant in some kind of revengeful tease.

Like the tease Cameron had played with my inner thigh.

See, you're betraying Richard even now.

I'd sabotaged this contract ever being signed.

Laughter carried from the garden and music drifted in, the lyrics singing something about being beyond saving.

"Thoughts?" said Richard.

"Does this mean—"

Richard's sternness intensified. "Mia, once this is signed you will abide by its law. Understand? There can be no resistance."

"This still stands?"

"Of course. Your submissive training will begin immediately upon you signing it."

"You changed your mind?" I stared at his beautiful face, his kind eyes. Even after what had just happened, he forgave me, was promising to take me where I needed to go.

Give me what I needed.

"A lot of consideration went into this decision," he said.

I wondered if Cameron's advances had stirred his jealousy, forced Richard's hand. Cameron's genius had worked again. This contract was proof. I read the first few lines and a thrill shot up my spine.

This was really happening.

Richard reached out, his fingers finding and lifting a fountain pen from his desk. "Know this, Mia," he said with an assured nod. "I want this more than anything. For you. For me. For us."

"I want it too," I said, taking the blue marble colored fountain pen from him.

I'd never used a fountain pen before. I hoped I wouldn't smudge my signature. I stepped forward and laid the contract on the desk and slid off the lid.

"This will ensure our compatibility," he said. "Our future

together."

"Thank you, Sir." Tingles spiraled in my chest and I beamed at him. "You're not going to put me on a leash are you?"

"Not my thing, Mia."

I gave a nod of reassurance and stared down the contract.

Richard pressed against my side, his scent of ocean and expensive cologne lighting my senses. Would we begin my training right now? As soon as I'd swept my signature across this expensive looking paper?

He leaned across me and flipped to the last page. "This is my only stipulation."

A short gasp escaped my lips.

He gave an elegant sweep of his hand. "I cannot tell you how much pleasure this gives me."

Blinking, I tried to make sense of what I read.

"There's no other way forward," said Richard firmly.

I examined the last page over and over.

Under the title of master, Cameron had signed his name.

CHAPTER 12

RICHARD SECURED THE diamond collar around my neck.

It was the most beautiful piece of jewelry I'd ever seen. The stones caught the light and twinkled prisms of every color.

"Cameron chose this for you," said Richard.

My fingertips traced the edges of the silver, its tightness owning me like the one who'd given it.

"You must wear it at all times," said Richard. "Never take it off without your master's permission."

"I cannot tell you how much pleasure this gives me," Richard's words rang in my ears.

Holding the contract out in front of me, I said, "I don't understand."

"Your new master waits. Take him his drink."

"You told Cameron to go down on me?"

"Correction: gave him permission," he said. "He would never have touched you otherwise."

"Why?"

"An easier transition for you."

"You both decided this without me?"

Richard looked tense. "You went to his house, Mia."

"To ask him to talk to you," I defended myself.

"I understand."

"Are you ending our relationship?"

"Do you want that?"

Tears stung my eyes. "No."

"I'm glad to hear it. Look, if I'm going to be blatantly honest

I find the process of training a submissive...challenging."

"Have you found someone else?"

"Don't be ridiculous."

I wanted to ask about Jasmine. About that text. My mouth froze.

"Mia," he said. "This is a wonderful opportunity."

You're getting rid of me? Getting me out of the way?

"I told you I like my submissives already trained," he said. "You have specific needs that require a specific set of skills—"

"Give me more time."

"I'm doing this for you. For us."

"I thought we came from the same fucking star!"

"Mia."

"I went to Cameron to see if he might help me get through to you. To see if he might persuade you."

"And to learn how to become a good submissive too. That's what you told him."

"I might have given him that impression."

"Some part of you wants him to train you." He raised his hand. "It's okay to admit that."

My body betrayed me by responding to facing Cameron again. This ache low in my belly, this longing, a yearning so intense I dared not turn my attention to it for fear of losing myself within the vortex that was Cameron Cole.

I wasn't ready for *him*. I'd never be ready for someone like him. Fantasizing about a BDSM relationship with Cameron was one thing. The reality of it was completely another. This man was hardcore. A self confessed sadist.

Richard gestured to the contract. "Read it and sign it."

I stared at Cameron's name as though his signature held equal power.

"Cameron is a world renowned dominant," said Richard. "You're a very lucky young lady."

Dizziness came in waves. "Why can't you train me?"

"All the reasons I've explained. I'm too close to you."

"You doubt my obedience?"

"You could say that. Mia, you just told the director you hate him."

Oh fuck, I did.

"You're impossible to train," he said. "Cameron is the only one who can. He's the only man who can tame you."

"I don't need taming."

"In my world you do." He swept his hand threw his hair. "You're out of control."

"Because I got a tattoo?"

"It's on your body. I love everything about your body."

"Why are you doing this?"

"I promised to love you. Protect you. Die for you, and right now I'm failing you." He stepped back. "I can't stand to see you hold onto this pain any more. I can't get to it, Mia, and God knows I've tried."

"If you love me how can you give me to another?"

"It's because I love you."

"Do you really believe he can help me?"

"Most ardently."

I'd beaten myself up believing I'd let Richard down, yet he'd given me over to Cameron like a plaything. Something to be shared like that tortilla chip that Richard had dipped into that creamy guacamole on Cameron's plate. Sharing me had always been a given. I was nothing more than an erotic delicacy.

I feared Cameron, yet that low dull ache tightened in anticipation of the pleasures he'd bring, and to prove it my panties were getting wetter by the second. My sex throbbed delightfully with thoughts of Cameron.

No...

I tussled with trust. Refused myself the pleasure of what I wanted most. This impossible dream was coming true and it terrified me.

"Mia?" Richard shook me from my thoughts.

"Yes?"

"As far as I'm concerned you're not ready for someone of this caliber," he said. "Prove me wrong."

He came into focus again and I fought this sensation of slow motion.

"Cameron sees your potential," he said.

Cameron wore his arrogance like a shield, and from what I'd gathered he used it to keep everyone at arm's length. He was the last person on earth who could save me. Even if everyone raved about him. Worshiped him, for goodness sake.

"There is no alternative," said Richard. "Your new dominant and I have made this decision for you."

The sting of defeat.

"Your actions from here on are imperative," he said.

My voice lost its will to speak.

"After two weeks, you will be returned to me," he said. "Primed. Obedient. A perfect submissive."

A thrill of excitement at the possibilities. Would I be trained at Chrysalis? Would I sleep in Cameron's bed? Wake with him? Eat breakfast with him? Be near him at all times? Would he hold me in his arms and tell me he'd protect me? Soothe me. Not push me away like Richard was doing now.

Trust this Mia, go with this, you want this…

No, the truth was glaring. I'd be handed back to Richard when Cameron had gotten bored with me. And what happened when Richard became bored with me too? I'd be replaced with that pretty young thing Richard had taken to Pendulum. A girl not as rebellious. A better fit.

Yet my body insisted there was only one man who could get to me, get to this, whatever *this* was, only one man who knew the art of surrender.

Cameron.

No.

I refused to let go of this resistance, forbade myself to give away my power.

It's all you have left.

"Do you like your collar?" he said, handing me the contract.

"Yes," I said, weighing this small victory.

"I'm glad to hear it." He pointed to the contract. "Give this to Cameron."

Slowly, I turned and made my way into the kitchen.

I prepared their drinks in a blur.

Finding that silver tray in the top left cupboard that Cameron had been so specific about, I placed beside it two crystal tumblers and filled them to the brim with bourbon and threw in reckless chucks of ice.

The scrape of ripping paper sounded impossibly loud as I tore up the contract into a hundred little pieces. I glanced back to make sure Richard wasn't watching. He was still in his office, probably assuming I'd obediently headed off to my new master.

After scattering the pieces upon the tray, I rested both tumblers upon the torn up fragments of delicious rebellion. I picked up the tray and headed out into the garden.

Passing small crowds of guests, some eyed me with curiosity, others were too engrossed in conversation to notice me. Rounding the blue pool that I had wanted to dive into all night and swim laps in, I headed towards the left hand corner of the garden, admiring the twinkling string lights and their attempt at emanating mystery.

With my head held high, I approached Cameron and Ethan. They still chatted away. They turned to look at me.

"Mia, that's a fine piece of jewelry," said Ethan. "A beautiful collar."

"Thank you." I raised the tray. "Sir."

Cameron lifted one of the glasses and handed it to Ethan. He took the other one for himself. Both he and Ethan dipped their fingers into their tumblers to scoop out chucks of ice and threw them onto the grass behind them.

Satisfied their drinks were now in better shape, they sipped their liquor as though nothing was out of the ordinary and I hadn't drenched their bourbon in daring cubes of defiance.

Ethan grinned. "Chilled to perfection."

"There's room for improvement," said Cameron.

"So you say." I raised my chin higher.

Cameron gestured to the tray. "That's our contract I take it?"

"Sure is."

Cameron held out his hand to Ethan. "Lighter."

Ethan reached inside his pants pocket and handed his cigarette lighter to Cameron.

"Mia, bring it over here please," said Cameron, gesturing for me to set the tray on the table.

I took the few short steps alongside him and placed it down, heart fluttering, watching with fascination. Cameron flicked open the lighter and clicked it several times, bringing it close to the tray. A small flame kissed one of the pieces of paper and a flash of flames burst up as the others caught fire too. Orange and yellows licked the air searching for oxygen—

Like my lungs were doing now.

Black smoke billowed. The silver base was singed with a pungent scent. He'd escalated my attempt at rebellion.

"I never signed it," I said breathlessly.

Cameron towered over me. "That's a given."

Whispers carried...

"I take it you don't approve," I said.

"Correct."

I raised my chin high. "The arrogance of genius."

"And how would you know?"

This was like playing chess with a master.

"Ms. Lauren," said Cameron, his glare intense. "When you change your mind, and trust me you will, you will present yourself to me and offer your most sincere apology. You will of course be naked, wearing only your collar. And maybe, just maybe, I will reconsider my offer."

"To train me like a dog?"

Gasps resonated around us.

"To fuck your pain into oblivion, Mia," said Cameron fiercely. "Should I ever deem you worthy of me again."

CHAPTER 13

LIGHTS FROM THE party blinded me.

The same ones I'd lovingly hung from one end of the garden to the other, taking my time to get them just perfect. The beam so bright it placed me at center stage.

With my heart twisted in knots, I took the walk of shame away from Cameron and the other guests, disorientated, shaken, lost and made my way down towards the end of the garden. Clicking open the latch, I trudged down the pathway that led to the beach.

I'd ruined my chance of being taken under Cameron's wing, and had no idea why. Self-examining my angst, I tried to reason with my will.

My need to hold onto my control.

For weeks I'd wanted what Cameron had just offered, yet I'd reacted so aggressively to him. Fear had taken over and sabotaged my moment, along with mistrust that gnawed into my heart. My thoughts were too foggy to see through.

The evening breeze caught my tears and stung my face.

I reasoned that revelatory text from Jasmine had given me every right to be mad. It proved my suspicions.

Turning slightly, I looked back up at Richard's home. It emphasized his wealth and privilege. I should have known my relationship with a member of high society could never last. I'd merely been a distraction. A gift given by another man to ease Richard's heartache, and once he'd healed I'd be no longer needed here. There was no room for a commoner like me in his world.

Kicking off my shoes, my feet sunk into the sand and I walked towards lapping waves. The ocean made me feel even smaller and truly insignificant; nature's statement of supremacy. Over the last few months I'd come to know a thing or two about supremacy in a society I'd never fit into.

Swiping away tears, I failed to hold back these sobs.

The ocean's grayness went on forever and waves crashed over the shoreline, lapping over my feet, stinging my ankles with its coldness. The sound of rolling waves seemed even louder at night. Foam frothed over my feet, only to be drawn back again in a watery tease.

I'd pushed back so violently I conjured fury in Cameron. Or perhaps his expression had been disappointment? Anger maybe? Well earned disgrace? I'd rebelled in front of all his friends and was sure to have ruined our friendship. I'd never be able to face him or Richard ever again.

I'd lost everything, probably my job too.

"How's the water?"

It was Scarlet, and she was right behind me, having snuck up quietly. In one hand she held a bottle of champagne and in the other two crystal flutes.

"Cold," I said, stepping back onto dry sand.

"Apparently glass is forbidden down here." She beamed mischievously. "But being naughty feels so damn good doesn't it?" She raised the glasses. "Thought we'd celebrate."

Surely she could see I'd been crying? She wasn't showing any sign of annoyance, so maybe she hadn't overheard my outburst.

"Not sure I have anything to celebrate," I said, wondering if she'd been sent down here by Cameron to chastise me.

Being berated by a dominatrix was going to round out this evening nicely.

"I love your collar," she said. "It's exquisite."

My fingers traced the edge. Despite its snugness, I'd forgotten I was wearing it. "I can't keep it."

"Why ever not?"

"Well..." my voice wavered with emotion.

"It was gifted to you. Of course you can." She stepped

closer. "Mia, you do realize those are real diamonds?"

"Richard mentioned something about them being real."

Scarlet shook her head. "Those boys are so decadent."

"How much do you think it cost?"

"Several million."

"Dollars?" My legs almost buckled.

I had a vision of Richard stomping over the sand and demanding this choker back. Maybe that was why Scarlet was here. To make sure I didn't run off with it.

Tipping the champagne bottle, she poured two glasses of bubbly and handed me one. Taking a sip, it tasted refreshing, and I took several more gulps, needing the buzz to kick in and take off the edge. With my left hand, I reached around to the back of the collar and fiddled for the catch.

"No, don't take it off." She took a sip. "You look beautiful in it."

I dropped my hand to my side. "I won't be allowed to keep it. Maybe you can give it back to Cameron for me?"

"Only your master may remove it. Surely you know that?"

"He's not my master," I said. "I screwed up—"

"If you don't learn to love yourself, Mia, you'll end up hating yourself, and if that's the message you're sending out into the universe, God help you."

"You were in the garden a few minutes ago?" I said.

"I was, yes. I overheard everything."

"Between me and Cameron?"

"Yes," she said. "It was an interesting interaction between a master and his new submissive."

"I'm not his submissive." *I blew that chance.*

"Then why are you still wearing his collar?" she said.

"He'll probably tell me to take it off."

"Did he?" She took in the ocean. "I never heard him say that."

"I made him angry."

She smirked. "You certainly gave him good reason to deliver the mother of all punishments."

I swallowed hard.

"The ultimate punishment," she said. "The ultimate gift."

I marveled at her belief I'd not blown this chance.

"Once you've signed your contract, you'll be hot housed at Chrysalis," she said.

"I ripped it up."

"Print off another one."

I blinked at her. "This hot housing is what exactly?"

"T.P.E." On my confused stare, she added, "Total power exchange."

"All the time?"

"Yes."

"So I'll stay at Chrysalis?"

"For at least two weeks," she said. "Under Cameron's supervision."

"What kind of things will I be asked to do?"

"Whatever your master deems necessary. He'll go over his expectations."

"Did Cameron send you down here?"

"No. As your mistress at Enthrall, and as your friend, I want you to make the best decision." She mirrored my stance. "I want you to be happy."

"I want that too."

"What's holding you back?"

"I'm scared of losing control."

"Cameron will guide you through the process of handing over all control to him."

"What if I lose myself?"

"First you have to find yourself." She measured her words. "Have you?"

"No."

"Chrysalis is a place where such an endeavor is possible." She threw in a smile. "And in L.A., that's quite something."

"How do you know who you really are?" I said.

"Well, if you have to ask."

A small rogue wave washed over my feet.

"You push the boundaries of your existence," she said.

I was in awe of her. Her beauty, her confidence, her worldliness.

Scarlet's expression softened and kindness exuded from her beautiful face. "Mia, I'm twice your age and know a thing or two about life." She raised her hand in protest to my reaction. "I've lived all over the world. I've flown in private jets and hung out with movie stars. Spanked quite a few of them too." She winked, her sassy expression turning serious once more. "I've scuba dived in the warm waters of Bali and eaten lobster from china plates in Dubai." She raised her hand in a warning. "I've prayed in the temples of Nepal and I've swum the shores off a private Hawaiian island at dawn, alongside wild dolphins. And yet nothing, and I mean nothing, equals the high of being with a master who can take you to the height of pleasure and hold you in a state of bliss for hours." She stepped closer. "Love is the only true treasure in this world. And along with it, blinding sexual pleasure. The master who gave you that collar is the only one who is capable of releasing that love within you." She downed the rest of her drink. "Cameron's an extraordinary man. He's also the only one who can ensure you reach your full potential. He just offered you the chance of a lifetime. Don't fuck it up."

"I just did."

"That's not what I witnessed."

"What did you see?"

"His greatest challenge."

"And Cameron doesn't mind that?"

"He finds the opportunity exhilarating."

"Have there been others like me?"

"You are amongst the privileged."

"Why now? Why are you encouraging me to submit to Cameron when all I've ever heard from all of you is to avoid him?"

"Because, Mia, you weren't ready for him before."

"And now I am?"

"He deems you ready. That's all we need to be assured you are."

"Is Cameron everything you say he is?"

"You have two choices: undergo Cameron's method or remain in therapy for many years and hope it works eventually."

"He's that good?"

"And he's chosen you. Agreed to transform you. Dedicate his time and effort into seeing you break out of your chrysalis."

"And no one else can do this?"

"No." She smiled. "Before the butterfly emerges from its cocoon it must first retreat from the world. Next, it becomes completely transparent, revealing everything about itself. It knows to become still, vulnerable, surrender to its metamorphosis and only then when this transformation is complete can it break free from the chrysalis."

Ocean waves crashed on the shoreline as a dramatic backdrop to her words.

Scarlet swept her hand through the air. "The color of your wings will be extraordinary. You will blind those around you with your beauty and you will shine brighter than any star. Cameron will transform you into a masterpiece."

All that remained was this breeze and the echo of her meaning.

"What about Richard?" I whispered.

"Who placed that collar on your neck?"

"Richard."

"There's your answer." Scarlet held out her glass to me. "Hold this."

I took it from her, wanting to believe that I hadn't burned my bridges and angered Cameron beyond repair.

If this was the only way to get Richard to love me again…

"Well Mia." Scarlet's voice sounded faint, distant. "What's your answer?"

My fingertips traced the diamonds, feeling the snugness of the choker.

Scarlet held up a black velvet blindfold. "Cameron will expect you to be wearing this."

"When?" I said.

"The moment you surrender completely to him."

CHAPTER 14

THIS BEVERLY HILLS manor tucked away on north Alpine Drive was a striking statement of superiority. Having visited Cameron's cozy Venice Beach property weeks before, I found it a relative understatement for a billionaire. So I wasn't surprised to find this statement of privilege.

Exotic foliage surrounded the house, and the fountain in the front was so dramatically lit up it was hard to tell whether it served to welcome or intimidate.

I'd found the front gate open. A relief considering my taxi had just driven off.

I'd visited here less than a week ago and Cameron had caught me upon entry. He'd led me up to one of his spare rooms and handcuffed me to his bed. All that had been done in silence.

In the throes of madness, I'd found my way back. This visit promised to be different on every level. My thoughts tussled with my belief that I was here to get Richard back and at the same time the bright flame that was Cameron lured this wannabe butterfly. This yearning kept me moving towards the house, towards the unknown.

A walled security camera above the doorway scanned the entryway. My arrival had been noted.

The front door was open. I removed my coat and flung it over the end of a foyer table, glancing at a stack of letters addressed to Cameron. I rested my handbag there. The only items inside were my comb, makeup, and contraceptive pills. The basics I'd need for my new life. I placed the envelope next to them. It contained my contract, yet to be signed.

Listening for any sign of life or even a guard dog that I may have missed the first time, I made my way in. The foyer's checkered black and white marbled flooring oozed masculine power, and that central low hanging chandelier eclipsed everything around it. It swept out of the stucco ceiling and merged with circled larger crystal droplets below, then fell into a perfectly formed V in a decadent beacon of indulgence.

Paintings hung on stark white walls. A few of them were floor to ceiling in size. The largest of them all was hung on the far left wall and depicted a man being attacked by angels. Dark clouds swarmed around them in a sinful theme, warning about indulging in the taboo. Or maybe I was reading too much into what looked like a Renaissance piece. Maybe it was merely where my head was.

About to escalate into the forbidden.

Taking my place in the center of the foyer, I wrapped the black velvet blindfold around my eyes, willing time to pass and my master to find me.

Other than these high-top stockings, I stood naked in the center, ready to apologize for my outburst at Richard's party and hoping he'd accept it. Accept me. It had only been one day since my eruption and Cameron's stark invitation.

I wanted this above all things.

These white high-top lace stockings were my last act of rebellion. The current Mia still had some fight left in her, and challenging Cameron pushed all my pleasure buttons. Five inch strappy heels added height to what I hoped would be a regal air, and *his* diamond encrusted collar felt like it owned each breath, catching each inhalation as though he already possessed me. Merely the thought of him caused exquisite spasms down there and my exposed nipples hardened, the buds peeking through strands of hair cascading over bare shoulders.

Despite such vulnerability, empowerment wrapped her arms around me and made me feel strong, free even, and in total control of my destiny. Thoughts of what Cameron would do filled me with excitement. An unquenched desire. I'd never felt more ready for him.

For this.

My heart thundered in my chest at seeing him again, feeling his hands on me, and hearing his commanding voice. Preparing to fall to my knees and show him my willingness to submit made me lightheaded.

The muffled sound of laughter. A door opened.

I ripped off the blindfold and stared in horror at the stunningly beautiful twenty-something woman. Her tall, slim frame was dressed in an elegant evening gown, and her long black hair fell down her back.

She saw me.

Oh shitity shit.

My thoughts raced out of control as I wondered who she was and how she was connected to Cameron. Oh please tell me this isn't his girlfriend. She was certainly elegant enough to meet his impossible standards. What if she was his current submissive and I was too late? I considered bolting for the door.

She strolled towards me in slow motion, or so it felt in my dreamy haze of mortification. She was probably Cameron's type. There was a similarity in those deep chestnut eyes, her refined nose and full lips just as hauntingly beautiful.

"Hello there," she said, reaching out to squeeze my arm reassuringly. "Are you one of Dr. Cole's patients?"

I shook my head.

She seemed to cheer at that and she took in my body, showing a mixture of awe and surprise. "Who are you?"

"His friend?" I struggled to articulate more.

Her gaze rose and fell over my nakedness.

The words that would best describe a submissive's role scuttled away out of reach, hiding behind my fear that she knew nothing of Cameron's other life.

"Are you his girlfriend?" she said.

"You're not?"

She giggled. "God, no. That would have been awkward for us. I'm his sister. Is he your beau?"

"I'm sorry?"

"Your boyfriend?"

I gave a nod.

Kind of, or maybe that was a no. It was definitely a no.

"You're very young," she said, her cheeks flushing as

though only now taking in my nakedness.

Everything about her screamed privilege, from that confident air to her designer dress that hugged her fine figure and showcased her upper classiness. That refined elegance that the moneyed possessed.

"I'm Willow." She held out her hand.

I shook it. "Mia."

"We have to hide you away before—" She spun round to face the door she'd come out of.

Oh no.

An elegantly dressed woman of sixty or so closed the door behind her when she saw us. I wanted to run, hide, my embarrassment lighting up my bright red face. My moment of empowerment dissipated.

I was fricken naked for goodness sake.

Cameron had told me his family was coming to town. That glass of champagne I'd drunk earlier to calm my nerves had addled my memory and skewered my judgment.

The older woman neared us, her elegant shoes clicking on the marble, echoing her strides with short, sharp clips. Her long black skirt fanned around delicate heels, and her blue chenille blouse enhanced her grey-blue eyes. A fine silver necklace caught the light. She emanated class and a regal air of authority.

If I wasn't already naked, I'd feel it now.

"To whom do we have the honor?" she asked calmly, admiring my collar with intrigue.

"Mia is Cameron's girlfriend," said Willow.

"My dear." She eyed me with a dignified grace. "You look like you've stepped out of the Musée du Louvre."

The word 'sorry' wouldn't come, refusing to leave my lips along with all the others that should have been offered to apologize for my presence.

Willow snapped back to me. "Mia, I'm delighted to introduce you to my Aunt Rose."

Oh no.

Aunt Rose scrutinized me as though assessing the value of a thoroughbred. She didn't flinch, didn't blink, and showed no signs of surprise or distaste. These women really did know how to deal with anything. A Cole trait it seemed.

"Delighted to meet you," said Aunt Rose as she reached for my hand.

Her grip was firm, persuasive, and I had a sense of where Cameron's confidence came from. Even the Cole women were impressively composed.

"My grandson has exquisite taste. If not emboldened." She raised her chin. "There you are."

Cameron stood a few feet away. I could have sworn he appeared out of nowhere, his ability to sneak up disarming. His beautiful face was a welcome view, and at the same time it was devastating to be caught like this by him.

His rage was inevitable. His denial he knew me was a real possibility. And I wouldn't blame him. I'd go along with it. Try to lessen his embarrassment, not to mention my own.

Cameron's expression was serene. "I see you've had the pleasure of meeting Mia Lauren," he said, casually tucking his hands into his pockets.

"She's quite lovely," said Aunt Rose.

"An exquisite find," said Cameron.

Aunt Rose turned to him. "Where have you been hiding her?"

"If I had my way, in a cage," he muttered.

"What was that dear?"

"They just got engaged!" announced Willow. "Isn't that wonderful?"

Cameron's eyebrows rose sharply and he glared at his sister.

"Willow, you've ruined the surprise," said Aunt Rose. "Look, Cameron was going to announce it over dinner. You stole his thunder. Willow, you are naughty."

Willow glared back at her brother, their silent scream shared with each other.

I felt terrible about the confusion. "Actually, I'm—"

"She's sorry she's late," said Cameron. "Mia, you're not forgiven."

"Don't be ridiculous," said Aunt Rose. "She's missed nothing."

This was all very surreal, me standing here with nothing on except high-top stockings and a collar and hanging out with Cameron's relatives like I was at a garden party and my nipples weren't on show along with my nether region.

Not five minutes before, I'd been ready to kneel at my new master's feet and surrender to my fate. Yet my fate was currently staring me down as Cameron's glare liquefied my insides.

Aunt Rose turned to study me again. "Cameron, you've outdone yourself. She's extraordinary."

"Thank you, aunt," he said, his glare fierce.

"A rare beauty." Aunt Rose affectionately brushed a strand of hair back over my shoulder. "Willow, get some clothes on her before your father sees her and has a coronary." She turned back to face me. "Mia, welcome to the family. I look forward to getting to know you."

In a daze, with Cameron's hand gripping my upper right arm, I was escorted up the sweeping staircase and away from the foyer. Willow followed and both she and Cameron held an uncomfortable silence until we were in one of the bedrooms. The same one I'd been handcuffed in three nights ago.

Cameron dragged a soft throw off the bed and wrapped it around my shoulders. He pointed to the bed. "Sit."

With all confidence lost, I did as he commanded while watching the brother and sister dynamics in fascination and with gratitude the focus was no longer on me.

I'd really fucked up.

"Don't look at me like that," said Willow to Cameron. "I saved you." She poked his chest with her well manicured fingertip.

"Willow, you've confused saving with sabotaging," he said.

She looked defiant. "You had a naked woman in your foyer. I had to come up with something."

"I am here," I said.

Cameron threw me a glare.

Feeling the full force of his annoyance, I flinched, wondering if now was a good time to make an exit. Though the threat of bumping into other family members made me sit still.

"I had to think on my feet," said Willow.

"Stupidity is a close cousin of dangerous," said Cameron.

She rested balled fists on her hips. "Where's my thank you?"

"Why did you have to tell Aunt Rose we're engaged? Mom will know immediately we're lying. Father will be on my case all night."

She lit up with excitement. "Tell them you're having the ring designed by Robert Procop."

"You've lost your mind." Cameron blinked at her. "Trust me, I'm an expert on this. Your brain's not firing on all cylinders."

"You're the great professor." She smiled mischievously. "You'll think of something."

"Go and get her one of your dresses," he seethed, glancing at my feet. "Something to match her shoes. You're about the same size."

"Oh Mia," she said. "I'm so happy you're here. These things are so tedious, and now I have a friend to hang out with. You are so much fun." She blew a kiss to her brother and disappeared.

Cameron paused, staring at the carpet.

"Sorry," I said.

Cameron went to speak and then paused, commanding even the silence. His thoughts took him away from me.

A knock came at the door.

Willow entered with an elegant black dress on a hanger. "How's this?"

"You had to pick the sexiest thing in your wardrobe?" said Cameron.

Willow looked hurt. "It's Stella McCartney."

"It's beautiful," I said.

Willow brightened and smiled back at her brother. "See."

Cameron stepped towards her. "Thank you."

"The only reason I'm not wearing it," she said, "is because Daddy disapproves of me wearing anything off the shoulder."

Cameron closed his eyes for a second. "Willow, you've outdone yourself. Now run along and let Mia get dressed."

"It's not like I haven't seen her naked," said Willow, looking like she wanted to hang out with us a little longer.

"Mia and I need a moment," he said. "We'll rejoin you in a few minutes."

She waved goodbye and I watched my lifeline leave the room. Cameron made his way over to the door and locked it.

"I am so sorry," I said, again. "Truly I am."

"For what?"

I gestured to my outfit, or lack of it.

"Other than wearing stockings, you obeyed. A punishment will find its way to you no doubt for that particular indiscretion." He tilted his head. "Your timing was…interesting. Timing is something I can teach you."

"Did I embarrass you?"

He blinked at me as though assessing my words.

"Your aunt?" I said.

"Did she look embarrassed to you?"

"Well…not exactly."

"My aunt was a nurse in the Vietnam War, so you'd have to do a lot worse to ever get a rise out of her." Cameron caressed his brow. "We're going to have to make it look like we're lovers, Mia."

I gave a sharp nod.

"We can pull this off. It's doable. We just have to be convincing. I don't want my aunt disappointed." He shrugged. "She's open-minded but won't tolerate lies."

"Of course."

"I love my sister, but God, Willow is incorrigible."

There came a little guilty relief that Cameron's wrath was redirected at Willow. Even with his family present, Cameron oozed enough intensity to power a city. Or entire country for that matter.

"I can act affectionate towards you," I reassured him.

His stare found mine. "In a couple of weeks I'll inform them we called the engagement off. I'll tell them it was you and not me. They'll expect it. It will come as no surprise."

"You've been engaged before?" I wanted to learn more, see beyond the wall thrown up before Cameron.

"Get up," he said.

I pushed myself to my feet and glanced over at the off the shoulder black dress.

"Not yet," he said. "Come here."

Staring up at him, I felt small, vulnerable even.

As though sensing this, he took my hands in his. "Richard printed you off another copy of the contract?"

"It's on the table in the foyer. In a white envelope."

"You consent to everything?"

I gave a sharp nod, not ready to tell him yet that form still awaited both our signatures.

"If you give yourself over to me completely, I will give you the world, Mia."

"I only want to please you."

"Be sure you do." He let go. "I will see to it that when the time comes for me to return you to your master, you will rule his heart." There came that glint of emotion, though it was quickly gone. "Mia, you are about to cross a psychological threshold unlike any other."

"I want this more than anything."

He looked menacing. "I will take you further than you have gone before. What will be left of you is that which you do not believe exists within you. I will destroy you. I will burn away this façade and I will reveal the true Mia."

I gave a slow, steady nod as my mind raced after his words, causing a rift in my mind, a need within me pushed out by anticipation.

"By the time I've finished with you," he said, "you won't know which way is up or which way is down."

My legs wobbled and I hid my shaking hands behind my back.

"Innocence will be a stranger to you. Are you prepared for this?"

"Yes."

"There's one more issue," he said. "I have no use for safe words."

Blinking several times, I ran that scary detail through my brain.

"Did you hear me?"

"That's fine."

"It doesn't appear so. Talk to me."

"What if I want you to stop?"

"Do you trust me to know what you need?"

I gave a nod.

He gave a shrug. "There will be no stopping."

Holy shit.

"Do you wish to continue?" he asked.

"I promise to do everything you ask."

"The present moment has its privilege." There was a shift in his stance, a darkening in the way he looked. "You are ready."

"I need this more than anything." My body relaxed into the mood, responding to this crackling electricity that set my nerves on edge and sent a shockwave of aliveness into every cell.

"Show me," he said.

I hesitated, full of doubt that I had what it took to please him.

"Mia." His tone was stern, as was his gesture. "Now."

With trembling hands, I eased apart my labia to reveal my clitoris, my fingertips brushing against that small nub and sending a pulse of pleasure. I tilted my hips to better show him, my heart thundering in my ears.

"This pussy is mine," he said. "Let there be no misunderstanding. I own it. I own you. I am a demanding master. If I wish to fuck you for the twentieth time in a day, you will present yourself to me."

"Yes."

With merely his words, he was making me wet, yearning for his touch upon that most delicate place I showed willingly. I remained obedient, poised and ready to please him, pleasure him, having never felt so aroused.

"Mia, from here on in you will submit to me."

Eyes wide, my fingers leaving my labia and pressing my chest in denial, I covered my breasts.

"Do we have a problem?" he said.

I shook my head *no*.

"Never cover yourself again. Understand?"

Reluctantly, my arms dropped by my sides and I fought this real urge to cover myself.

He studied me, his sternness lifting. "Good. If I deem you worthy, I will showcase you at Chrysalis. I will also consider taking you with me to Paris. London. Milan. Hong Kong. But only if you quickly grasp the art of submission."

A flutter of excitement tingled in my chest. "Thank you."

"First, you must obey me in all things. Am I making myself clear?"

I am going to come right here, right now.

And he hadn't even touched me. "Yes, Sir."

Enthrall Her

"Vanilla is not usually in my repertoire." He caressed his chin thoughtfully. "However, for our purpose this evening it will prove sufficient." He motioned for me to turn around.

The sound of his jacket coming off and his shirt being removed was followed by the unzipping and removing of pants. He sat back down behind me upon the end of the bed. A condom packet ripped open.

The softest sigh escaped me.

Blood rushed through my ears as my body trembled in anticipation. Staring dead ahead at the door, a calmness descended and the room ceased to spin. I gave myself permission to dare see what was on the other side of the gateway to his world. An abundance of promises. I couldn't wait to visit Chrysalis again. The first thing I'd do was swim naked in that large red lit pool. If I was allowed.

This perfect moment of madness made me feel more beautiful than I ever had, beholden to a brilliant, beautiful man who knew my limits and was going to push me beyond them. My flesh burned for him. My heart sang. Never had I felt more alive.

A thrill shot up my spine when his strong hands wrapped around my waist and pulled me firmly backwards, keeping my back to his front. He eased me down onto his naked lap. Facing forward, I was grateful to not have to look into that fierce gaze. Cameron could see beyond anything I'd ever show him and only he would know how badly I needed to be reprimanded, whipped and scolded, given the punishments I'd yearned for and freed from this anguish. His was an unrelenting grip.

His enormous erection pressed into the arch of my back. He was rock hard, an impossible size. No way was he going to fit. *No way.*

I was going to disappoint him...

Cameron pulled my legs apart and helped me straddle his thighs. He fully exposed me. Resting my head back against his chest, I swooned, full of need, willing myself to have faith in this moment and not pull away in terror at this impending pain.

His fingers tapped my clitoris. "A fine instrument must be honored. Cherished. Mastered." He played delicate beats along my wet cleft, stilling for a moment in a sensual tease, before tracing up and down as though I was indeed an instrument and he was a gifted maestro, strumming, tweaking, and tapping as my clit throbbed wantonly beneath his touch. My hands resting on his thighs, my fingernails buried deep in his flesh, my trembling legs dangled over his.

Daringly, and needing to know I could do this or maybe just needing to get the pain out of the way, I rose up until the tip of his cock found its rightful place at my entrance and I hovered there, gathering my confidence. Taking steadying breaths, I willed myself to relax.

His firm grip around my waist eased me down a little onto him and gravity did the rest as his full length slid into me, his girth stretching me wide, filling me. I leaned forward, gasping in pain as he owned my pussy with his endless shaft, my thighs shaking violently.

"Shush," he soothed, remaining still and giving me time to adjust. He caressed my hair, running his hand down the full length of my locks to calm me.

The pain eased into delicious throbs as his hardness twitched. His fingers sought my clit again and found their rhythm upon it, lifting this internal burn. A dazzling completeness flooded me. My moan filled the room and my body trembled with this mind blowing pleasure.

He yanked my hair. "Do you believe you are worthy of this privilege?"

Exhilarated by the sting at my scalp, my core tightened around his length, sending short, sharp bursts of delight down there.

"Answer?" He yanked my hair more, sending a thrill of excitement into my chest.

"I want to be worthy," I barely managed, terrified he'd pull out and leave me bereft.

If he sent me away now, surely I'd die from never having had him come inside me. Rocking my hips, I yearned for his approval.

"Remain still," he said.

I did as he ordered, wanting to do anything to make sure I'd please him and ensure this would last an eternity. Those firm fingers found my breasts, and just as they had done with my pussy they began their delicate strum upon my nipples. I arched back, wanting to give more of myself to him. My channel clenched around him, worshiping his cock, milking it.

"If I wish to fuck you for the twentieth time in a day, you will present yourself."

He elongated my nipples, tugging and squeezing, twisting and sending bursts of blissfulness all the way down my belly. I wriggled, wanting to ride him as hard as he'd let me.

"Be still," he said firmly. "Trust." His fingers paused, as though waiting for me to obey, to still, to have him control every nuance, even my breathing.

Fighting this urge to ride him, I stilled and gave myself over.

"Better." He nuzzled into my neck, burying his face in golden locks. "Move your hips in a circle."

A moan of defiance escaped me as I circled, thighs trembling, my toes just off the floor and pointed like a ballerinas as though this was our dance of sex. His hardness swelled within, hurtling me towards the edge.

"Slower," he commanded. "A wider circle."

As though using the timing mastery of a metronome, he tweaked the very end of my nipples with sensual strums until my mind splintered into a million fragments of nothingness, climbing ever higher, leaving me behind and peaking in an intense plateau, stretching outward, upward, on and on into the stratosphere.

Unbidden, my moan echoed as I climaxed, my thoughts scattering, my body shuddering. My head fell forward and I stilled.

"Continue," he ordered.

And still I circled, my pelvis moving as though it had always known this secret rhythm that had lain dormant. Quivering upon his lap, my mewling filled my ears as seconds dissolved into minutes and minutes into an eternity.

There was nothing but a brilliant light...

He whispered something about a beginning, about starting slow, about rewards and punishments.

We were a rhapsody, an embodiment of the erotic, this never-ending plateau rising higher. My heart beat against my ribcage like exultant sparrows trying to escape. The only noise was that of my gasps and Cameron's whispers as I struggled to obey and maintain this slow continuous circling. Reeling from the touch of his fingers delighting themselves with my nipples, never ceasing their play, he dragged out these sensations that threatened to go on forever as my pussy squeezed in adoration.

Only he and I existed as everything else fell away.

I groaned loudly when I came again, "Master."

He thrust upward and his breath hitched as he shot his heat inside me, his unyielding hands cupping my breasts, his fingers pinching my nipples to take me higher and keep me there.

Nothing but silence; bliss.

Wrapping a long strand of my hair around his wrist, he yanked my head back and towards him, capturing my mouth with his and kissing me leisurely, his tongue taking ownership of my mouth, pillaging, possessing, and he came hard again, jerking his seed into me. Another orgasm hit me and Cameron slammed his hand over my mouth to muffle my scream as I moaned my climax against his palm and bit into his hand.

Terrified I'd pass out and never recover, I whimpered my useless cries.

Collapsing back upon his firm chest, I tried to return my breathing to normal, though doubted anything would ever be normal again. Feeling him inside me, so firm, so taut, so safe, I wanted to stay connected forever.

Gazing upward at the blurred stucco ceiling, tears stung my eyes with how complete this felt. How perfect.

My head lolled to the side.

"Look at me." He tipped my chin up to better see my face. "Yes, good. That's the look I was going for."

CHAPTER 15

"THAT WAS VANILLA?" I whispered breathlessly.

"Now keep that look up," said Cameron, "and we may just be convincing."

He slid out of me and I felt bereft when separated from him. Our division caused me to swoon with longing, aching from this throbbing between my thighs. This soreness was the purest proof of us.

Cameron stood behind me, lifting me up as he went. My legs gave way and he caught me, turning me round to hug me into his chest. Breathing him in, and spellbound to be this close still, I crumpled before him and he whisked me up into his arms and carried me around to the side of the bed and gently laid me upon it.

I leaned up and wrapped my arms around him, refusing to separate just yet, burying my face in the crook of his neck. I needed this intimacy, this affection.

Cameron ran his hand up and down my back and waited for me to gather my strength, my courage to let go. "You were very brave, Mia,' he said. "Continue to show this kind of courage and you'll do well. You'll please me."

He pulled away and reached for the blanket. "I'll permit a few minutes." He rose and took a step back, peeling off the condom and ambling away, disappearing inside the bathroom. He took his clothes with him.

Being here felt dreamy, and despite the initial embarrassment of my arrival I relaxed. The welcome warmth of the blanket lulled me. I must have nodded off because when I came around Cameron stood at the foot of the bed, his face serene, his usual stern demeanor lifted.

"Was I asleep?" I said.

"For a few minutes." He turned from me and straightened his tie in the long mirror. "Dinner's in ten minutes."

I sat up and brought the blanket with me, easing off the bed and wrapping it around me.

"Cold?" he asked.

I gave a nod.

"That's the problem with big houses. They don't keep their heat."

"Did you grow up in a house like this?"

"Much bigger."

And this place was vast. I wondered what that must have been like. "Hide and seek must have been a blast," I said.

Cameron arched a brow. "Never played it."

"You missed out."

He fiddled with his cufflinks. "I doubt it."

Feeling slightly minx-like after my endless orgasm, I let the fur blanket slip from my shoulders all the way to the floor and stood before him with my head held high in a defiant stance. Pushing back felt so damn good.

He perused my nakedness, his eyelids heavy, his tongue sweeping his bottom lip. Cameron neared me, his hands reaching out for my left stocking top. He eased it up and then his fingers moved over to my right stocking top and tugged that one too. His touch felt heavenly, setting my cheeks ablaze again.

His sternness put me in my place.

Cameron strolled over to the other side of the room and opened a drawer. He withdrew a flat black box and returned with it. He slid the catch open and lifted the lid. A delicate bracelet lay within, resting on soft burgundy velvet, and tiny glinting diamonds encircled the band.

"It's beautiful," I said.

"Give me your wrist." He threw the box upon the bed.

His fingers made quick work of fastening the bracelet around my left wrist. "Never take this off."

It was so beautiful. I twisted my wrist in awe. "Can I keep it

Enthrall Her

when I go back to Richard?"

"That's another thing," he said. "Don't mention his name."

"Am I still allowed to call him?"

"Out of the question."

A wave of panic. "But—"

"Get dressed. We have a performance to pull off. Disappointment will bring the kind of punishment you're not ready for."

"What kind?"

"That cage I mentioned earlier." He eased the black dress off the hanger. "It's real. Now take a few minutes to freshen up and then get this on. Meet me downstairs. Prepare yourself, Mia. You're about to know the true meaning of interrogation. Guantanamo Bay is nothing compared to my family."

I needed to pee.

"I'll be right there beside you," he said.

"My underwear?"

"I don't see the problem."

"Perhaps I can go back home and get them—"

"There's no time." He turned and left the room.

Great, he'd have me face his family braless and pantyless. Examining the dress, I was reassured to see inlaid cups within the material. It was a small miracle. I gave a heavy sigh to rally my courage and headed into the bathroom.

Not mentioning Richard was going to be hard. He was all I thought about, and we were training me for the very purpose of sending me back to him.

I could smell Cameron on me. I gave myself permission to swoon. After all, Richard had granted it, and I was going to have to endure weeks of this and goodness knows what else Cameron had in store. This crush on him might actually be a godsend.

Not surprising, the bathroom was luxurious. Its white walls and pink marble had a feminine flair with a glass wall divider between the bath and shower. I mulled over whether he'd had an interior decorator. I made myself giggle. Cameron was hardly the type to hang out at Home Depot picking out tiles. The type of woman he ended up with would probably be used to all this decadence and wouldn't flitter an eyelid at heated marble flooring.

You're only here to be trained, I reassured myself. *You must become everything that Richard wants you to be, and then you'll be good enough for him. Cameron's merely your instructor, your professor extraordinaire. If what just happened is anything to go by, this might even be fun. Fricken fantastic actually.*

Staring at my reflection in the mirror, gripping the edge of the sink, I still felt the pinch of pain where he'd stretched me wide; a throbbing of pleasure. A delicious lingering soreness.

If Cameron was going for a freshly fucked and caught in the headlights kind of look, I was right on point. Pulling a comb through my hair, I tried to tidy myself up and not cause any more embarrassment. I hoped this evening wasn't going to be one of those situations that would haunt me for the rest of my life. Joining one of America's most distinguished families for dinner and not messing it up was going to be a challenge. Thank goodness Cameron had promised to be right there beside me. Meeting the family was reserved for the fiancé types and certainly not the new submissive. I wondered if his family knew he was into kink.

I certainly gave them a hint of it tonight.

Surely Cameron wasn't serious about putting me in a cage? That wasn't mentioned in the contract, along with all the other hard limits I was about to sign my life away on. Perhaps we'd get a chance to talk about those later tonight. I wondered if we were going to dive right into the deep end of BDSM. Cameron's family being in town was actually a reassuring distraction, though I could do without having to have dinner with them right now.

After freshening up, I reapplied my makeup, softening my eyeliner and applying gloss to my lips, going for subtle and pretty. The good girlfriend look.

Back in the bedroom, I dressed in the off the shoulder gown and it felt silky smooth against my skin. From my reflection in the mirror, it was super sexy too, maybe too sexy. Willow's haunting words about her father not approving of it caused a wave of panic. I was heading into this already compromised.

I fluffed my spiraling curls, fairly satisfied my locks concealed my naked shoulder. Stealing a few more seconds, I admired my new bracelet, and knowing it had come from him felt wonderful.

What we had just done had to be classed as a position from the Kama Sutra. That was the longest orgasm I'd ever had. That toe curling validation was what I'd needed to reassure myself I'd made the right decision. Just the thought of it made me throb in all the right places. I forced all thoughts of intimacy out of my mind and I put my game face on, making my way out.

Careful not to trip in these strappy heels, I descended the staircase, again taking in this beautiful foyer.

Lingering outside the door where I assumed the family had gathered, my hand rested on the handle. I doubted I could go through with this. The front door was within easy reach. That's if I could get my legs to work and be prepared to face Cameron's wrath the next time he saw me.

"Mia?"

Aunt Rose stood a few feet away. "We're in the anteroom."

Pretend you know what and where that is, my muse berated.

"Oh right," I answered my muse and Aunt Rose simultaneously.

"I love that dress on you," she said. "Stella McCartney, last season?"

I didn't want to share it wasn't mine. "Um, yes. Sorry."

"A woman who respects money has nothing to apologize for." She fiddled with my diamond collar, spinning the catch to the front. She tightened it and spun it back around. Her slim cold fingers repositioned the choker halfway up my neck. "Head high. Wear this with pride."

My brows arched in a question.

"Oh, I know exactly what this is," she said. "Would you like me to let you in on a little secret?" She brushed the locks away from my shoulder, exposing my bare flesh. "Mia." She leaned in. "You hold all the power."

Aunt Rose was not only beautiful but awesome too, and though I didn't quite believe her words they left a nice, warm feeling. A shared moment to ease this tension.

"Are you curious where Cameron gets his tenacity from?"

I gave another nod.

"Then come meet his mother," she said. "You're in for a real treat."

I was going to have to remember how to talk and fast.

Cameron appeared from across the foyer and calmly, taking his time, he strolled with his hands in his pockets. He looked so handsome in his black-tie and so refined wearing that perfect bowtie. His hair was ruffled just so in a hint of rebellion to all this formality.

I'd need to hold his hand when we walked in.

"Do you see the way he looks at you, Mia?" whispered Aunt Rose.

Searching Cameron's face, I tried to read what she was seeing. He was perhaps acting a little less arrogant, but I assumed that was for Aunt Rose's sake.

"He's very taken with you," she whispered.

Yet she'd not used the word love. Surely she was expecting to see love in his eyes. Maybe she was smart enough to see through our ruse.

"Thank you, Aunt, for taking such good care of her," said Cameron, planting a kiss on each of Rose's cheeks.

"My pleasure, dear."

"Both of you look stunning tonight," he said.

Aunt Rose winked. "Almost didn't recognize her."

He smiled. "May I be permitted a moment with my fiancé?" Cameron rested a hand on my lower spine.

When his heady cologne reached me, it lifted my mood and made me tingle all over. Cameron beamed that heart stopping smile my way, making me want to stretch my hands around his waist beneath his jacket and press my cheek against his white shirt and snuggle in. Though leaving a smudge of makeup on that crisp, white shirt wouldn't go down well.

As Aunt Rose headed off, I wondered if she knew about Cameron's penchant for pain and about Chrysalis. She certainly knew what this choker meant. "Your aunt is so cool."

"Let's not use slang tonight," he said. "Or for that matter ever again."

"Does your aunt know about Chrysalis?"

He gave a *don't be ridiculous* look.

Aunt Rose was intriguing. That glint of amusement made me feel like I was part of a secret club of women. Thank goodness for her being here. She might actually be the advocate I needed

Enthrall Her

when Cameron slipped back into intensity. I really liked his sister too and had to thank her for lending me this beautiful dress.

"Can I sit next to Willow?" I said.

"Will that help you feel more at ease?" he asked.

"Yes."

"Then no."

"But—"

"I need you focused."

"Oh, I'm focused."

"You really do look stunning." Cameron stood back. "When in doubt, smile sweetly."

"What's an anteroom?"

"We gather there before dinner. It's connected to the dining room." He gave a flash of concern.

Avoiding his sudden sternness, my concentration turned to the black and white marble flooring, admiring its perfect symmetry. Maybe that was why everything in this foyer was so unsettling. Each and every piece emanated not only wealth, a raw masculinity, but also flawlessness. Raising my eyes to the decadent chandelier, I admired the thousands of small crystal droplets forming a sweeping centerpiece of superiority.

All this square footage was daunting. I'd thought Richard's home was amazing with its four bedrooms and dramatic ocean views, but this was palatial. I'd never feel safe enough to fall asleep on my own.

"I can't take my eyes off you," he whispered.

He assessed my face and body with approval.

"You like the chandelier?" he said.

"It's striking."

He brushed his thumb over my bottom lip. "You are."

My lip swelled beneath his touch and I nipped at his thumb.

Cameron's eyes closed for a few seconds. "You are sublime," he said huskily. "Let me savor this. Don't dare refuse me this by denying your own beauty."

His words left me breathless.

"I'm recalling that image of you in the foyer. Naked, except for your choker and stockings and ready to submit to me…"

Subspace, I'd slipped into it so easily again, a place where nothing else mattered. Feeling like a million fireflies ignited me from the inside out, I gave the deepest sigh.

"You're training will bring me the greatest joy, Mia."

I needed to break this intensity, this sudden urge to fall at his feet and worship his cock in my mouth. "How often do you stay here?"

"It depends on what I'm doing. Or who I'm doing it to."

"Will your family be visiting your Venice Beach house?"

He looked amused. "No, they fly back to Long Island in the morning."

"Which house do you prefer?"

"My job is to challenge you, Mia. That's why you're feeling this way."

My lips trembled as these moments unfolded. Arriving here had been dreamlike, as though I ran on ahead of reason, fearing I'd change my mind if I gave it too much thought.

"You like the beach house better?" I stuttered.

"The authenticity of the beach house is refreshing. I prefer this house, as I do Chrysalis, for their ability to transform those within."

"Your submissive?"

"Earlier, I offered you a taste of how you will be treated. How did you find the experience?"

"I liked it." *A lot, actually.* I blushed. "What are you celebrating?"

"We're not."

"Are you going out afterward?"

"This is how we dress for dinner."

It was impossible not to show my surprise. I was still haunted by that time Cameron had visited my studio and caught me moments before I'd dived into a Pot Noodle while wearing pajamas. Our lives were oceans apart and every second in his company highlighted that.

"Look at this as an adventure." Cameron took my hand in his and led me towards a door. "One where you get to study us."

My panic rose. These people would spot my lack of culture in seconds.

He opened a door and gestured for me to go on ahead. Even the door handles were exquisitely fashioned. We entered a large mirrored dining room with a low crystal chandelier hung directly over a long dark wooden dining table, infusing decadence into an already lavish space. A prism of color burst down upon the room.

What was it with all these chandeliers? A rich person's thing I supposed. They were so pretty, yet intimidating at the same time. Maybe it had something to do with my childhood being all about hand me downs. Most of the time our bare light bulbs lacked shades or fixtures and glared fluorescently to illuminate both our lack of money along with our class. Thinking about that now really wasn't helping. It merely served to highlight the gargantuan chasm between our worlds.

Cameron was focused on me.

The mahogany high-backed chairs were empty. The table setting looked like something out of one of those luxury magazines I'd flipped through at the grocery store but couldn't afford. Starched finely folded napkins were placed next to delicate blue and white china plates rimmed in gold. It all looked too perfect to use. Numerous crystal glasses, several at each place setting, caught the light. People really did live like this.

"Will we be eating in here?" I said.

"Yes."

"You eat like this every night?"

"Not always." He gestured for me to step towards the table. "We don't have much time, so please listen carefully."

"Can I have some water, please?"

"Soon." Cameron looked intense. "We will be having five courses."

"Five?"

"Mia, I need you to listen." He gestured. "Silverware. You start from the outside and work in. You know this, right?"

"Yes."

"Good. Richard's taught you that much."

I frowned at him. "You have a chef?"

"No, Mia, I just have enough time to finish chopping vegetables." He arched a brow. "Of course I have a chef. Did you just roll your eyes?"

I rubbed my eyelid, careful not to smudge my mascara. "Have something in my eye."

"If we had the time, I'd slam you over the table and punish you from behind for insolence."

I was half startled and half in wonder.

"Now, where was I?" Cameron eased locks of my hair forward to cover my naked shoulder. "It's imperative you watch my father's lead. He will be sitting at the head of the table." Cameron pointed. "You do not begin to eat until he has taken his first bite. When my father has finished eating, so have the rest of us."

"Is that a Cole tradition?"

"Standard etiquette." Cameron continued with a serious air, no irony, just his voice trailing along with a list of demands I was to strictly adhere to. "No leaving the table during dinner."

"What if I need to visit the restroom?"

"Hold it." He wagged a finger. "Using your cell phone—"

"I don't have my phone—"

"Slouching, arms on the table, leaving the table, using the wrong fork, using the wrong wine glass, are all indicative of—"

"Being lower class."

"I meant us not having spent time together." His fists clenched by his sides. "Never again describe yourself in such a manner. Am I clear?"

"But you'd never date beneath your class, Cameron."

"What did I just tell you?"

"They'll know something's up."

"No, they won't." He glared at me. "Class is a word that I have no use for."

"It's just that your aunt's pretty smart."

"As are all my family. They're very open-minded." He cocked his head. "My father's a bit of a curmudgeon, but—"

"What's a curmudgeon?" On his response, I added, "See, you think I'm uneducated."

He shook his head. "Again, that's not what I meant. I would have prepared you for an evening such as this—"

"Yes, but if I had class you wouldn't need to."

He slid a fork closer to a plate and then slid it back. "Mia, I understand that throwing you in the deep end is unnerving." He looked up at me. "And I may come from privilege, but I never act like it."

Cameron did have a point, but he was shaking my confidence with all this talk of etiquette and rules and who eats first and when to stop eating and when to breathe. "I've never played these kinds of social games before."

"It's just dinner."

"Yes, but do you really need three glasses each?"

He pointed to them. "One is for your water. The other two are for wine. One for red and the other white."

"I thought you weren't meant to mix red and white wine?"

"We pair wines with the menu." He gave a wry smile. "Mia, we're only pretending to be engaged. A lover's tiff may hint we've been together a while but let's not over do it."

"I didn't sign on for this."

"You will do what I say and when." He lifted my chin with a fingertip. "That is what you signed on for."

I pouted, refusing to budge on this.

"God, Mia." He clenched his teeth. "Your mouth is so fuckable when you're angry."

Okay, that didn't help either. "That Guantanamo Bay comment sent me reeling."

"It was a joke."

"Can't you tell them I have a headache?" I begged. "Tell them I had to retire to bed early." I too could talk upper class.

"You'll be a pleasant distraction." He took my hand again. "You'll do great. Follow my lead. They're actually rather friendly once you get to know them."

Why the hell had I chosen tonight to break through my fear and turn up at his door?

"Trust me," he said, "I would rather be back in that bedroom with you silencing that smart mouth of yours, but duty calls."

Despite this impending fear, this might just prove invaluable in learning more about Mr. Mysterious. As long as I remembered not to pass out from terror and fall face first into my dinner. "Please don't tell me the main meal is something I've never heard of," I said, "or have no idea how to eat. Like a strange shellfish dish I need a degree for so I don't poison myself."

He threw his head back in a laugh. "We have a menu, so you can quite happily choose from that." He flicked a stray hair out of my face. "Ever resist my plans for you again and I'll be choosing everything you eat from here on in."

We headed towards the side door.

"I like you choosing my food for me," I said. "It makes me feel…"

"Cherished?"

I leaned into him.

"I haven't even begun to cherish you, my darling Mia."

A delicious tingle twirled up my spine.

"You're wrong about me," he said. "I couldn't be prouder to show you off."

"Why me, Cameron? Why did you choose me?"

"You are the epitome of the sacred feminine," he said. "Holding the evolution of your beauty within my hands brings an ecstasy like no other. You are an intoxication I refuse to live without."

Enraptured by his words, I desperately wanted to taste his mouth, have his arms wrapped around me again, his strong hands explore my body. This yearning for Cameron was growing more intense, as though he'd awoken these once dormant desires to be erotically enslaved by him, this insatiable need to be ferociously possessed.

"Soon, Mia," he said. "Soon."

How easy it was to slip into subspace when he was around. This out of body experience caused my body to tremble. This arousal swelled my breasts and tightened my core in anticipation of what else he had to show me.

Life was never going to be the same.

"Ready?" he said.

"As I'll ever be."

He gave a devilish laugh. "Once more unto the breach dear friends, once more."

"I don't want to know what that means, do I?"

"It's from Shakespeare's King Henry." His grip tightened. "The king spoke those words right before entering into the Battle of Agincourt."

"Please tell me the king didn't die."

He grinned and reached for the door handle.

CHAPTER 16

WE WERE GREETED with smiles.

"Here she is," said Aunt Rose, throwing me a welcoming wave.

Cameron's father was the first to rise, approaching with the presence of a man of his standing. Owner and CEO of the billion dollar empire Cole Tea Incorporated, the company Cameron was due to inherit. He easily intimidated with that smart tux and extraordinary height. He towered over everyone.

He held his hand out to me. "Mia, this is a real privilege. Thank you for joining us."

There was that familiarity of Cameron. Same chestnut eyes that glinted with kindness, salt and pepper hair and a handsome refined face.

"It's a pleasure to meet you, Sir," I said, feeling the strong squeeze of his hand.

"Please, call me Raife," he said.

"That's Cameron's middle name," I said, smiling.

Cameron beamed at me and it was a relief I wasn't embarrassing him just yet.

"And Granddad's too," said Willow.

The kiss on each cheek came from his mother. "I'm Victoria," she said. "This is such a lovely surprise." She studied me with that familiar Cole laser-sharp perception. Her auburn hair was coiffed to perfection in a chignon. She was tall and elegant, with a timeless beauty. She was where Cameron got his looks from. She had that same intensity.

Victoria took in my dress and glanced over at Willow, seemingly recognizing her daughter's Stella McCartney. "My son never tells us anything, Mia, so you'll have to apologize if we seem a little out of the know."

"This is a perfect opportunity to learn more about you," said Aunt Rose, giving me another hug. "Cameron is so very naughty keeping you so hush hush."

"More like protective," said Cameron, amused.

"He's such a rogue," said Victoria. "How long have you been dating?"

"A while," said Cameron, gesturing to the dining room. "Let's go through, shall we? I for one am starving."

"We went shopping in Santa Monica," said Willow, taking my arm and guiding me through. "I've promised to take Aunty to Rodeo Drive next week. I do love your choker."

As we made our way back into the dining room, I ran through all that Cameron had told me and made a mental note to follow his lead when it came to cutlery and which glass was used and when. I also reminded myself not to drink too much and start to believe our lie. No wonder the family seemed so guarded. Their son was quite a catch and the chance of women hunting him down for all the wrong reasons was a real possibility.

Cameron directed me where to sit and lifted my chair forward. Once settled, he planted a kiss on my cheek. The waft of his cologne alighted my senses and flashes of what we'd just gotten up came flooding back. He acted so demure now, regal even, so different from in the bedroom when he'd stunned me into submission.

After nudging his aunt's chair forward, he took a seat next to mine. My stomach did a flip when he rested his hand on my thigh, giving it a squeeze as though letting me know he was still in command. I hoped he wasn't going to pull that trick of pain on my thigh he used on me way back when. Squeezing my thighs together, I hoped he got the message.

In true fine dining tradition, we each chose a meal off the creme and gold menus, and much to my surprise I was allowed to choose my own. I decided on the Pacific Swordfish. Cameron chose the Kobe beef, as did his father. With the orders taken and our glasses topped up, I actually began to relax. This was a family affair that I'd never experienced before. A family all sitting around for dinner and catching up on their news. So different from my childhood of grabbing a bite to eat in front of the TV or taking it back to my room when my parents argued. I wondered if Mr. and Mrs. Cole ever disagreed, though the way they shared affectionate glances I doubted it.

Cameron's conversation with his father was about oil refineries and barrels being brought in by rail. Apparently suppliers were eager to tap an isolated market. Something about dwindling supplies in California. I had no idea that California was the third-biggest refining state in the U.S. To be honest, it was a little boring, so I honed in on what Mrs. Cole had to say. She and Willow were talking about their trip to Europe a few months ago.

"We can't wait to visit Italy again," said Victoria. "Mia, how do you find Milan?"

"I've never visited," I said. "But I'd love to."

Cameron's hand rested on my upper back and I felt the brush of his fingers pulling through my hair and making me tingle.

Two waiters appeared out of nowhere and I was so thankful for the interruption. We were served our appetizer of caviar upon thin crackers. All three of them. I was grateful for this small portion and hoped the rest of the meal was like this. Following Cameron's lead, I took a sip of champagne after taking my first bite of caviar, surprised with how the tang of bubbles went so well with the caviar. The combination popped on my tongue and burst with flavor. I beamed at him, unable to hide how much fun I was having.

Despite not belonging in their world, I was made to feel welcome. The ease of conversation between all of them revealed that Cameron had indeed come from a happy and what appeared to be a well adjusted family. It was interesting to watch them interact, but the most fascinating relationship of all was between Victoria and Willow. Their mother and daughter connectedness, their frequent shared glances of affection to each other. Willow seemed to have had an extraordinary appreciation of how lucky she was to have a loving mother.

Shoving down my regret for never having anything close to this with my own mom, I reached over and rested my hand on

Cameron's thigh.

He leaned against me. "Can I get you anything?"

"No thank you." I sipped my champagne.

"So, how did you two meet?" asked Willow.

"It's a long story," said Cameron. "One we won't bore you with."

"Why do men always think these things are boring?" said Aunt Rose. "You of all men must know how much we adore hearing about your adventures, Cameron."

"Let's just say the first time I saw Mia she took my breath away. The rest is history."

"That's lovely," said Aunt Rose.

"History is always skewered," said Raife.

He earned himself a tap of disapproval from his wife.

The waiters reappeared, their timing perfect, and placed our meals before us. Glancing over at Cameron and reassured I had the right knife and fork in hand, I took a bite of swordfish. This was delicious too and I threw a glance over at Cameron to thank him.

He leaned back in his chair. "I'm so glad you're here."

"Me too," I said.

"How's your swordfish?"

"Delicious. How's your steak?"

"Rare."

"You like it rare," I said, throwing him a smile.

"I find that I do," he said, proving he too recalled that first evening we'd had dinner together.

It was kind of fun to fake that Cameron had picked me out of zillions of hopefuls and I'd stolen his heart. He seemed to approve of my loving glances and we shared intimate gestures of affection—him holding my hand, me resting mine on his thigh.

"Have you had the pleasure of meeting Richard Sheppard yet?" said Victoria.

I froze mid-sip, glancing over to Cameron.

"As expected, we all get along great," said Cameron.

"Isn't he divine?" said Aunt Rose. "Why isn't he here tonight?"

"Last time I brought him to dinner at your behest," said Cameron, "you accused me of being gay."

I burst out laughing, relieved that everyone else was laughing too.

"You two boys are so close," said Victoria. "Like two rogues in a pod."

"And remember, Mother," said Willow. "We don't use Richard's real last name anymore."

"That's right," said Victoria, looking over at me. "Terrible business. You probably know all about it?"

I gave a nod, realizing they were alluding to the illegal activity of Richard's father and the suffering it had caused him.

"Richard's one very brave man," said Cameron. "And, as with all of life's challenges, he's come out of it stronger."

Aunt Rose leaned over toward me. "Cameron's holding off the announcement until you get the 'you know what.'" She glanced at my ring finger, as though excited with keeping our secret.

"I wanted to apologize for earlier," I whispered. "In the foyer."

"Oh my dear," said Aunt Rose. "Nothing to apologize for. Men need to be kept on their toes, and a little display like that ensures the furnace burns ever brightly. Besides, I always was a fan of Michelangelo." She winked at me.

She really was lovely. I felt terrible guilt about keeping up with this lie. I'd never been one for mistruths and it felt wrong to lead Aunt Rose on like this, especially as she was so incredibly nice.

"What are you two whispering about over there?" said Victoria.

"I was complimenting Mia on her choker," said Aunt Rose. "Cameron has exquisite taste."

"He most certainly does," said Victoria warmly. "And exclusive too."

Cameron shared a look with his mom. It was fleeting. He turned once more towards his dad, continuing what sounded like a tense conversation.

"Just give it some thought," said Raife.

"Dad, we've been over this," said Cameron.

"And we are yet to come to a satisfactory conclusion."

"What you are essentially asking me to do is give up

medicine," said Cameron. "A profession I have studied for years and one that I excel in. I'm a good doctor."

"Your mother and I do not underestimate what it is we are asking of you, Cam, but—"

"Don't bring me into this," said Victoria.

Raife went on, "What I was going to say is that our business has been in our family for generations. Had your brother shown more of an interest…"

My thoughts drifted with the revelation of a brother. There was so much more to learn.

"Maybe later," said Cameron, "I'll become more involved. When I'm ready."

"We need a firm hand at the helm now," said Raife. "Learning the business is essential."

"What about my commitment to my patients?" said Cameron. "They've grown to trust me."

"Surely you can transfer them over to another psychiatrist?" said Raife. "They won't be left without care."

"Won't the business be less stressful?" said Victoria. "Less dangerous."

"There's no danger in the work I do," said Cameron. "It's medicine."

"What about that time you were attacked?" said Raife.

"My patient was psychotic," said Cameron. "It wasn't his fault."

"Oh, well that's perfectly fine then," said Raife.

I sat up straight. "No one cares more for their patients than Cameron."

He flashed a glare my way.

"He even visits his patient's at home," I said. "And if they can't afford him, he doesn't charge them. Surely that makes him a special doctor?"

Aunt Rose beamed at me. "Why Cameron, she's lovely—"

"You go to their homes?" said Victoria.

"Let's check on dessert." Cameron grabbed my hand and pulled me to my feet. "Rumor has it that chef has gone all out because you're in town, Mom. Mia and I volunteer to be the official tasters."

"Can I come?" asked Willow.

"No," said Cameron, firmly leading me out.

We headed off across the foyer, my heels echoing around us.

"I wanted them to know what an amazing doctor you are," I said, trotting alongside him.

"Mia, I've handled my family and their lack of support for my career for a lifetime. I really don't need any help."

"Your dad seemed to understand."

"That wasn't understanding, Mia. That was the wisdom of leaving it alone until they've broken me down and I have no choice but to relent and become CEO of Cole Tea."

The kitchen was all dark wood and stainless steel. Pots and pans and other cooking implements were stacked next to the dishwasher. A short, young man with blond spiked hair wearing a chef's outfit was busy putting the final touches to a tray of desserts. He stood straight and faced Cameron.

Cameron threw a wave his way. "Mia, I don't expect you to understand."

"Tea versus saving lives," I said. "I understand the situation just fine."

"Freddie, dinner was extraordinary," said Cameron. "I can't thank you enough."

"Always a pleasure, Sir," said Freddie.

"My entire family is raving about the food. You have a gift."

"How was the Kobe?" asked Freddie.

"Cooked to perfection," he said. "I love that wine you selected to go with it. "The Valpolicella was pleasingly complete."

"I'm happy to hear that," said Freddie, pointing to the desserts. "The best is yet to come."

"So it seems," said Cameron. "Again you've spoiled us. Do give my regards to Sissy."

"It will be my pleasure, Dr. Cole."

"Would you mind giving Ms. Lauren and I a few minutes?" Cameron beamed at him and watched him go. Then Cameron's jovial demeanor evaporated. He leaned against the table, his thoughts seemingly elsewhere.

"Maybe your family will come round?" I said, breaking the silence.

"I wish."

"You have an older brother?"

"Yes."

"Well, isn't he meant to take over the family business?"

"Henry is a little unconventional."

"In what way?"

"He's...complicated."

"Surely they should be giving him a hard time and not you?" I said.

"What the fuck!"

"What?"

"I can't believe I am having this conversation with you. We've both seem to have forgotten why we are here. There will be no derailing of your training no matter how much you use the devious nature of your gender to manipulate me."

"That's unfair. I was trying to help."

"If this is you helping, please cease immediately."

"You're the one who forced me into this dinner party. I'm the victim here."

He burst out laughing. "You're right of course. Dining with my family may be classed as one of my crueler punishments."

"I happen to really like your family."

He ran his hand through his hair. "It doesn't exactly help that they find you adorable."

"That's a good thing, right?"

"Yes and no. Well, we came here to sample dessert."

"I thought you just wanted me out of the room?"

"What made you think that?" He rolled his eyes. "Well we're here now."

There, upon two silver platters, was a selection of chocolate brownies, individual pots of cream brulee, and several slices of chocolate gateaux.

Feeling mischievous, I leaned over and dipped my finger into one of the pots of crème brulee, breaking through the sugary crust and bringing the yellowy crème to my mouth. "Mmmm. Delicious. I want this one."

Cameron neared me, that fieriness all too familiar. "Actually, I've already laid claim to that one."

"Really?"

Cameron eased my dress off my shoulder and pulled it down

farther, exposing my breasts. He reached over and dipped a finger into the same pot of brulee and scooped up a little, bringing it over to my nipple. He smoothed it over my areola, causing me to throw my head back. His mouth met my nipple and he sucked, lapping at the cream and sending shockwaves of bliss into me and downward, his teeth grazing.

"That's misuse of the chef's hard work," I said.

"That isn't," said Cameron. "But this is."

I arched a brow.

"Open your legs." He scooped a larger portion onto his finger. "Lift your dress."

Mesmerized, I obeyed, hiking my dress up and around my waist, realizing that these lack of panties had been part of Cameron's plan all along.

His grin matched mine.

"You wouldn't dare."

"Never dare me, Mia."

Delicately, he brought his brulee covered fingertip towards my clit and rubbed it over the small nub. I gasped in pleasure. My thighs shuddered at his touch.

He flashed me a devilish grin.

And lowered himself to his knees, bringing his head between my thighs, his tongue licking at my pussy, fast and unforgiving. My fingers grabbed his dark locks, holding him there against me as I climbed ever higher, stunned by his tenacity.

Trembling, I could hold myself upright no more and let go of him and lowered myself all the way back onto the table until I was staring up at the ceiling. My thighs wrapped around his shoulders. Arching my back, my hair spilling around me, I tossed my head from side to side, panting for him and writhing.

His tongue sent me hurtling into outer space and I gasped for air, my climax owning my breathing like he owned my clit. His masterful thrumming brought wave after way of ecstasy.

With expert flicks, he brought me down slowly, and I let out a long sigh of satisfaction, all tension gone.

Cameron rose to his feet and tugged down my dress. His face came back into focus. I pushed myself up onto my elbows.

"Your responsiveness pleases me," he said.

I sat up and dangled my legs over the edge. "Does this mean

I'm forgiven for my faux pas?"

"There are just so many to choose from."

"I know how to make up for it." I reached for the pot of brulee and lifted it off the tray and set it on the end of the table.

I slid off and lowered myself before him, kneeling at his feet.

"Well this should be interesting," he said.

Reaching up, I unzipped his pants, easing him out in awe of his raw beauty, that hefty erection rising out of dark curls.

Breaking away from his glorious display of manhood, and still surprised that it ever fit inside me, I threw him a seductive glance and turned slightly, reaching up and easing a dollop of cream brulee onto my fingertip. Turning to face him once more, I spread the dessert around that dark purple head, taking my time to delicately lavish it.

"I see forgiveness in your future, Ms. Lauren," he said through clenched teeth.

A heady rush filled me when I caused him to instantly harden.

"Balls first," he said.

They twitched in my mouth as I suckled and licked, worshiping his testicles. Beneath my touch, I felt the muscles of his thighs flex. My fingers found their way, wrapping around the base of his cock, sliding up and down leisurely. I could wait no longer to have him in my mouth. The taste of him mixed with the crème was too delicious. His maleness mixed with the sweet sugared vanilla made me swoon. Taking him all the way in, deeper still, I set a rapid pace, needing to hear his sighs of approval.

His hands fell to my hair, his fingers curling and tugging at my locks. Their pull was just about unbearable, his desire to control the rhythm undeniable.

"Mmmm, delicious," I said.

He shoved me back to his cock. "Don't fucking stop, Mia." He yanked at my hair, pulling at my scalp, forcing me faster.

The feel of him, the taste of him, so clean, so pure, the knowledge that it was me pushing *the* Cameron Cole to breaking point was exhilarating. Gazing up at his serene face, his eyes closed as he moaned with pleasure.

"Flick your tongue beneath the head," he said.

Making a circular motion, I obeyed.

"That's right," he sounded husky. "Very good."

I gripped firmer, working him harder, concentrating on nothing but pleasing him, taking him all the way into my throat and farther still.

His hips pumped. "Mia, I'm close."

My own longing rose with each flick of my tongue, each downward twisting thrust. My hand worked in unison with my tongue as I filled my mouth with him, my lips pouty and tight. My sex responded, clenching and spasming in this ecstasy brought on by his.

Cameron went rigid. His warmth entered my mouth and I swallowed all of him, grateful to have this privilege of his seed flowing into me. Needing him to know this, I moaned longingly for him.

He remained still, with his left hand cupped over his eyes. I sat at his feet, staring up at him, needing to know I had pleased him.

"Sir?" I whispered.

Cameron shook his head and blinked down at me. "Beautifully executed."

I beamed up at him.

"I shall have to thank Chef," he said huskily. "Looks like the crème brulee was a hit."

CHAPTER 17

INTRIGUE CAME WITH the early morning.

I'd stayed in Cameron's guest bedroom, unable to sleep, rolling around and around in that big bed, my mind racing with all that had happened. I went over every interaction, every detail from dinner last night with his family, trying to remember if I'd embarrassed myself.

The highlight of the evening was dessert with Cameron in the kitchen. My sex clenched when I thought of it. I was actually enjoying my first days as his submissive. It wasn't as scary as I'd anticipated. Though the plan to leave for Chrysalis later this morning made it hard to relax too much.

Dressed in this plush robe I'd found in the bathroom, I went off exploring, down the central staircase, through the main foyer and along the hall. More paintings were hung here, and these too were religious themed. None of the images were in any way comforting. A conscious decision on Cameron's part probably. No one looked happy in any of them. Maybe that was the point, the message being that abstaining from temptation brought unhappiness. And as though right on cue, the end painting was of a young, pale maiden being taken by a white winged angel, his halo illuminating the canvas. I stared at his muscular physique. The way her head was thrown back in ecstasy. This one had to be about God's blessing on young lovers, or so the artist had perhaps led us to believe.

I continued along. This place was vast. I wondered if Cameron ever got lonely.

Enthrall Her

The strangest noise—

It sounded like metal clanging against metal and feet skidding along a hardwood floor. After pausing for a few seconds, I opened the door.

This was a gym with hardwood floors and bright florescent lighting. At the far end were two men and they were fencing, their faces hidden beneath meshed white masks and both of them dressed in white. The tension was taut between them. They lunged at each other, their feet making quick work of leaping forward and backward with lightning speed. Their thin long swords were held out before them as they struck their opponent's weapon again and again, the clanging echoing. Aggressively they plunged at each other with a swift grace.

"On guard!" the taller man shouted, and again he tucked his left arm behind him, his right holding his sword out in front. He jabbed his opponent on the shoulder and leaped back.

I slid just inside the door, mesmerized.

More agile strikes—

This was fierce. Violent. And yet beautiful. Sexy even. Their male physiques warred with one another in a dance of death.

They stopped in their tracks and their masked stares fell on me.

"Sorry," my voice echoed. "I was having a look around." As if that made it any better.

The shorter man removed his mask, revealing a young, handsome face.

He strolled towards me, taking his time to amble across the sparseness of the hall. "I was losing anyway. You did me a favor." He slipped off his glove and held his hand out. "Shay Gardner." His handshake felt firm.

"Mia Lauren."

It was hard not to be thrown by his grin and that handshake that went on a little too long. His outfit was so masculine. The other man pulled off his mask. It was Cameron, looking fine in his fencing suit and swaggering with the stride of the victor.

"I was going in for the kill, Mia," said Cameron. "You arrived just in time."

"Cole," said Shay. "This lucky streak will end, you do realize that?"

Cameron gave a low bow. "Always a pleasure, Mr. Gardner."

"I'll see you later at Chrysalis, Mia," said Shay. "I hear it's your first day?"

"Technically yesterday was Mia's first day," said Cameron.

A tingle of nerves resonated from my chest and outward and I blushed wildly.

Shay headed out. It was nice to know there'd be a familiar face at Chrysalis. He seemed friendly enough. I wondered if he was one of the dominants. He certainly used a sword like one.

"That was very impressive," I said.

Cameron flipped his sword downward. "We'll have to get you into the sport, Mia. Something tells me you'd excel at a parry." And on my confused stare, he added, "A blade work maneuver to deflect or block an attack."

I gave a wry smile. "It's very early."

He shrugged. "We have a long day ahead."

Cameron showed an odd indifference, as though last night's mischief with me and a pot of crème brulee never happened.

"Is your family still here?" I said.

"They left early this morning."

The Cole's were all early risers it seemed. Still, at least I didn't need to make polite conversation over breakfast and pretend like I wasn't off to a BDSM manor that their son owned.

"Sorry I didn't get to say goodbye," I said.

"They send their regards. Breakfast?"

"Yes please."

He headed towards the door. "Freddie will prepare you something. I'll meet you in half an hour in the foyer. We have a car picking us up at 8AM. You will find a dress in your wardrobe. Wear it."

"You're not eating breakfast with me?"

He looked surprised. "Why would I?"

I turned and looked back at the room. This show of manliness was probably a good representation of what I had to look forward to. All this testosterone and strength vying for power.

After eating only a few bites of yogurt and muesli, I hurried out of the kitchen, thanking Chef Freddie for my breakfast as well as the delicious coffee, and ran to my room to get ready. The last thing I needed was to be late and incur a punishment right out of the gate.

I grabbed my handbag and made my way down.

I found a stern looking Cameron waiting for me in the foyer at five minutes to 8AM, and I followed him out to the waiting Lincoln Town car.

The journey to Chrysalis felt dreamlike.

Sitting beside him in the back of the car with my hand in his made me feel safe and readier than ever for my new adventure. I stole glances his way, admiring how serene he looked, how peaceful.

The fingers of his right hand scrolled down his Blackberry while his left hand held mine, his thumb caressing and relaxing me.

He wore a three piece suit and his hair was neatly combed this morning, reflecting a level of control that was unnerving. Everything about him, even his highly polished shoes, looked flawless. So well thought out yet effortless.

I'd dressed in this Ralph Lauren sleeveless Pointelle-knit flare dress, matching it with strappy heels. L.A.'s mild weather was going to be a blessing if Cameron was going to continue to dress me like this. Luckily his taste was exquisite.

Just as it was for music. A string quartet oozed from surround sound speakers. Everything with Cameron seemed masterfully orchestrated. This elegant music was part of that and it caused chills to prickle the tiny hairs on my forearms as it emphasized the foreignness of his world.

I felt my power slipping away.

"Warm enough?" said Cameron.

I gave a nod that I was and resisted the urge to scoot closer to him and snuggle.

This crackling electricity between us was impossible to ignore. Not that I wanted to pretend it wasn't there, and from the way Cameron's gaze lingered on me from time to time he must have sensed it too. Entering into this agreement had taken the kind of courage I didn't know I had, and feeling this connection with him, seeing glimpses of his affection, made it easier.

Chrysalis appeared on the horizon, and just like that came

the return of Cameron's brooding intensity, his hand lifting from mine and his demeanor authoritative again. Caressing my right hand, I soothed the ache of having him no longer holding it, missing the warmth of his touch.

The land surrounding the manor provided the kind of privacy only the rich could afford, as did the services offered within. Clients booked themselves in here for weeks, and a few for months at a time apparently, and I was about to join these daring guests as I too took up the challenge of learning to become a good submissive.

The Lincoln came to a stop outside the front of Chrysalis and I stared out of the window to admire the vast hilltop Bel Air property that looked more like a grand hotel than a private house. And I suppose in many ways it was. Soft lighting highlighted the French styled château with its high arched windows and pristine pillars.

Fear lodged in my throat, quickly followed by doubt. That air conditioning had overly chilled the car.

Cameron leaned forward. "Leo, please inform the staff we're here."

"Yes, Sir."

He handed Leo my handbag. "Have this taken to Ms. Lauren's room, please."

"Sir." Leo tucked it under his arm.

Cameron settled back and waited for him to exit and then turned to face me. "How are you feeling?"

I exhaled in a rush. "Good. Excited. Ready."

"I'm looking forward to beginning your training too," he said. "Your discipline is well overdue."

Low in my belly came that familiar quiver, a delicious anticipation, and Cameron gave a nod of appreciation as though he'd picked up on it.

"Does my training begin now?" I said.

"It begins when I say it begins. Your attitude in the past has been unacceptable. Rebellious. Disrespectful."

"But I—"

He raised a hand. "Never interrupt me again. Are we clear?"

I shrank back, and despite some part of my brain telling me it was wrong to allow him to talk to me like this, it felt exhilarating and strangely safe. "I was merely going to say—"

"Mia, this is not a game of who the fuck is in charge," he snapped. "Do I have your attention?"

I gave a quick sharp nod.

"Good." He gave each cuff a tug. "To enter this house one must abide by its rules. Each and every person entering Chrysalis must first undergo a background check. They also sign an NDA. No one, and I mean no one, enters this property without my express permission. Doing so results in being expelled."

"I understand," I murmured.

"This is no ordinary house. This is no ordinary life you are embarking on. From the moment you enter those doors, you will strive to be a willing and well-behaved submissive."

Never had I felt more ready to enter those doors. I'd visited here only once before and caught a glimpse of what went on inside. I was so happy to have Cameron by my side, even if his master persona was a little terrifying right now. His alpha-maleness was off the charts and it was making me giddy. I tried to fight off this arousal, fearing it might cause me to lose control or say something embarrassing, like beg him to take me right now, right here in the car, like a wanton hussy. My body ached for him, and even though he was close I needed him closer. My hands trembled with need.

"No rebellious response?" He sounded surprised.

"I thought you wanted me to be good?" I'd been around his pheromones too long and they were addling my brain.

"I'm not used to your obedience." He gave a roguish smile. "Before we go in, I'd like to explain Chrysalis." He reached for a bottle of water and unscrewed the top. He handed it to me.

I looked around for a glass.

"Society deems that drinking from a glass is most appropriate," he said. "Certain cultures have deemed sexuality merely a mechanism for reproduction."

"Like the Catholic Church?"

"Many, many religions, in fact. Imagine if you will, that you discover at a young age you have a predilection that society deems evil." He waved his hand. "I'm only referring to acts involving consenting adults. Here at Chrysalis we only role-play with healthy minded men and women who want to play safely.

As well as care for those with certain sexual dysfunctions, impotence for example, or the inability to orgasm. As a way of ensuring a cure."

"People come here for treatment?"

"Some," he said. "Very often clients have tried everything else. Some have even undergone painful surgical procedures. All of which failed."

"So their issues can be either psychological or physical?"

"One affects the other. The work we do here is controversial but we have a high success rate."

"It's like a clinic then?"

He gave me a sympathetic look.

"Or perhaps something else all together?" I said.

"We do love to put labels on people and places, don't we?" he said. "I'm not talking about you personally but society in general." Cameron's voice sounded clipped, intense. "Let me tell you a little about our heritage. Our founder was threatened with imprisonment in London in 1905 because of his unusual fetish. He came to America and later began a secret society for like-minded individuals."

"What was his fetish?"

"Never ask anyone here that question. Understand?"

"Oh, okay. Will you always be this controlling?"

"Mia, I will parade you through the house naked if you continue to push back."

"I'm sorry... can't help it."

"You will learn to."

I bit my lip, trying to suppress this low ache in my belly, and lower still that delicious tingling, that longing to be touched by him.

"That's better," he said. "I see in your future a public punishment if you continue with this rebellion."

I squeezed my eyes shut, but it didn't help.

"Do I have your attention?" he said firmly.

My eyes shot open and I gave a nod.

"Throughout history, men and women have been persecuted for their inherent sexual desires."

"Why did they tell people about them?"

"Their innate desire to see their fantasy realized brought the wrong kind of attention."

"People can be cruel, can't they?"

"You were so sheltered in Charlotte," he said. "Sometimes I think you're younger than you are. It's not a criticism, just an observation."

"You seem older too," I said.

"Older than what?"

"Thirty."

"I'm thirty-four."

"But you went to Harvard with Richard?"

"We weren't in the same year, Mia."

I felt stupid and held back on a blush. "Don't change your mind about me. I so want to be here."

"Good."

This revelation stunned me, not only because I'd assumed they were both in the same year at university but also because he was thirteen years older than me. A man of the world, a sophisticate, and he'd proven on more than one occasion nothing fazed him.

"You've never been married?" I asked.

He seemed unaffected by the question. "No."

For some reason that made me happy.

Cameron continued, "Chrysalis is considered a sanctuary. We have guests visit from all around the world. It's an exclusive society that has a detailed screening process for members." He removed his BlackBerry from his pocket and glanced at the screen. He shot off a text and returned his phone to his pocket.

"Human sexuality is complex," he went on. "A kaleidoscope of erotic colors, ever changing, ever evolving—" He took the bottle of water from me and unscrewed the lid. "During your time here, you will be introduced to every aspect."

I stared at the water like it was the last bottle on earth.

Cameron took a sip, his lips encircling the tip, and though he may not have known it he even made that look sensuous. "Chrysalis is a safe, nurturing house that offers its inhabitants the opportunity to live out their desires, needs, and predictions in a non-judgmental environment." He raised the bottle. "Spring water. Delicious. It's refreshing, don't you agree?"

"Yes."

"Thirsty?"

"Yes."

"You have a need? A thirst that needs to be quenched?"

I gave a nod.

"What if I told you that you would never drink water again?" Cameron peered out of his side window and looked up at Chrysalis. "You would feel as though you were dying."

"I understand."

"Here we honor those whom society has yet to understand."

"If they can afford it." I regretted that one.

"Our members tend to have a higher level of intelligence and therefore lean towards the upper salary bracket. We welcome bright, beautiful, and open-minded individuals."

My attention drifted to the front door. Soon I'd be meeting many of those members and mingling with them for weeks. I hoped they'd like me and I them. If they were anything like the guests at Enthrall, I was going to like it here.

Cameron looked thoughtful. "During the Second World War, a young code breaker was hired by the British government at their code breaking center in Bletchley Park. By all accounts, he was a sweet, kind man. He was remarkably intelligent, so much so that he flourished in the field of cryptanalysis..."

I was working hard at following his words, but it was a challenge with my imagination scaring me over what we might be getting up to soon. Where was he going with this?

Cameron paused, as though sensing my daydreaming. "His name was Alan Turing. Alan devised a number of ways to break the enemy's ciphers, or codes. He was mainly responsible for decoding the Enigma machine. Now, the Enigma contained all of Germany's codes."

I sat forward, riveted

"The Enigma was brought back from Poland after Germany invaded. It was stolen by some very brave men off a Nazi U boat. When Hitler sent a message in the way of a command to his U boats, Britain could pick up that message, interpret it, and learn of Germany's plans. Such knowledge allowed the British government to instigate counterintelligence actions that would save millions of lives."

I stared at Cameron in awe and excitement with how much

he knew and everything I'd learn from him.

"Considering the critical work Turing did for an entire nation," Cameron added, "essentially helping Britain win the Second World War, can you imagine how he was rewarded?"

"He was given the Nobel Peace Prize?" I said wistfully.

"No, Mia, they prosecuted him for homosexuality, and as part of his treatment administered female hormones, which was essentially chemical castration." He shrugged. "Prison terrified Turing, so he chose the alternate prescribed treatment. He suffered a terrible ordeal."

"That's horrible." My thoughts scattered. "But I don't understand."

"You've understood greater than most."

"After all he did?"

"Had Turing been around today, he would have been celebrated," said Cameron. "Though we still have a long way to go. Being gay is perfectly normal. Society is realizing that. Societies preconceived ideas are more open than ever to the truth that normal isn't just what you and I deem it to be."

"So many of your clients here are gay?" I asked.

"Yes."

"Are you?"

He beamed at me. "If I was, I'd be in my element here."

"But your relationship with Richard is so…"

"We're exceptionally comfortable with each other."

"It's a bit like how close I am with Bailey."

"Exactly. Supporting Bailey when she came out was an extraordinary gift."

"She's my best friend. I love her."

I didn't want to talk about Bailey right now. The last thing I needed was to be reminded I wasn't going to be seeing my best friend for a while. Apparently I was forbidden to call anyone while I was here. The thought of it made my fingers twitch for my phone that was back in Malibu.

"You're delightfully bi-curious, Mia," said Cameron. "This we can work with."

I blushed wildly. It was more of a fascination with what the dominatrixes got up to with their clients than wanting to engage in any sexual shenanigans. Cameron had found me bent over on

Scarlet's spanking bench, so his imagination must have run wild with what was going on in her office. I still had so much more to learn.

Initially, Richard had gone all out with my BDSM education, giving me numerous reading materials. Thanks to him, I'd read some pretty interesting books. One of them being 'The Story of O' by French writer Anne Desclos, under the pen name Pauline Reage. She'd written her novel in 1954 about a fashion photographer seduced into the world of BDSM. I'd found it both arousing and disturbing at the same time, mainly because of the extent of her sexual torture. Seriously, this book had anal stretching in it and no way was I going to allow anyone to do that to me. *No fucking way.*

"You've gone very quiet," said Cameron.

"You're okay with me crossing out those things for my hard limits?" I said, making sure he'd made a note of them.

"Let's discuss the details later."

My heart took off at an alarming rate. "Are you going to be training anyone else while we're here?"

"No."

I swallowed hard, trying to feign I wasn't having a panic attack.

"As the director," he said, shaking me from my freaking out, "it's my responsibility to ensure our clients' needs are fulfilled. Here, we specialize in healing and acceptance."

"I want to be part of that."

"You'll be at the center of it. There will be times when you will be called upon to assist with my clients."

"I would very much like that."

"After much consideration, I have decided to take you on as my new secretary. This will ensure we continue to work closely together. I require a willing, open-minded assistant who is also my submissive, who trusts me."

"What about my job at Enthrall?"

"It's not going anywhere."

My thoughts spiraled with the kind of things Cameron had in mind, yet I knew he wouldn't push me too far, not on my first day anyway.

My mind screeched to a halt. "You'll hire a new secretary at

Enthrall?"

The thought of a newbie hanging around Richard sent a wave of panic.

"You're merely switching places with Lady Penny."

It was too late to not show my relief.

"You're going to be a good fit," he said. "I saw your potential for what we do here during your interactions with Monsieur Trouville. Or rather how he reported he felt after interacting with you."

"Monsieur Trouville is one of your patients?"

"Yes. Though we refer to them as clients. They either stay here or have sessions at Enthrall."

"I helped him?"

"You did. Trouville had a remarkable breakthrough after interacting with you at Enthrall."

"Breakthrough?"

"Yes. I can't say too much as his case is confidential."

"But I didn't do anything." I blushed. "In fact, I kind of lied to him. I let him believe I had those Venus balls in."

"You made him feel normal, Mia. Which of course he is."

That made me wonder what his fetish was.

"He's desperately fond of you," said Cameron. "When you improve a man's life, you improve his work, and Trouville's work is highly important."

"What does he do?"

"Monsieur Trouville is one of the world's most preeminent astrophysicists," said Cameron. "Trouville's findings on the study of black holes is remarkable. He continues to awe the astrophysics community. He has an interesting theory on black hole behavior, believing they swallow the occasional star in order to protect them."

I stared through the window again, skyward. "It's a bit like what you do here." I turned to face him. "You take us under your protection for a while. Until you're ready to let us go."

Cameron closed his eyes and his expression shifted to unreadable. "It's time."

Trying to still my shaking hands, I followed him out.

When he slammed the car door behind me, I jumped. Never had I been so nervous yet never so exhilarated. My heart thundered like a thousand starlings scrambling for freedom.

"Frightened?" asked Cameron.

My expression held nothing back.

"As expected." He took the few short steps up towards the carved dark wooden door, turned the handle, and opened it. He gestured for me to go on ahead. Of course I'd walked through this door before, but never under these circumstances. Entering now meant relinquishing control. The unknown had never loomed so close.

My intuition screamed at me to get back in the car.

"After you," he said.

Soft lighting came from dramatic inlaid ceiling sconces, showering the foyer with shards of white and emphasizing the central staircase sweeping up and heading off in opposite directions.

I took in the marble pattern, bold and uncompromising, as were the striking blood red velvet drapes behind us, easily complimenting the surrounding upholstery. A visual symphony of shape, texture, and color all ingeniously exuding Chrysalis's power.

His power.

"You like me being frightened, don't you?" I said, turning to Cameron.

"Yes," he said darkly. "I do."

CHAPTER 18

THE HARRINGTON SUITE was as I remembered it.

A lavish ballroom situated on the west side of the house and probably the biggest room of all. The last time I'd visited I'd naively sneaked in, hardly noticing the décor. I'd been too mesmerized by the erotic vision of a beautiful naked woman being taken hard on that long central table by two masked men, both of them half stripped out of their tuxedos.

I'd fought off my arousal long enough to get the hell out, only to be caught leaving the room, and ten minutes later presented to the director, like the trespasser I was. Lucky for me the director was Cameron. The shock that this renowned psychiatrist ran this place, as well as Enthrall, had never left me. A connoisseur of the dark arts, whatever that actually meant. I'd been told his erotic skills equaled his brilliance as a doctor, which was a heady combination.

It didn't help that he was standing a few feet away watching me, his hands casually tucked inside his pants pockets and that fierce intelligence reflected in those deep chestnut eyes.

We'd only just left the safety of the Lincoln and here was our first stop on our tour. This empty room was a regal reminder that they partied hard in the lap of luxury. Those memories brought with them an arousal, a thrill, those sensuous scenes replaying in my mind like a forbidden dream. I was now part of this world and my guide was the man who ruled this house.

"What do you remember?" he asked.

"There was a crowd," I said. "People were watching."

"What were they watching, Mia?"

Turning from him, I made my way farther in.

The high stucco ceiling and long sweeping drapes gave a palatial air, formidable even. Understandably, last time I'd not noticed the black and white photographs in heavy frames lining the walls, these dramatic renditions of men and woman dressed either in tuxedos for the men or the finest underwear, or a lack of it, for the women. All of them masked. Members caught in real life poses, all of them elite, rich. Otherworldly.

"Mia?" he said.

I pointed, cheeks flushing. "There was a woman on this table. Two men were making love to her."

"They were fucking her." He shrugged. "Semantics."

"They were sharing her," I whispered.

"Do you want to know the meaning of what you witnessed?"

This place had a way of silencing me. *He* had a way of silencing me.

"Ruth was being returned to her master after being trained," he said, "by one of our senior dominants."

I tried to make sense of his words. Ruth, that mysterious brunette with the grace of a dancer, had writhed in pleasure, spellbound by those capturing her, pleasuring her, and in front of all those people. Ruth's eyes had met mine as though needing to share her experience.

Was he suggesting that I too would be taken by both Richard and him in this manner? The thought of it both terrified and thrilled me. My legs wobbled and I willed myself not to show any weakness.

He neared me and grasped my shoulders. "There's a real risk you may become infatuated with me. Don't. This is not about love. This is about surrender. Yours."

This room was bigger than I remembered it. The vastness impersonal and lacking intimacy. In here you could be swallowed up and no one would notice.

Cameron lifted my chin. "I say this to prepare you."

"I don't see myself falling in love with you, if that helps," I said. "I belong to…"

His eyes crinkled into a smile. "Correction. You now belong to me."

Enthrall Her

I stared at the plush carpet and willed his intensity down a notch.

Cameron came closer and brushed his thumb over my mouth. "While you are in this house, don't think of him again. Am I clear?"

"Yes," I said, my heart wilting.

He grasped my arm and led me out of the room. "As my submissive, you will be granted certain privileges. You'll be considered BDSM royalty. Do not take advantage of such a position."

His intensity caused chills throughout my body, my psyche warning me this was it.

Outside, I glanced left and right down the sweeping hallway. Hardwood floors led off in either direction. The scent of fresh pinewood and incense filled the air. Cameron closed his eyes and I felt the shift in his demeanor.

Disquiet seeped into my bones.

He opened his eyes again and zeroed in on me like a predator. "Mia."

"Yes?"

Cameron slammed me against the wall, using his body to hold me there. "Last time you came here," he gripped my wrists, raising my hands above my head and holding them there, "I caught you trespassing. That time, I had no choice but to let you go. Deny you the punishment you deserved."

Shadows dance over his striking features and I saw the truth in his eyes. That he held all the power.

He looked intense. "Now that you are mine, everything changes." Cameron's lips met mine, forcing them open, his kiss furious, his tongue battling for domination and finding it. This need within me was so powerful, so intense, I moaned into his mouth, slipping towards surrender. He was breaking down my defenses, the severity of his hold weakening me.

My thoughts spiraled out of control as memoires flooded in, distracting me from this, our first kiss at Chrysalis. Cameron had promised to get to my pain but there was only one way for him to do that. I'd have to tell him about what really happened that day, share the shame of what I'd done. I'd risk losing him forever and sabotage my chance of going back to Richard. When Cameron learned the truth, his wrath would turn from domination to hate.

I turned away. "No."

"Life is a series of moments." His tone was silky, refined. "Don't be frightened of this one."

By now, Richard was probably nestled at home with that young woman. An ache settled in my heart. My stomach twisted in knots. It had been so easy to surrender to Richard, his boyish charm, his gentleness.

This was different.

What was being offered by a world renowned dominant promised no end of pain. The kind I wasn't ready for.

"I have to go home," I said.

Cameron's right hand gripped my wrists above my head and with his left he tugged at my dress. "Lift."

Giddy with this adrenaline rush forging through my veins and causing me to shake uncontrollably, I obeyed, feeling his right hand trailing up the inside of my thigh.

"Shush," he soothed, his fingers exploring.

Cameron's hand came down hard on my pussy and I jotted with the shock, the pang of pleasure hit me right on my clit.

"This is your home now," he said.

I gave a sharp nod and Cameron's hand delivered another slap, sending astounding pleasure there and alighting my sex, sending me spiraling.

"And while you are here, you will obey me in all things."

My moan echoed. "What if anyone sees?"

"Then they see. You arrived at my Beverly Hills home wearing stockings, Mia. When I distinctly remember giving you orders to the contrary."

"And I'd do it again too," I burst out.

His hand came down hard, shooting pleasure into my core. "Rebelling?" His slaps became short, sharp and resounding. "Be still."

"No."

"Then I'll still you." His fingers explored further, entering and circling, pressing my g-spot, suspending all my thoughts.

Not wanting this to end, I begged him with my eyes. Despite this urge to fight back and not give up my dreaded secret, his fingers owned me right now and he was luring me closer, finding a way to weaken my resolve.

His thumb flicked across my clit. "Who does this belong to?"

"Me."

"Is that right?"

I clenched my teeth. "Yes."

"What about your body?"

I turned my face away, letting that serve as my answer.

It was difficult to concentrate with those slow, heavy thrusts of his palm making me throb. Swooning with pleasure, my channel pulsing and aching for him, my head lolled to the side. His fingers were doing something masterful to my clit now and I lowered my gaze to see.

"Do you agree to obey me in all things?" he said.

"That depends."

"On what exactly?"

"If I like what it is you're ordering me to do."

He let out a wolfish laugh. "It's just a matter of time before I have you on a leash."

"Never."

Cameron continued with this devastating pace, his hand punishing me.

I moaned. "Can I come?"

"You're not so impossible to train."

"That proves you don't know me."

"I know you better than you know yourself, Mia."

I shot him a look, trying to read the truth in his words. "Let me come."

"Let's be clear on something," he whispered close to my ear. "If I'm going to make you come frequently, you will never hold back on me again? Am I clear?"

Heeding his words, I let go, leaning forward into the pleasure, allowing the climax to sweep over me, shuddering, wanting and needing to be held like this forever. Cameron continued his mastery, holding me at the height of climax as though he had the power to hold me there forever.

"Who do you belong to?" he asked.

A shiver ran through me.

As though sensing my need to fall from this dazzling

precipice, he slowed his pace and led me down, guiding my recovering with expert circling, bringing me back into the now.

"This moment is not meant for you." Cameron slammed his body against mine with a deadly grace. "You are the most beautiful creature I've ever seen, and until now I've had to give you up, until now."

We were replaying that scene from the first time he'd caught me trespassing here. That time he'd resisted taking me against the wall. He'd merely held back on his passion and guided me out of the back of the house, amongst the partygoers, and delivered me to Richard.

But not tonight. Not now. This was our chance to replay that chemistry between us, trust where the seconds dared to take us. My desire to please Cameron overwhelmed me and my thoughts scrambled, trying to remember what I knew about him, about this place. I pushed against him, panicked by my imminent surrender.

Cameron stilled, his expression remaining taut, his frown deepening. "You dare to defy me?"

It didn't make any sense. I'd surrendered to him back in his Beverly Hills home and been rewarded with astounding pleasure, yet here, now, I'd lost my will to submit.

"I belong to me." I said it with the same volition with which he'd demanded I was his.

"Careful."

I glared at him. Yes, I wanted to let go, but something deep within me refused to go there. My body wanted this, but my mind denied my release, this freedom, refusing to let him in. Refusing to let go. My past dictated each decision despite what I wanted.

He gripped my wrists. "You're playing with fire."

"Apparently you like to watch us burn?"

"You don't know what it is to burn." His hands grasped mine above my head again. "My advice to you is submit. Now." His twisted his lips arrogantly, his erection digging into my lower abdomen.

His expression revealed the inevitable.

"You will never know me." I sobbed, out of the fear it was true.

Cameron looked dangerously virile, his unequaled strength

holding me in place, unmovable. "Defiance will bring a harsher treatment." There came a flash of aggressiveness, that dangerous stance, that pressure of his firm body against mine.

My instincts were screaming at me to get the hell out. "Can I see the rest of the house now?"

With his defenses down, I'd slip out the back and make my getaway when no one was looking. This plan I liked. It calmed me.

He let go and stepped back. "Time to sign your contract."

I backed away, putting distance between us, unease surging through my veins as I tried to remember how to breathe. My feet came through for me despite these high heels, carrying me swiftly down the hallway and away from him and onward into the foyer. I moved towards the front door, blood surging through my veins and my heart thundering.

Cameron was fast, fast enough to close in and cut me off.

He stood between me and the exit. "Where do you think you're going?"

"Hadn't given it much thought."

He stepped back to give me some room. If I wanted to turn and leave, I could. He was giving me the space I needed to be sure.

"I'm sorry to have wasted your time," I said.

"She knows, Mia."

"Who? What are you talking about?"

"Your subconscious. She knows we're close."

"What does that mean?" But I knew.

Cameron really did believe he had what it took.

Scarlet's words came back to me, *"Before the butterfly emerges from its cocoon, it must first retreat from the world. Next it becomes completely transparent, revealing everything about itself."*

"I've made a terrible mistake," I said. "I should never have come here."

He held that calm demeanor. "It's time."

"What if you end up hating me?"

"Where I am taking you, there is no room for hate."

Tears stung my eyes. I wanted, needed, to believe that.

"Do you want to know why I like it when you're afraid?" he

said.

I froze, every taut muscle on high alert.

"Mia, your psyche knows that change is imminent. Fear stands between you and your future. Your freedom from pain." He held his hands together as though in prayer. "Do you trust me?"

I wanted too.

Bolt through that door and get the hell out.

My heart wished it was possible to run and stay at the same time. Intrigue mixed with trepidation addled my brain. Cameron was the most beautiful, most brilliant man I'd ever known and he was offering me a lifeline to freedom. Was he? Or was it sex leading me into danger? The thrill of submitting to him weakened my resolve.

"I will be with you every step of the way," he said.

It wasn't going to work. I was going to lose everything.

Consequences. There was always an aftermath that followed when getting close to someone. A predictable regret that you'd allowed your heart to open and let them in.

"Slow your breathing," he said.

Steadying my trembling hands, I took in the foyer. This place might have very well been my only chance, yet I had no way of knowing if I'd survive it, or end up permanently damaged even more than I already was.

"It's time to heal."

I didn't like it one bit. Weren't we just meant to be fucking? Hard? All over this house? And sometimes in front of people, if that was what got his rocks off. Wasn't I just meant to be crawling around on all fours at the end of a chain and doing what I was told so I could get back to a life that promised to be happy?

If only I deserved that.

"It's time for you to think differently," he said.

"How?"

"As Carl Jung so succinctly puts it, 'if you think along the lines of nature then you think properly.'"

"How does nature think?" I whispered.

He held out his hand to me.

CHAPTER 19

"POSSESSION IS THE ultimate pleasure," said Cameron, admiring my nakedness from a few feet away.

Had he spoken those words prior to securing me to the Saint Andrew's Cross in the center of Chrysalis's dungeon, I may well have put up more resistance. This free standing crisscrossed board would allow him full access to my body from every angle. He'd seduced and coaxed me to follow him and I'd gladly held his hand all the way down here, taking the short journey from the foyer into the lowest depths of Chrysalis. Passing door after door, each room begged to be investigated, but we'd not stopped to peek in any of them. We'd entered the room at the end of the hallway.

The dungeon of his choice.

Cameron had undressed me and I'd willingly let him, lifting my arms above my head as he'd stripped me. I'd obeyed like a well trained sub as he unhooked my bra strap and removed it. After nudging me back against the fixture, he'd positioned me spread-eagled with my wrists and ankles secured within leather straps. He'd pulled them tight to ensure movement was impossible.

Operatic music bestowed a sensuous backdrop of soprano's dramatically vying for attention, an extension of this already exotic mood.

That daring decision had led me to this.

Rising from subspace, I opened my eyes as though awakening from a dream. Spellbound, my thoughts spiraled out of control. My body trembled with need and a lust for him to be closer. All I wanted was to have him inside me. That was the only cure I needed. I saw that now.

Five minutes ago, though it could have been longer, I'd been weighing the pros and cons of bolting out the front door and somehow, in true Cameron style, he'd casually led me into his red walled playroom.

I'd walked beside him willingly.

This dungeon was unlike any I'd seen, decorated with the decadence I'd come to expect from him. Several oriental-styled cabinets were flush against each wall and probably contained all sorts of whips, paddles, and other accoutrements. Mirrors and contemporary artwork hung between bronze sconces, providing an ethereal air. Low lights showcased the ceiling fixtures that were perfect for the art of suspension, dangling submissives and leaving them vulnerable, their body's secured with rope or chains or whatever else the dominant desired. The wonder of floating would ensure they remained in subspace. Sharp hooks were fashioned on the end of some for those with a overly masochistic leaning. I offered a silent prayer he'd never use those on me.

I wondered if, after our session, I'd get to recover on that regal four poster bed with its carved posts. It was artfully strewn with drapes and chains and leather cuffs, just in case the submissive got too comfortable.

A rush of excitement flooded my veins and my trembling limbs struggled to be free from these leather bindings. Twisting my wrists, I was shocked by the sting to my flesh. Being ensnared was mesmerizing. These straps felt agonizingly tight and trying to escape them was thrilling.

I was soaking wet, and my scent gave me away.

Cameron dragged what felt like a whip along my backside, sending spasms into the center of my universe, soothing, luring, seducing me to surrender.

His handsome face came into focus and shadows danced over his beautiful features, his stern stance proving he ruled the room. He held up the whip for me to see.

Cameron had stripped off his jacket and shirt and was now naked from the waist up, his black pants hanging loose over his hips, revealing his muscular sculptured body, that incredible toned torso flexing as he moved.

He snapped the whip. "Are you worthy of this?"

"If you deem me worthy, Sir."

"I do."

The strike to my left thigh made me flinch. He continued on, strike after strike, circling my body with the ease of a predator overwhelming its prey. The stinging left bright red welts and they burned and hummed when his strike left them. The snap of the crop between my thighs made me jump. With his left hand, he eased apart my labia and flicked the leather strap across my clit. I let out a cry, and a groan of need. Working at a steady pace, he snapped it continuously until my moaning hinted I was close. He raised the whip to my pelvic bone and slid it along my abdomen, up and over my nipples.

Satisfied I'd calmed, he again lowered the whip, torturing my pussy once again with the curl of leather, teasing and striking, flicking and patting.

He ceased those delicious strikes, his face reflecting the triumph of masculine control. "Mia, you are soaking wet. Good girl."

I shuddered when he squeezed my clit between his thumb and forefinger. "Who does this belong to?"

"Well as it's on my body, I can only assume it belongs to me," I said.

He threw the whip down and disappeared behind me.

Oh no. I really was out of my mind.

The rustle of an envelope being ripped open.

He reappeared, holding what looked very much like my contract. "See this?"

It was the same one I'd placed on his foyer table, being the good submissive I'd hoped to become.

"Untie me," I said, "So I can take a closer look."

Cameron flashed a heart stopping smile. "Nice try."

My mouth was dry and thirsting. "We were going to go over the hard limits, remember?"

Cameron's gaze left the contract and held mine. "As your dominant, I deem which hard limits are appropriate."

That was confusing and a little scary, but as we were role-playing. I lowered my voice, trying to play along. "Sir, perhaps we could just discuss them then."

He blinked at me. "No need."

My breathing was now ragged. "I mean before we go any further?"

"Any further?"

"Before you do anything else," I said. "Before we start."

He glanced at the whip on the floor. "We've started. You gave your consent after you trespassed into my Beverly Hills home. Selective memory, Mia?"

"Cameron. Sir—"

"There's been a change of plan," he said darkly, throwing the contract into the air and letting it spiral to the floor. He stepped forward with lightning speed, firmly gripping either side of my head and attacking me with a kiss, forcefully crushing my lips. He stole my reason, my will to fight, his lips forcing my mouth wider open only to deliver brutal and dominant strokes of his tongue lashing mine, punishing, controlling.

He broke away.

I came up for air. "We'll start slow, right?"

Cameron looked thoughtful. "We'll do silence. How about that?"

His mouth met my nipple and he dragged his teeth along its pertness, grazing and elongating, sending a shockwave of bliss.

"Safe word," I said quickly. "We didn't agree on one."

"We talked about this, remember?"

"Remind me."

"Shall I define silence?"

This was meant to be about trust, opening up, savoring sensuality with your partner. Richard had told me that. This, whatever Cameron was doing here, was far from the reaches of my understanding. This was off the charts.

This was mind blowing.

"Yield, Mia," he said. "I've promised you pleasure. It comes in many forms."

My heart pounded against my chest. Blood roared through my ears.

He whispered close to my ear, something about the rewards of surrender, and he fingered my sex and it rippled around him, clenching. He withdrew his fingers and I groaned my disappointment. Then he eased those damp fingers into my mouth and I suckled, tasting myself and swooning at this erotic act.

"This is what I do to you," he said. "Trust your body. Trust your mind."

"I need this." I yearned for release. "Please, Sir."

He strolled over towards the cabinet and reached inside. He removed a long, thick leather strap.

Cameron was behind me now and I knew what was to follow, needing this more than breathing itself. He was going to purge my pain.

The first strike to my buttock made me jolt. Another and another came fast. His masterful strikes now found my thighs, my lower back, my sex, helping me ease into the rhythm. Sensations poured into my flesh. Interwoven sparks of pain and pleasure, making it impossible to separate the two. Aware of only this, lost in an inner landscape of nothingness, I was absorbed by this well crafted tempo of bites to my skin.

He used his hands, taking his time to caress the stings, soothing this burn, pinching this soreness, lulling me.

When he applied the sharp spiked nipple clamps, I gritted my teeth, wanting to prove I could endure this delicious agony. They punctured the edges of my areolas, shooting orgasmic pleasure between my thighs. He tugged each one and then together, sending stabs into each sensitive nub, and my juices trickled down my inner thigh.

Eyes bleary, I watched him fetch the delicate vibrator, and with a flick he'd fired it up. He traced it over my belly and lower still. The vibration felt heavenly against my skin, as though he'd prepared my flesh simply for this.

The sex toy met my clit and thrummed away.

"Oh, God," I burst out.

He pulled it back. "Did I give you permission to talk?"

"No, Sir, sorry Sir."

"May I continue uninterrupted?" he warned.

A quick nod, then I squeezed my eyes shut, exalting when that buzz found my pussy again, circling and bouncing and pressing until all thoughts scattered out of reach. The climax swept over me and I gasped, hoping Cameron would allow me this. My lips formed a pout.

When I opened my eyes, he was studying me with that same scrutiny. "What do you say?"

"Thank you, Sir," I managed.

"Good girl." He lay the vibrator down on a back table. "Do you think you are worthy to come again?"

"Only if you deem me ready, Sir."

He eased off the clamps. First one and then the other.

My body trembled with the letting up of this pang. He massaged my nipples to soothe their sting and ran his thumb over each one, sending me into a near climactic trance. Firm fingers pinched their pertness, sending a shiver of pleasure low in my belly.

He reached into his pocket and there was that rip of a packet, followed by him swiftly freeing himself from his pants. That threat of his erection, that sleight of hand as he rolled on the rubber. He released my ankles from their leather cuffs and brought my legs up and wrapped them around his waist. My wrists tugged hard behind me, still well secured in their straps. I was suspended against him.

He thrust fiercely, entering me, mercilessly owning my sex, sending shockwaves of pleasure. Obsessively, I clenched him, letting him know he was mine just as much as I was his. I moaned as I drew closer to another orgasm.

Sliding in and out, he slowed now to let me know he was master. My wetness allowed his sensuous glide.

"You haven't begun to see what my dark nature has in store for you," he whispered.

Thrusting again and again, he was pounding into me, possessing me, and my soul screamed for this to be so. Arching my back, my hair tumbled behind me as I writhed in this bliss. I stuttered for air while my trembling thighs gripped him and pulled him in.

He pushed deep and deeper still and I feared the pleasure wouldn't hold off the pain of his forcefulness, this fine line between agony and bliss raising me towards another climax. Our perspiration soaked bodies slapped together, making the only sound other than our primal cries. Our throaty moans mingled, willing each other on, competing to be heard.

All consuming.

"Mia," he said hoarsely, "you will never leave this room."

Unraveling, I struggled against him, trying to process, having believed I could cope with whatever he had to throw at me, reveal to me. Do to me.

This frantic pummeling, his ability to enter me, enter my mind, getting closer to that secret place, that dark chamber hidden away in my consciousness…

Cameron was virile, with that blaze of authority. His pupils dilated to large black circles of primal want. A trickle of perspiration trailed down his forehead as he assumed frenzied control and he fucked me into oblivion.

I was captured completely.

Exalted, moving ever higher into the stratosphere.

My mind fractured into a million pieces of nothingness as his words buried deep inside and I reached within to comprehend, screaming my orgasm. I'd reached an impossible summit where I was mesmerized by the scattering of thoughts, the disappearing of consciousness, gliding through nothingness.

A euphoria unlike any other.

Free…

CHAPTER 20

COLLAPSING AGAINST HIM, I fell into his arms.

Surrendering.

My wrists stung from their leather bindings, but they were now free. Weak and spent, my legs failed and buckled. He caught me and picked me up in his arms, swiftly carrying me over to the bed where he lay me down. He pulled the chenille over me.

Pressing my face against his chest, eyes squeezed shut, I was grateful for these minutes that followed, this gentleness. The way he eased sweat soaked locks of hair away from my face. Fulfilled and ever so sleepy, my body thrummed with lingering pleasure, my flesh tingled.

"What's the first letter of the emotion that haunts you?" he whispered.

My body tensed. "G."

"Guilt," he murmured. "Not so uncommon."

I closed down again, shuddering away the feeling. "You didn't mean it?" I lifted my head off the pillow. "That I'm not allowed to leave this room?"

"Shush," he soothed. "Sleep."

Cameron spooned behind me, wrapping his arms around my waist and pulling my back tighter against his front. His hand ran up and down my right arm.

Never had I felt such freedom, which Cameron had given me, and my heart ached for him though he was right here. There was no way he was not letting me leave. That was unethical and illegal too.

No way.

I replayed every second of every detail of Cameron's mastery, reimaging that delicious pain balanced with pleasure. The richness of ecstasy was too much to endure, and I understood that only with torment could there be a transcendence of mind and body. A freeing of consciousness. Now I understood.

"Sleep, Mia," he said.

"How do you know I'm still awake?"

"Your breathing."

I let out a satisfied sigh. "Are you going to sleep?"

"No, I'm going to watch over you while you do."

"I think you might be the perfect man, Cameron," I said, smiling.

"I can live with that"

"Humble too."

"I have my moments."

"You sure do."

He chuckled. "I'm just warming up."

"I was right then."

"About what?"

"Death by fucking."

"Interestingly enough, that's part of the process."

I turned my head to better look at him.

"The façade that is Mia Lauren is just that, a façade, and I can't wait for you to let me in."

I yawned. "I just did."

"You didn't, but you will."

My body became rigid, that veil once more coming down.

"Every part of you is delightful, Mia. Even the conflicted part. The aim is to get you to like it too." He kissed my shoulder. "Now sleep. I won't tell you again."

"Yes, Sir." I relaxed against him, liking how that word made me feel so safe.

Dozing off, I gave in to the tiredness.

If I dreamed, I didn't remember it. I did however remember what had unfolded in this room, my sensitized skin an easy reminder. Stirring awake, my muscles ached and my sex throbbed.

Stretching, I was yanked back. The longest chain dangled from my collar and spiraled off down the edge of the bed. Bolting upright, I lifted the chain and gave it a tug. It was attached to the far wall, and though it was long enough to allow me to roam the room it was not long enough to let me leave it.

I leaped off the bed.

Cameron stood a few feet away. "Good, you're awake."

"I don't like it. Take it off." I tried to reason with my panicked thoughts. This was not happening. "Unlatch it."

"Why would I want to do that?" he said.

"Because I'm asking you to." I trotted over to the wall and gave it a firm tug. The thing was welded to the wall.

Holy cow.

Judging from his white shirt and jeans, Cameron had left me sleeping long enough to shower and change. It made me feel grungy. I needed to take a shower. Clean my teeth. I needed to pee.

"I need to freshen up," I said.

"There's a bathroom in there." He pointed.

Fiddling with the collar, my trembling fingers tried to unhook it. I traced the shape of a padlock at the back of it. Out of which came the end of that long chain. "What the fuck is this?"

Cameron looked fierce. "Is this how you greet your master?"

Blood red walls. Cabinets full of instruments of pain. Suspension hooks waiting to capture a submissive and hang her up irrevocably.

I dropped to my knees and lowered my head in submission, waiting for him to unhook me. Resting my palms facing up, I calmed my shaking hands, doing everything in my power to make him believe his mastery was working.

"A lie to oneself," he said softly, "is the cruelest lie of all."

"Sir, I submit to you."

"And a lie to your master brings the harshest of punishments."

"Lie?"

"Do you belong to me? All of you?"

My head snapped up and I still couldn't answer.

"Bend over the bed, Mia." He gestured.

Rising to my feet, I made my way to bend over it, offering my butt to him. My hands reached out to the comforter and gripped it with both hands, trying to steady their trembling.

"Ass higher," he said.

I curved my spine, showing more of me.

Seconds past, maybe minutes, and then the strike of his hand met my ass with a shocking sting.

I flinched forward. "Thank you, Sir," I managed, squeezing my eyes shut and trying not to move. *Keep it together, Mia*, I rallied myself. Just show him you'll play along. He'll calm down and before you know it you'll be wearing a fancy dress he's picked out for you, sitting opposite him in the dining room, and choosing something you've never heard of from a menu.

The slap to my butt was hard and the strikes that followed came fast. Squeezing my eyes shut, I went with him, caught in this slipstream, amazed how even now I enjoyed his touch, his ability to lull me. The spanks sent ripples of pleasure between my thighs, bringing me close.

"Good girl," he said. "Turn around."

I stood before him, trying to read his face.

Cameron removed two strands of silk from his pocket.

"Hold your arms out wide." He used the strips to secure my wrists to either side of the bedposts, tying the knots you'd expect from a consummate master. No way was I getting out of these.

Being bound by this chain and strung up with my arms stretched out wide caused a wave of exhilaration. I was beholden to his aura, his presence vivid and unsettling.

Naked and vulnerable, I watched him stroll over to the other side of the room and grab hold of a chair. He dragged it back and placed it in front of me.

"Now." He sat and crossed one leg over another. "Let's begin." He reached into his inside shirt pocket and removed a notebook and pen.

Oh no, he was going to do this now.

"What do you want to know exactly?" I said, hurrying this along.

"The truth."

"I've always told you the truth."

"Actually, you've skirted it. But you're forgiven."

"Maybe it will be easier to open up if Richard's here?"

His face tensed.

"Sorry," I said. "I need some fresh air, Sir."

He looked solemn. "You are not leaving this room until you have shared with me the truth of what happened that morning. Holding onto it is poisoning you." He swept his hand wide. "None of this would be necessary if you opened up to me."

My lips trembled.

"Though it may very well be that this event remains subconscious," he said.

"What does that mean?"

"You are keeping it from me perhaps because the truth remains elusive even to you."

"What if we can't find it?"

He placed his pen nib onto his notebook, poised to write. "You told me you'd come to terms with your past. Yet you do not seem to have forgiven yourself for chasing your father away?"

I yanked at my silk restrains. "My dad left me. He walked out on us when we needed him the most."

Cameron removed a pair of round rimmed glasses and put them on. He looked so devilishly handsome, as though nature had cunningly bestowed him with the upper hand.

He nodded thoughtfully. "This still causes you pain?"

"No shit."

"Then you lied to me," he said. "You told me you were over it."

"What? No, I mean, I am. It's just that you're trying to make me feel like it was my fault."

"I'm merely mirroring what you told me."

"It's confusing."

"How does that make you feel?"

I shrugged. "I don't know, confused."

"Confused?"

"I waited every day," I said. "Expecting him to return. Sometimes I'd play this game where I'd imagine him coming through the door with presents. He'd be pleased to see me and so sorry about all the confusion. And he'd kind of changed. Into someone a little nicer. Like he was happier. Less angry." The words tumbled out like the darkest confession.

I waited for Cameron's reaction.

"Interesting," he said. "So I understand correctly, you feel guilty over making your father leave?"

My gut wrenched.

And to think he was meant to be a genius doctor.

"Unless I misunderstood what you where saying?" Uncertainty marred his face. "Does guilt not indicate you were at fault?"

"You weren't there," I yelled. "I was fourteen! How could I control that? How could I?"

"Explain."

I glared at him. "They argued all the time. He wanted my mom to stop doing drugs and she wanted him to stop drinking. They blamed each other. He hated the fact that he had to marry her when she got pregnant with me. I overheard him telling my mom that one night."

Cameron made a note. "Just to clarify, you led them to drink and drugs?"

What the fuck.

"No, I didn't. They chose to do that. You can't blame that on me."

"Yet you do?"

I flinched. "Not like that."

"Either you do or you don't."

"Maybe I had something to do with it. It's hard to tell."

"Something to do with it?"

"Sometimes they seemed unhappy when I was around."

"What were you doing to make them unhappy?"

"Just hanging out. I don't know."

"Were you rebellious?" he asked.

"No."

"You merely breathed in the same space, I take it?"

"Yes." I hissed at him. "Cameron, I don't like this. Please untie me."

"You mentioned overhearing your parents arguing about you? How did that make you feel?"

"Did you really study at Harvard?" I snapped. "I'm fucking naked."

"Yes, I was valedictorian of my class." He raised his pen. "You *are* naked before me. Hence, you are naked before me. See how that works?"

"No, actually. This seems very unprofessional."

"That kind of professional doesn't work with you, Mia." he said. "Though I am willing to send you to yet another therapist to prove my point."

"Let's do that. How about booking me in this afternoon?"

I wondered if Richard and the girls knew that Cameron's techniques were this messed up. I had willingly stepped right into this fucked-up fuckery.

He peered at me from over his professorial glasses. "We were discussing your sparring parents and their grand ability to triangulate."

What did that mean?

"Apparently." He made a note. "You became their victim because they were not brave enough to face off with each other."

"I was caught in the middle."

"Undoubtedly. Answer me this, what kind of man turns away from his only child when she needs him the most?"

"I don't know."

"What kind of man?"

Tears welled. "It wasn't my fault."

Our eyes locked and I felt within the releasing of this dreadful tethering. "It wasn't my fault." Only this time I believed it.

Cameron rose and came towards me, untying the straps and wrapping his arm around my waist.

"I'm not to blame," I whispered, holding onto him and burying my face against his chest, my tears wetting his shirt.

"Subconscious," he whispered. "Did you hear that?" He rested his chin on my head. "Not to blame."

After I collapsed against him, he lifted me up and nudged me back to sit on the edge of the bed.

Cameron sat beside me and kissed my cheek. "Now, let's continue."

I looked up at him. "I think you found it. My shadow thingy."

"That wasn't it, Mia." He wiped away one of my rogue

tears. "Your shadow complex is very predictable. It offered up an obvious truth in hope that we'd believe that was it. A clever distraction. Self-preservation is the greatest instinct of the mind."

"What are you saying?"

"How about I go and get you something to eat?" he said. "It's best we settle in. Looks like it's going to be a while before we illuminate the anomaly."

"It was my mother's death," I stuttered. "I admit it. It's obvious, now that I come to think of it."

"Ah, the final flailing of the psyche." He pressed his hand to his chest. "My ego is wounded."

"There's nothing else to say."

"Other than the truth."

"Sir, have you ever spoken to another therapist about your technique?"

"Why yes, Dr. Raul and I went over your case."

"No, I mean did you tell her about this room? This chain? About keeping me locked up in here?"

"She expressed her intrigue."

"She didn't try to stop you?"

"And prevent us finding a solution? Goodness, no."

"Can I come with you?" I said. "Pick out something to eat?"

"No, my darling. Your homework is self-exploration. And in here you'll have no choice but to go within."

My mouth felt dry. "How long will I have to stay in here?" I tugged on the chain. "Like this?"

"That, my sweet Mia, is totally up to you." He paused by the door.

A sob caught in my throat. "What if it fails?"

"My profile of you indicates otherwise," he said. "It's not only guilt you feel."

"How do you know?"

"I see it in your eyes."

I slinked down on the edge of the bed, my head bowed, this chain clinking around me. "Yeah, it'll be interesting to watch you work out what I'm feeling exactly."

"You just showed me."

"Showed you what?"

"Your shame."

I scowled at him. "For what?"
"For what you believe was an unconscionable act."
He left me alone in the dungeon.

CHAPTER 21

HE FED ME chocolate covered strawberries—

In reward for me ceasing my screaming. I'd attacked where the chain met the wall with my heel, trying to dig out the hook. Until he confiscated my shoes.

This red walled dungeon became my safe dwelling. These matching lace bra and panties were my only clothes.

Together we sat on the four poster bed with me leaning up against the headboard, and him in front of me with his legs crossed, in the lotus position, bringing the rich fruit to my lips. I licked chocolate off his fingertips.

Cameron wrapped a blanket around my shoulders and tugged it around my body, and if it wasn't for this long chain dangling from my neck, we could have been two lovers wasting the day away talking and snuggling.

If he really did believe I'd committed an unconscionable act, he didn't show it. The affection he lavished made me feel more like I was someone who deserved to be pampered.

Throughout the days that followed, Cameron fed me each meal, whether it was the Italian dish the chef had cooked up or the crepes for breakfast. He bathed me in the shower, dressed me, held me when I cried, and wrapped his arms around me. He pleasured me too, taking his time to see I came frequently, providing orgasms that stole my breath and brought us closer.

His only stipulation was I wasn't allowed to touch him. This was the worst punishment of all. I longed to run my hands over his body, touch his face, grip him when I came, but I wasn't allowed.

Whenever I faulted and forgot this rule, I was punished with the lick of leather. When I endured my discipline well, I was rewarded with pleasure.

How quickly the mind adjusts and accepts that which it cannot change, soon learning the futility of rebellion.

Still, pushing back was all I knew.

"I have a gift for you," he said, reaching over for the wrapped present.

I ripped off the paper and held up the book. "Goddesses: Mysteries of the Feminine Divine?"

"Joseph Campbell," he said.

"Why are you giving me this?"

"It's an important book," he said. "Once you've finished reading this one, I'll bring you another."

"How long do you intend to keep me in here?"

He raised my chin and kissed my mouth, nipping my lower lip.

Minutes turned into hours, and days into an unfolding of sharing with him all that had happened in my childhood, every detail, every moment relayed with the passion of one who'd lived it. Hoping that at any moment he'd be satisfied I'd spilled enough.

Hours unraveled.

I read the books he bought me and we discussed what I'd learned, and I marveled that I could still smile, or laugh, or find him endearing.

Despite everything.

Until my need to purge the rest of it became too great.

"I'm ready to tell you," I said. "It was the morning of my mother's death." I readied for his reaction. "I fell asleep, while she lay dying on the floor."

His expression remained serene. "That's hardly a sin."

"I wasn't there to help my mom when she needed me." I confessed my terrible truth. "I was in the bathroom."

"Someone else was in the house?" he whispered.

"My mom's dealer."

Cameron looked thoughtful. "See, that wasn't so bad, now was it?"

"I couldn't help her." My fingers scrunched up the blanket, kneading the material.

"What else do you remember?"

"It's all a bit of a haze." I rubbed my arm, a familiar ache taking me back to that day.

"A blur of memories?" He glanced at my right arm.

"Yes."

"Ethan's coming over tonight for drinks," he said. "Dominic will bring you your meal."

"Can I leave now?"

He scratched his head. "Something's not adding up."

"What are you talking about?"

Had he any idea how hard it had been for me to tell him that?

"Any requests?" he said flatly.

"What for?"

He slid off the bed. "Dinner?"

That was it. I'd lost him. Turned him away from me so swiftly that everything we'd shared, everything we'd planned to do here, was now meaningless.

"You hate me, don't you?" I whispered.

"Hate is a very strong word."

"I can see it on your face."

"What you see is perception. You've given me something to work with."

"I don't understand."

"You don't need to," he said gently. "Because that's my job."

CHAPTER 22

DOMINIC NEVER DID bring me food.

With no way of judging time, I could only guess it was midnight. Curled up in a ball on the bed, I sobbed into my pillow. Cameron had years of training to hide his reaction to a client when they blurted out their despicable truth. His stone-faced expression gave nothing away.

Only his desire to leave.

I couldn't blame him. I'd feigned that I was a well-balanced woman who belonged in his circle of friends. Deserved to date his best friend even. But I was a weak and shameful girl. I didn't belong here. Didn't belong anywhere.

The only comfort came from dipping into that book he'd given me about Goddesses and hoping that one day I too might find something beautiful inside.

The door handle turned. Cameron's silhouette showed in the shadowy darkness.

I raised myself up and slid off the bed, making my way around to see him. Needing to see he'd forgiven me. Or perhaps a sign of understanding.

He entered.

A sharp pang of fear. "What is that?"

"A sandwich," he said, holding out the plate. "Peanut butter and jelly."

"Don't," I said, realizing. "I'm begging you."

"One final step, Mia." He closed the door. "Come here."

Nearing him, I took the plate.

Tears sprung into my eyes and my sobs came hard and fast. "Please, Cameron, Sir."

"Lead the way." He gestured.

"I can't."

"Every step of the way, I am with you. Just as I promised."

Dazed, and with all power gone, I headed towards the bathroom door. Once inside, I waited for him.

Cameron wandered in behind me, his hands casually in his pockets, those round rimmed glasses making him look superior. Truth hinged on his ability to dare to push further.

Survival hinged on my ability to push back.

Staring down at the white bread and sticky spread within, I couldn't understand how he knew. Sliding down the wall, I rested the plate on my lap. Despite this gnawing hunger, no way was I eating this.

It's a coincidence, my intuition reassured me, he doesn't know. Can't know.

Cameron was barefoot too, having kicked off his shoes before following me in. He slid down the wall opposite, mirroring what I'd just done.

"Take a bite," he said.

It tasted better than expected and the sweet and salty texture melted on my tongue. This sandwich had been my meal on *that* day.

That awful day.

I awoke from this trance he had me in. "But how?" Then I realized. "Do you know someone in Charlotte?"

"Ethan went for me."

I swallowed this awful stickiness. "You sent him?"

"He volunteered. We had dinner tonight to talk about what he found." He gestured to the bread. "At least it isn't moldy this time."

My eyes shot up to meet his. "But how..."

"White bread was the only food in the house. Other than peanut butter and jelly." He gave the deepest sigh. "At 10AM that morning you left school. You walked home and arrived soon after 11AM."

"I don't understand?"

"School records," he said flatly. "You argued with your

mother soon after, according to the neighbors."

"Ethan went to my old house?"

"Yes."

My lips trembled. "The same people still live there?"

"Same neighbors, yes. Ethan also visited the sheriff's office. He was very obliging."

All of it had been reported, documented, yet the core of the secret was never to be aired.

Never.

I took comfort in that.

"May I continue?" he said.

The room closed in.

"After the long walk home, you were hungry." He gestured to my plate. "Your mom made you a sandwich. Peanut butter and jelly."

"How did you know?"

"Sheriff Bradshaw documented what was found in the kitchen."

I was amazed those records still existed.

"Your mom's dealer was scheduled to come to the house before twelve," said Cameron. "He always came on a Thursday."

"The neighbors told you that?"

He shrugged.

"They knew he was a dealer?" I said.

"No. Your mom never went out and there was only one visitor to the house, apparently. Every Thursday, like clockwork. Same time your neighbors cut their lawn. Your mother had to get her drugs somehow. I deduced that's who he was. You confirmed it."

I made a mental note to stop giving so much away.

"You argued with her around 11:30 AM," he continued. "Apparently you were pretty loud. Very agitated. Understandably, I might add. You were angry with your mom. Probably trying to talk her out of taking her next hit?"

That was true.

Nosy fucking neighbors.

"You went silent around 11:50AM." He gestured for me to take another bite. "According to the police report. Your mom had filled a prescription, which you collected for her from the pharmacy the night before. Ambien. Twenty-five pills started off in that bottle. Yet forensics only found twenty-three. Only one faint dose level was found in her system upon post mortem. She'd metabolized it from the night before. Which meant someone else also took one."

"I didn't."

"Actually, you did," he said. "In the kitchen they also found two silver spoons with what turned out to be the residue of Ambien. There's only one reason to crush a tablet. Either it's because it's too big or because you want to slip it into someone's food."

I blinked at him, trying to keep up.

"Your mom made your sandwich that day because she wanted you quiet. She dosed your sandwich."

"What?"

"Ambien will not only send you to sleep, it places your brain into a haze afterward. The common side effect is forgetfulness."

My lips trembled and I dreaded what might come next. The big reveal, the terrible truth proving my guilt. "I'm willing to give Dr. Raul another try," I said. "If she'll have me."

"You woke up in the bathroom," he said. "But not from sleep. You'd taken a hit of cocaine."

"Cameron, please—"

"Allow me," he said calmly. "When you finally came around, you saw the discarded needle by your side."

The very needle the police had found because I'd failed to hide it in time. Tears stung my eyes. Shame seeped back and forced me to look away and not see his disgust.

"What happened next?" he said softly.

"She was dead."

"You found her on the floor of the living room?"

"I called 911 and hurried to clean her up," I said. "I didn't want them to find her like that."

"At fourteen years of age, you're not taught how to resuscitate."

I wiped away another tear, trying to hold back on this tidal wave of emotion causing my throat to tighten.

"The paramedics could see she'd been gone for a while, Mia. Even if you had attempted to resuscitate your mom, you couldn't have brought her back."

"Had I not been high," I snapped, "I might have stopped her from taking it."

"And you were very high," he said. "That's why you did your homework after the police arrived. So they wouldn't look into your eyes and see your pupils."

Slapping my hand to my mouth, I suppressed a sob.

"Nevertheless they took you to the hospital," he said. "And a forensic nurse examined you. All part of the process of assessing a crime scene."

The emergency room had been busy that night. The nurses had been kind enough though, patient, and despite hurrying around me they'd given me the courtesy I didn't deserve.

Cameron stretched out his long legs. "In the forensic nurse's report, she noted the puncture wound in the crux of your arm. She assumed it was from where labs had been drawn. But labs weren't drawn until twenty minutes later, which proved the needle had punctured prior to your arrival. The forensic nurse missed it. Especially as you were the one who told her it was from where you'd had blood drawn. You were savvy at fourteen, but you didn't do yourself any favors." He reached into his upper breast pocket and held up a syringe. "Recognize this? It's a ten cc and was found in the bathroom." He leaned forward and rested the needle beside me. "Show me."

I reached for the needle. Using the precision with which I'd drawn it up that day, a skill learned from watching my mother no doubt, I pretended to flick out the bubbles and then hovered the needlepoint close to the crux of my left arm.

"How many times had you shot yourself up before that day?" he asked.

"It was the first time," I admitted.

"Interesting. You've never been inclined to use drugs since?"

"Never." I wiped my runny nose with the back of my hand and, relenting to his cruel and pointless request, hovered the needle close to my arm.

"No, no," he said. "The puncture wound was in the right arm."

I took the syringe in my other hand and angled the

needlepoint at the crux of my right arm. It felt awkward and I fumbled to position my fingers on the injector. It really didn't make sense and I wanted him to know that. "But I'm right handed."

The shockwave hit me. If this was what it felt like to drown, I now knew it. The memory of that day cleared like rain clearing fog.

That stale breath. That scarred face. That snake tattoo. "*It will make you feel better,*" *he'd soothed with his soft southern drawl. An uncompromising strength.* "*Take your medicine now.*" *The sting of a needle.*

My tears streamed, and my throat constricted against words that had never been spoken. I'd been too drowsy to protest. Too weak to shove him away.

Cameron gave a nod, his expression kind. "It was the Ambien that caused you to forget."

"Are you saying?" I swallowed hard. "I didn't inject myself?"

"No, my darling," said Cameron. "You didn't. Your fingerprints weren't on the syringe."

CHAPTER 23

AN OCEAN OF tears.

Off came my collar and I was released from that long, dangling chain.

Cameron wrapped me in that blanket and carried me in his arms out of the dungeon and up into the foyer and beyond, rising up that sweeping stairway. Burying my face into his chest, I wept, soaking his shirt, gripping him like a lifeline.

Inside the marble tiled bathroom, he made quick work of removing my bra and panties and lifted me into the pre-drawn bathtub. Bubbles foamed and water sloshed around me and over the rim.

When he stripped off his clothes, I let out a sigh of relief, grateful he'd be close again. Quickly, he joined me inside this warm cocoon of water, lying with his back against the tub and pulling me face down on top of him. My front rested along his firm body, my left cheek on his chest. I breathed him in, still and quiet and savoring the hypnotic rhythm of his heartbeat. Safe in his embrace.

Despite feeling as though I'd been trapped down there for a lifetime, it had probably only been three days, but being stuck in that cocoon of change had felt longer. Leaving my past behind, I refused to think of it now and have it encroach on what was surely perfection. Old feelings dissipated, scattering to the far corners of nowhere, leaving me whole and healed. If I'd believed I'd surrendered before, I was naïve. *This* was surrender, this feeling of being completely beholden to another, needing nothing other than Cameron.

It was too late. I was smitten, lost, having willingly given myself over to this miracle of a man. Now I understood why everyone held him in such high regard. His brilliance was blinding and right now he was my knight in shining armor.

He peered down at me. "How are you doing?"

"Oh fine," I said.

He kissed my head. "That morning, right after you got home from school, you found your mother's dealer in your house. You called 911 to report him. According to the police records, your mother answered the door when the police arrived and tried to talk them out of coming in. They were reassured it was a misdial."

My call for help had gone unanswered.

"Your mother made the worst decision of her life," he said. "She left her dealer alone in the bathroom with you. He probably reassured her he'd talk you out of talking to the police. I imagine she had no idea he'd inject you."

"It was his fingerprints found on that needle in the bathroom?" I asked.

"Yes. After your mother died, he disappeared."

"How did you find out all this?"

"Ethan subpoenaed each and every report. We both read everything, from the coroner's findings to the police records. We discreetly made inquiries to your school. That's how I found out what time you left that day. The forensic reports were precise. Once correlated, they clearly formed a conclusion."

"You are both so clever," I said, awestruck.

"Ethan's office wields some impressive legal power. I flew him out on my private jet."

"You have a private jet?"

"Yes." He kissed my lips. "One of us needed to be there to gather all the information. Chat to the neighbors. That kind of thing."

My body tensed and Cameron's hand caressed my back.

"Ethan's very discreet," he said. "Very trustworthy. He's been through a lot himself so he knows how important it is to work through a difficult issue. He's very fond of you."

"I can't believe my mom let that happen to me."

"She made what she'd believed was the best decision. Calmed you by putting Ambien in your sandwich. You were heavily sedated by the time her dealer injected you. Maybe he thought they could blame the drugs on you if the house was raided. Accuse you of being a wayward teenager."

"I'm going to find him," I said. "I want justice."

"I have my private investigator looking for him, Mia."

"Will it be hard to prove?"

"Perhaps." He sighed. "I wish I could travel back in time and rescue you from that house."

I shifted against him. "You're rescuing me now."

"From here on in, I'm going to protect you. Prevent anything bad from happening to you ever again. Possessive, I know, but now you're under my protection."

"Don't send me away," I said. "I'm not ready to go."

His embraced tightened. "It's imperative you listen very carefully to what I have to tell you."

My heart sunk with those words, as though I already knew.

"You can't stay in Chrysalis after tonight," he said. "You're very vulnerable. It would be exploitative of me."

My stomach bunched into knots. "We'll still see each other?"

But it isn't enough.

"Of course. Tomorrow morning, a car will take you home." He kissed my forehead again. "It's for the best."

My tears fell onto his chest, and despite swiping them away it was useless.

Cameron lifted me up and lowered me again so that I now rested with my back against the other end of the tub. He reached for a sponge and squirted bath gel onto it. He bathed me, sweeping the sponge over my body in sensuous circles. In a dreamy state of relaxation, I merely lay back and allowed his nurturing. Too many times he broke my gaze, but I refused not to look at him, wallowing in the warmth of his tenderness and needing more of this beautiful man.

Beside the bath, I waited patiently as he took his time to dry me with a soft plush towel. He wrapped my body in another and led me into the bedroom that I vaguely had a memory of entering.

"You'll sleep here tonight," he said.

The large central bed strewn with throw pillows was luxurious, and despite this exhaustion and need to climb under the covers, I was reluctant to let him leave. The interior designer had gone all out, making the room cozy with its light colored furniture and feminine touch. It was all very extravagant.

Not that I cared.

He removed a pink satin nightgown from a dresser and gestured for me to approach. With my arms up, he slid the low V of the chiffon ruffle Babydoll over my head and tugged it down.

"I won't be far away." He gestured. "Just a few rooms down. In you go."

"You won't sleep with me?"

"No. Get in, Mia. You need to rest."

I scrambled onto the bed and pulled the comforter up and over me. A knock at the door caused me to freeze.

"Perfect timing," he said, giving a heart-stopping smile. "How about we break the house rules and have dinner in bed?"

Seriously, did this man know what he did to me?

He opened the bedroom door and exchanged a few words of thanks with whoever was there. Cameron opened the door farther and wheeled in the food trolley strewn with two silver domed lids. The bottle of white wine had been corked and he merely had to pour two glasses. He handed one over to me. It was strange to have him serve me food. He was used to be waited on.

As though reading my thoughts, he said, "You need privacy tonight." He took a sip of wine, his tongue brushing over his bottom lip.

I was jealous of that glass, coveted his fingertips tracing along that stem, wanting them on me.

Dinner in bed felt so decadent, and thoughts of Scarlet and her love of being naughty came to mind, her words of what happened to butterflies and their stages of transformation. Cameron had stripped away this façade of pretense, ensuring my transparency, yet I felt robbed of what should follow. Shouldn't there be another stage? Something about a transformation? I felt stunted, as though I'd successfully emerged from my Chrysalis only to have no idea of where to go from here.

Despite my appetite being subdued, my stomach growled.

Sitting next to each other on the bed with our backs against the soft leather headboard, we ate from our plates resting on our laps, enjoying the delicious meal of fresh salmon with hollandaise sauce and asparagus. Despite my hunger, I only manage a few mouthfuls.

The wine tasted crisp and fresh and was a nice distraction.

"Thank you, Cameron," I said.

He grinned. "I didn't cook it."

"You know what I mean. Thank you for caring enough to do everything you've done for me."

"So you're out of the 'you're a bastard' phase?"

"I'm still not quite sure how you did it, but I feel... reborn."

"Can't have my submissive sad, now can I?"

But I wasn't his submissive anymore, and my heart wrenched with the thought. I refused to cry again, couldn't have him see me weak and validate his theory I wasn't strong enough to stay.

He turned to better look at me and rested his head on his hand. "Eat, Mia."

Cameron still made my insides coil and then liquefy. I took another bite of salmon, hoping his stare would cease its penetration.

So now you want to look at me, Mr. Cole? Now that I'm dressed in a Babydoll and in bed with you? All I could think of was if he planned on making love to me. Maybe a goodbye fuck? I really needed him inside me right now, and the thought of all this small talk continuing for much longer caused a shiver.

"Cold?" he said.

I took a sip. "The wine's warming me."

Cameron placed his glass down on the bedside table. "I'm so proud of you. You faced your demons bravely and now you can move forward and live the life you're destined for."

"What kind of life is that?"

"Whatever kind you want it to be."

"I want it to be here with you. I want you to continue my training."

He leaned over and ran his fingers through my hair. "You'll feel differently in the morning. Get some sleep."

"Can we talk about it?"

"The decision is made."

That was it then. The decision was made. Yet again I'd been removed from the process. I feigned understanding, not wanting to cause a scene and validate his doubt.

"How are you feeling?" he said.

"Content." I gave a half truth.

Leaving here wasn't going to be easy.

"Goodnight, my darling." Cameron climbed out of bed. "Maybe I'll drive you home."

He gave me a drop-dead smile before leaving.

In a fog, I found an assortment of toiletries in the bathroom and took my time to use each of one, like the Estee Lauder cleanser and face cream and the gold colored hairbrush. I cleaned my teeth with what looked like a titanium toothbrush. Maybe I'd be allowed to keep it as a souvenir? A piece of Cameron.

My fingers traced where my collar had been. I missed it terribly. Had I not been so tired, I'd have snuck downstairs and back to that dungeon to retrieve it and put it back on.

The thought of having to leave here, leave him, made me want to scream, and clenching my fists into balls, I stared at myself in the mirror.

"If you don't go after want you want now, you never will," I told myself.

Cameron had been very persuasive. His look of intention proved that changing his mind would be impossible. I could add Mr. Stubborn to his list of titles.

I headed back into the bedroom and climbed onto the king size bed, wondering if I'd be able to sleep knowing he was a few doors down. Tucked under the covers, I peered upward, not surprised to see the chain and leather cuffs waiting for some lucky submissive. Jealous of this faceless girl that would get to be secured within them by Cameron and have his precious time, I willed myself into nothingness.

And drifted off.

With no clock in here, it was impossible to judge the time.

But it was still dark outside.

I checked to see no one else was wandering the corridors and began my search, not wanting to be caught wearing this see-through Babydoll. Three doors down, I found Cameron's bedroom.

He was in bed, resting back against a tall leather headboard and wearing those round rimmed glasses, looking all scholarly while reading from an iPad. All he had on was PJ bottoms, his chest naked revealing that muscular torso. Whatever he was immersed in gave me the time to admire this delicious eye-candy. The man who I desperately needed to be my master.

I quietly closed the door and made my way around the other side of the bed, tiptoeing as I went.

His chestnut gaze found me.

"You can't sleep either?" I climbed onto the bed beside him.

"Love breaking rules, do you?" He leaned over and pulled the comforter back. "I'm going to have to keep a very special eye on you."

"There are all these noises outside my room." My toes curled at being close to him again. "This place isn't haunted is it?"

"Not as far as I know," he said. "No one has ever died here."

"There's always a first time."

He laughed. "Please don't tell me you have a hidden agenda, Ms. Lauren."

"Only to be the best submissive you've ever had."

"Mia—"

I sat up. "No, hear me out, please. You revealed to me what really happened to me and now I remember it. The shame and guilt I've had all my life never needed to be carried. All that wasted time. All those years I held back on what I wanted because I didn't believe I deserved it."

Cameron placed his iPad down by his side and then shifted position to look at me.

"I deserve to choose what I want to do with my life now," I continued. "That's my prerogative. My heart is telling me to stay. To be with you. To have you show me all that you can. And I refuse to leave. I am not leaving. You're not kicking me out."

He blinked at me. "Keeping you here is out of the question. It would be unethical. I'd be taking advantage of you. You need to be far away from this place."

"Look at me," I said. "You've seen everything I've been through. How unfair life has treated me. Choices have been taken away. Lies told. Now I see the truth. I want this. Never am I happier then when you are mastering me, guiding me into subspace. I belong here. It's helping me heal. You know it is. You would never have given me to Richard had I not—"

"Given is a strong word. You have free will."

"And I want to stay here."

"Sleep on it."

"Throw me out and I'll camp on the front lawn."

"You are so stubborn, Ms. Lauren."

"I know what I want and I know what I need."

He sucked his bottom lip, looking thoughtful and so damn handsome in those round rimmed glasses.

I poked his ribs. "Am I or am I not your fucking submissive?"

"Did you swear at me?"

"Maybe."

"You must listen to me."

"I can help you with your clients."

"You're still talking?"

"Yes, evidently I am, and no, I won't change my mind in the morning."

"I can still hear you."

"Because you gave me the courage to speak. I see what you do here. I see the importance of your work. This is no ordinary manor. It saves lives. I am in awe of what you accomplish and how you do it. I am so proud of those who come here as their authentic selves. This place is more than I ever realized. More than I ever knew possible. I will be proud to stand beside you as your submissive. Because I understand that the woman who holds that title represents the sacred female who has overcome life and gives herself over with full consent because she can. She is the epitome of the empowered. Now I understand. I own my sexuality."

"Mia." His tone was commanding. "Yes, you do—"

"I deserve this title. Have I not proven that I am strong enough to hold it? Have everyone here know that I am yours." I pointed at him. "Your equal."

"I'm delighted that you understand how we honor the role of our chosen submissive—"

"Am I worthy of this title?"

"Undoubtedly, but if you will be quiet for just one second—"

"No, no, only my master can silence me."

He was holding a manila folder.

"What is that?" I said.

"A contract."

I sucked in a gush of air. "Our contract?"

"Maybe."

Blinking at him, I realized he'd needed to see my strength, needed to hear from me that I wanted to stay. "Tell me it is."

His stare was intense.

I fell against his chest, planting kisses there, my body trembling against him. "I'm still your submissive?"

"The matter is still under consideration."

With more kisses, I worshiped him, showing how much I wanted and needed this. I reached down for him, my fingers feeling beneath the waistband of his PJ's and farther down and soon finding him, wrapping my hand around his silky hardness.

He caught my wrist and pulled my hand away, saying, "There's plenty of time to prove you're a good submissive."

My heart leaped with joy.

"You've come a long way," he said. "Your experience may very well be an asset."

My tears returned but they were of joy, of relief, and resting with my ear over his heart I was soothed by its strong and steady beat. "So I will get to sign one after all," I said, exhaling after an eternity of waiting for him.

"We need a clear and concise agreement. It's essential that you're completely congruent with all that I ask of you during your training. " He raised it. "Perhaps if you still feel the same in the morning, we'll go over it, should you have any questions."

Tomorrow. I'll still be here.

Despite being this close, I yearned to be closer, and would count the seconds until his affectionate words turned into tender touches.

Having a contract before would never have been practical. I saw that now. It had been imperative that I believed he held all the power. This piece of paper meant I still had some say over what happened to me.

I let the happiness in.

"I need you to understand clearly what it is I'll be asking of you," he said.

I didn't know if I'd be able to wait now, and certainly not after him saying something like that. But I gave a nod that I would, and to be honest I was a little sleepy after being drawn down into this glorious feeling of relaxation. I had never felt so liberated, and it wasn't just from that room either. Cameron had liberated me from myself. *My past.*

I gave a drawn out sigh of satisfaction and Cameron responded with a boyish grin. His beauty and strength made my heart dissolve and I wondered if this was what it was like to lose yourself to another. There really was no choice in the matter. It kind of snuck up on you and stole whatever it desired. He had to know the effect he was having on me. Everyone caught in Cameron's wake fell at his mercy. There was no escaping becoming infatuated.

"I'm looking forward to you continuing my discipline," I whispered.

He curled his fingers and brushed his knuckles over my cheek. "Sweet Mia."

"When do I get my collar back?"

"When you've proven yourself worthy."

"Not tomorrow?" I wanted everyone to see me wearing it so they knew.

"We'll see." He caressed my arm.

"Thank you, Sir."

"Your skin is like silk. I can't stop touching you."

His caresses soothed. "Scarlet told me you're very select on who you choose as your sub," I said. "I'll never take being here for granted. I know I haven't always been easy."

"Apologizing for being so defiant?"

"I suppose I am."

"We have made progress." He scrunched locks of my hair and tugged, the sting just bearable.

"I can tell you now I don't want any anal stretching."

"Has our feisty Mia returned?" he said, amused. "Anal plugs are a soft limit here."

"What does that mean?"

"We can't have ass play if we don't prepare you first. It's more preparation then stretching."

"So I don't have any choice?"

"That look in your eyes that begs me to fuck you will be the same look you'll have when I insert your anal plug."

I buried my face into his chest, my face ablaze.

He ran his fingers through my hair. "God, you're beautiful."

I peeked up at him. "Even when I'm bright red?"

"I'll take a Mia Lauren in every color, please." He swept his hand over my back, chuckling.

I beamed at him. "How old were you when you first discovered you were into kink?"

"Sixteen."

"What happened?"

"It's just something you know. You're drawn to riskier images of sexuality and the idea of vanilla doesn't appeal."

"Have you ever been in love?"

"Am I being interrogated by my sub?" he said darkly.

"I want to know everything there is to know about my master. So I can please you."

"Obey me in all things. That is how to please me." He tapped my shoulder. "Up you get." He climbed out of bed. "Let's get you back to your room."

"I can't stay with you tonight?"

"No, Mia. Cardinal rule. We never sleep together. It prevents us from forgetting our place. Our relationship is master and sub. We will never be lovers. And as only lovers sleep together, we must sleep apart."

Heavy hearted, I took his hand and let him guide me out and back down the hallway.

That small quiet voice reassured me at least I'd won tonight's challenge of persuading Cameron to let me stay.

We soon made it back to my room.

He pulled back the covers. "In you go."

My heart almost leaped out of my chest with joy when he got into bed beside me. I forced myself to hold back on telling him what he meant to me, nervous he'd feel it necessary to withdraw his affection. I couldn't have coped with that right now.

"At no time while you are under my supervision will you be permitted to pleasure yourself," he said. "Understand?"

I willed his stare to focus on something other than me.

"Mia?" he said firmly.

"I won't touch myself," I muttered, assuming he knew his words turned me on. Oh, the irony.

"I won't be able to sleep," I said, defiantly.

"I have a cure for that."

I arched a brow, wondering what he had in mind.

Cameron flipped back the covers. "Bring up your legs." He eased my nightgown up my thighs, hoisting it around my waist, and I lifted my butt to assist. He moved each of my legs to bring up my feet and position the soles so that they touched each other. My thighs were spread wide, completely exposing my pussy.

"Proof that less is very often more," he said.

Despite all we'd done and shared, having him dressed in PJ bottoms and me virtually naked beside him with everything on show made me blush wildly.

Cameron sat up beside my waist and crossed his legs. He placed his middle finger in his mouth and sucked, wetting the tip. Then he placed his finger on my clitoris. I raised my head to better see. Ever so slowly, he moved his finger in a small circling motion over that tight little bud.

"Remain still," he demanded sternly. "Understand."

I hadn't moved yet, but the order made me want to. "Yes, Sir." I eyed him suspiciously, wondering what he'd do next.

Yet his finger circled excruciatingly slow, keeping an even pace, his concentration only breaking for a smile when he saw my reaction. Stunned by the pleasure building there, gaping in awe, my bliss rose beneath his touch. His small encircling continued slow and sure as his fingertip massaged my clit with perfection.

Of course I'd touched myself down there before, but this, this was different. I'd never thought to go slow. My body had always yearned for faster flicking.

"Where did you learn this?" I stuttered.

"Silence."

Spasms overwhelmed my pussy as it throbbed, gratified by

his sternness. Willingly I submitted, resting my head back on the pillow.

"Don't bite your lip," he said. "You don't have my permission to balance the pleasure with pain."

"It's too much."

"Obey."

Dying from pleasure was a real possibility right now.

His finger continued, languidly circled my clit. "I ordered you to stay in your room. Consider this your punishment."

Cameron sent me hurtling into the stratosphere, rising ever higher. My eyes squeezed shut. The pleasure was a delicious torment.

The world slipped away.

Higher still I climbed, caught in an erotic vortex, a whirlwind of bliss, mesmerized that it was merely his fingertip encircling and never ceasing that was keeping me there, held midair in this climax. I was beholden to him, my pussy clenching and relaxing and clenching again, my hips fighting this urge to pump against his finger.

Stunned, my eyes shot open to again see the proof that all he was doing was circling my clit slowly. It wasn't only Cameron's skill that was remarkable, it was his patience, his desire to see this experience fully realized for me as he waited out the time it took for this never ceasing orgasm to play out. Minutes passed gloriously, dissolving into what could have been half an hour as I surrendered to this endless orgasm, panting, moaning, and trying not to writhe. My thighs trembled.

Both my scent and his cologne filled my nostrils. My every thought led back to him.

Endlessly riding this crescent, the pleasure radiated to my nipples, forcing them to become pert from this sublime bliss. I brought my hands up to cup them and soothe their rapture, their wanton desire for my master.

"Arms by your side," he whispered.

I was caught in a blinding grip of paradise and sucked in air, trying to fill my lungs with oxygen as though I'd forgotten how to.

With limbs weak and trembling, I began my descent, freefalling back to him. He brought me down from this impossible pinnacle with strokes, and slaps, and caresses, his fingers exploring and proving once more he'd mastered the art of touching a woman.

His woman.

"Beautiful submissive," he said firmly. "Who do you belong to?"

"You, Sir." My head crashed back onto the pillow.

"And your clit. Who does it belong to?"

"You, Sir."

He gave a nod of approval and pulled me into a hug, wrapping his strong arms around me, and I collapsed against him, spent.

Falling asleep felt so easy.

CHAPTER 24

WIPING THE SLEEPINESS from my eyes, I stared out of the bedroom window and looked down into the sweeping, well-tended garden of Chrysalis.

That was Cameron down there, wearing goggles while swimming laps in the enormous pool, his strong shoulders and arms pulling him through the water like an Olympian. He glided with ease, showing remarkable breath control during what looked like a grueling breaststroke.

I'd awoken this morning to find him gone. True to his word, we'd slept apart. He was probably right about keeping our distance at night. I was already infatuated with him as it was. Spending twenty-four hours with each other would send me over the edge.

I was happy to be free of that dungeon. I marveled that Cameron and Ethan had gone to all that trouble for me. They'd spent time, their precious time and expertise, to decipher the documents and discover what had really happened. Had I never met Cameron, I'd have probably spent the rest of my life believing I'd injected myself that day. I wasn't ready to leave him. Couldn't cope with the thought of separating from him just yet. I needed more time.

Needed him.

Signing my contract would be my way of proving that I was ready to stay here. Sitting in the corner lounge chair with the paperwork resting on my lap, my mind drifted off to thoughts of Cameron. I forced myself to bring my concentration back to the six pages of signing my life away.

A knock at the door startled me and I leaped to my feet.

It opened and I brought my hands up to cover myself. This Babydoll wasn't sufficient enough.

I recognized Dominic immediately. He was Cameron's right hand man, or so I assumed. The forty something short, bald man who wielded his authority with a sinister air. He had a handsome face but a very slight feminine air.

"Welcome, Mia," he said sincerely.

His kindness threw me. "Hello Dominic." I swallowed hard. "May I call you Dominic?"

"You may. How did you sleep?"

"Really well." My cheeks flushed with what had been the catalyst for a good night's sleep.

Facing Cameron after each intimate event never got any easier. It was like my reset button returned to zero each time he showcased one his erotic tricks.

"Your clothes for the day have been laid out on the central isle in the wardrobe," said Dominic. "Meet me downstairs in the dining room."

"I don't know where that is."

He raised a brow. "I'll return for you in half an hour. That should give you enough time."

"Thank you."

"Bring your contract."

With him gone, I made my way over to the walk-in wardrobe, wondering how much of Mr. Scary I'd be seeing while I was here.

My jaw dropped.

Cameron must have known all along I was going to stay. The vast wardrobe was filled with clothes of every assortment and every color, and as I ran my hand along the hangers they were all my size. My inner shoe goddess, who'd evidently lain dormant until now, screamed herself awake when she saw the shoes. There was enough of a collection here to send a Beverly Hills housewife apoplectic.

Oh great.

Despite there being endless outfits to choose from, I'd been allocated a sweetheart pink corset, high-top stockings, and panties. I'd not given any thought to what would be my day to day uniform. Maybe I could request an addendum in my contract? Something about being allowed to wear fucking clothes.

After taking a long, cleansing shower in the cream tiled bathroom, I dressed in what I hoped my master had chosen for me. If there'd been a mistake and this was meant as evening wear, I'd be laughed at. The heels were comfortable, but then again they were Jimmy Choo shoes. I grabbed my contract.

Dominic was waiting for me outside.

"How does this look?" I gestured to my clothes, or lack of them.

"Just dandy." He turned on his heels and headed off.

His nod of approval was only slightly reassuring. Still, I was grateful he kept his eyes forward and didn't letch. We made our way down the sweeping staircase and I gripped the handrail, careful not to trip. I couldn't wait to be reunited with Cameron and looked around the foyer, hoping he'd appear any second and throw me one of his reassuring smiles.

My heels clipped along the marble flooring, echoing, emphasizing the enormity of the place. The red-headed, Chanel wearing receptionist barely looked up as we passed her, and it made me wonder if it was out of politeness or training.

"All staff are submissives in training," said Dominic, answering my rambling thoughts. "It keeps them focused in-between sessions." He gestured we were going left. "Have you been given a tour yet?"

"Not yet."

I've kind of been locked in the dungeon for a few days, as you well know.

The dining room was as expected. It contained a long carved table with ten or so chairs on either side. All very formal. The floor to ceiling window overlooked the garden. Having not gone outside for days, I hoped I'd be allowed into the garden today. How easy it was to take freedom for granted. I crooked my neck to see the pool was now empty. I couldn't wait to have a dip in there myself.

Think of this like a holiday chalet, I mused, one where a really hot guy wants to spend all his downtime playing with you.

Don't think about that now. And certainly don't think about Cameron's penchant for pain.

A shiver ran up my spine.

Dominic fiddled with a panel on the wall. He raised the temperature, taking pity on me no less. Scarlet had once told me that submissives were pampered by their masters, especially when they were well behaved. I made a mental note to try to be good. Though last night's small rebellion of visiting Cameron's room had brought the most exquisite punishment, proving that being naughty had its benefits sometimes.

"I took the liberty of ordering you an omelet," said Dominic, shaking me from my thoughts.

"Thank you." I sat where he pointed and placed my contract to my left.

That gut wrenching rock that had been lodged in my chest all my life was gone. The feeling I'd accepted as normal. This dreadful ache had disappeared. My shoulders relaxed, my body easing into this new state of peace.

Dominic dragged a chair up close to me and sat.

A young waitress entered, quiet and respectful. From the short length of her hem and her demeanor, she too was a submissive. I wondered if they'd be time to make friends with her.

"Thank you, Alana," said Dominic.

She laid before me a plate with a perfect looking omelet and buttered toast. Taking her time, careful not to spill the tea, she rested a cup to the left of the table setting and next to that a glass of orange juice. She gave Dominic a cup of tea too.

If she found my outfit odd she didn't show it, and she certainly didn't react to Dominic's wave of dismissal. She left.

"As Chrysalis's attorney," began Dominic.

"You're an attorney!"

"Yes, I oversee the official organization of Chrysalis. I ensure all who enter here prove they are willing participants. Hence your contract." He reached into his jacket pocket and handed me a pen.

"Can I be sued if I don't abide by it?"

He looked annoyed. "Do you intend not to?"

"I want to add in there about being allowed to wear clothes.

Not just underwear."

"Turn to page three."

Of course I knew what was on page three. Something about my master deciding on what I ate, how I dressed, and how I spent my days. Total power exchange.

"Problem?" said Dominic.

"I'd like to talk to Cameron about it."

"Firstly, you will address your master as Sir, and secondly—" he paused, his gaze locked on the door.

"Is my submissive causing trouble already?" said Cameron.

I braved to look back toward the doorway and watched Cameron walk in casually. He'd dressed in a black suit and tie, his morning swim having given him the edge of unnerving alertness, even more than usual. That side parting in his hair producing a refined and formal air.

I gestured to my corset.

"You may speak," said Cameron, tucking his hands into his pockets.

Resisting the urge to glare at Dominic, I said, "This outfit—"

"You're quite right, Mia," said Cameron, pulling up a chair beside me.

"Really?" I said.

"A black corset next time." He turned to Dominic. "I fucking hate pink."

"Thought you loved pink?" said Dominic.

"No. You love pink," said Cameron.

"I thought she looked pretty," said Dominic. "For a girl."

Cameron frowned. "She looks like a doll."

I gave a wave. "I am here." At their glare, I bit into my toast.

"Maybe she's missing a bow?" quipped Dominic.

"It's too early for fool-fuckery," said Cameron.

"Speak for yourself," said Dominic. "I've been up for hours. Working."

"You are so fired."

"Thank God for that." Dominic rolled his eyes. "Put me out of my misery, why don't you."

My gaze bounced from one to the other, caught up in their drama.

"Go check on the ponies," said Cameron.

"That's where I'm headed now."

"Ponies?" It came out before I could stop it, and somewhere in the far reaches of my addled brain I remembered that newscaster, Andrew Harvey, who I'd met at Richard's party, and his pony play fetish. "Can I come see them?" I threw in, trying to save my embarrassment, though in no way wanting to see them.

"Later," said Cameron, clearly amused.

I reached for a slice of toast to lessen my angst and it took all my strength to take dainty bites and not shove it into my mouth.

Cameron stared down at the table. "What is that?"

"Our contract," I said in-between another bite.

"It's not ripped into a hundred pieces," he said dryly. "I didn't recognize it."

I placed my toast down and licked my fingers. Picking up Dominic's pen, I flipped to the last page of the contract and swept my signature across from where Cameron had earlier signed it. "There you go." I threw the pen back towards Dominic.

Dominic picked up his pen like I'd contaminated it and slid it back into his breast pocket. Cameron gestured for the contract and I handed it over to him.

He flipped through the pages. "You didn't cross anything out. Impressive."

"I was allowed to?" I wondered if I could do it now. "I meant what I said about the you know what."

"You're in good hands." Dominic gave a smile and it looked like he was trying extra hard to hold it.

"How's breakfast?" said Cameron.

"Delicious."

"You haven't touched your omelet?" he said.

I sighed. "Still working my way round to it."

"Eat," he said firmly.

I sat in silence, taking my time to eat my omelet while eavesdropping on their conversation. I wondered how many times Cameron fired Dominic as a form of entertainment. Guests were arriving tonight apparently, and they went over the details of who was on the list and which rooms were best for whom.

Dominic seemed satisfied the contract was signed and took it from Cameron. He walked out with my written agreement and I seriously considered running after him and asking for one more look.

You're doing this for Richard, I reassured myself.

I shuffled in my chair, questioning my motives, my muse hinting that being around Cameron was mesmerizing and the idea of having to leave him eventually filled me with dread. A wave of guilt washed over me.

I willed my feistiness to stay in its box.

Cameron rested back in his chair. "Mia, while I'm at work you will oversee my office. Dominic will go over all the admin."

That made me feel better. I really did need a purpose, and filling my day with taking care of Cameron's office would be interesting.

"Shall we walk?" he said.

I took a last swig of orange juice and headed out with him. We made our way westward towards the Harrington Suite, and onward until we reached the end of the hall. Cameron opened the door for me and I went on ahead.

We'd stepped into a library with floor to ceiling mahogany shelves strewn with every conceivable type of book. From volumes that went on forever to stacks of hardback novels at the far end. A deep burgundy leather sofa and several matching armchairs positioned on a large rug rounded out the gentleman's club theme. The table at the back with its throne-like chairs looked perfect for meetings.

"Very nice," I said.

Being alone with Cameron was both nerve-racking and exhilarating.

There was a marble fireplace and a fire burned in the hearth and it filled the room with the scent of pine. I scurried over to it and held up my hands to warm them, grinning back at Cameron.

He joined me by the fire, and with one hand casually resting on the mantle and the other tucked in his pocket, he regarded me intently.

"Have I done something wrong already?" I said.

"I'm sure we can find something."

I blushed. "Do you have to go to work?"

"Yes, but I'll be back later. Dominic will provide a tour of the house. While I am away, he holds all authority." Cameron cocked his head. "You're quite safe with him. You're my prize possession and he'll protect you in that regard."

"He's gay?"

"He most certainly is."

For some reason that cheered me up, though Cameron's prized possession comment brought mixed emotions.

"I found those clothes in my wardrobe," I said.

Cameron shrugged it off. "It was imperative the decision to remain here came from you. You are here for you, right, Mia?"

I frowned at him. "Of course. Why?"

He shook it off with a wave of his hand, his stare not leaving me.

"Am I allowed outside?" I said.

"You're free to wander the grounds."

"Am I allowed to swim?"

"If you like. I'll see you have everything you need. However, I have one stipulation."

A wave of uncertainty swept over me as my brain tried to cope with the threat of another challenge.

"During my time away from Chrysalis, you will undergo an intensive education. Tutors will be brought in and you'll study English, French, math, foreign affairs, geography, and etiquette. All lessons will take place in here." He swept his hands wide. "No one will disturb you. Subs are forbidden from entering. Other than you of course."

I was still hanging on the threat of math. I fricken hated math. "Why?"

"Because it will please me."

"Will I be allowed to wear clothes?"

"Of course. Your tutors will know nothing of your position." He gave a nod. "You will not impart any personal information to them. Merely attend their class."

"I don't understand why any of this is necessary?"

"While in Charlotte," he said, "Ethan had the privilege of reviewing your education."

I looked up at him coyly and full of embarrassment.

Ethan had no right. Wasn't that private? Meant to be sealed and not revealed to anyone? Or, more likely, disposed of when you left school?

"These same classes will continue after you leave here," he said.

My lips trembled with doubt. "You don't think I'm good enough?"

"Ridiculous," he said. "This is about a second chance."

"Second chance?"

"I believe we can get you into the university of your choice." He stepped closer and took my hand. "I have a friend at Berkley—"

"I'm not sure. It's too late for all of that."

"Mia, did you really think that all we'd be doing is fucking?"

"Kind of."

He beamed at me. "No, my darling, that would be doing you a disservice."

"Maybe we can drop the math?"

"No. We can't. Apparently you excelled in French," he said. "And as I intend to have you accompany me to Paris, you'll be required to speak fluent French."

Paris?

He lifted a loose strand of hair out of my face. "You don't have to choose fashion. It was merely a thought. I saw your drawings and wrongly assumed perhaps?"

That's right. I'd stupidly left out my sketches that time he'd visited my apartment.

"And later," he added, "I'll arrange an intern position with the designer of your choice."

"What if they don't want me?"

"Why wouldn't they want you?" he said. "The recommendation would come from me."

"Do you always get what you want?"

"Always."

"You have that kind of power?"

"Without question."

"Even the New York fashion houses?"

"Worldwide. I prefer to call it influence. I want you to be happy. I'd like to see you excited about your future."

He really needed his head examined. That kind of future

belonged to the privileged, the chosen few.

"Everything will be taken care of," he said, as though reading my doubt. "The entire course would be care of a scholarship. Consider it a gift."

Feeling my life spiraling out of control, I said, "Please don't make me do lessons. It'll ruin everything."

"In what way?"

"Everyone will laugh at me."

"No one will know. Only you, me, and Dominic."

"What if Dominic lets it slip?"

"He's the most trusted and loyal staff member I have. He's worked for me for over a decade. When it comes to secrets, he's the gatekeeper."

I eyed him suspiciously. I wasn't used to nice Cameron. I'd expected to be taken through my paces this morning. Perhaps even forced to learn to crawl elegantly beside my master, but not this.

He arched a brow. "Thoughts?"

"What kind of etiquette?"

"Samantha Harding will visit twice a week and guide you through skills that will make you feel more comfortable in certain social gatherings."

Great, lessons in how not to be common. My confidence took a nose dive. "Thank you, Sir." I sounded annoyed.

"Mia, it is not my intention to obliterate your personality but rather to exalt it."

The scent of leather mixed with Cameron's heady cologne, the crackling and sparking in the fireplace, those endless books stacked high—all were a clear reminder of how little I knew.

"But I'm your submissive?" I muttered.

"As my submissive, you will attend every party that I attend. Every event. When you are permitted to speak, I can't have you boring my guests, now can I? You reflect me. They are highly educated socialites and demand intellectual stimulation."

Amongst other kinds of stimulation, no doubt. "On one condition," I said.

"Go on."

I fisted my hands and placed them on my hips defiantly. "I will get the chance to teach you something." Though what that was right now I had no idea.

His jaw flexed. "This I have to see."

"So it's a yes?"

"Apparently."

That was surprisingly easy.

"You get one attempt to enlighten me." He looked amused. "And I will do my best to endure it."

"Does this mean I'll get my GPA?"

"In-between me fucking your brains out, yes."

I beamed at him, unsure which one I was happier about.

"Let there be no misunderstanding," he said sternly. "You are mine for two weeks, to do with what I will. I own you. I say when you eat, what you wear, and when you take your next breath. Do you understand?"

I gave a quick nod.

"You're going to make me late for work, Mia." His expression caught me off guard. "Because, my sweet sub," his voice was low, husky, "I can't keep my hands off you." He stepped closer and reached around to the back of my head, grabbing a fistful of locks and bringing me towards him, crushing his mouth against mine and kissing furiously. Obsessively.

I raised myself onto my toes and opened my lips wider, letting him in, offering his tongue whatever it wanted from me, no longer battling but resigning to these gentle sweeps, the deepest affection playing out. Never wanting this to end, I held him to me firmly, gripping his shoulders as though my life depended on it. Captured against his firm chest, his erection digging into my stomach, I relinquished in his arms.

He pulled away and stared into my eyes, confusion marring his face. An unfamiliar expression. "I really will be late."

"Sorry."

Cameron's fingertips caressed his lips.

Had I disappointed him? He'd closed his eyes. A wave of emotions crossed his face.

Trying to read him, desperate to do what would please him, I lowered myself to my knees.

His firm hand rested on my head.

Stillness. The crackling of embers. My master above me.

"Thank you for letting me stay," I said softly.

"By the time you leave this house," he said, "you will have learned the true meaning of empowerment."

"Yes, Sir."

He headed for the door and turned to face me when he reached it. "I'll be back around 4PM. You will wait for me in my office. I will expect you to be in this exact same kneeling position by my desk and holding the whip you will find on it. You will be naked."

"Did I do something wrong?" I asked nervously.

"You questioned the clothes chosen for you," he said sternly. "Defiance will not be tolerated." Cameron's hand gripped the handle. "After I've finished with you this afternoon, you'll truly understand the meaning of sorry."

He left the room.

My legs wobbled and gave out from beneath me and I staggered back towards the leather chair and crashed down into it.

He'd never kissed me like that before.

CHAPTER 25

THE DUNGEON LOOKED smaller.

My chest constricted as I replayed the scenes from the last few days of being locked in here. I'd been holding off for years visiting those twisted memories, and they'd hung like a dark cloud over me, waiting to entrap me in an abyss. I could never have faced the truth on my own.

Or perhaps ever found it.

Despite having never been more scared in my entire life during what Cameron had done, I'd come out of the experience feeling surprisingly renewed. I had a new respect for what butterflies went through. Maybe that's what Cameron had meant when he'd enticed me down here with romantic words of how nature thought. As far as I was concerned, nature always kicked butt and took no prisoners.

Time had stood still in here. What had come out of it was an understanding of his controversial technique. I imagined there'd be no article in the Journal of Clinical Psychiatry on keeping young women locked away and using S & M to reveal their deepest darkest secrets. Yet it had worked.

I missed him terribly. I'd be counting the minutes until he got back.

Cameron even possessed my thoughts. My mind revolved around our kiss. My lips still tingled from it. He'd just rendered me virtually useless with that heart-stopping embrace in the library before heading out for work. I'd taken advantage of being left alone for a few minutes and had made my way down here in search of my collar. Not least because it was worth a small fortune apparently, and the thought of losing it made me anxious.

I couldn't find it anywhere. Not even in the oriental cupboards filled with torture devices of every assortment. The collection of intricate ropes and chains distracted me for a while as I imagined Cameron wrapping me in these.

I braved the bathroom and was in an out of there in seconds.

"There you are." It was Dominic, and considering I'd gone wandering off he didn't look annoyed.

"I'm looking for my collar."

"It's locked away in your master's safe," he said, gesturing me out of there.

"I was hoping for it back."

"All in good time." His eyebrows lifted. "Care for a tour?"

"Yes, please." I strolled beside him, thrilled to finally be able to see behind the curtain.

We started with the other dungeons. Leaving behind the one I'd become intimately acquainted with over the last few days, we entered the first of many playrooms fit for socialites. No expense had been spared with each and every Saint Andrew's Cross, spanking bench, and even the Louis Vuitton trunks screamed opulence.

In one of the larger dungeons, Dominic walked me through a private screening room with full length one-way mirrors, should any guest wish to sit in any number of burgundy armchairs and privately watch a session. There was even side tables for their drinks.

"Champagne is served," said Dominic, as though casually guiding me through a movie theater.

I was riveted listening to Dominic's confidence, proving this was all so normal for him. Like any other day. For me, this felt like a revelation. A private tour of one of the world's most secret societies.

The scent of polish and leather did funny things to my head. My panties were now damp from all the possibilities of what could happen if Cameron brought me down here.

I pointed at the one way mirror. "Do you know you're being watched?"

"If you're in this room, you might suspect it," he said. "Do you like being watched?"

I flushed wildly.

"You signed off on it," he reminded me.

That's right, in my contract. I'd been too hasty and scribbled away my choice in the matter, eager to please Cameron.

Our tour continued and we moved on to the office and conference room where any mistress or master could conduct business dealings. Subs were banned. So this was going to be my first and last visit inside the swanky office area.

Chrysalis's generously decked out gym was tucked away in the far eastern corner, and already several staff were making use of the facility. The spa and salon came as no surprise. This place was five star everything. No expense had been spared to indulge guests. In-between all this decadence were stylish art-filled public spaces that oozed tranquility. The many walled alcoves strewn with handcuffs hanging from within was proof that submissives would be showcased at the will of their master. This was no ordinary hotel.

The dining room was unadulterated opulence. A halo of soft lighting complemented the all white table clothes, lavish gold settings, and sumptuous burgundy chairs. The aura was warmed by all the dark wooden paneling, offering a luxurious and intimate experience.

No wonder you had to be rich to play here. The money that had gone into Chrysalis must have been exorbitant. It was all very intimidating, and if you weren't submissive when you walked through that front door, all this excessive finery would take you the rest of the way. The word compromise probably wasn't welcome here.

"There's also a private dining room," said Dominic, "should a master wish to entertain his sub alone."

"Will I eat with my master?"

"If it pleases him," came Dominic's vague reply.

I trotted after him, out of the restaurant and up the sweeping foyer stairway.

"A tour of the bedrooms," he said.

We made our way to the top of the central staircase.

"That way is off limits to staff." He pointed. "No one will ever disturb you."

Recognizing the door to my bedroom, a little way down and beyond that was Cameron's. The room I'd found him reading in last night, those dreamy round rimmed glasses making him look so fricken intelligent and equally as hot. Cameron really was a sublime combo. I couldn't wait for him to get back.

"Dr. Cole rarely stays here," said Dominic. "Don't get used to always having him around."

The punch to my stomach felt real. Knowing he was just a few doors down had been the only reason I'd gotten any sleep. "Where does he stay?"

"Beverly Hills," said Dominic.

That swanky house I'd trespassed into twice now.

I tried to give the impression I was fine with this.

All of the bedrooms were decorated lavishly with big luxurious comforters. As expected, they were decked out with every accoutrement a master and slave might need, from the thick drapes to ensure privacy, to ceiling harnesses and beds strewn with handcuffs and chains. In one room a gothic central brass light fixture hung low, enabling suspension. My heart fluttered as I remembered Cameron's threat of that being in my future. Just the thought of it turned me on, and with my *no touch* rule, the only relief I'd be getting was at the hands of my master. He had to know what an order like that did to a girl.

Dominic was staring at me and I was glad he couldn't read minds.

"Cup of tea?" he said.

I giggled. After all this intensity, a beverage seemed so mundane.

"What about the ponies?" I said, heading back down the stairs.

"Off limits for now," he said. "That environment is carefully managed. We require all our handlers to show maturity." He gestured down the north hall. "Those rooms are off limits to submissives. You are forbidden from entering that hall without your master's permission."

"What's down there?"

"The private quarters of the masters."

"Quarters?"

"Accommodations," he said. "Where the doms can take their

subs and be assured of privacy. You don't go down there. Ever. Even if you hear screaming." He gestured farther down. "The auction room is down there too. Again, do not enter that room without your master. These rules are there to protect you."

Hoping I'd never be auctioned off like a painting at Sotheby's, I followed Dominic past the foyer reception.

We stepped into an elevator east of the foyer. The carpet was green velvet. The full length mirrors reminded me of Enthrall. Same designer, I mused, my mind trying to grasp why there were four buttons and not three. There were only three floors. The bedrooms, the foyer ground level, and the dungeons.

"There's four buttons," I said.

"Are there?" said Dominic.

My curiosity spiked and I made a mental note to investigate this mystery next time I was alone.

Within minutes we were in the state of the art kitchen with chrome everything and a large table at its center. The place was empty, but I imagined when guests were here the kitchen would be thriving. Chrysalis really did remind me of a luxurious resort.

Dominic set about making us tea.

It was no surprise when he placed the cup of Earl Grey before me. My master's favorite, and with the Cole emblem on the teabag tag, I knew it was one of his family's. After rummaging in the fridge, Dominic brought out two small cakes.

He placed them on china plates and handed me one. "Cream slice?"

"Yes, please," I said, accepting the silver spoon from him.

Taking a bite, I rolled my eyes in ecstasy.

"Best pastry chef in L.A." said Dominic, taking a bite and smiling broadly.

"So everyone will be arriving tonight?"

He glanced at his watch. "Staff arrive around noon and guests arrive around 7PM."

"Where do you live?"

"Palos Verdes."

"Do you have a view of the ocean?"

"Yes."

"Are you married?" I said. "I mean, do you have a boyfriend?"

He smiled at that. "Two naughty children." He reached into his inside pocket and showed me a photo of two cute Pomeranians.

"What are their names?"

"He's Gladstone." He pointed to the one of the left. "That's Harriet. They're brother and sister."

Despite devouring my cream slice at an alarming rate, Dominic was polite enough not to react. "Have you worked for Cam…Sir, long?" I said.

"Fifteen years. I was a burned out attorney with a penchant for twinks." On my confused stare, he added, "Pretty young men."

"So he helped you with a double whammy," I said. "A new job where you weren't as stressed and—"

"Pretty much."

"My master has been very kind to me too," I said. "He's a bit scary at times, but I know he has my best interests at heart."

"He's a very special young man," said Dominic. "You're a very lucky sub." He leaned forward as though about to let me in on a secret. "There's a long line of submissives who wished they were you. Some of them will be here later tonight. Don't let your guard down."

I paused mid-bite.

"Chrysalis's party is next Saturday. You'll be showcased by your master. That should squish any saboteurs."

"Saboteurs?"

"Girls who want you gone so that they can get their crack at the whip, as it were." He gave a knowing look.

Nudging my plate away, my appetite now gone, I was full of regret for eating half a cream slice that sat on my stomach like a rock. I'd hoped for a sisterhood, not jealously.

"Your first lesson will begin this afternoon," he said, moving on as though his last statement hadn't thrown me. He gestured to the way I was holding my spoon. "Etiquette."

Despite his kind smile to lessen the blow, I still felt dejected. I was probably doing all sorts of things wrong and had no way of knowing. You don't know what you don't know, as Richard always reminded me. Perhaps I was one big mess and the only reason Cameron had taken me on was he couldn't bear to have a lost cause amongst his circle of friends.

Just what was I to Cameron? Friend? Submissive? Current work in progress? For some reason, I really needed to define us.

"Everything all right?" asked Dominic.

I beamed at him. "Just dandy."

"Fancy a game of tennis?"

"I've never played, I'm afraid."

"Well then, best get you changed into some clothes and get you on the court."

"Chrysalis has a tennis court?"

"No, we'll be playing in the pool," he said dryly.

"Like water Polo," I quipped. "Only with rackets."

"Look at you, Ms. Comedy."

"Can I go for a swim later, too?"

"Sure."

I rose to my feet. "I'll wash up."

"No need. We have staff for that."

"I don't mind."

"Mia, you will be spoiled while you're here. Best get used to it."

Dominic was my new bestie, and despite us being opposites he was all I had right now in the way of company. The idea of learning to play tennis filled me with excitement. Never in a million years would I ever have believed I'd be doing that here.

The day was starting to look up. Passing the time like this would make waiting for Cameron to come back from work a whole lot easier.

"Just bitch-slap those mean subs." Dominic winked at me. "That should put them in their place."

Yes, I was really going to enjoy spending time with Dominic.

CHAPTER 26

I'D NOT EXPECTED this.

My tennis instructor was not Dominic. My first clue to this was when Dominic met me outside my bedroom and was still dressed in his snappy pinstriped suit. Though he insisted on me putting on a short, white skirt, T-shirt, and expensive Nike's, making me look like I should have some idea on how to hold a racket. Dominic led me down the pathway behind Chrysalis and onto the sprawling tennis courts, where he introduced me to Cage Everson, a buff and tanned thirty-something with an accent I couldn't place. German maybe? That sweatband around his forehead threatened this may not be quite as enjoyable as I'd first anticipated.

"Don't get any ideas," whispered Dominic. "He's mine."

"Don't worry, after he sees I can't hit a ball he'll lose all respect for me."

My lesson began and I didn't do too badly, considering I really was such a newbie to this sport, or any for that matter, having never participated in any athletics before. Other than running in school.

Cage had to be playing at fifty percent because there was no sign of any competitiveness, merely a focused instructor. He went over how to hold my racket correctly, how to hit a ground stoke from behind the baseline to land it deep in the court over the other side, and how to get my opponent to stay behind their baseline to prevent them from attacking. After I'd gotten used to my strike zone, I actually found it easier to hit the ball over the net.

I couldn't wait to tell Bailey and Tara about my new adventure. Hell, I might even challenge them to a game if I got good at this. Maybe I'd even get to play with Cameron, but something told me he'd be amazing at this. The thought of having to face off with him made me miss a ball.

"Focus, Mia," shouted Cage from the other side of the net.

Sorry, I was busy musing about what kind of punishment I have coming from the man paying your salary. He's kind of a delicious distraction.

Those hours I'd spent cycling my bicycle around Studio City when I'd lived in my dinky apartment were coming in handy. It turned out I wasn't as unfit as I'd suspected. Even Dominic, who sat patiently on the sidelines, seemed pleasantly surprised when I hit the ball.

It made me wonder what other activities Cameron had arranged. This wasn't so much a finishing school as a starting one. For me anyway. I was being groomed, and despite my ego taking a battering, there came a smidgen of pride.

I, Mia Lauren, was playing tennis at one of the swankiest clubs in Los Angeles and had my very own personal instructor. And from the way Dominic's eyes never left Cage, he too was impressed that Mr. Universe didn't work up a sweat. That, and Dominic's obvious crush.

My first class was a success.

Jumping up and down in exhilaration, I shouted, "Wimbledon, here I come!"

Which amused Dominic and Cage, and they laughed alongside me. I was informed that my next lesson would be in two days. This was going to be a regular occurrence.

Taking a dip in the enormous pool was my next activity. I was so excited to be swimming that I giggled for the first four laps, much to Dominic's annoyance. He had again chosen my bikini and again he sat close, though this time on a lounger while sipping Sangria.

Taking another lap, my attention drifted to the large house and I considered how it could be transplanted to England, to rest amongst their rolling landscapes, the ones I'd read about in Richard's coffee table books. He'd promised to take me to

Britain and I couldn't wait for our trip. Maybe Cameron would come along too. He'd told me he had a club in London. Maybe all three of us could visit together?

My thoughts wandered further to the scariest place of all: the future. Would Richard be pleased with how my training had turned out? Would these new skills I was learning endear me more to him?

A housekeeper opened one of the upper bedroom windows. The place was coming alive with staff in preparation for the arrival of guests. I wondered how long before I'd be allowed to wander about unaccompanied. I really enjoyed Dominic's company, but it was starting to feel like I had a babysitter. Maybe Cameron was nervous I'd leave while he was away. I really had meant it when I'd told him I wanted to be here.

After swimming thirty lengths or so, I joined Dominic at poolside and dried off with the plush towel he'd gotten ready for me. I wrapped a fresh one around my waist. The Californian sunshine made it possible for us to eat lunch out here, beneath this dark green awning. Hungry from my morning's activities, I devoured my shrimp salad and actually finished eating before Dominic.

"Look!" I pointed to the two elegant peacocks cresting the lawn.

Their blue necks and heads contrasted with the lush grass. Upon their tails was a spectacular spray of color.

"There they are," said Dominic. "Wait till you see the male dance. He's quite the show off."

"They're beautiful," I said. "Everything here is beautiful."

"Are you aching yet?" he asked. "That was quite a match with Cage. You really gave him a run for his money."

"The swim helped." Raising my glass, I took a sip of Sangria. "So will this. Jeez, Dominic, I can't keep this up or I'll turn into a lush."

"It's your first day. We wanted to spoil you. You'll have to get used to being pampered. It's what we do here."

"You're all being very nice."

"Think of yourself like a racehorse, my dear. You're the master's property. Truly, his most prized possession. I've never seen Dr. Cole so eager to discipline a sub."

Resting my glass against my lips, I stared at him, speechless.

"Don't look so abashed," he said. "You're the one who went looking for your collar."

That much was true, but comparing me to animal stock was humiliating. Yet the thrill of Cameron considering me his prized possession softened the blow. Dominic had merely been tasked with watching over the goods, it seemed.

He glanced at his watch. "You have a ninety minute massage in the spa at 2PM."

"A massage?"

"Let's make our way over there now," he said. "It's time to get pummeled within an inch of your life."

"Will it be one of those hot stone massages?"

"I'm sure we can request that." Dominic swept his hand wide across the silhouette of the house. "Mia, if you haven't already figured it out, you soon will. Anything is possible here. Absolutely anything."

CHAPTER 27

WAKING FROM MY doze, I looked around to get my bearings.

That's right, I'd been pampered with hot stones for the last hour and a half. My achy muscles had been warmed and relaxed and I truly knew the meaning of spoiled. This, along with my sporting activity from earlier and that tall glass of Sangria, had all done their part to make me drowsy.

The soothing scent of sandalwood filled the air. I swung my legs around from the massage table and reached for my glass of lemon water, the ice now melted. I took several refreshing sips. My eyes adjusted to the low shadowy lighting. Soft music flowed from hidden speakers, all lending a high-end air. A candle burned in the corner. The black and white print of Chrysalis's symbolic shield encased within a black frame served as a reminder that a submissive was in here at their master's discretion.

The post nap grogginess lifted and a slow, steady dread seeped in.

What the hell was the time?

I leaped off the table and scrambled into the terry cloth gown, my inner clock sensing it was late afternoon. I ran through the empty reception and caught sight of the wall clock pointing to 4:15PM.

Oh no.

Gripped by terror, I bolted out of there, hoping with every cell in my body that traffic had slowed Cameron down. I sprinted down the hallway.

Then I burst into his office.

Oh fuckerty, fuck.

I paused in the doorway, frozen by his austere glare. Cameron leaned back against his office desk, his arms folded as though he'd been in this pose awhile.

Waiting.

"I'm sorry," I burst out. "I fell asleep." My eyes flitted to his desk and I caught sight of a glint of diamonds. My collar sat next to the whip I was meant to be holding.

Cameron turned his head to look at it. Though the frown that followed hinted I may not be getting it back today. Or maybe never. He really looked pissed.

Quickly, I shut the door and moved towards him, shrugging out of this terry cloth gown and letting it fall behind me, leaving me naked. I dropped to my knees and bowed my head low.

"Too little, too late," he said darkly. "Wouldn't you agree?"

"I'll make it up to you."

"And how do you propose to do that?"

"A punishment of your choosing, Sir?"

"As opposed to your choosing?"

"What I meant was—"

"Silence."

"But I have to explain." I looked up at him. "I had a tennis lesson. Thank you for that by the way, and then I went swimming. And then Dominic took me to the spa for a massage—"

"Mia," snapped Cameron, "My interest ends right where those details begin."

Silence actually was a good idea.

"I hate being late," he said. "So you can only imagine how irked I am when I set an appointment and it is broken. My time is valuable."

My tears welled as frustration set in. He was right. Cameron had been so kind to me today and I'd selfishly only thought of myself.

"Stand up," he said.

Rising to my feet, I considered running out of there and finding the sanctuary of my bedroom. Cameron grabbed my arm, proving there was no escape now as he dragged me towards the back. He reached up high onto his toes and grabbed a long dangling chain attached to the center of a four foot horizontal bar. A padded leather cuff sat at each end.

Instead of fear, all I felt was relief that Cameron would punish me and then perhaps return to the kinder version of my master. His jaw tensed in frustration, that severe expression of fury revealing his sternness wasn't letting up anytime soon.

Yielding to his tug on my arms, I let him pull my hands out, stretching them wide to either side of the bar and securing my wrists into the leather cuffs before pulling the straps tight. He stood back, his stare sweeping from my toes to my head as though assessing his next move.

Despite this rousing excitement at being at his mercy, I hoped there wouldn't be too much pain. Blinking through these stirring emotions, I tried to control this heady fevered flush, this low ache in my belly. He brushed his hand over my cheek and I swooned at the welcome touch of affection. A show of kindness I yearned for.

Cameron left me hanging. He ambled over to a dark paneled cabinet and within seconds music flowed. Rock blared through hidden speakers.

My master was back before me.

"Permission to speak," I said.

He paused, as though mulling over my request.

"I really am sorry," I blurted. "Please forgive me."

"It's under consideration," he said. "Do you rile me up on purpose?"

"No, never, Sir."

"Mia, I give you all this." He swept his hands wide. "All of it. Whatever is mine is yours. And in exchange I get you. It's quite simple. All that I ask is your obedience."

"I only want to please you, Sir." And really I did, yet in pleasing him my heart selfishly soared.

His touch returned, his hand lifting my chin, sending shivers, a pulse of pleasure, yet he'd done nothing yet.

Cameron's expression was full of longing. "*My* submissive." He made it sound so beautiful, so full of promise.

"Sir."

"I'm going to use a bull whip on you. Your behavior calls

for it." He strolled with the elegance of a panther, his hand reaching for a long whip, its handle made up of thick crisscrossed leather. He carried it back to me.

"Thank you, Sir." I exhaled in a rush, eyeing it suspiciously.

Cameron dragged the end across my lips. "I do believe this may prevent any further episodes of lateness."

With him standing behind me now, I squeezed my eyes shut, waiting for the first sting. His fingertips dug into my shoulder and he dragged his nails down my spine, pausing on my butt to clench it firmly. His hand lifted...

The snap stung like hell and I yelped after the air came back into my lungs.

When another strike came, I flinched forward and lost my footing, but the bar prevented my fall. The whip struck again, though this time softer, merely causing a warm tingle across the back of my thighs. When the whip snapped against my sex I jolted upward, gasping at the shock of pleasure. He worked a steady rhythm, a hypnotic whipping and stroking as he marked my body, leaving red welts that tingled deliciously. My skin warmed beneath each contact, awakening.

To think I'd believed the horse whip was harsh. This was taking punishment to an entirely new level. Its snap was like a sharp edged sword striking my body. I gritted my teeth, determined to prove I was strong enough for this.

When it became too much, I gave a thin cry, "Mercy, Sir."

He halted, merely patting my sex with the end of the whip and quite possibly using this to show his approval that I willingly accepted my discipline.

He resumed whipping, establishing a rhythm, a tempo that was easy to fall into. My mind focused on each and every strike and forgot everything else, pushing out all rogue thoughts, all reasoning...

"We ease pain with pain." came my silent mantra.

I rocked with the pain. Breathed with the pain. Until all that was left was liberation.

Exhilaration swept over me that I'd found a pathway into my master's life. All the roads I could have taken, yet I'd ended up here, fate leading me to this, Cameron's perfectly timed touches of both leather and hand ethereal.

Nothing came close to this.

His hands running up and down my body took their time to explore, alighting nerves, stirring senses, until there came an explosion of shocking sensations as his firm caresses ignited this quickening, this aliveness.

An indescribable centering of body and mind.

Cupping my breasts, he tweaked my nipples, aiding their pertness, sending twinges of delight through each one. The pinches sent spasms of bliss right into my sex.

This dampness between my thighs proved his touch was perfection. Letting out a long protracted moan, I swung towards him, desperate for my body to be against his.

"Very good," he said.

I arched my back, pressing my breasts farther into his hands, my thoughts having long ago scattered from reach. All that I wanted in this moment was him, his guidance, his commanding of me, and I gave myself over willingly, my eyes sharing that which he seemed to already know.

"I'm going to lower you to the floor," he said. "Sit."

After doing as I was told, the chain slackened above and I watched in fascination as Cameron unhooked my wrists. There came a sense of loss, right up to the point when he used those same shackles to secure my ankles.

It happened fast. The chain pulled at a dramatic rate upward. My body lifted off the floor feet first. The room now hung upside down. My legs spread wide, making my sex easily accessible. My arms stretched down towards the ground and my fingertips were inches from the carpet. Locks of my hair covered my face.

If it was possible to be thrilled and terrified at the same time, this was it.

Cameron tested the cuffs tautness around my ankles, as though checking I was safely entrapped. He gave several hard slaps to my butt. The sting sent short sharp bursts of thrills into my core. He was behind me now, doing nothing, merely watching, waiting, taking his time as though letting my anticipation grow.

How quickly words fell away. How easily time no longer mattered.

Cameron ran his hand between my thighs, a finger trailing

along my wet sex. "Good girl." He slapped it. "But I do believe you can do better."

I moaned. "Yes, Sir."

This was the true meaning of vulnerable. This was subjugation in all its glory. The blood surging into my head caused elation. This floating was overwhelming, this and the hypnotic stimulation Cameron was bringing to my clit with his steady strokes.

"Release will only be permitted if you please me, Mia. If you obey."

My teeth dug into my lower lip; I'd do whatever he asked.

The inverted image of Cameron walked back to his desk. From there, he fetched a long box and made his way back to me. "You will silently endure this. Do you understand?"

Crooking my neck forward and swinging slightly to better see, I caught sight of what looked like a pearl necklace. Only the beads were fewer in number and larger. My breath hitched when Cameron's fingers explored me, easing apart my swollen lips, and slowly he inserted the line of balls into my vagina. Soft spasms encircled them, my pussy eagerly welcoming this fullness, this delicate process made easier with his expert flicking of my clit in-between inserting each ball.

With my ankles shackled and spread wide and fixed in their bindings, it was hopeless to struggle, or even try to close my thighs. I was hopelessly his to do with what he willed.

I reached out for Cameron's legs and rested my head against them, hugging him into me to try to find solace. This stretching within created pulsing waves of ecstasy.

"I do not remember giving you permission to touch me," he said.

I let go and swung back. He caught me, stilling the chain.

Leaving the beads in, Cameron resumed whipping me, sending me further into a trance. He circled around me like a predator stalking his captured prey. The slice of pain balanced out these delicious ripples of bliss inside me. The soft end of the whip struck my sex repeatedly, sending shockwaves down the string of spheres, and he tapped rhythmically as though reading each and every response, pausing just shy of my release.

He threw down the whip. "Ready, Mia?"

Cameron's fingers neared my sex and he gave the beads a gentle tug, pulling them out slowly, the balls bursting out one by one. I gasped and shuddered with the blissfulness of them leaving my body, like a sensuous massage deep inside, rippling along my channel and out. My pussy instinctively tried to hold onto each one. My groan echoed, only muffled by the music.

"Oh," I moaned my joy.

"You will remain silent," he demanded, and again began the process of filling my vagina with the beads. Tension built as his fingers worked their magic. In-between inserting those welcome balls, he kneaded my clit, pushing me to the brink.

Tranced out, beholden to his gentle fondling, I lost count of the times he inserted those beads inside me and then pulled them out again, bringing a delectable sensation of an impending climax that never was. He merely left a delightful rippling as he tugged those beads from me.

With the beads fully inserted yet again, Cameron's mouth met my clit, his tongue sending me hurtling to the edge, dazzled and unbidden, and I cried out, begging him to let me come.

Yet he pulled me back, denying my release.

"No," I groaned, my body riddled with need. "Please, Sir."

His lips trailed down the inside of my thigh, planting soft, gentle kisses there, and then he began his descent down the other.

He pinched my clit, hard. "Who does this belong to?"

"You, Sir."

"That is correct," he said, his tongue circling upon it.

"Let me come, please, Sir."

"Only good subs get to come." Pulling the chain, raising me higher, he positioned my face directly before his groin.

"I can be good."

I let out a long sigh of gratitude when he unzipped his pants. Rising out of dark curls, his cock was proud and inviting. Swinging forward, that small movement was all it took to encase him in my mouth, opening wider to welcome his enormity. He was rock hard yet velvety smooth. Mesmerized, I closed my eyes, savoring him. If power had a taste, this would be it. Spellbound, I took him all the way in, sucking firmly, working him passionately, moving my head backward and forward to fully pleasure him.

Those beads were once more inserted.

His grip tightened around my ankles. "Mia," he said huskily. "It's good to see my submissive knows how to please me."

A moan served as my answer as I tasted that small bead of his arousal, letting me know he was close. I took him farther still to the back into my throat, daring my breathing to find its own way. I needed this more than him, beholden for this chance to gratify my master, my dom, my everything.

My entire being exalted when his mouth once again met my clit and his tongue danced and lapped with the mastery of one who knew what it needed. Against his thickness, I moaned, his cock twitching in reflex against the vibration.

Shaking violently from my intense climax, I forgot to breathe. My mouth clamped down and worshipped him in a frenzy of powerful strokes from my tongue, proving to him I knew he owned me, wanted him to.

Coming still and shuddering violently, immersed from head to toe in searing euphoric pleasure, my sex exalted with delight at its collection of beads and my master's thrumming tongue.

It flashed through my mind whether I could swallow upside down or not, but this was quickly answered when he came into my mouth, flooding me. I gulped him down, hungrily licking and sucking and wanting to prove I was capable of doing anything he asked of me. He was the only man who had ever truly understood me, never ceasing to enthrall with his flair for wonderment.

He stilled, resting his head against my left leg. His grip on my ankles finally relented.

Stillness returned to the room, a dreamy tranquility. Even the music faded.

Pride swelled that it had been me who had rendered him peaceful. Minutes passed and I forced myself to wait for him to rouse.

After a flurry of activity, I was standing again. My wrists were back in their cuffs, my legs shaky as they found their footing on the ground. Those beads still deep inside me caused me to swoon, and a post climax flush heated my flesh.

"Good girl," said Cameron, his eyelids heavy, the back of his hand brushing across my cheek. "You exceeded my expectations."

My gaze settled on my collar.

He gave a reassuring smile. "First, I will showcase you as my new sub during my staff meeting. If your behavior is pleasing, I shall return your collar to you." Cameron strolled away, zipping up and casually returning to his desk as though we'd not just had the most incredible upside down sex ever.

He was going to leave me like this, completely naked, strung up and vulnerable, and clearly post fucked.

And with those beads still inside me.

CHAPTER 28

DISTRACTION.
That was the best way to cope with this.
Looking around Cameron's office, I tried to gather more information from the décor and hoped that an interior designer hadn't placed too much of his or her own touch to throw me off the scent.
These leather cuffs chaffed my wrists. I remained dazed from the shock of having been hung upside down and what had followed. Everything Cameron did was breathtaking.
He sat on the edge of his desk as though he was gauging my reaction to my imminent showcasing to his staff. I wondered how many of them there would be. Having to face them afterward would be excruciating.
You want this, my muse tried to rally me. *You're playing in the major leagues now.*
Those beads were still inside, causing my sex to twinge delightfully. My wrists smarted, a raw forbidden sensation that sent me reeling. My nipples stood pert from all this sensual tension.
I wondered if Cameron had chosen the dark blue damask wallpaper on the far wall. Or the leather furniture. Or that expensive looking Persian rug in the center. The one his large mahogany desk rested upon. All of it was centered perfectly. The bookcases stacked high rounded out his private domain. Upon the central table sat a large sleek computer, a few manila folders neatly filed beside it, a selection of pens, a paperweight and his

briefcase. The phone rang once and he pushed a button, sending it to voicemail.

His focus fell upon me once again.

Having Cameron calmly stare at me like this caused shivers, and a sense that he was waiting for me to speak. There was nothing to say, not really. During this last hour, everything I'd ever wanted to express to him had been. Though not with words.

Braving to hold his gaze, I hoped he'd read that from me. He always saw more, delving into a part of me that even I couldn't reach.

That burn of his stare was too much.

There was a framed black and white photo on the wall to my left of an old man with a mustache. A kind, intelligent face that I couldn't place.

"Carl Jung," said Cameron, pushing away from the desk and strolling towards the photo. "Psychiatrist and psychotherapist. Father of analytical psychology. Jung was also a pioneer in sexual therapy."

My brows shot upward.

"That's right. All that I do to you is well thought out and based on science."

Unsure whether to be happy about that or not, I shifted my footing, finding Jung's face once more.

"Don't worry," said Cameron. "I'm only using this technique on you."

He'd used it on Richard too, and I wondered what exactly he'd done to him to free him of his demons. It had certainly freed me of mine.

"Jung first used sexual therapy on his patient Sabina Naftulovna Spielrein." Cameron arched a brow, as though judging my reaction. "She was in pretty bad shape when she first turned up at his hospital in Vienna. He healed her, using a very similar technique to that I used with you in the dungeon."

It was hard not to gape at that revelation.

Cameron tucked his hands into his jacket pockets. "His work with her was so successful that Sabina went on to become a psychoanalyst and teacher herself, influencing psychiatry and offering a profound insight from a female perspective." He looked down. "I'm afraid the Nazi's SS Death Squad murdered her in 1942. A terrible loss."

"Like Alan Turing," I said, remembering that brilliant cryptologist who came to a terrible end.

Cameron gave a nod.

It made me wonder if everyone Cameron admired died horribly. My mind tried to wrap around what that might say about him.

"Sex merged with science," he said. "Who'd have thought?"

You, evidently, my kinky master. Still, his technique had worked, and staring at Jung's portrait I now had someone to blame as well as to thank.

"You have the most exquisite body, Mia," he said. "You've been bestowed with stunning beauty." He raised his hand. "I'm not just talking about an exquisite face. Of course you have that. An unmatched beauty. But more importantly your soul shines. You have the kindest heart. So forgiving in nature. A loving spirit." He moved closer, pulling me against him.

I leaned into him, weakening in his embrace, these leather cuffs preventing me from wrapping my arms around him. I nudged up my body closer.

Cameron broke away and my body missed the warm imprint of his, yearning for his return. He poured iced-lemon water into a tall glass and brought it back to me. After he tipped the glass, I sipped, grateful for the refreshing drink.

He placed the glass down.

Gently he eased loose strands of hair out from my face. "Your body is a temple." He raised my chin and kissed me, nipping my lips. "It houses the soul. It deserves to be worshipped. And nothing gives me more pleasure than to do just that."

His words sent me into a spiraling mess.

"Never be ashamed of your nakedness," he said. "You are a rare masterpiece."

A knock at the door startled me.

Begging Cameron with my eyes, I let him know I didn't want this. Couldn't bear to be showcased, objectified. From the armchair a few feet away, Cameron dragged a chenille throw off one of the chairs and brought it back. He wrapped it around my body to cover me.

"Yes," he called out towards the door.

It opened and Dominic appeared. "Are we ready?"

"Push the meeting back an hour," said Cameron. "Mia will not be joining us after all."

"Got it," said Dominic, quickly leaving and shutting the door behind him.

I gave the softest sigh of relief.

"I may be a sadist." Cameron brushed his lips across mine. "But as it turns out, when it comes to you, Mia Lauren, I'm a possessive sadist." He reached between my thighs and gave the string of beads a short tug.

Moaning from the burst of pleasure, I leaned against him, needy for more.

"Only good girls get to come," he whispered.

I sighed with longing. "I promise to be good."

"See that you are." He lifted my chin and that fierce chestnut gaze held mine. "Because nothing gives me more pleasure then to watch you when you come."

CHAPTER 29

"LEAVE THE ROOM and come back in."

Samantha Harding made it an order.

Resting my hands on my hips, I mulled over whether being showcased naked was preferable to spending an hour's lesson with etiquette's go to girl. God, she was bossy. I'd clocked her age at around mid-forty and she had the uncompromising confidence that women of a certain age carry. She was pretty though, and very sexy, and something told me she'd be a match for any of these alpha males circling Chrysalis. Her blue silk blouse and pencil skirt screamed L.A. elegance. Teaching people how to act classy was a lucrative business apparently.

"I need you to walk back in like you own the room." She raised her hand to cut off my reply. "I know you don't actually own this library, but pretend you do."

I obeyed and left, stealing a few moments to rest my forehead against the door, this inner glow surely showing. The tryst with Cameron left me heady. He'd led me to the edge of coming and hurtled me over into blinding oblivion.

I wondered what he was doing now and if he ever thought of me in-between our sessions. Despite leaving his office an hour ago and taking a long hot shower, my skin still tingled. Those strokes of his whip left faint welts, but those were now covered up by my jeans and cashmere sweater, thank goodness. Having to explain to Ms. Control Freak why my body was marked might send her over the edge. From what I'd gathered, Samantha was a feminist.

"You can come back in now!" she called out to me.

Holding my head high, I reentered, trying to pull back on what felt like arrogance.

"No pouting," she said. "Walk with self-assurance and others will treat you with respect. Of course there may be a few people who will be threatened by such aplomb. Deal with them with patience. Kindness. Sincerity."

There was no time to mull over Samantha's words of wisdom. We'd already moved on to fine dining, and she'd organized a table setting at the back of the library. We went over everything from waiting for our partner to assist us with our seat, to how to choose from the wine list.

Of course I'd had a crash course in this when I'd joined Cameron's family back in his Beverly Hills bachelor manor, and Richard had even offered a few tips on how not to embarrass myself at expensive restaurants. So I was quick to grasp all of Samantha's pointers and she even looked impressed when I correctly held my champagne glass by the stem in a pretend toast. That one had come from Cameron, when we'd dined at Chez Polidor in-between him squeezing the hell out of my thigh.

Flushing brightly, I tried to get my thoughts back on track. We'd moved onto what was considered passé, according to Samantha—the inability to hold an intellectual conversation.

"There's no excuse not to remain well-informed with current affairs with so many news outlets." She sat beside me. "You'll be socializing with some of the greatest minds in the world. We need to prepare you." Samantha picked up a remote control from the end of the table.

Behind us, a wooden screen drew back, revealing a 40inch television.

She flicked it on. "Time for a little geography."

I blinked at her, hoping I'd be able to remember all this.

"Mia, by the time this journey is complete, you'll not only be gorgeous, you'll be brilliant," she said. "You'll have the pick of any man you choose." She raised a long manicured finger and pointed it at me. "My darling girl, you'll conquer the world!"

It turned out that Samantha Harding was actually pretty amazing. As our class continued, I got to know her better and actually started to really like her. She'd been respectful enough not to ask any questions about my relationship with Cameron. Though she had shared some insight into her own life. Samantha was happily married to a photographer and they had two children. She also was a fitness fanatic and was shocked to hear my tennis coach was Cage Everson. Cage had in fact played at Wimbledon, she went on to inform me, and had even won a championship a couple of years ago. I wasn't sure whether to be happy about that or not, since my next lesson with him loomed. He must have been costing Cameron a small fortune.

Leaving the library with a leap in my step, I was actually starting to feel my confidence rise. I wondered if Cameron really knew what he was doing. On the one hand, I was being asked to submit to him, bow at his feet and freely offer myself in subjugation, and at the same time he wanted me to evolve into a woman who'd pass as a socialite. Independent and freethinking. Despite the arousal he brought merely with his presence, it was a heady combination of mind-fuckery.

The sound of Cameron's raised voice drifted. A door slammed down the north hallway. I headed off to investigate.

And stopped in my tracks when I saw Cameron heading fast towards me. He looked equally surprised to see me.

As he got closer, a dull ache hit my gut. A flurry of panic—

There was a smudge of red lipstick on his white shirt.

"Lesson over?" asked Cameron.

"Samantha's amazing," I said, swallowing this lump in my throat. "My head's spinning, to be honest."

So this is what it feels like to drown.

"She's very smart," he said. "Yale grad. Nice too, which you don't always get with that kind of smart. She's a bitch free zone. I like her. I knew you would."

I swallowed again, trying to dislodge what felt like a boulder. "I do like her."

Cameron frowned, his gaze leaving mine and finding that lipstick. He stared off as though deep in thought. "Yeah, great." He leaped forward and grabbed my hand, pulling me back the way he'd come.

My tears welled and I reasoned as merely his submissive I had no right to jealousy, yet the idea of him touching another woman made me sick to my stomach.

"I would say it's not what you think," he said, opening a door. "But right now it would sound like bullshit."

"It's fine," I said, "I understand. It's my mistake."

He jerked my arm back. "No, Mia. Never see something like this and blame yourself. Do you understand?" Cameron looked furious. "Have some fucking self-respect."

There, at the back of the room, was Shay, Cameron's fencing buddy, and he was dressed in leather pants and not much else. He was barefoot. From the look of things, he was taking his pretty submissive through her paces. The brunette was sitting at his feet, subjugated. She had a streak of red in her hair and her hands tied behind her back. Her breasts pushed forward and showing off their nipple piercings.

"Hey Cole," said Shay, turning to face me. "Hey, Mia, how's it going?"

"Fine," I managed and threw in. "Pretty amazing actually."

"Shay, I need you to explain this to Mia." Cameron pointed to the lipstick.

The girl raised her head, her eyes sparkling with mischief. She knew I was hurting. I could see it in her eyes. She looked triumphant.

Shay studied me and his expression changed. He'd apparently caught this devastation I was failing to hide.

"For fuck's sake," Shay shouted at her. "Explain it. Now."

She was attractive in a hard kind of way. The tattooed rose on her shoulder was pretty. It matched her bright red lipstick.

Shay rolled his eyes. "Arianna made a pass at Master Cole. I was here when it happened. He dodged it. Cole was only in here to discuss the party." He glared at her. "Fucking minx. That's why my bitch is on her knees."

"Happy?" said Cameron calmly to me.

With an embarrassed nod, I turned on my heels and headed out, my tears stinging.

"Shay, make sure that's the last time your sub misbehaves," Cameron's voice trailed behind me.

Finding out that Cameron had been intimate with another woman would have brought me to my knees. I was so far gone and hadn't seen it coming. Of course it now all seemed so obvious. The letting go. This complete submission. This feeling of being unable to breathe unless he was in the room. This sense of loss when he wasn't. This need to be closer to him even when he was inside me.

The pain of losing him stuck in my throat. Anger welled that I'd allowed this to happen. The obviousness of it. How does a girl share such intimacy with a man and not fall for him? Cameron had to know this. Surely he didn't believe his warning not to fall for him could prevent my heart from breaking when this was over?

"Mia." He caught up with me halfway down the corridor and grabbed my arm. "Never walk away from me." He flinched when he saw my tears. "Mia?"

I was riddled with confusion.

"Surely we just cleared this up?" He pointed to his shirt.

Sharing my feelings now would very likely end this. With every breath, I betrayed Richard. And despite his betrayal, my guilt refused to lift. How, I wondered, could Richard feel okay about Cameron being with me? Doing all those things to me? Richard had warned me that Cameron had the ability to tie his subs up in more than just knots. Yet he'd given me over to him without hesitation.

"Tell me your thoughts," said Cameron. "Mia, have I not earned the right to them?"

I licked my lips to moisten the dryness of fear.

"These thoughts are hurting you," he said. "Let them out."

My lips trembled. "I know you both see other women. It's just hard for me."

"Not true," he said firmly. "I just proved to you without a shadow of a doubt how this lipstick got here."

"I meant Richard."

"This triggered a fear for you?"

"Kind of brought back a memory."

"Of what?"

My gaze shot to his.

"Mia, Richard's waiting for you. He loves you and would never hurt you. What is going on here with you and me is an arrangement. He's mature enough to allow this to happen. He wanted this."

"I know he's seeing someone else," I muttered. "I saw them

together."

"What? When?"

"And I saw a text from her on his cell. Some girl called Jasmine. I know you lie for him. He's your best friend."

"Jasmine Tate?"

I let out a sob. He'd just confirmed my worst fear.

"Were they sexting?" he said.

"No."

"I've never lied to you." He seemed to measure his words. "I admit to being overpowering. It's who I am. But I've never feared the truth. And neither should you. Knowledge is power after all."

"I know what I saw."

"When did you see them together?"

"Outside Pendulum. Richard forgot his phone. So I had Leo drive after him."

He looked shocked. "Leo told me you missed Richard."

"I lied to him. I knew Leo would tell you. I had every intention of giving Richard his phone back but then I saw him and Jasmine together. The way they were with each other. They were holding hands."

"Leo didn't see him?"

"I had him park around the corner."

He stepped back. "That's the same day you got your tattoo."

I flinched at that revelation.

"No, no, no, Mia. You've got it all wrong. Richard was merely escorting Jasmine into the house. He didn't stay. I know this because I met him there and we went for drinks at The Strand. Right after I left you sleeping on the couch."

"Why did he take her there?"

"As a favor. It's how it's done at Pendulum. Her master was out of the country. I fucking hate the place."

"Is it a club?"

"Not exactly."

"Well, what is it?"

"We'll take the Benz. Fly up and speak to Jasmine personally," he said. "She lives near Big Bear. I'll let her know we're on our way. It's best we have her explain Pendulum."

"Just tell me."

"Not while you're in this state."

"What happens in there?"

Cameron was too busy dragging me along the hallway to answer.

CHAPTER 30

THE BLADES SLICED through the air as we banked right over the crest of the hill. This safe feeling of being suspended high in the air was the illusion of flying in a helicopter. My heart was firmly lodged in my throat even though I had full confidence in Cameron's piloting skills. He controlled his EC145 Mercedes-Benz with the same self-assuredness he dealt with every other aspect of his life. His fingers wrapped around that gearstick proved his ability to control at will.

Cameron weakened my resolve, throwing heart-stopping smiles my way in-between flicking switches here and there and occasionally speaking to a discarnate voice from air traffic control. Their chatter wafted clearly in my headphones. Their verbal sparring revealed they were already acquainted.

This adventure brought back memories of when Cameron had flown me to Napa Valley to see my father. This memory encroached on our precious time together, so I pushed it far from my thoughts, refusing to go there. A tried and tested coping mechanism that I'd come to appreciate. Time with Dr. Laura had helped me come to terms with that at least. Cameron had taken me the rest of the way by shining a light on the truth and proving I wasn't to blame. Out of my time spent at Chrysalis, I'd always have that.

Every second with Cameron was precious and I wanted no other thoughts to come between us. This was my first time outside that Bel Air manor and I wanted to savor it. Savor him. He didn't need to know I was falling for him. Knowing him, it might end my training, and I was so far in, the thought of abandoning it sent me spiraling. The only time I felt centered was during a session. I wasn't willing to give this up. Not after I'd come so far and risked so much.

Our descent was smooth.

Cameron eased the Benz down onto a grassy bank, leaves, twigs, and earth scattering. We were landing behind an enormous property. The house was all glass and white walls, the yellow lighting dispersing shadows and almost making the place look mystical. In any other circumstance I might have been impressed, but knowing who we were coming to visit threw me off balance.

The whir of the propellers came to a stop.

Leaving behind the safe refuge of the warm cocoon of the Benz, Cameron assisted me out of the cabin and placed me firmly on the ground. He took my hand and we headed towards the back of the house. Leaves spiraled around our feet, the autumn chill making me wish I'd worn warmer clothes.

Jasmine waited for us on the back steps of the property, the helicopter having announced our arrival. Her big smile and wave would have been a welcome greeting if I didn't loathe her. Envy saturated my thoughts that she'd stolen time with Richard.

As we got closer, I could see her appeal. Jasmine was strikingly beautiful. The kind of pretty where despite wearing no makeup she looked like she was. Long blonde hair, big brown eyes, and naturally rouged lips oozed elegance with a hint of elf. Dressed in a T-shirt and skimpy shorts, she either didn't care how she looked or was using her long lean legs to lure Cameron.

Still, holding onto that strand of hope I was mistaken about her and Richard, I forced a polite smile. Cameron remained close to my side as though ready to police any unforeseen outburst on my part.

Yes, but you are here with your master, who just so happens to be a sexpert. One who frequently takes you through your erotic paces. So you're a fine one to talk.

Double standards came to mind. Guilt lessened as I reminded myself ours was an agreement arranged by Richard. Very different to Jasmine making moves on my man. Was I about to meet the woman who'd stolen his heart?

There were so many questions.

The myth that was Pendulum was growing ever more intriguing. Knowing we'd have to wade through the pleasantries of a first meeting, I tried not to show my frustration. I needed to know, now.

"I've made Cosmopolitans," she announced with an accent I couldn't quite place. She kissed Cameron on each cheek.

"Thank you, Jasmine," he said. "I'm flying, but I'm sure Mia would love one."

Need more like.

"Especially after that." Jasmine stared at the helicopter. "To what do I owe the honor of having Master Cole visit?"

"Shall we go inside and talk," he said. "It's freezing out here."

"Now I am intrigued." She offered her hand to me. "Mia, I haven't heard anything about you. Seems like you're a well kept secret."

Cameron's arm came around my waist and he pulled me into him. "Jasmine's Irish. Did you guess?"

"Why are you living here then?" It came out wrong, but I didn't care.

Jasmine laughed. "I'm a model. More work here." She beamed at Cameron and headed on inside.

He hugged me tighter as we made our way through the open plan house. Hardwood floors and crisp white walls revealed a minimalistic taste and the size of the place screamed money. I wondered if this house was hers. Cameron sat on the central cream couch and I ambled off towards the bay window to check out the view. Jasmine circled the bar and got to work on our drinks.

There was a large flat screen TV on the wall behind the bar. Cameron grabbed the remote from the coffee table and turned it off. He stretched out his arms on either side, making himself comfortable.

The view was spectacular, breathtaking really, but I was in no mood for a landscape of endless snow covered trees. I turned around to face the room again. "What's Pendulum?"

"Whoa," said Cameron, flashing his irritation. "Mia, not so fast."

Jasmine ceased mid-pour and glared at him. "What is this?"

He rose to his feet and rounded the bar towards her. "An issue has arisen and I need your help to clear it up."

She looked unexpectedly vulnerable.

"Let's start with the truth," he addressed us both. "That's always the best way to proceed."

Oh God. Here it comes.

"Why don't we sit down?" He gestured to the round table.

"Pendulum doesn't exist," said Jasmine. "That's pretty much all you need to know." She handed me the Cosmo.

"Really," I said. "So how come I saw you enter the place with Richard Booth?"

She sat opposite me and took a leisurely sip of her Cosmo. "Were you spying on us?"

"No, I was going to give Richard his phone back."

She rolled her eyes as though choosing not to believe that. "Phones aren't allowed."

"You mean in the place that doesn't exist?"

"Cameron, you know the rules," she said.

"Mia believes you're having an affair with Richard."

"This is why you're here?" She looked relieved. "It's unlike the great Cameron Cole to care about gossip."

I couldn't bear to read the truth in her face.

"Mia, you can be rest assured I've never been intimate with Richard Booth. Ever," she said. "My master's in London. Richard was kind enough to step up as my escort. My master asked him to take me as a favor."

"Jasmine, everything discussed in this room will remain private," said Cameron. "You have our word."

She shuffled in her seat. "What about the clause?"

"I've spoken with the board," he said. "They've permitted this meeting."

That didn't sound sinister at all.

Jasmine chewed her lip. "What's your thing, Mia? What gets you off?"

I looked to Cameron for his support.

"We're still working on discovering her tastes," he said, "But Mia thrives under domination."

I glared at him.

Cameron reached out and picked up my drink. "Jasmine is

about to reveal a very personal aspect of herself." He took a sip of my Cosmo.

Damn, despite being annoyed with Cameron right now, he even made sipping a Cosmo look hot. That lick of his lips, that glint of appreciation, the way he ruled the room when it wasn't even his.

"Well done," he said. "Best I've tasted in years."

"Sure you don't want one?" she said.

With a shake of his head, he declined.

"Want another?" Jasmine asked me.

"Maybe later," I said, my throat dry despite my drink.

"What do you say, Jasmine?" said Cameron.

She took a large sip of Cosmo. "Oh, go on then."

"I'll kick us off," said Cameron. "Spoiler alert. Jasmine's a nymphomaniac."

She beamed at him. "A happy nymph."

"And why is that, Jasmine?" he said.

"Because I get to live out my fantasy in an intense experience that is Pendulum." She turned to me. "You two are fucking then?"

"We are," said Cameron.

"Lucky you." She arched a brow my way.

"The reason Pendulum doesn't exist is because…" Cameron gestured for her to continue.

"It's a house for unique clients who seek an S & M experience," she added. "Those who hold public office—politicians, lawyers, sportsmen, senior bankers, you get the idea. Both married and unmarried men and women who can never be discovered having any links to BDSM." She watched my reaction.

"We are discreet at Chrysalis," said Cameron. "But if you're being tailed by the press, you're compromised. Which in turn means we're compromised. We discourage unwanted attention."

"And there's also the controversial issue," said Jasmine, "of Pendulum being unsupervised."

"The subs are alone in there with no one to monitor the play," Cameron threw in.

Again, she feigned horror.

I swallowed, hard trying to ignore this cranberry and vodka

rising in my throat. "And Richard encourages this?"

"Contracts are signed," said Cameron. "Consent is given."

"That's how you know Richard?" I said.

"We met at Chrysalis when my master took me there for training," she said. "The night you saw us, Richard was escorting me into Pendulum. He began the role-play per a preordained script. You get the picture. He's the unforgiving top dropping off his bottom at a private residence because she's been so disobedient. She needs harsh discipline. And boy do you get it at Pendulum." She held her hands up to cover her face in mock horror, her high-pitched tone mimicking distress. "Oh no, this can't be happening to me. What's going on? Who are you?" She beamed at me. "That's my kink."

Scrutinizing her, I tried to see if she had any idea of the risk. "I take it the women are carefully screened?"

"I like to think so," said Cameron.

"If Mia's so hung up on Richard," said Jasmine, "why are you fucking her?"

"I'm training her."

Jasmine smiled at me. "How's it going?"

"Great," I said. "Why did Richard take you to Pendulum?"

"She's a firecracker, isn't she?" said Jasmine.

"She really is," said Cameron.

"Rick escorted me inside and went over the rules with my new dom."

"He doesn't like being called Rick," I said.

She smirked. "My master asked this as a favor of Richard, because he couldn't be there. This was a one off favor. Richard was reluctant but I begged him. Nagged him really. Once I got settled in and my dom took over, Rick left."

My hairs prickled on my forearms.

She pouted suggestively. "Want to come in the Jacuzzi with me?"

"Maybe next time," said Cameron.

I downed the rest of my drink.

"If it's something you want to try," said Jasmine. "Pendulum, I mean, we can arrange it."

"No, thank you," I said.

Jasmine wiped a trickle of liquor from the side of her glass and sucked her fingertip. "One day the client could be wearing head to toe latex while fucking you like an animal," she said, "and the next day you see them on television accepting their Oscar, or winning the NBA, or on the cover of Forbes magazine after being promoted to CEO. It's a hoot."

My imagination ran wild with what they did to her in there. Though somewhere in the far reaches of my addled brain, I remembered Cameron had told me he didn't approve. If using a whip on a woman re-wired her brain, I wondered what being trapped in there might do. Yet Jasmine seemed so normal, sweet even, and now that I no longer wanted to gouge her eyes out, she was actually pretty cool.

"So we're all good?" said Cameron.

"Your master," I said to Jasmine. "Why didn't he escort you in?"

"There's a general election going on in London." She beamed at Cameron. "He's kind of busy."

"He's a politician?" I said.

"Now there's a glorious bunch of deviants if ever I met one," said Cameron. "The members of British Parliament take perversion to a whole new level."

"I'm thinking of moving back," said Jasmine with a glint of mischief. "Nothing better than getting my kink on with a young fucked-up and frisky lord."

"And your master doesn't mind sharing you?" I said. "That's his kink?"

"It's right there in our contract," she said cheerfully. "And I never want to disappoint him." She dragged her teeth along her bottom lip, flirting with Cameron.

He gestured to the window. "You've got quite a view."

"Still nothing matches east coast autumn colors," she said. "Or should I say fall?"

The pleasantries continued as though there'd been no discussion of Pendulum. My thoughts screeched all over the map as I realized this conversation had never happened.

Yet I still had so many questions left for Cameron, and began asking them as soon as we were back in the Benz, placing miles between us and Jasmine.

"Let's talk about it over dinner," he said.

Those thoughts and more ate up my brain as darkness closed in around us. The view of lights on the horizon called us home. Though when we began our descent, I recognized nothing. The landscape was covered in snow.

"Where are we?" I said, my toes curling with excitement.

"You only ate a salad for lunch," said Cameron, his voice husky in my earpiece. "I imagine you're hungry."

I seemed light-years away from eating that shrimp salad beside the pool. Time really didn't matter when it came to spending it with Cameron. And the fact he was keeping track of what I ate once again reminded me just how much of a control freak he was. Cameron had been at work when I'd eaten lunch with Dominic. I wondered if there was some kind of note-taking going on while I was at Chrysalis. Someone keeping track of my every move. The thought made me shudder.

We landed within a shrouded opening of a snow spotted forest. The trees strained away from the force of the propellers, their white covering scattering and revealing the greenest leaves. When the blades stilled, Cameron removed his mouthpiece and directed me to do the same.

"This is the plan," he said. "Go hunt us something to eat. Bring it back skinned, please. No rabbits. I'm rather fond of rabbits."

I smirked at him.

He leaned over and unbuckled my seatbelt. "I'll get to work on the fire."

"Please tell me you're joking," I said.

He looked affronted. "Submissive 101."

What the fuck.

"Or." He smiled. "We can see what chef packed in our picnic basket."

"Picnic?" I screeched with excitement and peered behind me, and there, on the backseat, sat a wicker basket.

Cameron reached into the large black bag beside it and took his time removing two coats, a couple of tartan scarves, and two hats. He handed me a pair of boots.

Beaming at him, I pulled on the hat and slid on the chenille gloves. The thick coat was my size, as were the boots. This was fricken fantastic. Like the best date ever fantastic.

Carrying the hamper between us, we scrunched our way through the thicket, following a beaten path. There came the fleeting thought I may not be the first sub brought here, but I shoved it far away, refusing to have any negative notions encroach on our adventure.

I let out the deepest sigh when I saw the view.

A grand lake spread out before us, its surface twinkling with its icy covered layer.

It was breathtaking.

Birdsong burst up around us and the occasional rustling of leaves proved we were nestled deep within nature. As though both starved for this, me more than him probably, we stood stock still, staring out at the lake. A ripple here and there hinted that somewhere beneath that great body of water were fish.

Taking a lungful of fresh air and breathing in the freshest scent of woodland, I couldn't remember being so happy. Cameron opened my mind and heart to new experiences and we'd even flown here in a helicopter. My life had changed irrevocably because of him.

"Now is all we have," said Cameron wistfully. "Learn to cherish it."

I really was speechless. I'd never expected anything like this. I'd been so sure we were heading right back to Chrysalis.

Cameron found us a patch free from snow and laid down a thick blanket. He removed his gloves and threw them beside him. Reaching into the basket, he rummaged through it. He withdrew two plates and placed upon them perfectly cut salmon and cucumber sandwiches, home baked chips, along with stuffed olives and a selection of dips.

I pulled my hands out of my gloves. "You certainly know how to wow a girl."

"Why thank you, Ms. Lauren." He poured two glasses of sparkling water and handed me one. "I thought it best we went somewhere private. A debriefing after Jasmine's revelation."

Oh, so this wasn't a romantic picnic for two? My heart sank at the thought he'd merely brought me here to talk about Jasmine's proclivity and that place.

"You look surprised?" he said.

"Not sure there's anything to talk about."

He studied me in that usual probing way of his, his squint revealing he'd sensed the truth. "It's only natural for us to become fond of each other."

After everything we'd gotten up to, fond sounded like a betrayal. My appetite waned.

"You'll always be one of my most extraordinary encounters," he said.

It sounded so dry, so formal, so Cameron. Seriously, did this guy have a one sentimental bone in his body?

I relented to his lead. "Thank you for taking me to meet Jasmine. You were right about hearing it directly from her."

"Even though I don't approve of Pendulum, I respect those who wish to partake. Despite my concerns."

"What if the girl changes her mind halfway through?"

"There's a pre-selection that involves intensive training before a sub ever enters."

"But if she needed to leave for personal reasons?"

"The request would be honored." Cameron topped off my glass. "We're talking professional men who want the best for their sub. Again, they all consent. No one enters Pendulum unless they're an established submissive with a cleared mental health background, and a track record of excellence in S & M."

"Do you clear them?"

He waved his hand. "I have no connection with that place, other than knowing many of the members. Any intensive unsupervised environment is risky." He looked out at the lake.

"What is it about Pendulum you don't like?" I said.

"The clients are powerful men with a lot to lose."

"And you're sure Rich—" I hesitated. "Has never taken a woman there?"

"There's always a history. A previous lover. Unless of course we're talking about someone like you, Mia, who is innocent and then there's no man to be jealous of."

"You didn't answer my question."

"I already did." He peeked inside the hamper. "Richard has never been a member of Pendulum."

"But you were once?" I said. "Weren't you?"

CHAPTER 31

CAMERON'S FIERCNESS LESSENED to reticence. "I should be more careful."

Despite taking a sip of water, my mouth stayed dry.

"Her name was Arabella," he began. "She was nineteen. Too young." His frown deepened. "She slipped through the cracks at Pendulum. It was early days for the club and it was still finding its feet. Her bi-polar condition went undetected until stress brought it out. By the end of the second week Arabella was a mess. I was woken up at 1AM by a distraught member and begged to come to Pendulum." Cameron gave a sigh. "I was never a member myself. I merely bailed one of them out. As you can imagine, due to the nature of the club, the police were never called. There was never an official report. The man who fucked up was a congressman. Arabella was safer for it to all go away."

"What happened?"

"Upon my arrival, I found Arabella agitated."

"What did you do?"

"Talked her off the roof. And then sedated her."

"Oh my God," I said. "Was she going to jump?"

"She threatened to."

"What happened to her? Is she okay?"

"She is now. I hospitalized her for several months and, after her recovery, recommended she leave L.A. She followed my advice. She was paid off. She's now an associate director of a Ritz Carlton in Seattle. Not that she needs to work. That was one hell of an expensive mistake."

"This congressmen?"

"Leave that well alone, Mia." He crossed his legs, getting more comfortable. "For self-preservation's sake."

This really was a dark world I'd entered. One where the privileged few got whatever they wanted. Dominic had confirmed their place in Bel Air was where unusual tastes could be explored. "It makes Chrysalis sound tame."

"It's a sanctum. Running Chrysalis and Enthrall within very specific parameters assures safe role-play. We take into consideration the mind, body, and soul of the individual. Yes, what we do is considered deviant to some, but we cater to the needs of clients who cannot be served elsewhere." He took my hand. "What I did with you in the dungeon was finely executed after I'd profiled how well you'd respond. As you're happily sitting here with me, I can only assume you want to be here."

"More than anything."

"I'm glad we had this talk."

I tilted my head. "Talk about what?"

His nod showed his approval.

"You do realize this is a very romantic setting?" I said.

"It's just us eating food near a lake."

"For someone so brilliant," I said, "you seem to be out of touch with your feelings."

"I'm not denying that I enjoy your company." He popped a stuffed olive into his mouth. "It's rather pleasant."

"Me or the olive?" I arched a brow.

"I'm merely proceeding through your training," he said. "It would be foolish for either of us to develop feelings for each other. I am, after all, priming you for another."

"But you must know," I said. "All this affection. All this fucking. The way you are with me. Your generosity. Your kindness. Your patience. Spending all this time with you is deeply affecting me."

"I'll merely be a blip on the horizon of the number of lovers you take in your lifetime," he said.

"And that's all I am to you?" I released the words in a rush. "An impending blip?"

"You are...my finest work."

"Cameron—"

His raised his hand to cut me off. "Your reaction time during a session. We need to cut it down. I need to see you comply to my order with an immediate response. No hesitation."

God that was hot.

His threat to intensify my training made my insides liquefy and my thighs weaken. Running my hand through my hair, I tried to soothe this unbidden desire to pounce on him and kiss him hard on the lips.

I caught his subtle smile, a glimpse of the all too elusive playful Cameron.

"What else have you got hidden away in that picnic basket?" I said. "Any chocolate?"

He dug around. "It's imperative that I honor my best friend's trust, Mia." Cameron pulled out a bar of Godiva chocolate. "And as I'm the most hedonistic man you will ever meet, I must also protect you from me."

"What if I don't want protecting?"

"You don't have a say in the matter." He peeled open the packet and snapped off a square and handed it to me. "The last thing we need to do is fracture reality."

Swallowing, I remembered to breathe again.

"Don't be concerned if you're falling in love with me," he said. "We'll cure that problem with your next session."

Blushing wildly, confused yet aroused, I looked away.

CHAPTER 32

CAMERON HAD REDUCED love to a problem.

Why was I not surprised? A man so remarkably talented at getting clients in touch with their own feelings seemed pretty sketchy when it came to his.

We'd flown back from Big Bear in silence.

Upon our return, in true master and sub style, I'd been firmly escorted by him through Chrysalis and brought down here, into a vast tiled room with a space cut out of the center like a small paddling pool area, only without water. A large cage sat within it. Big enough for a person.

A *'what the fuck,'* I'm not going in that, kind of a cage.

I'd been stripped down to my bra and panties.

The unusual décor would have been enough to make me want out of here, but there came an even greater threat, along with all this sparseness. That long coiled hose held by Master Shay, the nozzle pointed directly at me.

My thoughts sparked in all directions and I managed to catch one of them, which questioned the temperature of the water, quickly followed by how much this was going to hurt.

With Cameron's last words ringing in my ears about curing my affection for him, I found it hard to stay calm.

He might just be onto something.

Of course he looked gorgeous. Both he and Shay were barefoot, their only clothes their black pants, their muscular, naked torsos on show and rippling with the kind of power needed to keep me in here. If I ran, they'd catch me.

And I'd signed off on this. Given permission for these two sexy rogues to live out their fantasy. Still, intrigue equaled my arousal. Cameron looked hotter than ever as he paced in his overbearing master mode, all lean muscle and mental superiority.

Electricity crackling in the air. An overbearing sexual domination. My short, sharp breaths revealed some part of me was exhilarated to be locked in here with them. I was getting off with being vulnerable and at their mercy, the promise of forbidden pleasures just out of reach.

As I've already mentioned," Cameron sounded strict, "your response time needs refining."

It was hard to believe this was the same man who'd flown me to Big Bear to put my mind at ease. Now he was about to perform some kind of water torture.

"This is how we will proceed, Mia," he said. "I will give an order and you will obey. Should there be a lapse in your response time, you'll be punished." He gestured to Shay, who was seemingly taking this all too seriously.

"I'm not going in that fucking cage," I told them.

Cameron's jaw tensed. "What was missing there?" He stepped towards me. "I'll give you a clue. Sir, and permission to speak."

"Sir," I muttered. "May I speak?"

"You may."

"Please tell me I'm not going in that." I pointed to it.

"Kneel."

I dropped to my knees. I was nothing if not a quick learner and the threat of that cage had my head spinning.

"Rise," said Cameron.

Snapping my head up to get a read on him, I was caught by his eyes darkening yet giving nothing away. His right hand gave a subtle gesture.

The shock of cold water blasted my abdomen.

The burst forced me to slam my mouth shut and breathe through my nose. Scrambling backward onto my butt, my arms flailed for balance. Shay turned off the hose and smiled defiantly.

From a quick glance at both of them, they were getting off on this.

"Stand," snapped Cameron.

Soaking wet and freezing, I rose and bowed my head. A recollection stirred, about finding a book in Cameron's office on Ian Pavlov, and his research on conditioning. He was famed for training dogs with electric shocks. Funny how these psychology types were really the ones who needed their heads checked.

"Kneel," came Cameron's sharp order.

Fighting this rebellion, I relented and lowered myself to my knees, water trailing off my body and forming a pool.

"Stand," he snapped.

I was on my feet again. The threat of cold was all I needed for my reflexes to respond.

"Turn around."

Despite my quick reaction, there came that pressure pounding my flesh, stinging by buttocks, and stunning me into a bent over pose of resistance. My eyes squeezed shut, my lips pressed together, and that sting of force pummeled my flesh.

The water stopped.

"Come here, Mia."

Facing Cameron again, I relaxed against him, resting my cheek against his chest and drawing comfort from his warmth. A shiver. A sigh. My body reacted to his embrace.

"Good girl." Cameron nudged me away and stepped back. "Now kneel."

I stepped closer, needing another hug—

A burst of cold sprayed me, only this time directed at my breasts. I brought up my arms to protect myself and sank to my feet, holding my breath until the water stopped.

"Up," ordered Cameron.

Trembling, I begged him with my eyes.

"Lie down," said Cameron.

What. The. Fuck.

Shay turned the hose on me again.

Arms protecting my chest, I scrambled towards him in some kind of out of body experience, slipping and skidding my way along, leaning into the full force of the water and soon closing the gap. Grabbing hold of the hose, I yanked it out of Shay's grasp and struck it against his chest. I kneed him in the groin.

"Mia!" shouted Cameron.

Shay faced the wall, cupping his balls as he slid down.

Cameron sprang towards us and skidded across the floor, his arms out on either side as he flailed for balance. His feet gave way and he lost his footing, slipping backwards and landing hard on the ground. He laughed hysterically.

"Get your fucking sub off me," shouted Shay, and despite rolling around on the wet tile he too seemed to find this hilarious. "What the fuck was that?"

I turned on Cameron, skidding over to him. "Don't you ever do that to me again." I slumped to my knees beside him and thumped his chest. "It's not funny. You guys are messed up."

"I know you'll be surprised to hear this," said Shay, "but my erection's gone."

Cameron's laughter rose louder. He couldn't speak, but merely stared up the ceiling, clearly finding delight in this entire spectacle.

"What made you take this one on?" Shay pushed himself to his feet. "She's un-trainable."

"I lost a bet." Cameron beamed and pulled me on top of him.

"Bastard." I thumped his chest again.

"Mia, you can't take this all so literally," said Cameron, grabbing hold of my wrists.

"You're not the one having cold water sprayed on you," I snapped.

"I'll leave you two at it then." Shay headed out, shaking his head and still cupping his balls.

Cameron rolled on top of me, pressing his soaked torso against mine. "My feisty angel, you are so beguiling."

Wrapping my thighs around him, unable to resist his firmness, I squirmed beneath him. "What did you expect?"

"Not that," he said, shaking his head, amused.

We stilled and stared into each other's eyes.

That sheen of water on his chest glistened. That firm hold of my wrists held above my head, his strength dominating my movement, caused me to weaken.

"Be a good girl and take off your panties," he said, lifting off me.

Pouting my annoyance, trying to feign I was more pissed off then I was, I eased them off my hips and down, throwing them across the room. Cameron slipped off his pants and underwear and was soon lying back on top of me, maneuvering himself between my thighs. His firm body brought a welcome warmth.

With one hard thrust, he buried himself deep inside and I arched my back in pleasure.

"You don't deserve my cock." He moved his hips in a circle. "But I'm giving it to you anyway."

"Thank you, Sir." I dug my nails into his back. "Oh God," I moaned, quickly getting close. This fullness, these thrusts banging me into the tile, caused my insides to melt and my thighs to tremble.

He paused mid thrust and leaned on his elbows and peered down at me. "If I make you come hard, will you forgive me?"

"I'll consider it."

"Consider it, Sir," he corrected.

"Sir," I added through gritted teeth.

He slid out of me and there was a terrible emptiness.

"Sir." I grasped his arms. "I forgive you. I forgive you."

Cameron chuckled and slid back in, filling me again, stretching me wide and creating delicious spasms that radiated outward and upward. These whirling tingles captured my body with need. He pounded me towards the steepest edge, deep and hard.

Nothing mattered but this. Him. I held onto this man, remembering his words from Big Bear, that 'now was all we had.'

Now.

I screamed my climax, digging my fingernails in farther, fiercely scratching at his back. His warmth filled me, sending me into a spiraling dive into nothingness. I buried my face against his neck, taking short sharp breaths as his scent of dominance filled my lungs.

Lying still now, feeling his breathing slowing, I luxuriated in him. This completeness was a nice change from all that craziness.

He pulled out of me and glanced over at the cage.

"No," I said.

"I might as well be in there," he whispered. "That's what you do to me."

That dark revelation was so fleeting it caused me to doubt

he'd even spoken it. Cameron was on his feet and pulling me up to mine.

In a flurry of movement, both of us soaking wet and not caring, we wrapped ourselves in plush white towels then made our way through the house.

We lingered outside my bedroom door before separating.

Parting was getting harder.

CHAPTER 33

CAMERON MET WITH his friends at the bar in Chrysalis's lounge.

I wasn't invited.

The evening was mine to do what I wanted. He'd invited me to visit the screening room to watch a movie and mingle with the other subs. Still undecided, I took my time to shower and change into this Cameron approved halter-neck black dress and pumps.

Not wanting to show off my post fucked glow to anyone, I made my way toward the privacy of the kitchen, in need of a snack.

I stood in the doorway, thinking twice about entering.

"Come in." The woman gestured. "I'm Pilar." She went on to tell me she was Chrysalis's housemaid.

"Mia," I said.

Pilar was plump and pretty, her maid's uniform showing off the creases of a long day of work. I guessed her age around fifty; her beautiful olive skin luminous. I wasn't the only one happy to be here it seemed.

"Hungry?" she said.

I gave a nod that I was and followed her direction to take a seat at the kitchen table.

"Savory or sweet?" asked Pilar.

"Savory, please."

She rifled through the fridge.

I rose to my feet. "I can get it."

"Then I'd be out of a job," she said cheerfully.

I was feeling proud, despite the weirdness of what Cameron and Shay had intended in that tiled room. My rebellion had been the last thing they'd expected. It made me laugh. The look on their faces had been classic. My inner goddess gave me a high-five.

Rain came down hard against the window, the wind blowing leaves up against it. I wondered how safe it was to fly in this weather. Luckily Cameron and I had missed it several hours ago. The weather report was no doubt all part of a flight plan. Cameron looked so sexy when he flew his Benz. That man had style. Enough sophistication to make an ex-girlfriend stalk him. He had an addictive quality. Despite considering gate crashing him and his friends at the bar, I willed myself not to embarrass myself. He really was inside my head, causing havoc to my dignity.

Pilar placed before me a selection of vegetables and dips. I peeled off the lids of each one and munched away on the delicious selection. "Have you worked here long?" I asked, and took a bite out of a spear of broccoli.

I assumed Pilar had seen all sorts.

"Ten years," she said. "Dr. Cole has been good to me."

"I like him." I wondered if she knew about his extra-curricular activity. Having worked for him for a while, she must have suspected something.

She sat opposite and rested her chin on her hands. "You like it here?"

"I really do." I dipped a carrot into the pot of Ranch dressing. "You must be pretty open-minded to work here?"

"What do I care what people do?" she said. "No one gets hurt. I get paid well." She leaned forwards and whispered, "Dr. Cole is putting my son through school. Top school in Brentwood. He pays for everything."

"Your son's father doesn't mind?" I said.

"He's dead. Died years ago."

"I'm so sorry."

"I'm happy now. There's a lot to be grateful for."

I popped a baby carrot in my mouth. "There sure is."

"You're not going to the cocktail party?" she said.

"What party?"

She twisted her mouth, as though unsure.

"I think you mean the one coming up," I said. "It's not tonight."

"Dr. Cole is a good man."

"I feel the same way," I said. "Cameron may be stern, but he's really helping me in so many ways."

Pilar shot to her feet. "You're his submissive?"

"Yes, why?"

She grabbed my plate and carried it over to the sink and tossed it in. "Dr. Cole is very specific about what you can eat."

"What are you talking about?" I said. "These are vegetables."

"You can only eat when he says you eat."

"What?" I went to express my annoyance—

Arianna strolled in.

"I should be getting back," I said, rising quickly. "Thanks, Pilar."

Even if she had snatched my food away, I liked her. It wasn't really her fault that Cameron's precedent had everyone on their toes around me. Pilar gave a nod, seemingly too busy to care as she loaded the dishwasher. It was hard to tell what had rattled her more, me eating an unapproved snack or Arianna.

Arianna's burgundy corset looked amazing on her, as did that rose tattoo balancing elegance and edgy. Her collar was a strip of velvet. She looked extra dressed up tonight. Her hair and makeup were professionally done, like she was attending an event, a party.

That familiar curl of doubt crept in.

I went to leave and Arianna held her hand up, pressing it against my chest. "Not so fast."

"Please get out of my way."

She shrugged casually. "I have a message for you."

"Oh?"

"Richard Booth is here. He wants to see you."

"What?" I shot a nervous glance at Pilar.

Pilar smiled. "Tell Mr. Booth I'll make him a sandwich."

"Yeah, he's not allowed in this part of the house, Pilar," said Arianna. "Not while his sub's undergoing training with Master Cole."

Pilar tutted her disapproval. "He'll catch his death out there."

Arianna laughed. "If he comes in here, he'll catch his death when Master Cole sees him. Richard's not allowed to interrupt her training." She pointed at me. "Which apparently isn't going well."

What the fuck.

Shay, her master, had evidently shared the details of our catastrophe in the water room.

Pilar scurried away, seemingly finding the contents of the fridge interesting.

"Where's Richard?" I said.

"By the pool," said Arianna. "Waiting for you under the awning."

I wanted to ask Arianna not to let Cameron know he was here, but something told me it wouldn't make any difference. "Please, tell Richard to go home."

"You tell him," said Arianna.

Pilar closed fridge. "Maybe, Ms. Arianna, you should get Dr. Cole to handle this?"

"The ultimate cock block," said Arianna, turning on her heels and laughing her way out. "This should be interesting."

Had it not been raining, I'd have been tempted to leave Richard outside. If I wasn't allowed to mention his name, seeing him sure as hell wasn't allowed.

After thanking Pilar for my half eaten snack, I headed out. A chill ran up my spine when I caught sight of Arianna just outside the kitchen. She leaned against the wall. She puffed on a cigarette and glared at me as I passed her. That rendezvous in that tiled room with her Master would turn an already jealous Arianna into a liability.

"Where's your collar?" she called after me.

I turned. "Sorry?"

"If you're Master Cole's sub, why aren't you wearing his collar?"

Telling her that I still had to earn it wasn't an option. It already felt like she had one up on me. Her familiarity with Chrysalis, the staff, and the other members.

"That's between me and my master," I said.

"He's tolerating you until he can give you back."

"Why do you say that?"

"I've seen him with subs before. He's different with you. He takes no pleasure in your lack of submission."

"I submit," I said, even though it was none of her business.

"Looks like defiance to me." She glared. "Why are you even here? For his money?"

It was my turn to glare back. "No."

She took a long hard drag. "Learn to obey or you'll be out."

I kept walking, quickly putting distance between us.

I really believed I was making progress. Even if our last session had ended abruptly and rather disastrously. Other than that one, Cameron had always seemed pleased at the end of our sessions, and I'd come out of them exhilarated. It wouldn't have surprised me to learn that Arianna was sabotaging a master and sub relationship that she coveted. Despite Dominic's suggestion to bitch-slap her, I could only assume that wouldn't go down well. If subs fought with each other, they were out.

The thought of seeing Richard distracted me. I wondered if he was even here. Making my way out of the house, I used the awning for cover, intending to merely throw a wave his way and let him know I was fine. Then get him out of the rain and home safe.

There he was.

My beautiful Richard. His clothes were soaking wet and clinging to him and his golden short locks were squished damp on his head. His face lit up when he saw me. He was dressed in a tux.

Was this why I was banned from the bar? Cameron was meeting him. Perhaps to provide an update on how things were going.

Hopping through the rain towards me, he looked so playful. That boyish charm showed on his handsome face. "Hey you." He beamed, ushering me back inside.

"I'm not sure about this," I said.

He dragged his sleeve across his brow. "You look amazing. God, I've missed you."

"Oh Richard." I wiped a sodden strand of hair out of his face. "I've missed you too." I glanced down the hallway.

Enthrall Her

"How's it going?" he whispered. "Are you enjoying yourself?"

"It's pretty intense," I said. "But I know you'll be happy with everything I've learned." And now that I knew there was nothing between him and Jasmine, I could relax around him again.

He nudged me up against the wall, biting his bottom lip and looking oh so sexy in that vulnerable way of his. "It's been hell without you. Staying away is impossible. I want you to know that. Enthrall isn't the same without you. Even the clients miss you. And the girls, well they talk about you all the time."

I laughed. This felt like two kids meeting behind the schoolyard. So deliciously forbidden. "I have so much to tell you," I said. "Master Cole has arranged for me to do classes. Did you know about those? Math and stuff. I hate math. But he thinks it will help me get into a great fashion college."

"He did mention it." Richard grinned. "And I can help you with that too."

"I'm even doing etiquette classes. Samantha Harding—"

"What happened to your collar?" he said. "You shouldn't take it off."

"Well—"

"You look amazing. I mean radiant."

"Are you doing okay?"

Richard stared past me. "Oh fuck."

Cameron stood at the end of the hallway, his expression hard to read. The only sign giving away his disapproval came from his dark, fiery eyes. Cameron was also wearing a tux. The kind reserved for parties.

"We are so busted," said Richard.

He grabbed my arms and leaned in, pressing his lips against mine, stealing a kiss, passionately taking his time to savor these last few seconds. A flash of memories. A feeling of familiarity. I was safe in his arms.

Then came a wash of fear that he was doing this in front of—

"Booth," yelled Cameron, stomping towards us.

Richard pulled away and threw up his hands, grinning at him.

Wide-eyed and a little shaken, I took interest in the ground. Cameron's stare hopped to Richard and then back me.

"It's my fault," said Richard. "Don't blame her."

Cameron's glare hinted he didn't quite believe that.

"Come on, Cole," said Richard. "I missed her."

"We have to get you a dry jacket," said Cameron. "This won't do. Where's your tie?"

Richard smirked. "You can't be that pissed with me, surely?"

"Mia," said Cameron sternly. "Go to your room."

"Mia, wait," said Richard. "Five minutes, Cameron, please."

Cameron shot me a look.

With a nod of compliance, I headed off, forcing myself not to look back and get either of us in any more trouble. That response time training served its purpose and I hoped I'd get points for that at least.

Touching my lips where Richard had kissed me, relieved he'd not forgotten me, I made my way down the hallway.

My old life had been put on hold, yet here, now, after Richard's stolen kiss, confusion set it. I didn't know how anyone could ever live a lie with an affair. Knowing Richard wanted me under Cameron's tutelage sent my mind doing cartwheels. Looking from one beautiful man to the other had caused a wave of unknowing. Despite Cameron's expression scaring the hell out of me, he'd handled this with his usual controlled style, calm and determined.

When I made it to the foyer, I paused.

Several guests mingled in there, all dressed in their finery. Men wore tuxes and women wore cocktail dresses, and there were a few in elegant lingerie. Proof there was an event going on that I'd not been invited to. They gave me a passing glance.

Head down, I ascended the staircase, up and along, soon making it to my room.

Falling back onto the bed, I stared up at the ceiling, my mind spiraling, trying to understand why Cameron hadn't invited me.

He didn't think I was ready.

Thinking quickly, I stripped out of my dress and flung it across the room. Next, I removed my bra and panties and pulled on my high-top stockings and high-heels and then climbed back onto the bed.

I reached up and pulled down the long chain, easing my wrists into the leather handcuffs. Sitting up and parting my thighs slightly, I faced the door.

Arianna was wrong.

I knew how to please my master.

CHAPTER 34

CAMERON SHUT THE bedroom door behind him.

He carried a glass of liquor, the ice clinking. His eyes locked on mine as he took a leisurely sip. Shifting position, my arms aching from holding this pose for fifteen minutes or so, I broke his steely gaze.

Moving slowly, deliberately, he leaned back against the wall and slid down it, balancing his drink as he went.

"Master," I whispered.

"You believed you'd lost him?" he said softly. "When you saw Richard and Jasmine together that night?"

I gave a nod.

"That's why you let me bring you here to Chrysalis," he said. "In hope of winning him back?" He watched my reaction. "It was very brave, Mia. But unnecessary." He pointed to my hummingbird. "An expression of wanting to fly free from the pain of heartbreak."

Another nod.

"Have I in some way soothed your psyche?" he said. "Enlightened you to the truth?" He gestured his need to hear me speak.

"You've given me so much," I said. "I don't know how I'll ever repay your kindness."

"You already have."

"Everything has changed," I said. "Nothing will ever be the same again."

"It can be."

"How?"

"Richard's in the bar. You can go home with him tonight if you like." He waved his hand casually. "I'm not a complete monster, Mia."

"Sir, I want my collar back."

"The one who puts the collar on you..." His expression softened. "I've decided to wait for when I return you to him."

"I want it to be you." I swallowed hard. "I need it to be you."

He stared into his glass, his frown deepening.

"Sir, I belong to you."

Confusion marred his face. "He shouldn't have come. He's brought doubt."

"Not for me."

"I promised him." He shook his head, as though shaking off a thought.

"I'm close, Cameron. I can feel it."

"Feel what?" he whispered.

"I need you to guide me the rest of the way." I gritted my teeth. "I am not leaving."

"What do you want, Mia?"

"I'm ready to leave this room as yours. Show all of them that you have conquered me."

He ran his fingers through his hair.

"Surrendering to you is the only time I feel free," I said.

He looked thoughtful, cautious even. "You're an interesting challenge."

My heart thundered when he raised his eyes to mine. Since that first day I'd met Cameron at Enthrall, I'd yearned to see him look at me this way. Those dark chestnut eyes fierce, possessive.

"Perhaps we should talk this through?" he said.

"Words aren't needed. Not for us."

He rose to his feet. "God, you take my breath away." He looked serene. "I have never known a pleasure more sublime than you."

I pulled my wrists out of these handcuffs and rested my hands over my heart, needing to prove he'd taught me well. Offering everything I had, I honored the art of submission. "Yours, Sir," I whispered.

Opening to him, I gave my body, my heart, my mind.

He set his drink down on the dresser and faced me again, his eyelids heavy, his stance changing to that of master. "Yes, you are mine."

This ache in my heart was too much. I slipped off the bed, moving slowly, deliberately, towards him and lowered myself to my knees, leaning forwards on the carpet in a low bow, my hair spilling over my arms and onto the carpet.

The deepest sigh escaped me. The air crackled with electricity. The truth filled my heart and soul that I was *his*.

Time passed over us, knowing what we needed was this.

"Mia," he whispered.

Sending shivers up and down my spine, my flesh prickled with an unbearable need. I yearned for his touch, for him to take me in his arms.

The sound of footfalls moved away.

Cameron left the room.

Doubt crept into my bones, yet a small quiet voice reassured me to remain still, wait for my master's return. Trust this moment. Trust him. This transformation loomed closer than ever.

Seeing Richard again reminded me how much I loved him, yet I needed my master more. Cameron had mapped a pathway into my soul and our connection was too profound to ignore or turn away from. My yearning was never greater for Cameron's approval, his affection, his ownership.

My thoughts scattered as I wondered if this would ever be enough. Could I love a man who would never love be back?

He does love you. His eyes tell you what he refuses to say.

Cameron was the air I breathed.

And I knew he'd come back for me.

Merely a minute passed when the door opened again. Footfalls neared.

Cameron knelt before me. "Lift your head, Mia."

The sensation of his fingers securing my diamond collar around my neck felt divine.

"So be it," he said. "We'll see this through."

The tightness of this choker brought a sense of safety. A sense of belonging.

"What about your meeting?" I said.

"Fuck the meeting," he said. "It's time to showcase my new

submissive."

He entered the wardrobe and soon reappeared carrying two white boxes. He rested them on the bed. Cameron removed the lid from the first, taking his time to ease apart the delicate tissue paper. He removed the lingerie. In a ritualistic fashion, proving he'd been saving this exquisite outfit for me, he dressed me in this elegant and well fitting corset, its tassels made from Swarovski glass beads. Even the delicate panties he put on me were decorated with crystals. His hands felt warm and luxurious as they moved over me, dressing me in a way that proved I was his.

He knelt at my feet and eased on the ivory satin shoes.

Cameron stood beside me in the bathroom as I applied fresh makeup, tussling my hair until he gave a nod of approval that I was ready.

He opened the second box.

Within lay a beautifully crafted venetian mask, feathers bursting out from the top in a spray of white. He assisted me with mine, then removed his own mask from his pocket and placed it on.

With his strong hand holding mine, he led me out and along the hallway and down the stairwell. Admiring glances from the guests swept over us.

Peering up at my master, my fingers held his hand firmly. My heart burst in awe that he'd chosen me.

I felt more beautiful than I ever had.

We entered a cocktail lounge and I looked around for Richard. I didn't see him. In the corner was a piano player playing the keys softly, providing a musical backdrop that allowed the ease of conversation. To our far left, it was no surprise to see a couple making out on a black velvet lounger. A few guests had gathered before them to watch.

I assumed this couple's tender touches, their tame show of affection, would soon be ramping up in a more erotic display.

Cameron removed two glasses of champagne from a tray offered up by a waiter and handed me one of the flutes, while taking a sip from the other.

The room was filled with fifty people or so, all chatting away, seemingly knowing each other well. They greeted

Cameron warmly, and when he introduced me they offered words of welcome, making me feel I belonged. Their respectfulness proved the honor of what it meant to be Cameron's submissive.

He was strangely quiet. I felt his scrutiny on me, as though he judged my every move, my every reaction.

"You are incandescent, Mia," he said, raising my hand to kiss my wrist. "I wish you saw yourself as others see you. As I do." He held me close to his side, his arm wrapped around my waist possessively.

For much of the evening, it seemed that we were the center of attention. Cameron was surrounded by friends, old and new, and they all deferred to him during their conversations. Only now that he was wearing a mask did I realize his stark beauty was the least of his eminence. His stature, that self-assuredness, that ability to handle anything or anyone was what made him so enigmatic.

I wasn't the only one mesmerized.

Shay stepped out of the crowd, holding a martini with a single olive. He looked so handsome in his tuxedo and mask, so different to that man who'd tried to drown me earlier.

I stared at him warily.

"Mia," he said, moving close and towering over me in a possible attempt to gain his power back. "You look divine."

I glanced at Cameron for permission to speak. With a nod, he gave it.

"Thank you, Sir," I said, scanning the room. "Is Arianna here?"

"What is it with you two?" said Shay. "Maybe we should shove you in a mud bath and let you fight it out."

Cameron beamed at him. "Not while she's wearing that. I had it imported from Venice."

My brows shot up in surprise.

"Really," said Shay, eyeing my corset. "It'll take the kind of will I don't have to get her out of that quickly without snapping something off." He locked eyes with me and dragged his olive off its stick with his teeth.

Cameron took a sip of champagne. "I like a challenge."

"I don't think Arianna likes me," I whispered to Cameron.

"She's a little unruly, but Shay finds her pleasing," said Cameron.

I scanned the room. "This is all very tame."

Other than the couple on the lounger, nothing else was going on.

Cameron turned to Shay. "I'm conflicted," he whispered to him.

Shay gave a look of understanding. "Do you want me to show her?"

"No," said Cameron. "It should be me."

"Show me what?" I said.

Cameron held his hand out for me. "You remain silent. You remain by my side. Show no reaction to what you see. Understand?"

A chill caused the fine hairs on my forearms to prickle. I gave a nod.

We set our glasses down.

Together, we walked across the room towards the double doorway. Shay gave the door three solid knocks.

It opened.

A stocky, tux wearing, masked doorman gestured our entry was permitted.

I'd not been shown this part of the house during my tour. And as the doors closed behind us, I could see why.

The décor, the artwork, even the black velvet drapes revealed this was the heart of the sanctuary. With my hand holding Cameron's tightly, and flanked on my right by Shay, we made our way down the dimly lit hallway.

"Welcome to Chrysalis," said Shay.

Another door.

The lighting dimmed.

An Italian styled ballroom. It was vast, with a high ceiling. Balconies ran along each side. Pillars here and there emphasized the greatness. The grandness. This room was even larger than the Harrington Suite. Rich burgundies and deep reds draped the luxurious furnishings and complemented the lavishly accented pieces.

The music was dramatic, the scent of incense pungent. That, and the rich aroma of burning wood. There was a large fireplace with a huge mantle. Within the hearth, golden flames danced, embers sparked—

Here and there, people were fucking.

Twos, and threes, and sometimes more. Some of them naked, others fully clothed. Oral sex, frenzied for some, others gentle. Everyone was in the throes of passion. None of them cared about the three of us who walked through with the casualness of viewing an art gallery.

Cameron's hand squeezed mine and I woke, as though rising from a dream.

We walked onwards, strolling beneath an arched doorway into another room that was darker. Smaller. Though just as inviting.

Two women knelt before a man, pleasuring him, his hands upon their heads in a show of approval. His erection was lavished with affection from two eager subs. Their soft cries of gratitude found us in the dimness.

Behind us, another scene played out. An erotic display that stole my breath—

A masked man was sitting on a leather couch, and a blonde woman wearing a half mask faced forwards. With her back to him, she rode him slowly, his cock disappearing inside her, only to show once more on her upward glide. Her bright red lips pouted in ecstasy. She wore a submissive's collar.

A jolt of pleasure spasmed low in my belly. I shot a look at Cameron and he returned a slow, steady nod.

My arousal had never felt so forbidden.

This act of passion was so beautiful, so pure, and as I dared myself to continue watching, stilted by uncertainty, I knew the honor of what it was to witness their lovemaking.

"Master Cole," said Shay, "May I?" He gestured to the couple.

"Mia?" said Cameron. "What do you say to Shay's request?"

"Yes," I said breathlessly.

"Thank you, Mia," said Shay, his pupil's dark and feral, focusing once more upon that couple. That lick of his lips proved his intention.

"What about Arianna?" I whispered.

"She's being well taken care of," said Shay, flashing a smile at Cameron.

"She belongs to Scarlet tonight," said Cameron.

There was no time to consider what Scarlet and Arianna might be doing right now. I was too mesmerized by the couple and their leisurely fucking. The way he tweaked her nipples and cupped her breasts. Their eyes were full of wonder.

Shay shrugged out of his jacket and threw it over the end of the couch. He loosened his necktie and neared them.

He sunk to his knees in-between the woman's outstretched thighs.

Cameron pulled me so that my back was against his front, and his hand slid beneath my panties. My blush burned my face. He'd feel my wetness.

His palm cupped me there. "Do you want to watch?"

"Yes, please, Sir," I managed, my head resting back on his chest, my eyelids heavy.

Cameron's touch sent a shiver through me.

"So wet." His fingers trailed along my sex. "Obey."

"Yes, Sir." My thighs trembled.

The woman peered down at Shay through her mask, and her eyes lit up when she looked beyond him and saw us.

Shay kneeled before her. Leaning forwards between her thighs, his tongue lapped at her sex. She gripped his locks, her eyes heavy with lust.

My own sex clenched.

Shay's tongue lowered to lap the balls of the one she rode. The man threw his head back. His fingers gripped her breasts and pinched her nipples.

Shay returned to her clit.

I marveled at her discipline, her ability to rise and fall, following the orders of her master to continue her slow gliding motion. Her thighs trembled, and her whimpering revealed her closeness.

I jolted with the shock of Cameron's fingers easing apart my cleft. They strummed their steady rhythm upon my clit, and my pussy squeezed in pleasure, quivered. His steady massaging and flicking continued, while his other hand wrapped around my waist.

Shay firmly gripped the woman's hips to assist her upward

glide, then he brought her down hard on that man's cock. His mouth delivered a frenzied punishment of pleasure to her pussy.

This was a brilliant symphony of sex. Their lovemaking was stunning.

Her thrusts downward became more needful as she peered down at Shay beneath heavy lashes.

"It's beautiful," I said. "Now I understand."

Waves of intensity came one after the other and I moaned in pleasure. This dampness between my thighs grew, in time with the sure rhythm of Cameron's fingers matching that of the rise and fall of the submissive. Her eyes now closed as she neared.

Cameron shifted his hand, his thumb now strumming my clit as he fingered me forcefully. My sex clenched around his fingers as they thrust in and out, and my breath became ragged. My hips rocked to his frenzied pace.

I rode his hand.

I didn't care who saw. All I wanted was to ride out this bliss, exalted that Cameron was allowing me this.

Shay masterfully bestowed sucks, nips, and licking flicks. His expert timing took on a fierce pace—

A clash of swords. Cameron and Shay fencing. That virile fight so intense, so powerful, so arousing.

My thighs shifted farther apart, my legs trembled.

I went with her.

Falling into the abyss, coming together, our groans rose ever higher. With incense in my nostrils, this heat rising from Cameron's touch scorched me from the inside out. I was lost in this dreamlike state.

Skillfully, he worked me towards another orgasm, whispering to me, "Submission is just the beginning."

"Master," I called out, another climax owning me.

My legs weakened and gave way.

Cameron picked me up and carried me out of there. And though I didn't recognize the route we took, I did recognize the foyer.

He carried me to my bedroom and threw me upon the bed. We ripped off our masks.

Cameron took me hard.

Both of us rolled around those tussled sheets. Both of us

were desperate to be closer. Still fully clothed, merely edging away that which wouldn't allow penetration, we joined in a frenzy of want.

Being apart was too painful.

His lips bruised mine. His cock buried deep. His passion was unlike anything I'd ever seen in him before. He rode me harder than he ever had. Pushing deeper, his pace grew virile, demanding. There was no time for leather or chains while both of us chased the high of being fucked by each other.

I screamed when I came.

He stilled, shooting his warmth into me. His gaze locked on mine in a show of power. "You are mine," he said huskily.

"I am yours," I whispered, staring up, realizing those chains above the bed had already entwined me, yet they hung there out of reach.

Eventually, I managed to slow my racing heart.

"I'm going to take you again, Mia," said Cameron fiercely.

"What? No." I shook my head, unsure, my body too consumed with exhaustion.

"Fucking is finished when I say it's finished." He rolled on top of me again and pinned me down. "This is about me worshipping you, in case you missed it."

Our lovemaking was a meditation, an endless display of unspoken words and unfathomable emotions we dared to feel. A giving over of everything and leaving nothing unsaid.

We lay in a tangled mess of disheveled bed sheets, this dampness beneath the purest evidence of us. Both of us spent.

Our breathing only now slowed.

Lying with my head on his chest, lulled by the sound of his heartbeat, sure and steady, I drifted.

"Before you," he whispered, "I never questioned."

CHAPTER 35

SLEEP CARRIED ME through to the morning.
Italian landscapes. Masked men in black tuxes. Strangers mouthing words to me I couldn't grasp, couldn't understand.
I'd seen behind the curtain.
Yet I knew there was more than this. My first glimpse into Chrysalis was a mere taste of its delicacies.
I stretched my arms wide, feeling that familiar ache from where Cameron's hands had been. That low pang between my thighs was a sweet reminder.
Daybreak burst its light into the bedroom, casting shadows. Clothes were strewn round and about—his jacket and pants, that white shirt, my corset with its Swarovski glass beads catching the morning light.
Cameron was still here.
Laying beside me and fast asleep, his face was serene and peppered with that five o'clock shadow. Ever so gently, I rolled onto my side and stared at him. It felt as though I was seeing this man for the first time, his vulnerability, his serenity. There was no fierceness. He was so beautiful and looked younger, peaceful even. That fluttering of eyelids proved he too dreamed.
Reaching out, I caressed his shoulder, needing to touch him and wanting to free him from sleep.
He stirred, blinking awake.
Cameron's gaze shot to mine.
He bolted upright and ran his fingers through his hair.
"It's Sunday," I said. "You don't have to go to work."

"I fell asleep," he said, turning his back on me and swinging his legs over the bed. "I'm so sorry."

"Why are you sorry?"

He leaped out, moving to his right to reach for a sock, his expression conflicted. An awful thud sounded when his toe struck the end of the bed.

"Fuck." He hopped, holding his foot until he lost his balance and fell back onto the bed.

"Are you late for something?" I said.

"No, Mia," he said, annoyed and caressing his toe.

"Then what's wrong?"

"Our arrangement," he said. "No sleeping together."

"Don't be ridiculous. It's a one off. No one died, for goodness sake. Get back in."

He glared at me.

I resisted rolling my eyes. "Get back in, Sir." I pulled back the comforter. "It's like eating a bar of chocolate. Once you've had one square, you might as well finish off the whole thing."

His face contorted in pain. "That doesn't make any sense."

I patted the bed. "Come on."

His shook his head in defeat and climbed back in beside me. I scrambled to the end of the bed and bent low, planting kiss after kiss to his toe.

He laid back, his frown deepening, his look of suspicion not letting up. "Ice would be better."

"Want me to get some?"

He waved it off. "It's okay."

I scrambled up again and landed on his chest, snuggling against him, sniffing in pure Cameron as I rested my head on him, relaxing once more and letting out a sigh of happiness. "See? This is nice."

"Don't get too comfortable," he said. "This will never happen again."

"Then I better make the most of it."

"I'm serious."

"So am I."

He wrapped his arms around, hugging me into him. "The whole bar?"

This part of the house was quiet. It was nice to imagine we

were alone, even though I knew we weren't. Somewhere, in the far reaches of the house, doms were waking their subs to prepare them for the day, and elsewhere staff were working tirelessly to accommodate the guests.

Finally, I broke this silence and said, "I want to know more about you."

"What you see is pretty much what you get."

"There's more to you. I envy your friends that know you well."

"What do you want to know exactly?"

"Why did you choose psychiatry?" I said. "Why didn't you go into your father's business?"

"Becoming CEO was a privilege reserved for Henry, my older brother. Life took a few hard turns for him and he's questioning his path right now."

"That's so vague."

"Henry's a recluse. He lives alone in a cabin in the woods."

Henry sounded a bit frightening.

"I chose psychiatry because I find the mind fascinating." He smiled down at me. "I take pleasure in making people feel better about themselves."

"Do you ever get lonely?" I said.

"I'm constantly surrounded by people."

"But I've never seen you in a serious relationship."

"I find them futile."

I lifted my head. "Futile?"

"In a relationship, the couple moves through the predictable steps that lead to either a breakup, or marriage, and then onwards, bound to divorce."

Jeez, he sounds like Richard. These really were two rogues in a pod, like Cameron's mother had said.

I felt wounded. "That doesn't sound very romantic."

"I'm drawn to the extraordinary."

"Such high demands, Sir."

"I've never met anyone who's ever inspired me enough to take that risk."

"Risk? Futility?" I chuckled. "What about love?"

"What is love to you, Mia?" He smirked. "No, really, I'm interested to know what you believe it to be."

"Love is where you can't help but want to be near the person. It hurts when they aren't around. They make you feel complete."

"But you're already complete." He sat up. "I should go."

"Love is God's breath," I whispered.

Cameron lay back down on his pillow, blinking up at the ceiling.

I rested my head back onto his chest and snuggled. Those soft caresses of his hand up and down my back lulled me.

"It was never that profound," he said softly. "Not with her. It was a long time ago. She believed our lives would be all about garden parties in the Hamptons and time wasted on yachts. She never imagined it would be about us offering our time in the inner cities. Or volunteering at halfway houses. Or patients calling me at odd hours and needing my time. Or me leaving her behind at a dinner party when I was called to the ER."

I studied his face, trying to read if he was still hurting.

"I thought she'd come round." He gestured to the room. "All this is an illusion. The only way to soothe my conscience is to do my bit." He raised his hand. "Don't ask me her name."

"Did she break it off?" I whispered.

"I did." A wave of his hand told me this line of questioning was over.

"You really are a dichotomy," I said. "This place. What I saw last night. Those people on that couch with Shay. It was all so..."

"I warned you I'm hedonistic. I'll never be accused of being puritanical."

"Despite last night seeming so forbidden," I said. "There was something beautiful about it too. The room was about worshipping sexuality, finding no shame in it, sharing in the pleasure of others."

"I like to think so," he said. "Would you ever conceive entering there again?"

"Yes, please. If I'm allowed."

He kissed my forehead. "Only senior members are invited into the red ballroom."

"Then I'm lucky I know you."

Cameron laughed. "I'll see if I can sneak you in again."

I smiled at that. "Thank you, Sir."

"Trust me, it's my pleasure."

"How did you meet Shay?"

"At a polo match in Surrey," he said. "It turned out we had mutual friends."

"Do you play polo?"

He scratched his stubble. "Yes."

"You really are very upper class."

"Don't let this well spoken, perfectly bred demeanor fool you." He dug his fingers into my ribs and tickled.

Giggling, I squirmed. "Oh, I've seen your tricks, Dr. Cole. I know exactly what you're capable of."

"You haven't seen anything yet." He poked some more.

Wriggling, I tried to escape. "I'm looking forward to today," I burst out.

"Why, what's happening?" He stilled. "You're choosing today to take me off on a Mia adventure."

"Don't expect too much," I said. "I can't afford anything too flashy. Still, I think you'll like it."

He looked amused.

"You will come with me, won't you?"

"I gave you my word, Mia. My word is everything. Unless you fuck up, and then I'm likely to change my mind."

"Don't change your mind about me."

"Why do you say that?"

"I want you to like me as much as I like you."

"Where did that come from?"

My heart, you idiot.

"I feel so very deeply about you," I said.

He let out a hesitant sigh. "There's so much I want to say to you." He looked down at me. "Sometimes, though, it's wise not to speak those words."

"Why?"

"Once they're out, there's no taking them back."

"Is this your way of letting me know you really are fond of me?" I said.

But he'd closed his eyes, seemingly drifting off into a doze.

CHAPTER 36

"WHY ARE WE here?" said Cameron, peering through the shop glass window of Pottery Play. "Oh, fuck, no."

I folded my arms. "You agreed."

He looked affronted. "What is it you believe you can teach me from this?"

"Come on," I said. "It's best if I show you."

"Mia, let's grab a coffee. Look, there's a nice bakery over there."

"Sir, you gave me your word."

"Not for this. What is this place anyway? And please call me Cameron when we're out."

"This is where people have fun." I opened the door.

Cameron followed me in, his jaw grinding with tension, that now clean shaven face taut.

"When was the last time you had any fun?" I said.

"The last time I spanked you," he muttered.

"No, I mean really."

"Really."

I gave his arm a nudge. "We had an agreement. You're a man of your word."

"Hey guys," said the blue haired host with Trish on her button. "How does that table work for you?" She gave Cameron the once over with a mixture of shyness and awe, her blush giving her away.

"Perfect. Thank you." I turned back to Cameron. "I'll take your coat."

I reached up from behind him and he reluctantly shrugged out of it. I hung it in the corner on a coat hanger. I placed mine next to his.

"How about I take math off the table?" said Cameron.

I patted his back. "Facing your fears is good for you."

Cameron's brow knitted together. "I should never have agreed to this. What the hell was I thinking?"

Ignoring him, I followed Trish, who soon had us set us up at a central table. I headed over to the counter to pay.

"I'll get this." Cameron reached into his pocket.

"No, I'm paying." I nudged up to him. "This is important to me."

"I don't want you wasting your money," he said, and on my glare, as well as one from Trish, he rolled his eyes and ambled away.

I chose a mug, and after some persuasion Cameron picked out a margarita shaped piece.

"This is how it works," I said. "After we're done, they glaze and fire them. We can pick them up in a few days."

Cameron scratched his jaw. "I'm not sure about this."

"Look, it's only an hour. And you did promise."

Glumly, he conceded with a nod. After choosing our colored pots, we took our seats. I slid between us some napkins, brushes, and positioned those multi-colored pots of paint within reach.

Cameron waved his hand at his margarita shaped cup. "Wouldn't it be better to have someone with an artistic flair do it?"

"That's not the point."

He shuffled in his seat. "Let's get this over with then."

"That's not the attitude, Cameron." I said. "You have to smile as you do it."

"Let's not go that far."

"Red's a good color for that." I nudged the pot of paint his way.

He rolled up his sleeves and removed his watch and tucked it into his shirt pocket. "Why don't you do both and I watch?" he said.

"Cameron!"

He picked up the paintbrush, studying it with an air of

contempt.

"Yay!" I clapped my hands with delight and pretended Mr. Intensity wasn't sitting opposite.

He dipped his brush into the pot of red paint and dabbed it onto his cup, turning it as he went. Choosing a bright blue, I swept my brush over my mug and sucked up the fact that this wasn't going too well.

Cameron's gaze shot between his legs. "Fuck."

"Did you spill some?"

He gave a crooked smile. "No, my balls just fell off."

Laughing, I pointed my brush at him. "See, the great Cameron Cole can have fun."

"I'm doing this for you, Mia, because I gave you my word." He flicked his brush at me and a spot of paint landed on my nose.

I wiped it off with a napkin. "When was the last time you were creative?"

He looked thoughtful.

"You didn't do art in school?" I said.

"It wasn't that kind of school."

"What kind was it?"

"Boarding school."

"One where you don't get to see your parents?"

"I visited home during the summer. On holidays, like Thanksgiving, Christmas, Easter."

"Were you lonely?"

"No, I had friends."

"Do you stay in touch with them?"

"A few."

I waited for him to go on, sensing he'd relaxed a little and might even be enjoying himself from the way he was taking his time applying strokes to the inside of his cup.

The doorbell rang and an elderly couple entered with what looked like their grandchildren. They soon settled across the room by the window.

Cameron finally broke his attention from the family, as though satisfied he'd gleaned all he needed to analyze them.

I searched his face, hoping for a sign he wasn't too annoyed with me.

"My best friend in school was a guy named Dabuku Reid,"

said Cameron, his voice low. "He was an exchange student from Sandton."

"South Africa," I said.

Cameron beamed at me. "Dabuku's an ophthalmologist now. He has his own clinic on Harley Street."

"Ha," I said. "I know where that is too. See, all this money you're wasting on me is paying off."

"Then it's not wasted."

"Did you stay in touch?" I said.

"Yes. I'm lucky we have, considering."

"Considering what?"

"I know you'll find this hard to believe, but there used to be a time when I was very competitive."

"No. You?"

"Careful." He arched a brow. "We had our mid-term exams. Dabuku and I were not only best friends, we were at the top of our class and highly competitive against each other. So, the night before our exam, I took him out and got him blinding drunk." Cameron shrugged. "He was too busy throwing up the next day to finish his exam."

"What happened?"

"He was expelled. They thought he was cheating. All those visits to the restroom."

It was hard not to show my sadness for his friend.

"It all worked out fine," said Cameron. "I phoned my dad and admitted what I'd done and he made things right."

"How?"

"My dad donated generously to the school."

"And your friend was reinstated?"

"He was. Dabuku completed his education care of my father's grant. He went on to study medicine at Yale and I went to Harvard. Every few weeks, Dabuku flies out to Africa to perform surgery on those who can't afford it. He's saved the sight of thousands."

"He sounds amazing."

"He is."

"Did he ever forgive you?"

"Yes, we're the best of friends still. We laugh about it now. You can only imagine the guilt I feel knowing that I might have prevented Dabuku from ever becoming a doctor. His legacy is exceptional."

"You were very brave to tell your dad," I said.

"Sometimes doing the right thing is hard but necessary."

"Your dad's proud of you. I saw it in his eyes when we had dinner."

Cameron flicked his brush again and paint landed on my cheek. "The only psyche around here that gets explored is yours."

"Hey." I wiped it off. "That doesn't seem fair."

He looked at his margarita cup. "This is a cruel and unusual punishment."

"You're enjoying yourself. Don't try to deny it."

"There may be some benefit to this time wasting activity, I suppose. I'm still figuring it out. It's like some excruciating science experiment that keeps on giving."

"Very funny." I pointed my brush. "Your lip just curled up. I'm sensing happiness breaking through your austere demeanor."

He shook his head and grinned.

"I still feel guilty when I think about what I did to Dabuku," he admitted.

"So you hold onto things too?"

"I try not to, but that was pretty selfish. Luckily I'm over my megalomaniac stage." He raised his brush. "Don't even try responding to that."

I beamed at him. "Was that your trigger that nudged you into kink?"

"No, Mia, I was made this way. I take a great deal of pleasure in S & M. As you very well know."

I flushed wildly, responding to that stark stare of his. "See? This is fun. We're getting to know more about each other."

"I don't think I've ever painted before," he said.

"How can you never have painted?"

"I have no idea."

"I'm giving you a first time for something too."

"So it seems."

"And nothing bad happened," I said. "You lived through it."

"I'm rather proud." He turned his cup around to show me. "A masterpiece if ever I saw one."

"Looks amazing. It's a good thing Van Gogh's dead."

"Why?"

I gestured to his cup. "If Van Gogh saw that, he'd chop off his other ear in a fit of jealous rivalry."

We burst out laughing.

"And you get to keep mine and I get to keep yours," I told him.

"Who says?"

"So we can remember this moment every time we look at them," I said. "When we had fun together."

He gave a shrug. "Whatever floats your boat."

Cameron made the final touches to the base of his cup. God he was beautiful. His confident air always had its expected effect. Everyone who crossed his path naturally deferred to him. He'd even received glances of approval from the grandparents across the room. As though merely his presence was enough to impress.

"You have a hidden talent," I said.

"So do you apparently." He admired my mug. "Pity it will never get used."

"Why do you say that?"

He held my gaze. "Thank you for this."

"It's my pleasure," I said. "I'm relieved it wasn't a total disaster."

"It wasn't a disaster at all," he said. "I haven't had this much fun since I stubbed my toe this morning."

I flicked a splotch of paint his way and it landed on his collar. I covered my face and peeked through my fingers.

"Thank God for that," he said. "You've been such a good sub lately, I've been running out of reasons to spank you."

I melted right there in my chair, my thighs snapping together, my brightly blush giving my happiness away.

CHAPTER 37

DOMINIC HAD US wait outside.

Arianna held a tray of glasses and I'd been tasked with the one with the Louis XIII Remy Martin Cognac. The tray was getting heavy and I was quietly freaking out about dropping this three thousand dollar bottle.

With both of us dressed in sweetheart corsets, suspender belts, and stockings, we'd been prepared like lambs for the slaughter.

We were about to enter the lion's den.

Despite not liking Arianna, I drew strength from having her here. I didn't want to enter that room alone. Not while those members of the board were having their meeting in there. Arianna had told me these were the exclusive board members who almost wielded as much power as Cameron. Apparently they convened on the last Friday of every month here in his office, where he hosted this grand collection of hedonists to discuss the governing of Chrysalis.

Samantha Harding's training was paying off. I'll be walking in there with my head held high and a confident air. My other classes were amazing too, and if any of those refined members were interested to learn that a formula was a rock star equation highlighting the relationship between different variables, or that Virginia Woolf was a once beloved secret member of the Bloomsbury Group, I was their resource. Though if I knew one thing about Chrysalis's members, they'd all be super smart.

Dominic knocked.

He grabbed the doorknob and turned it, gesturing for us to enter.

All but one of the men wore tailored suits. There were ten men, their ages ranging from thirty to sixty, all of them groomed to perfection. These men had money, their fancy watches and polished shoes also gave that away. Their arrogant glances toward Arianna and I proved they were used to getting what they wanted. Cameron sat amongst them, looking equally refined with one leg crossed casually over another. When he caught sight of me, he quickly rose and strolled over towards Dominic.

Cameron whispered to him, "What is she doing here?"

Dominic looked rattled. "You asked for two subs."

Cameron didn't acknowledge me. He merely glared at Dominic.

"Gentlemen, cognac?" offered Cameron, facing the others again.

Arianna was directed by Dominic to offer a glass to each man and I followed her around the circle, pausing briefly to pour their cognac. When it came to pouring Cameron's drink, he didn't seem to see me. He merely held his glass out for me to fill.

"Where's Booth?" asked one of the men.

"He'll be joining us next month," explained Cameron. "He's otherwise detained."

With a gesture of his hand, Cameron directed Arianna and I to stand back a little, poised ready should they require a top up. Knowing Cameron's decadent nature, this would be no easy wait. Though from what I'd gathered from that terse interaction with Dominic, Cameron wasn't expecting me.

The only clue to Cameron's aggravation with whatever they were discussing was him circling his signet ring. Chrysalis's emblem of a lion's face caught the light.

"It's time to monetize," said one of the men, his face handsome in a rugged kind of way, his salt and pepper hair hinting he was in his forties.

"Lance, we've discussed this issue before," said Cameron. "My concerns remain the same. We uphold the trust of our elite members. Their privacy is sacrosanct."

"Hear me out," said Lance. "What if we opened the club up to the public but hosted them at another establishment? Say a private residence?"

"Our members would not be comfortable," said Cameron. "With the crossover of staff, doms, and subs, there would be a greater risk of gossip. Other members mentioning who they'd seen and where. Privacy is our priority."

"They could all wear masks?" suggested another man, who sat on Cameron's right.

"Please," said Cameron. "Don't insult me. Look, we're financially stable. We always have been and always will. This desire to make more profit is tasteless. That's not what we're about."

"We could always break off, Cameron," said Lance. "Start our own club."

"All my staff would be forbidden from partaking," said Cameron. "You'd be left high and dry without the caliber you need to make it work."

"Perhaps we'd kick off in another city," said Lance. "Seattle."

"I see you've given this some thought," said Cameron. "Look, what you do in your own time and with your own money is your business. But it would be without my blessing."

"I'm talking about real competition for you."

"And I'm talking about honoring the code."

"Cole's right," said the man to his right. "These are fundamental changes." He addressed the group. "What Cole has created... There is a very delicate balance here."

"We've mastered a stable equilibrium," agreed Cameron. "Let us continue to thrive with the best intentions. Turning it into a money making scheme would take advantage of our clients."

"Another drink," said Lance, raising his glass.

Taking several cautious steps towards him, I tipped the bottle carefully and poured. He grabbed my wrist and pain shot into my arm.

I froze, terrified I was going to spill liquor on him. "Please, Sir."

The bottle tipped and Arianna caught it just in time. I threw her a glance of thanks, my wrist smarting from Lance's ironclad hold.

Cameron was on his feet. Quickly, he reached for the bottle

and extracted it from my grip. He placed it safely on the side table. "Lance, it's unlike you to be so avaricious. Let her go."

Lance narrowed his dark eyes. "A token gesture, perhaps?"

"I won't tell you again," said Cameron.

He released his grip and I stepped back, nudging up towards Arianna and gaining strength from her arm wrapping around my waist protectively.

Lance took a swig of his drink. "Later then? She can serve as my consolation prize."

"She's Master Cole's sub," blurted Arianna.

Cameron shot her a look so severe Arianna visibly flinched. "Out," he ordered.

She quick footed it out of there and I felt her loss, her strength gone, and went to follow her.

"Stay there," Cameron snapped at me.

Lance seemed to take pleasure from this revelation. "I'll tell you what, Cole—" He looked over at me. "What's your name?"

"Mia."

"Lovely name," said Lance. "Let me have her for one week and I'll reconsider."

A wave of terror washed over me. This really was a lion's den, and getting devoured by one of them was a real threat. Anger rose in my gut that I'd been placed in this kind of danger by Dominic.

Looking at Cameron, I pleaded with him to let me leave.

"Gentleman, I believe we've covered everything," said Cameron calmly.

"No negotiation?" said Lance.

"For God sake, Lance," said the man to Cameron's right. "Drop it."

Lance merely held his sinister grin.

Cameron turned to face me. "Mia, would you like to spend time with Mr. Merrill?"

I swallowed hard and shook my head a little too enthusiastically, causing a wave of laughter from the men.

"Sorry Lance," said Cameron. "You know the rules. No consent. No go."

"I imagine she'd enjoy Pendulum," said Lance, his attention back on me. "I can see it in her eyes."

"Gentleman, I believe we've covered everything," said Cameron.

Lance rose to his feet. "Think about it, Mia. Cole knows how to contact me. We'll set it up."

"She is a fine specimen," said one of the others. "Cole, where did you find her?"

I focused on the print of Carl Jung, drawing strength from his kind face, that look of integrity that was missing from this room.

"Same time next month," said Cameron.

They took the hint. All shook hands with each other and exchanged compliments. They left the room.

And I let out a long sigh of relief.

"You made eye contact with Lance," said Cameron. "That was your mistake."

"I'm sorry," I said. "I was trying not to spill his drink."

"Bend over the desk."

"It wasn't my fault."

"That's debatable."

I rested my hands on my hips. "You made me a glorified waitress—"

"Prove to me your training has not been a waste of my fucking time."

Quickly, I scurried over, leaned forwards, and bent over it. My hands trembled as my thoughts scattered. I was glad they'd gone, yet their cologne lingered like a pungent warning of the power they wielded.

With my eyes squeezed shut, I waited.

"Mia, I'm sorry," said Cameron, lifting me up to stand before him. "I shouldn't take out my frustration on you. Forgive me." He looked so worn, so harried.

I reached up and caressed his cheek. "You look tired. You work too hard, Sir. You need a break."

He ran his fingers through his hair. "What a mess."

"They've gone now."

"They'll be back. With the same agenda."

"Maybe Dominic can write up some legalese to help you?"

"What was Dominic thinking?" said Cameron. "Parading you in front of them."

"He wanted to make them happy, for you. Please don't be mad with him."

"You are so sweet. So forgiving. I'm an idiot. I should have asked you to leave. How could they not covet you?" He shook his head. "And yet I wanted them to. I wanted to see in their eyes that they knew they will never have you." He stroked my cheek and he chuckled. "I shouldn't be the only one to suffer."

"How do you mean?"

"Mia, our time together is drawing to a close."

"Let's not discuss that now."

He waved it off. "This meeting was a waste of time."

"It sounded like you had it under control," I said. "You made some very valid points and most of them listened."

"Greed is dangerous." He caressed the tension out of his brow. "I doubt Lance can be dissuaded."

"The others support you."

He looked sympathetic. "In this room. After they've left—" He threw his hand up in a frustration. "They're probably scheming as we speak."

"I'm here for you. I want to be here when things go well and when they don't."

"God, you're beautiful. I don't deserve you."

"Yes you do or I wouldn't be here."

"That's not exactly true." He turned away and ran his hand through his hair.

Slowly, I dropped to my knees before him and reached for his zip, knowing what he needed, what would calm him.

He pulled me up and nudged me against the desk. "No, Mia."

"I want to."

"Luckily for you." He kissed the end of my nose. "You negate my upper hand with your beauty."

"You always know what to say."

He strolled over to the door and locked it. "I've been meaning to give this to you for some time."

"What is it?"

"Now that I have a good reason to punish you." He gestured to the desk. "Lean over."

I rested my palms on the desk and pressed my butt out and

up. He tugged my panties down and I stepped out of them.

A small, square velvet box rested on his desk.

"You soothe me, Mia." He knelt behind me and leaned in.

Tugging my butt cheeks apart with firm hands, his tongue speared that delicate rosebud, circling and sending shivers. My face burned with embarrassment that he was touching me there. The intimacy of this moment forced me to shut my eyes and endure these foreign sensations. I covered my face with my hands.

Vulnerable. Forbidden. Decadent.

"They will never know what it is to have you, Mia." His tongue flittered, and his warm breath fanned there. "They covet everything of mine. Especially you."

Wanting nothing more than to please him, soothe with my body, I curved my spine and offered myself as I rested my hands once more on his desk.

I knew what was to follow. What had always been looming. He opened the box and the contents confirmed it. Inside lay a silver butt plug bejeweled with a large sapphire.

Arching my spine farther and widening my thighs, I showed I wanted this. I wanted to want this for him.

His left hand reached around and found my clit. "We'll take our time to prepare you."

Following through on his promise, he soon had me writhing on the end of his fingers, his frenzied pace taking me where I needed to go.

"I need it," I cried, begging for it, as though he knew merely dangling the promise of that round rimmed plug would spur me on.

Staring dead ahead, I felt the pressure of it at my entrance, the fullness, the strange sensation of pleasure and pressure as he twisted the plug in. My thighs shuddered, my sex tightened, and my short, sharp cries let him know I needed his fingers to finish.

"No, my darling." He slapped my butt.

I spun round to face him, confused.

"You will endure this punishment," he said. "Do not take it out. It's there to remind you who you belong to."

"But I already know," I said. "I belong to you."

He knelt at my feet and gestured for me to step into my

panties. He tugged them up my legs, pulling them back on and hiding that plug. Cameron rose to his full height, his hands reaching around my hips, his fingers delving beneath my panties, trailing farther to find and twist the plug. Slowly, around and around.

I moaned and rested my head against his chest, swooning with the sensations, this fullness, a drawn out need threatening never to lift.

His hands shifted to my buttocks and he squeezed me into him. "Soon, I will explore this uncharted territory, and only then, Mia, will you know what it means to be mine."

CHAPTER 38

I LIKED SPENDING time in here.

Cameron's office was a peaceful refuge. Although I enjoyed mingling with the other staff and clients, in here I was assured of privacy.

I took pride in being trusted with Cameron's emails, and even taking the occasional phone call from clients. Though most new inquiries were dealt with personally by Cameron. During the day, he worked at his clinic on Beverly Boulevard in Los Angeles, and I counted the hours to his return in the late afternoon. Cameron made balancing his clinic, his on-calls, and managing Chrysalis look easy.

I'd also been tasked with taking care of the smaller issues related to the day to day running of Chrysalis, like the one this morning where a valet had been caught snapping photos in the foyer with his phone. It pained me to report him to Dominic. The young man was fired on the spot.

Cameron had a vast collection of books, both in the library and here in his office. He encouraged me to borrow them, even his first editions that spanned an entire wall. There was nothing nicer than rummaging through Cameron's books, drawers, and cabinets, to feel his closeness when he wasn't here. He was a neat freak and everything was well organized. He had that in common with Richard.

Sipping a latte that Pilar had kindly brought in for me, I set about answering Cameron's emails.

Chrysalis was hosting a ball tomorrow night and guests were

still being confirmed and sent their tickets. The guests loved the exclusivity, apparently. This was to be the first ball I was going to attend. Cameron was going to choose my dress and we were going shopping this afternoon. A lady in Beverly Hills created one of a kind masks and Cameron and I were going to pay her a visit. I couldn't wait.

I was still getting used to this bejeweled plug. It was a pleasant reminder of him and the promise of what this token meant. Soon, he would be taking me the rest of the way. I swooned with the thought. My sex tightened in anticipation.

I tried to refocus and get down to some busy work.

Despite clearing Cameron's in-box, more emails kept coming in. Cameron was a popular man.

A knock at the door made me jump.

"Hey there," said Pilar, smiling.

"Thank you for my coffee," I said. "It's delicious."

Pilar came in, timidly glancing around Cameron's office as though she too felt smaller in here. All this dark wood grandness intimated.

My ass flinched as though she somehow might know what was going on with my butt and that sapphire plug. My face was ablaze with the thought.

She paused before the desk. "Your visitors are here."

I rose to my feet. "I'm not expecting anyone."

Cameron wasn't going to like Richard visiting again. My thoughts soared with how to deal with this.

"Who is it?"

"Ms. Bailey and her friend," she said.

I rounded the desk. "In the foyer?"

"The garden."

"Pilar, they haven't been screened."

"You're fine," she said. "Master Dominic's signed off on it and he arranges all the passes."

I thanked her and hurried out.

Damn, I still had this distracting thingy in. I shook my head, making a mental note to take it out as soon as I could.

Bailey sat with her legs soaking in the pool, her striking titian hair catching the sunlight. Her warm smile greeted me. There was no sign of Tara.

"Bailey," I called out, hurrying over to her. "Hey, how are you?"

"Mia." She pulled her legs out of the water and trotted towards me, grabbing me into a hug. "This place is fricken amazing. Are you really living here?"

"Yes, I got a transfer over as Cameron's secretary," I said. "It's temporary."

"Have you been working out? You look amazing."

"Swimming and tennis. That kind of thing."

"Tennis! Ha, that's, wow. Can you play?"

I shrugged. "I'm having lessons. I can just about get the ball over the net."

She laughed. "Tara's here. She's in the restroom."

Dread shot up my spine that Tara was wandering around inside. "I'm so sorry, Bailey, but you guys can't stay. There's this rule about being pre-screened. How about I meet you later?"

"What are you talking about?" she said. "It's me."

"I know that. I'm really sorry. But they're so strict here."

"Your boss won't mind, surely?" she said. "Tara used to work for him."

Pilar trotted out of the doorway carrying a large tray laden with three glasses of Coca-Cola and sandwiches.

"No, Pilar." I gestured. "We're not allowed."

"No, you have permission." Pilar set the tray down and laid out the glasses. "I was told to treat you."

"By who?" I asked.

"Hey, Mia." It was Tara and she was dressed in a polka dot bathing suit. "That restroom was something else," she told Bailey. "You have to see it. The taps are gold plated. I'm not kidding."

Tara's already exotic complexion, inherited from her Bengali mother, had caught the sun, her tan making her toned body look flawless.

"Hey, Tara," I said, giving her a hug. "How are you doing?"

"Fine," she said. "Nice place you got here. Talk about landing on your feet."

I smirked. "Very funny. I'm staff. I work here."

Tara folded her arms and gave a wry smile. I turned back to face Bailey, not wanting to know if Tara had an inkling about why I was really here. It was better not to go there.

"You don't mind, do you?" said Bailey. "I had to see you."

"I've been crazy busy," I said. "I promise to make it up to you. Hey Tara, you can't swim. The pool's for members only."

She was dipping her toe in the pool. "It's heated. It must cost a fortune to run this place."

"I have a message from Lorraine," said Bailey. "She's worried about you."

"Tell her I'm fine," I said, calling over, "Sorry, Tara."

"No one's in it." Tara pouted.

"Lorraine wants you to know she's in remission," said Bailey, dragging my attention back on her. "Her treatment worked. She's so sorry about everything and she really needs to see you."

"She already has," I said. "I told Lorraine I forgive her. I've put all that behind me."

"You're not returning her calls?" said Bailey.

"Lorraine made me believe my dad was dead," I snapped, a little too harshly.

Bailey folded her arms. "He threatened to cut her off financially and she needed the money to pay for her treatment."

I shook my head. "I helped pay for that."

"I know you paid for some."

Of course, the truth was that Richard had paid for it all. Wiping out her debt in one fell swoop of kindness, for me. He'd tried to do it anonymously but it hadn't been hard to work out it was him. I didn't want to go into that now. "Look, why don't you just give me a second to call Cameron and make sure this is okay."

There was a loud splash.

Tara swam across the full length of the pool.

Bailey ripped off her T-shirt and eased out of her jeans, revealing a swim suit. "If any members want to use the pool, we'll leave," she said. "I promise."

"That's not it," I said, my anxiety rising.

Bailey leaped in and when her head reappeared she splashed Tara, laughing at her.

Pilar returned with a large bowl of strawberries and placed them next to the sandwiches. "Go have some fun with your friends," she said. "Life's too short."

"Who gave permission?" I whispered to her.

"Dr. Cole."

"Really?"

She scurried off back into the house.

Relenting, I hoisted my skirt up around my thighs and sat carefully, not wanting to reveal my little secret or sit directly on it, then I lowered my legs into the warm water. This was actually a nice break from all that intensity. Power-play between subs and their masters went on 24/7 in this manor and it was rare to let my hair down.

I needed this. Pilar was right.

I relaxed a little.

Bailey swam towards me and rested her elbows on the side of the pool and began to share her news, filling me in on all I'd missed over the last two weeks.

She'd applied for a new job in a post-partum wing at Cedars Sinai. And Tara's first year as a nurse was going well. She was enjoying every second. After some reservations on my part, when Tara had first announced she'd wanted to follow Bailey's footsteps and go into nursing, I was relieved to see her so happy. See both of them happy. Bailey and Tara were so cute together. It was lovely to see them both.

Despite my best endeavors, my thoughts drifted to the fact that this was my last weekend here. My training was essentially over and I'd soon be reunited with Richard. Being around him was going to inject this kind of fun back into my life. Yet the thought of leaving Cameron caused gut wrenching pain. I tried to caress it away, circling my chest with my hand, while reassuring myself I'd get to see him around.

It was no consolation.

The thought that what we'd shared was about to end came crashing down around me. My friend's visit had shaken me into reality. Tears stung my eyes and I tried to focus on what Bailey was saying, nodding and smiling away.

They returned to swimming, allowing me time to return my thoughts to Cameron and wallow in every memory I had of him. Every detail. Every single moment shared.

Bailey and Tara unabashedly shared affection for each other.

Their kissing session went on for a bit too long. Still, I loved that they felt comfortable to be themselves around me. Remembering what Cameron had taught me about being in the moment, I made a concerted effort to relax and enjoy my friends.

"We're planning a trip to Vegas," said Bailey. "We're going to announce our coming out to our parents. It's a big deal."

"I'm so proud of you," I said, ruffling Bailey's hair with affection.

"We want you there," said Tara.

"It's a date," I said. "When is it?"

"Next month," said Tara. "We're going to book rooms at one of those fancy hotels on the strip."

"Count me in," I said.

Pilar re-appeared. "Mistress Scarlet says you have to come now."

"Sure." I eased my legs out of the water and pushed myself to my feet. "I'm sorry, guys. Something's come up. I'll be right back. Hang out here. Enjoy yourselves. But don't go in the house."

"Okay, Ms. Bossy Pants," said Tara. "What happened to our sheepish, Mia?"

"Very funny." I waved that off and followed Pilar back in.

Tara was right. My confidence had taken a leap. All those classes, all that schooling from Samantha Harding, had taught me what I needed to get by in a room full of socialites. No, not just get by but hold my own, helping me to pass off as a woman who belonged there. Cameron had given me the most incredible gift and I'd always be grateful to him. I couldn't imagine how I'd ever repay him.

I wondered what Scarlet wanted to talk to me about. The only drama of the morning was the firing of that valet. As head of HR, Scarlet probably had a few questions.

Dominic and Scarlet were waiting for me.

"Mistress Scarlet." I beamed a big smile, though it quickly faded when I saw her expression. "Is something wrong?"

"Oh, Mia," said Scarlet, shaking her head solemnly.

"It's not Richard, is it?" I shook my head. "Or Sir, whatever, just tell me they're safe."

"This has nothing to do with them," said Dominic. "And

everything to do with you."

A wave of nausea—

"You were clearly briefed on the rules prior to your entry into Chrysalis," said Dominic. "No background check means they do not step foot on this property."

"But Dr. Cole gave his permission," I said.

"He did no such thing," said Dominic. "Where did you get that idea?"

Oh no, it had come from Pilar.

And how much more did she need this job than me. I stared off, not wanting to believe she'd have lied to me like that. Not when the consequences were so high.

"Who was it?" insisted Dominic.

"I can't…"

Scarlet looked furious. "Privacy is our priority, Mia," she said. "We have the kind of guests here this week that will not appreciate this breech in our security."

"I understand," I said, trying to placate them. "It's just Bailey and Tara. And Tara was your secretary at Enthrall. I didn't invite them. Honest."

"And you had Pilar serving them," said Dominic, "when clearly she has enough to do."

"Mia, how could you be so selfish?" said Scarlet.

"I'm sorry," I said, heading towards the door. "I'll ask them to leave immediately."

"I'm afraid it's too late, Mia," said Dominic.

My mouth went dry, failing to form the words I needed to save me.

"Pack your things," he said. "A car will take you home."

"I need to explain this to Cameron. I mean, Sir." I moved towards his desk.

Dominic held up his BlackBerry. "Your expulsion came from Dr. Cole."

I let go of the phone.

"I'm sorry, Mia," said Dominic. "His orders are clear. You're to leave this afternoon."

"I didn't do anything wrong."

"She doesn't get it," said Dominic.

"I'll take care of it." Scarlet threw me a glare. "Seriously,

Mia. You took advantage of your position. You're no different from everyone else who works or plays here. You may be in the privileged position of being the director's sub but the rules also apply to you."

"Please, Scarlet," I said, "I'm so sorry."

"You must always consider the consequences," she said.

"My classes?" I said.

"Cancelled, for now," said Dominic.

Scarlet left the room.

Dominic peered down at the screen of his BlackBerry. "Don't bother packing."

My shoulders dropped their tension.

Thank goodness for that.

"Change of plans." Dominic looked straight at me. "Dr. Cole says he'll send your personal items on to you. He wants you out of here. Now."

CHAPTER 39

IF I NEEDED proof of just how much Chrysalis meant to me, this was it.

I was being wrenched out of the place I'd called home for two weeks. After being wrapped in a cocoon of sensual and therapeutic intensity, it was over. I was being pried out before I was ready.

A flailing butterfly, her wings not ready to fly.

Leo drove the Rover away from the manor, now and again glancing into the rearview as though checking on me but not saying anything. My inability to speak gave away I was close to breaking down and becoming the mess no one wanted to deal with.

Fuck, I still have that thing in me.

Spacing out, my thoughts ran over the last few weeks, the days that had bled into each other and my final hours. This made no sense. I'd never foreseen that shame would be the riding emotion I'd have when I left here.

I'd done my part, vowing to surrender with the promise of serenity. I'd honored the code of a submissive and pleased my master each and every day. A sense of betrayal filled me, with no one to blame.

Distracted by the slow traffic and stop and start of lights, I drifted off into a hazy doze.

Nightmares surged into my brain with the brashness of the uninvited. A tidal wave caught me in its wake and dragged me along, pushing me under, the flood forcing water down my throat, drowning me.

I jolted awake.

I gasped for air, as though the dream were real. My knuckles went white from gripping the seat.

The car stopped.

Blinking into the dusk, I found this wasn't Malibu. Leo had driven me to the wrong place.

"This isn't it," I said sleepily. "Sorry Leo, I thought you knew you were taking me home to Malibu." I felt terrible. He'd driven all this way to Cameron's Beverly Hills house.

"My orders were to bring you here," he said.

I sat up straight, reading his face in the mirror and trying to see if he was certain.

"Is Dr. Cole here?" I asked, full of hope.

"His car's here." Leo pointed at the black BMW.

Not waiting for Leo to open the door, I flung it wide, slamming it behind me and running the few short steps towards the front door. Realizing my error, I turned on my heels and ran to the driver's side of the Rover. "Thank you, Leo," I blurted out. "I forgot to thank you."

"Always a pleasure, Ms. Lauren," he said warmly.

Taking the few short steps back, my mind was a mixture of confusion and anticipation.

The handle turned easily.

Cameron rose from where he'd been sitting on the sweeping steps, his face hard to read with that usual intensity. That steady focus was locked on me.

Familiar black and white tile clicked beneath my feet. Above that was the low hung, sweeping chandelier. Before me stood this man whose unpredictable authority was wielded depending on whim, hinging on mood, desire, or passion.

"If there was any doubt I'm a complete bastard," he said. "You have unquestionable evidence now."

"You invited Bailey and Tara to Chrysalis?" I said.

"Yes."

"You set me up?"

"It appears so."

"Why not just ask me to leave?"

His eyes swept over the foyer in a haze of confusion. A look on him I'd never seen before.

"Dominic and Scarlet are really annoyed with me," I said. "I left there in shame. Why would you do that to me?"

"Your return to your master is scheduled for tomorrow night, Mia."

I hung my head low. "I know. It's hard for me too."

"In the Harrington Suite."

My legs wobbled with understanding. "In front of everyone?"

"Per tradition."

The Harrington Suite also represented the end of our extraordinary affair.

I swallowed hard at his revelation. Of course, that's what I'd witness when I'd first stepped into Chrysalis and this had been the warning Cameron had given to me on the first day. The thought of being taken in front of a crowd liquefied my insides and sent a thrill through me that was so intense it threatened to paralyze me. I'd reasoned it would only happen when I was deemed ready.

Was I ready?

I faltered.

My training was complete. An achievement of being successfully trained by one of the world's most distinguished masters. And I had failed him. Failed myself.

Cameron took a step towards me. "I can't prevent your return but I can control how it's done."

"You should have spoken to me first," I said. "You're always so insistent that we express our feelings, our thoughts. You owe me the same privilege."

"I now understand Richard's reservations," he said. "To think it was me who encouraged him to take you to Chrysalis and now all I want is you out of there."

"Why?"

His hand swept downward. "My reasoning is hard to define."

"Have I failed as your sub?"

Cameron closed the gap between us. "You have excelled."

"I don't understand," I said. "We've been working toward this day. Everything I've learned. Studied. Strived to be."

"You've exceeded on every level."

"Then what is it?"

He took a moment to gather his thoughts. "You've fallen in love with me, Mia. The dynamics have changed. The risk of emotion coming into play during a public session is too great."

"How dare you," I said. "You have no right to stand there and tell me how I feel."

Sympathy weighed heavily in his eyes. "I would rather see my own heart broken than ever hurt Richard." He cupped my face in his hands. "Do you understand what I'm telling you?"

"You can't bring yourself to say it?" I said. "Can you."

"And I never will say the words you need to hear."

"Then take me back to Chrysalis."

"I can't."

"What is this?"

"Indulge me. Let me show you."

My heart fluttered as I tried to reason.

"What I offer you is two days with me," he said. "Here in this house. Our final hours together."

"And then what?"

"We face the inevitable."

"I thought that's what you wanted?" I said.

"I only want what is best for you. For Richard."

"Be honest with me, Cameron. That's what I need from you now."

"This is how I feel about you, Mia." He sunk to his knees and lifted my skirt, easing my panties aside. That kiss, that tongue, Cameron's affection was spoken, though not with words. Grabbing hold of his head, scrunching locks of his hair in my fingers, I held him there. A moan escaped my lips.

This was power.

I'd conquered the one man whom everyone had deemed unreachable. Of course he would never admit it. He didn't have to. The promise of what was to follow between us might not have been enough, but it was all we had.

My head fell back and I looked up. "You do realize your chandelier looks like a cock," I said.

"Really?" He blew a cold stream of air onto my clit and then looked up. "I hadn't noticed."

"You've taught me so much," I whispered.

"You're an exceptional woman. The first ever to stand up to me."

"Yes. Yes to staying here with you. Yes to being fucked by you. Yes to whatever you deem I deserve." I brushed my fingers through his hair. "I am nothing if not a good submissive."

He rose to his feet. "The finest a dominant can have." He led me across the foyer.

We entered the dining room, the table now bare. Guided by Cameron, I sat on the end and he gently pushed me to lay back. He tugged at my panties, easing them down and off my legs. He threw them to the ground.

His eyebrows rose when he saw the plug. "You obeyed?" He gave it a twirl, then buried his fingers inside my vagina, simultaneously bringing ripples of delicious pleasure.

Cameron's heavy eyelids revealed his need matched my own. He eased out the plug and I immediately felt its loss.

"How could I not obey my master?" I shamelessly widened my thighs for him. "Even when I believed he no longer wanted me."

"I will always want you." Standing between my thighs, he unzipped his pants and brought out his cock, pressing the tip against that rosebud and easing it in a little way, his hands resting on my knees and widening my thighs.

I grimaced with that first shove. The shock of pain. That burn of pressure.

"This is just one of many privileges I'm going to miss," he whispered.

"Oh, God," I cried out at the fullness of him, my pussy flinching with jealousy, the pleasure rippling through me.

Relief followed when that burn inside dissipated, leaving nothing but pulsing bliss. He smiled down at me when he saw how I swooned.

"Let's pretend you and I will never end," he said, pushing all the way in.

"Yes," I said. "This moment is ours forever."

"This place is our sanctuary," he said huskily.

"You're my sanctuary."

He gave long, hard thrusts in and out, his rhythm steady, his eyes locked on mine and telling me everything I needed to know.

The world fell away. Time was finally ours.

That steady rise, that growing need, my climax nearing.

"Together," he warned.

"Yes, Sir." I lifted my head to watch his erection sliding in and out, his fingers strumming my clit in unison to his thrusts.

I flung my hands above my head, wanton, desperate for this never to end, all this decadence, all this power, all this pleasure.

Nothing would ever be the same again.

Screaming, I came hard, my head slamming against the table, though I didn't care. My hair spilled around me. His warmth filled me.

"See? I am yours," I said breathlessly, lifting my head. "You have conquered me."

He withdrew and cupped his face in his hands. "What you do to me."

"Cameron?" I whispered.

In a flurry of passion, he grabbed me and pulled me upright into a hug and we held each other tightly, still and quiet, soothed.

Never had I felt closer to him. I held onto every moment, my heart aching that these were our last.

Hand in hand, we toured the house, moving from room to room as he showed me what had always been a private haven for him. Each space held a reflection of who Cameron really was. A man who appreciated fine art. Simple colors. Unpretentious décor.

The grand foyer had been a ruse, it seemed.

"There's something I want to show you," he said, leading me into what looked like a study.

The room was smaller, yet no less impressive then his one back in Chrysalis. I gasped, my eyes taking in that mug I'd painted for him at Pottery Play. He'd placed it on its own shelf.

"You kept it?" I said.

"Of course."

"I'm speechless."

"I'm speechless that you're speechless," he said. "That's a first, surely?"

I beamed up at him, thrilled that day seemed to mean something to him.

One of the upper rooms served as an observatory of sorts. There was book after book on astronomy and a long telescope pointed out of the window at the stars.

"You're not spying on the neighborhood, are you?" I said in jest.

"Trust me, anything they get up to out there would pale in comparison to Chrysalis."

"That's true."

It had been Cameron's idea for Richard to take me to the observatory all those months ago. The planetarium, where I'd made love for the very first time. I realized now that it had been Cameron's way of sharing a private piece of himself, a glimpse into his secret world.

"This is the aperture." He twisted the end of the telescope. "It improves the focus of what you're looking at. Want to see the moon?"

"Yes please." Peering through it, Cameron's hand guided the direction.

Awestruck.

The moon's ridges could be clearly seen, its grayish light clearer than ever. It was beautiful.

"The night sky reminds us how small we are, Mia," he said. "We are nothing compared to the magnificence of the universe. That view keeps us humble."

I stepped aside and he peered through the lens. "Amazing that we landed a man on there, isn't it?" He raised his head and stepped towards the window, grabbing my hand to join him.

We peered out at the night sky.

He pointed skyward. "Do you know that we have more technology in our phones than the astronauts had on Apollo Eleven when they first landed on the moon?"

"Seriously?" I said. "Maybe they should have waited."

He burst out laughing. "And spoil all the fun?"

"A few more years and it might have been safer."

"Never wait for anything or anyone."

I closed the gap between us and buried my face into his chest, wrapping my arms around him, squeezing my eyes shut.

"I know," he whispered, dipping his head to kiss mine.

Feeling the comfort of his arms around me, I willed myself

to remember every second, every moment with him here.

"Let's add astronomy to your classes."

"I think my head might explode."

"Think about it," he said cheerfully. "Hungry?"

I broke away and looked up at him. "Shall we order in?"

He tut-tutted. "Not when we have a master chef in the house."

"Your chef's here?"

"I am the chef," he said. "Everyone else is banned."

I liked the sound of that. "What are you going to cook?"

"What would you like?"

We made our way down the stairwell. "What kind of ingredients do you have?"

"Let's see, shall we?"

Simple and elegant appliances made his large kitchen homey. Here and there, a touch of Italy. Warm blue tiles covered surfaces and dark wood furnishings finished off the room.

Watching Cameron move around the kitchen was surreal. He knew how to cook. This was a revelation. A man who'd grown up so privileged knew how to prepare Beef Bourguignon.

Sipping this delicious red wine while sitting at his kitchen counter, I savored not only the aroma of tomatoes and thyme bubbling on the stove but also the eye candy of my token chef. Cameron wielded a knife like a pro.

"Where did you learn to cook?" I said. "And don't say Paris."

"Paris." He took a sip of wine.

"No, seriously."

"I was a student, Mia. It was either this or starve," he said dryly. "My dad thought it best I live off a limited budget to develop my character."

"And quite a character it is."

"Careful."

"Looking for a reason to punish me?"

"With a feisty Mia in the house, I never have to look far."

I laughed and took several sips of wine, melting into this intimate mood.

"Do you own Charlie's Soup Kitchen?" I said.

He went to speak, yet said nothing.

I pointed at him. "I knew it."

"I may own the property they utilize."

"Bet you loved playing monopoly as a kid."

"I was more into the board game Operation." He looked sad. "I knew then I'd never make a surgeon. Kept ringing the buzzer and making his nose light up. Had to come to terms with it." He winked at me.

I giggled; he really was cute when he wanted to be.

"So how did you guess about Charlie's?" he said.

"Your body language when you talk about the place, your tone, the sub-text, that little twitch in your left eye."

"I'm not sure whether to be delighted or disturbed."

"You taught me all this, Cameron, so you only have yourself to blame."

"The most important question is, are you happy?"

"I've never been happier."

He pulled me into a hug and rested his forehead against mine, closing his eyes. Slipping into this loving pose, I wished it was possible to read his mind. Cameron broke away and returned to the stove. He set the heat to simmer.

With dinner cooking, he rejoined me by the central countertop and topped up my glass. The richness of dark red fruits along with mocha danced on my taste buds. Merlot, Cabernet Sauvignon, and Zinfandel had been blended together in an award winning wine. It was delicious.

This buzz soothed my soul.

Our conversation flowed easily.

The time it took for dinner to be ready passed with the ease of old friends spending time together and talking incessantly. Our laughter never ended. Our precious moments unfolded ever more richly for knowing they would soon end.

Those two days were everything I needed them to be and more.

We played tennis, and he won every match, of course. We hung out by the pool, swam, read our Kindles, and made out. We bathed together.

Slept together.

Ate every meal together, and watched movie after movie. We binged on season after season of TV shows at a time.

And made love in every room of the house.

Never had I felt closer to him in these unfolding moments. He was an obsession I never wanted to end.

This was more than goodbye. It was us paying homage to love.

CHAPTER 40

VOICES CARRIED UP from the foyer.

In the haze of waking, I rolled onto my side and slid out of bed. I pulled on one of Cameron's shirts, pressing my nose against the cuff and sneaking in a delicious sniff of cologne.

After making my way out of the bedroom and along to the top of the balcony, I peered down. I took in the foyer, still wiping the sleepiness from my eyes. I jolted awake when I saw Richard. He was dressed casually in jeans and a sweater, his hair disheveled. Cameron was standing close to him, his arms folded across his chest. He'd not made his morning run.

"Is she here?" said Richard.

"Yes," said Cameron. "You look good."

"You too," said Richard. "You look... different."

"I was going for a run—"

"You took her out of Chrysalis?" said Richard calmly.

"I thought it best."

"On the weekend, she's due to come back to me."

"We're returning tonight. That was always the plan."

"Are you and Mia engaged?"

"What? No."

Richard's face was marred with confusion. "Then why did your sister tell me—"

"No, Richard. It's a misunderstanding."

"Can you imagine how it made me feel hearing that?"

"God, I'm sorry," said Cameron "Where did you see Willow?"

"Rodeo Drive. She was with your aunt."

Cameron flinched. "It was a miscommunication."

"One you never corrected, apparently."

"I was being a rogue," he said. "Want some coffee?"

"No. Thank you. You were about to explain."

"We're not engaged. Have I ever let you down before?"

"No you haven't. Never. Why tell them you're engaged?"

Cameron ran his hands through his hair in frustration. "Willow was being incorrigible and I went along with it."

"That doesn't sound like you."

Cameron shrugged. "I fucked up."

"You expelled Mia from Chrysalis yesterday and brought her here?"

"Your reservations about the Harrington —"

"I need her back."

"She never left you."

"You and I both know that's not true."

"You asked this of me."

"And I'm grateful. From all accounts, her therapy was effective. She's calmer. More at peace."

"Please lower your voice," muttered Cameron. "She'll hear."

"You're right. Perhaps I should hide her away."

Cameron flinched. "I fulfilled my promise to you."

"I never asked you to fall in love with her."

My breath stuck. I was half terrified he'd admit it and half terrified he wouldn't.

Cameron turned to go. "I'll go get her."

"You didn't deny it," said Richard.

"I'm desperately fond of her," said Cameron. "She's a beautiful, vibrant, smart, kind woman. What man wouldn't be enamored?"

"I've never seen you like this, Cole."

"Please, let's not do this now." Cameron raised his hand in a gesture of insistence. "We must do what's best for Mia."

"Is this where you tell me she must decide? After an intensive weekend with you here?"

"There was no S & M."

"But you still fucked her, right?" Richard closed his eyes in frustration. "You told me you could handle her. I never once thought to ask if *you* could handle it."

"I have. Everything is fine. You're reading too much into this."

"Have you used these final hours to remove all trace of me from her mind?"

"That was never my intention."

I scurried along the balcony and down towards them, these endless steps taking forever to reach them.

"Mia," said Richard, his eyes lighting up.

Cameron closed his eyes and pinched the bridge of his nose.

I'd given away my eavesdropping, but didn't care. "I'm going back to Chrysalis." I ran to Richard and took his hands. "Cameron's always been clear about me returning to you."

"You still want this?" Richard's tone was shaky. "After all this?" He swept his hand in a gesture. "I can never give you this."

My hands slipped from his. "It was never about—"

"Richard, that's unfair," said Cameron.

"Then what is it about, Mia?" asked Richard. "You let him remove you from Chrysalis? You left there willingly."

Cameron's glare was locked on me. As was Richard's, and in that moment my thoughts fractured into a thousand pieces of confusion.

"This is my doing," said Cameron. "She's innocent. I took advantage—"

"No," I said. "I wanted this. All of it. Cameron, you've helped me so much. Richard, you were right. My time at Chrysalis has been cathartic."

"I didn't let you down?" asked Richard. "Pushing this on you?"

"No. I like the person I've become." I smiled over at Cameron. "I've never felt more empowered."

"Are you coming back to me?" said Richard.

I managed a nod, knowing it was what Richard needed to hear and having caught that subtle blink from Cameron.

"Kneel," ordered Richard.

I hesitated, my hands dropping from his.

"Mia," soothed Cameron, "kneel for him."

I sunk to my knees and bowed my head.

The silence that followed served its purpose and stunned me into submission.

Cameron approached and he knelt before me. "Go back with him. Your master will take good care of you now."

"But what about the ceremony?" I said, despite having once feared it, now it was all we had left of what we had been.

"Postponed for now," said Cameron.

"Have I done something wrong?" I said.

"Not you, Mia," said Richard. "Cameron's making this harder on everyone."

"Not true," said Cameron, rising to his feet. "It's a case by case situation."

"See, Mia? You're just a case to him."

Again that silent language shared between friends, a relationship seeming more fragile than it ever had been.

"That is correct," said Cameron with a confident nod. "This particular submissive has been one of my more interesting cases."

My hand shot to my mouth to stop a gasp.

Those black and white tiles were flawless. Polished to perfection. Not one smudge on any of them. The glint from the chandelier reflected.

Cameron looked down upon me. "I am thrilled with your progress, Ms. Lauren. Your response times are excellent. Your ability to obey your master exceptional." He paused, his brows raised as though deep in thought. "Richard, I do believe you'll be happy with her training. She enters subspace quickly upon command. Her aural skills are exquisite. My work is done."

A wave of lightheadedness overcame me.

The realization that all this had been part of the process caused my insides to curl into a tight ball. The terrible torment of a truth that had been glaring all this time.

I'd believed this delusion of my own making.

"Mia, rise," said Richard, and he held his hand out to me.

On my feet now, though a little unsteady, I reached out and took Richard's hand, dazed by his ocean blue eyes. I didn't want to look at Cameron. Couldn't cope with seeing that what we'd shared meant nothing to him.

"Go and get dressed," said Richard. "We're leaving."

"Yes, Sir," I said, and trotted up the stairs, shoving down this hurt where it belonged. A familiar ache that I knew so well. A familiar place that I'd long ago learned how to deal with.

Returning to the bedroom, I quickly pulled on my jeans. Those bed sheets were still tussled from a morning of lovemaking. There sat an empty bowl once filled with fresh fruit that Cameron had fed me for breakfast. This, his bedroom, where I'd never known a deeper sleep. My master's sanctuary that I would never know again.

Refusing to remove it, I tucked Cameron's shirt into my jeans.

I headed on out.

Back in the foyer, only Richard was waiting for me. I looked around for Cameron and didn't see him. Richard told me it was easier this way.

The journey back to Chrysalis in the front passenger seat of Richard's Rubicon Wrangler felt dreamlike. A surreal mixture of pride that I'd completed my training, but also a lingering sense that Cameron and I still had shadows to throw light upon. More time with him was a luxury I'd never know.

Leaving him was gut wrenching.

Despite Richard's accusation that all this decadence had drawn me towards Cameron, he couldn't be further from the truth. Cameron's blinding brilliance had been all it took. What we'd had was clung to and hidden deep inside where no one could ever reach it. It was mine to cherish.

Richard drove the jeep hard, as though each thrust of the gear stick represented his frustration that my thoughts were still in that house.

As though he knew.

"Cameron's not capable of love," said Richard, finally breaking the silence. "That's why this was a safe decision for us."

His words stung. "I was never part of the decision."

"You could have refused."

"I was scared I'd lose you."

He reached for my hand and squeezed it. "I had to make a choice. Do what was right for you. You needed to work on what was causing you pain. We knew it was subconscious. That only a doctor with Cole's skills—"

"Did you know how he was going to get me to break?" I said, turning in my seat to look at him. "In a dungeon that I wasn't allowed to leave?"

"Each case is different."

"Can you imagine my fear?"

"I knew he would never hurt you," he said. "He didn't, right?"

"No." *He loved me.*

And I'd allowed myself to love him too.

Richard pulled the jeep over to the curb and killed the engine. "Cameron helped you?" He searched my face for the answer.

"I feel different," I said. "Stronger. Clearer."

"He resolved your pain?"

"Yes, is that how he helped you?"

"No, it was different. What he did to me was…" He waved it off, refusing to share it. "Are you happier?"

I braved to look at him. "I've never felt more fulfilled."

He seemed relieved. "You want to continue with this lifestyle?"

"More than ever, Sir."

He closed his eyes for a few seconds. "Good."

"Cameron saved my life," I whispered it.

Richard reached inside his left jacket pocket for his BlackBerry and glanced at the screen.

"Is it Cameron?" I said. "What does he say?"

"You're in love with him?" murmured Richard, tucking the phone away.

"I'm in love with you." I reached for his hand, needing to feel his warmth, his affection, his approval. "I've learned how to please you."

"You're still wearing his shirt?"

I shifted uncomfortably.

"Mia." His tone was quiet, soothing. "The transition back to me must be swift. You're obedience must be sure. Without any questioning."

"Yes, Sir."

"You know you can talk to me?" he said. "You can tell me

anything?"

"Just take me home."

"Malibu?"

"Bel Air," I said. "Take me back to Chrysalis."

"Cameron won't be at the party tonight," said Richard. "It's better this way."

"I know."

"You will be presented to me. Everyone will witness that you are mine. And mine alone. Let there be no mistake, Mia, I am your true master."

"I know."

"In lieu of an affirmation in the Harrington Suite, which I might add you are in no way ready for—"

"But I am—"

"Cameron was meant to prepare you to excel in this level of intimate experience, and I can see from the reticence in your eyes that he fell short."

"That's not true—"

"Please don't interrupt me." Richard turned the key and steered the Jeep away from the curb, sliding back into traffic. "I've planned an event tonight that will see you returned to me publically, and will leave no doubt that you are once again my submissive."

Trying to read his expression, I waited. When I could wait no more, I whispered, "What are you going to do with me?"

"I'm going to auction you off, Mia," he said. "To the highest bidder."

CHAPTER 41

"THE ART OF Shibari," said Scarlet, "represents the honor of a beloved captured prisoner."

She'd brought me down to one of the red walled dungeons and instructed me to hold my arms above my head and separate my legs slightly in order for her to bind me in thick rope. She spiraled geometric patterns around my body and over my half corset. My breasts were bare, my nipples decorated with bejeweled gold bands and sapphire beads, their positioning bringing an erotic tingling to those already sensitized buds. Scarlet had first worked me over with a whip.

This was how I was to be presented to the members of Chrysalis.

I forced myself not to think of *him*.

Turning my attention back onto Scarlet, who weaved rope with precision, I begged my mind not to return to his Beverly Hills home. All those fond memories were now tainted by truth. Cameron's last words cut deeper than any knife. Tears stung my eyes as I recalled his final speech.

I'd merely been one of his cases.

Staring ahead, I willed this heartache to lift. Seeing him from time to time was all I had to look forward to.

I should hate him. But I couldn't. Cameron had freed me from pain and I held on to that at least.

The auction was imminent.

Scarlet looked stunning, dressed in her leather dominatrix bodice and stockings, her black gloves off for now for ease of tightening the knots.

"How does this one feel?" she asked softly, careful not to break the trance she'd lured me into.

"Good, thank you, Mistress Scarlet." I watched her nimble fingers as she crisscrossed rope between my breasts. Giving small gasps, I was soothed by the sensation.

She knelt before me and continued tying with an expert hand. "Shibari comes from Hojo-Jutsu." She looked up at me. "The martial art of restraining captives in Japan. These bindings were used by ancient samurai warriors to restrain their prisoners. This technique took a great deal of time and expertise and therefore proved that the samurai honored their captured prisoner."

"It feels dreamy," I whispered.

"I'm well trained in rope bondage," she said. "I'll soon have you rope drunk. Euphoric. During the auction, you'll be lulled so beautifully that everyone will be drawn to you. And the bids will no doubt be high. The money's going to Charity Wells in Africa, bringing safe drinking water to millions. It's one of Chrysalis's favorite charities."

It felt good to be part of something so wonderful. "And Richard bids the highest?" I said.

"Of course," she said. "Everyone here knows you're to be won by him. They'll honor his bid."

"And then I go home with him?"

"First, he'll take you to the master's domain in the dungeon." She tightened the rope around my left thigh. "Richard will wish to spend time with his prize."

"Mistress, why did Dominic have me sign that contract?" I said.

"It's a formality," said Scarlet. "If someone bids higher, it would mean you honor their bid and agree to submit to them. You would go willingly with them. You're just signing off on the auction. You know Dominic, always wants to get everything in writing."

"I suppose that's his job," I said. "Protecting the manor."

"Protecting the client too," she said. "And as we're transitioning you over to a new master, we need to ensure you consent to the transfer of power."

"Richard was always my master," I said. "He just had Cameron train me."

Our eyes met and Scarlet seemed to know it was the lie I needed to believe.

She tugged the rope between my thighs. "Get your mind on your new master." She pulled the rope up. "It's best you look forward."

I bit my lip. "I feel dizzy."

"The rope stimulates pressure points," she said. "Your Ki energy. Your life force." She caressed my thigh. "I feel it too, Mia. I'm sharing your flow, feeding off your rush." She brushed a strand of hair behind my ear.

My cheeks flushed as pleasure spiraled in my chest. "I like it."

"Perfection." Scarlet stood before me, admiring her handiwork. "You are an exquisite piece of art."

"Thank you for being here," I said.

"You've reached the level of an honored submissive, Mia. By now, you know how special you are. That we, the dominants, take pleasure in keeping you in subspace, freeing your spirit, and in doing so we free ours."

"It's dreamlike," I murmured.

She gave the rope on my lower abdomen another tug and it rubbed against my sex. "This is one of your seven chakras," she said, gesturing between my thighs. "Feel the vital energy building and allow it to move upward through your center and into your highest chakra on the top of your head. Think of it as a fountain spurting light." She leaned into my ear. "S & M is about raising consciousness."

"I feel it," I whispered, closing my eyes and surrendering to her rhythmic tugs, the sensation of rope vibrating.

"Is that nice?" she said softly, tugging some more.

"Yes, Mistress." I leaned into the pleasure.

The scent of jasmine and roses filled my nostrils; the scent of Scarlet.

"Cameron has transformed you into a masterpiece," she whispered.

Subspace, I slipped into it, freefalling, letting go, wishing I could stay in this place forever. I melted into the rope as though it had always been part of me.

The softest words stirred me from this trance. "You're ready." Scarlet clasped my hand and led me towards the door.

A jolt of excitement raced through me. I was about to take my rightful place here in Chrysalis.

The house was full of guests.

They'd stepped out of those photos in the Harrington Suite, or so it seemed. The men were all dressed in flawless black tuxes and the women wore an array of evening gowns, or merely elegant yet skimpy underwear. All of them were masked, all of them elegant, their conversations animated with the vibrancy of friends meeting again, distance worn easily away by a warm greeting.

Subs were not permitted to wear masks tonight, so there'd be no hiding.

The auction was going to launch Chrysalis's Ball.

Scarlet guided me through the crowd and into a larger room, where the auction stage was draped in black velvet.

Dominic was the master of ceremony. Beside him stood a young, pretty brunette who had just been won in a bid. Shouts from the crowd cheered her on as she was handed over to her new master.

And led away.

The lights were dim, the music soft and Gaelic sounding. As we moved forwards towards the stage, the crowd stepped aside for us. I stared straight ahead, my feet taking cautious steps up onto the platform, fearing I'd trip and embarrass Scarlet, or even Richard.

"Mia, you look beautiful," said Dominic, greeting us on the stage. "You've come so far from that wide-eyed girl who stepped foot in here two weeks ago."

With a nod, I let him know I appreciated his attempt to calm me.

Turning to face the crowd, I gazed at a sea of masks.

I looked for *him* in the crowd.

A hundred or so eyes stared back. An array of color, extravagant designs, all their emotions frozen by those blank masks. Hushed whispers. New audience members poured in.

Adrenaline surged through my veins as I took it all in. Those high crafted balconies on either side hosted even more people.

All of them focused on me.

Scarlet stood by my side, her left arm against mine providing strength that I drew from.

Feeling weightless, lightheaded, I found all of this surreal...

Now rope drunk, I understood that my half nakedness didn't mean vulnerable, and this was what Cameron had tried to teach me. My body was a temple, and here, now, I represented the sacred feminine. That which provided nourishment, forgiveness, beauty, and empowerment.

Standing tall and proud, confident with my sexuality, I no longer felt shame. Instead I understood the profoundness of elevating consciousness to shed the illusion of selfhood.

Emerging from this chrysalis, I was reborn.

The bidding began.

At the front of the stage, I recognized those ocean blue eyes, and despite the mask I knew it was Richard. Shay stood beside him, both of them wearing Mardi Gras masks. Richard threw me a wave.

Dominic was acknowledging each bid, guiding the audience through the process with a confident and methodical air.

The bid hit six thousand dollars.

Dominic swapped a wary glance with Scarlet.

She gestured to Shay, asking him to near the stage and she bent to whisper in his ear. "Call Cameron. Tell him."

I stared up at Dominic. "What's going on?" But I knew.

He stepped out of the crowd, and I knew those dark eyes, that salt and pepper hair, that regal stance of a man who belonged in the lion's den. The man who'd threatened to take me to Pendulum. Lance raised his hand and called out, "Ten thousand."

Richard threw him an annoyed glare and squeezed his way through the crowd towards him.

Lance and Richard kept their voices low and those around them seemed as equally fascinated as me. I didn't need to hear to know they were arguing.

"Twenty five thousand dollars," Lance called out.

Richard threw me a look of concern. "Twenty seven thousand," he shouted.

"One million dollars," shouted Lance, and he looked

triumphant.

"Any other bids?" asked Dominic.

An argument ensued, voices carrying over the din, but I couldn't catch their meaning.

"Sold," said Dominic, glaring at Richard.

I froze.

An already agitated crowd became a bustling array of men and women. Scarlet argued with Dominic. Shay argued with Lance.

Richard looked stunned.

"Doesn't Lance know?" I called out to Scarlet.

"I'll take care of it," she said, and turned towards the two suits joining us on the stage. "Please, wait." She frantically gestured to them.

The men looked like bouncers and behaved like them too. They grabbed hold of me and pulled me from the stage.

They led me out of there and through the foyer, towards the elevator. Despite trying to wriggle out of their grip, they moved with purpose. Their ironclad hold was unrelenting.

Lance strolled into the elevator behind us and quickly dismissed the suits. The door slid closed.

Richard placed his foot in the way, preventing the door from closing. "Lance, there's been a misunderstanding," he said. "I'm sorry."

Lance's grip tightened around my arm. "My bid was higher."

"No one's ever bid that high on a sub," said Richard.

"She's no ordinary sub," said Lance. "Look, I just donated a million to your charity. I'm the hero here."

"Mia's my girlfriend," snapped Richard. "There's been a mistake. This is a mistake."

"She still belongs to Cameron," said Lance. "I saw no transfer ceremony."

"Cameron gave her back to me this morning. We decided against a public display—"

"So it's okay for you to change the rules," said Lance, "but when it comes to other members we must abide by them."

Richard gave a thin smile. "Lance, she's a live wire. There's no telling what she'll do."

"I can handle her."

"Come on, man," said Richard. "This is fucked up."

"Just how I like it," said Lance.

"Mia, get out of there," snapped Richard.

I went to move, but Lance was too strong. With his other hand, he removed a keycard and slid it into the wall panel. Richard went to speak, but those two men who'd lugged me out of the auction room grabbed hold of him and pulled him back.

Richard lost it.

The door slid closed.

We descended.

"I've heard you can be a handful," said Lance.

"You have to take me back up," I said.

"There are rules. Stipulations. I won you fair and square."

"You knew Richard was meant to win me."

"The highest bidder wins. The rules got skewered along the way."

"What do you want from me?"

"Firstly, your silence."

"You won't silence me."

"You're in limbo." His eyes darkened. "Between masters. The perfect time for a new master to stake his claim on you."

"What about my consent?"

"Oh, you'll consent. I will be able to do whatever I want to you and you'll submit."

"Never."

The elevator stopped and the door slid open. I was manhandled out of there and along to the lowest level. The one I'd wondered about despite Dominic pretending it didn't exist that time I'd ridden the elevator with him.

I wished it didn't exist. This long hallway with wooden paneled walls. The same with the door at the end. The far eastern carvings in the wood reflected medieval images of torture, and if this was meant to illicit fear it worked. Lance used the same keycard and opened it.

"A connoisseur of the dark arts." Cameron's self proclaimed title.

And now I understood why.

Deep blood red walls. A medieval torture room, modernized

perhaps, but there were low hanging chains with hooks on the end of each one. Those strange contraptions, along with the numerous threatening looking collection of equipment. Rusty shackles. An antique rack in the corner with a wooden rectangular frame, rollers at both ends. The kind you saw in old movies where the victim was persuaded to talk with a twist of a handle.

A gallow.

There was a fucking gallow. The kind where the person is hung for stealing food, or something equally benign.

I refused to pass out and find myself trapped in any one of these. Gothic artwork was strewn on the walls, depicting men and women being subjected to severe pain from several devices that interestingly enough could also be found in here.

What the fucking hell?

No, I didn't want to believe it. Couldn't understand how this room had been here all the time beneath all this beauty. Those days when I'd spent pleasurable hours with Cameron immersed in what was probably the lighter sight of BDSM.

I went for the door, but Lance was too strong.

He struck my face.

Stunned, I offered no resistance when he dragged me to the center of the room and secured me to the spiked Saint Andrew's Cross. Tiny metal points dug into me, creating slivers of stinging pain across my back and buttocks.

The room came back into view.

His face.

My tears poured, unceasing.

Lance was going to rape me.

He stepped before me, his arms folded. "Submit."

"Fuck you," I said. "If you so much as touch me again, I'll report you to the police."

He laughed. "In less than a minute, you're going to ask me to fuck you."

"You're delusional."

"Richard Booth…Sheppard," he said. "Ah, see, we have a reaction."

"What about Richard?" I tried to stay calm, stay focused.

"What if the general public, namely those who lost their

homes and investments due to his father's illegal activity, find out that Richard lives in Los Angeles now?"

"You wouldn't do that," I said. "You're his friend."

"Do we look like friends?"

"No." I shook my head. "Please, Lance."

"You will address me as Sir."

"This is not how it's done, Sir. We're meant to trust each other."

"Look around you."

My eyes darted around, hating his connotation. "Please, I can't."

"You have thirty seconds to consider my offer," he said.

Lance seemingly got his answer. He busied himself, choosing the music for what was about to become the soundtrack to my pain. The atmosphere was set, the lights dimmed, the hypnotic lyrics flowed in a language I couldn't understand.

I screamed.

"Is that your answer?" he said, and he was back, tracing a forefinger across my throat.

The door opened.

He walked in with the sternness of a predator. The intensity of a man who knew he ruled the room and was ready to take the power back.

Cameron.

Richard was right behind him, as was Scarlet, Dominic, and Shay.

"Cameron," I called out to him.

He gave me a look of reassurance. "Has he touched you?"

I gave a shake of my head.

"That's lucky for you," said Cameron to Lance. "Get her out of this."

Richard rested his face in the crook of my neck, his expression full of relief. Fiddling with the leather straps, he quickly freed me. "Are you all right?"

"Mia consented," said Lance. "Didn't you?" He gave me the longest glare that shared his silent intent.

That threat still between us.

My lips trembled. "Yes, Sir, I did consent."

Confusion marred Cameron's face. "I doubt that."

"Tell them you want to come with me," said Lance. "That you're coming home with me. I won you in the auction. Tell them you are thrilled to be going home with your new master."

It was too late for me.

"Mia?" said Cameron, fracturing the silence.

"I want to go with Lance," I said. "It's what I want."

Cameron lifted my chin. "What did he say to you?"

"It's for the best," I said, throwing a glance at Richard.

Tears stung my eyes, but there was no choice. No way out. Richard was in too much danger if I refused to leave with Lance. The enemies of his father would come after him.

A flash of fury shone in Cameron's eyes. He stormed to the back of the room, pulling open metal drawer after drawer, searching, a clang of instruments, his fingers trailing through them. He came at me with a knife.

Lance staggered out of the way.

I flinched, gasping.

"The rope, Mia," said Cameron calmly, sawing through the Shibari knot on my shoulder, loosening it, and unraveling the others until he'd freed me. "I'm still your master," he said firmly. "I decide what you want and when you get it. Do you remember that?"

"Yes, but—"

He shook his head. "No negotiation." He looked over at the others. "Out." He rested his hand on Richard's shoulder. "You too, buddy."

"I'm not leaving," said Richard.

"Yes, you are. Dominic, you're staying," said Cameron.

Richard looked uncomfortable. His stare left me and found the manila envelope Dominic held. He shared a stare with Cameron.

They exited the room, leaving Dominic behind. I wished I could have followed.

"Lance," said Cameron. "Your money will be refunded."

"I don't want it," said Lance. "I want her."

"This is not going to happen," said Cameron.

"How about," began Lance, "you agree to open another house in L.A. and brand it with Chrysalis's logo? I run it."

"Out of the question," said Cameron. "We've discussed this.

You've been given my answer."

"What happens when members hear about how you and Richard bend the rules to serve your own needs?" said Lance.

"There will be no further mention of this," said Cameron. "Mia is coming with me."

"Everyone will hear about how you really treat your patients," said Lance. "The rumors of how you counsel your damaged clients. The Board of Medicine is going to have a field day with this revelation."

"Sir," I said. "Let me go with him."

"Mia," said Cameron. "I do not remember giving you permission to speak."

"It's over for you, Cole," said Lance.

"Or." Cameron reached out his hand.

Dominic placed that manila envelope into it.

Cameron slid out a piece of paper and held it up for Lance to see. It contained the image of a dove with a long sprig of green and gold between its beak.

Lance glared at the symbol. "I take it you have something like this on each one of us?"

"Insurance," said Cameron.

Lance gave me a sideways glance. "And what happens when the board finds out you're keeping secrets that threaten each and every one of us in this manner?"

"They won't," said Cameron. "Because you won't tell them. Your membership is withdrawn. You are no longer welcome."

"I'm a member of the board," said Lance.

"Were," said Cameron. "And if I ever see you near any member ever again, I will personally see that each and every one of your shareholders find out where their money is actually going."

Dominic stepped forwards. "Transfer all the money from the Cayman Islands," he said, "and return it to those whom it belongs to."

"That's extortion," said Lance.

"That's not the definition of extortion," said Cameron, grabbing hold of my arm and pulling me towards him. "This is the result of you threatening what is mine."

"I'm not going to hurt her," said Lance.

"No, this is me protecting you from her," said Cameron. "If I let go, you're in trouble."

"Fuck you," said Lance.

Cameron studied my face "Mia?" He caressed my lip with his thumb. "Is that a bruise?"

Lance cringed.

Cameron's nostrils flared, and rage filled his eyes. He swung wide, punching Lance hard in the face, sending him flying backward. "Ever touch any of my friends again and I will end you."

Hand in hand, Cameron and I strolled out of there, leaving Dominic to deal with what was left of Lance's eviscerated ego.

We stepped into the elevator.

And ascended.

In silence.

Cameron shrugged out of his jacket and wrapped it around my shoulders. The welcome warmth reminded me that even my bones had been chilled.

We jolted to a stop.

Cameron grabbed my wrist and led me out. The others were waiting in the foyer.

"Get her coat," he snapped to Scarlet.

"I'll take her home," said Richard.

"No," said Cameron, "you had your chance."

"What are you talking about?" said Richard.

"You call this protecting?" Cameron pointed to the elevator.

"You can't blame that on me," said Richard. "The auction went wrong."

"I'm taking her somewhere safe," said Cameron. "She needs time to recover."

"That much is clear." Richard pressed his hand to Cameron's chest. "Thank you for coming so quickly. I've got it now."

Scarlet removed Cameron's jacket and wrapped a coat around my shoulders. "It's mine," she told me. "Keep it." She handed Cameron his jacket back.

Cameron led me across the foyer and towards the front door.

"Where are you taking her?" said Richard.

"She's just been threatened." Cameron glared at him. "Get

out of our way."

Richard neared me. "Is this what you want, Mia?"

"I can't think straight," I said.

The fresh air hit us with a burst of cold. Cameron's BMW was idling right out front, guarded by a valet. He'd literally driven here and run inside. He guided me around to the passenger seat and opened the door, nudging me in. He rounded the car, climbing behind the wheel.

Richard banged on my window. "Get out of the car, Mia."

In a haze of confusion, I reached for the handle, but my door was locked. The BMW took off, shoving me back into my seat—

Leaving behind Richard, Dominic, Scarlet, and Shay on the steps.

Chrysalis, this cocoon of safety I'd grown to love, was soon behind us.

"Where are we going?" I said, tugging my seatbelt round.

"I should never have let you come back," said Cameron. "What the fuck was I thinking?"

"It wasn't Richard's fault," I said.

Richard's face, when we'd driven off, was haunting me, yet here was Cameron, driving with the passion I longed for. Accelerating around the corners too tight, our frantic speed matching his mood.

"You're angry with me?" I said. "Because I went willingly?"

He flashed a sideways glance. "I sent you away, Mia. I forced you away with cruel words that I didn't mean." That wave of his hand was a warning this conversation was over.

Gently, and trying to be discreet, I eased off those sapphire nipple rings, cringing at the awful ache where blood flooded back in. I tucked them into my coat pocket.

We drove on in silence.

Until I couldn't cope with the tension between us. "You have a gallow," I said. "Why do you have a fucking gallow?"

"They're pieces from around the world," he said, flashing an amused glance my way. "My predecessor collected them. They aren't used."

"They better not be," I said. "They look very dangerous."

"Prisoners were actually put to death on those things."

"You told me there aren't any ghosts in Chrysalis."

"Are you suggesting that discarnate souls followed the piece of equipment that they're killed on all the way from London to America?"

I shifted in my seat. "Have you never seen an episode of Ghost Explorers?"

"No."

"Maybe you should."

He reached out and grabbed my hand. "God I missed you."

"I missed you too." I reached for his hand and kissed it, pressing it against my lips, needing this to soothe me.

"Can I have my hand back?" He smiled at me. "I need to make a call."

I let go and settled back, listening to him speak with a concierge, asking about a suite. He was booking us into a hotel.

He hung up and gave a nod, as though satisfied with that decision.

"What was that symbol you showed Lance?" I asked.

"It's represents a bank in the Cayman Islands," said Cameron. "I'm sure you got the gist of what he's been up to."

"He stole all those people's money?"

"I was waiting for the right time to spring it on him," he said with a degree satisfaction. "You brought my agenda forward."

"Thank you for saving me."

He shook his head and said softly, "Mia, it's you who's saving me."

CHAPTER 42

STRETCHING LANGUIDLY, I awakened from sleep greeted with the scent of coffee.

The bed dipped and Cameron sat beside me, holding a cup. "Here you are."

I shifted up the bed frame and took it from him, wiping sleepiness from my eyes. "What's the time?"

"10 AM," he said. "I didn't want to wake you."

Looking around, I got my bearings. That's right. We'd gotten a room at the L'Ermitage in Beverly Hills.

He ran his thumb over my lip. "You have a bruise. People will think I did that to you." He shrugged. "How did you sleep?"

"Well, and you?" I blew on my coffee.

"Careful, it's hot," he said. "I slept a few hours."

I reached up to touch his face and brushed my fingers over his stubble. "You didn't sleep, did you?"

He seemed to relax with that. "Why, look at that?" He flashed surprise as he eyed the clothes on the chair. Brand new jeans and a cashmere sweater, and matching underwear. A new coat.

"Where did those come from?"

"The hotel fairy."

"Are shops open at this time?"

He gave me a look. For him, everything was open.

Cameron squeezed my hand. "I called Richard. Told him you're safe. We talked for a while. He understands."

"Really?"

He scratched his chin. "He wants what's best for you."

"Richard didn't take it well, did he?" I said.

"I told him I need more time."

"And how did he react to that?"

Cameron dragged his teeth over his bottom lip. "With the creative use of expletives."

"He freaked out?"

Cameron raised his brows.

"Oh God."

"I'll handle it. This is my doing."

"Perhaps I should call him?"

"He's not the only one who needs protecting, Mia. You do too."

"What's the plan?"

"Breakfast."

I gave a nod, allowing him these temporary moments to drag out, trying to avoid the inevitable that seemed to be stalking us.

Cameron took my mug from me and set it down. "I have something to tell you."

"Oh?"

He gave a nod and leaned in, cupping my chin and kissing me fiercely. I melted into him, giving myself over, our mouths tussling, our tongues caressing. His hands now gripped either side of my head. His mouth forced mine open. That lash of his tongue made my insides melt. My heart coiled from a sudden shiver.

He broke away and said, "You are extraordinary."

His words were laden with meaning.

"Your happiness is all I care about," I said.

"Then choose us something off the menu." He beamed at me. "I'll order room service."

A wave of joy. "Thank you, Sir."

We ate breakfast in bed.

Waffles, and strawberries, and more fresh coffee. And I licked syrup from his fingertips after he'd dipped a strawberry in it and fed the fruit to me.

I couldn't remember ever being happier.

We checked out of our room by merely leaving the key in there. We rode the elevator in silence.

Thoughts of leaving him again caused my insides to ache. I'd never hated the unknown more.

We stepped out of the hotel foyer, greeted by crisp morning air. Standing on the steps of the L'Ermitage, we waited for the valet to bring round Cameron's BMW.

We cuddled.

"You never did work out how nature truly thinks," he said. "Did you?"

"I have an idea. Not that I'm sharing it with you though."

"Keeping secrets from me?"

"Perhaps that's the way nature thinks," I said sheepishly.

"Very clever, Ms. Lauren."

"That's not the answer though, is it?"

He kissed my forehead.

"Well I'm going to say it, even if you won't," I said.

Cameron looked down.

I prodded his stomach. "Those were damn fine waffles, Sir."

He shook his head, laughing off my mischief. "I have a gift for you." He reached inside his jacket pocket. He handed me a small gift wrapped in silver paper.

Ripping it open, I pulled out the trinket. "A key ring." I admired the diamond encrusted double decker bus. "It's adorable." I wrapped my arms around him again. "It'll go everywhere with me."

"Actually, it's a clue." He broke away to tip the valet.

"Cameron?"

He lifted my chin. "Our plane is fueled and ready at LAX."

"Passport," I said. "I don't have…"

But from his expression, I gathered he'd already thought of that. Somehow he'd gotten it out of the Malibu house, and I wondered, "Does Richard know?"

"He's invited."

I blinked up at him. "We're going now? Right this second?"

"Travel inspires the soul." He gestured to the car.

A million butterflies were fluttering in my chest. "We don't have any luggage."

"We'll shop. Harrods is fun. Selfridges. No trip's complete without a visit to Carnaby Street. And I'm sure the Savoy will have a Christmas tree," he said with a smirk. "Even tinsel. The blue kind. The stuff banned at Enthrall."

My thoughts swirled. "We're staying at the Savoy?"

This is all so fast.

My thumb caressed the keychain. "Will we get to ride on a double decker bus?"

"The moment we arrive," he said. "And I thought you might like to visit The Tower of London. There's plenty of interesting antique torturous devices in there for you to peruse. I saw the way your eyes lit up when you saw that guillotine."

I laughed. "Please tell me it's not the same one Henry the Eighth used to cut off Anne Boleyn's head?"

"No, King Henry used a gifted swordsman."

"For a second there, I thought it had a tragic ending."

He grinned. "You are an obsession I never want to end, Mia."

"Sir, are you taking full ownership of me?"

He led me towards the car. "How does a man take what he already possesses?"

I grabbed his hand and squeezed it, letting him know I wanted this more than anything. "Thank you, Sir. For everything."

"This transformation is mutual, Mia."

I stared at him in wonder, recalling the mention of Carl Jung. "How does nature think?"

"Actually..." he said, guiding me around to the passenger seat. "Jung never clarified that statement. What does it mean to you?"

I almost responded, but a curiosity arose, leading me to say, "Something tells me you know the answer." I climbed into the car.

And waited for him to get in.

He settled into the leather seat and turned to face me, his eyes meeting mine. It was as though what Cameron saw helped formulate his words. "Nature brings light to darkness. Order to chaos. It fulfills its promise of bliss."

THE DEEPENING

The Enthrall Sessions

Enthrall

Enthrall Her

Enthrall Him

Cameron's Control

Cameron's Contract

Richard's Reign

ACKNOWLEDGEMENTS

A great deal of thanks goes to my husband. Your support and humor make each and every day special. You really are *my everything*.

My deepest gratitude to my editor, Louise Bohmer. You're always such a pleasure to work with and I treasure our friendship and partnership. You have rock star skills!

A big thanks to my dear friends Diane Eadie, Debbie Stone, Liz, and Cheryl.

My gratitude in abundance for all that you do, Shelly Knox Jimenez, Christine Christmann, and the awesome team over at *Books and Beyond Fifty Shades*, as well as Summer Daniels from *What to Read After Fifty Shades of Grey*. A big thank you also to Hazel Jones Godwin from *Craves the Angst Book Reviews*, your support and kindness mean the world to me. Sue Quiroz, you're such an inspiration!

The dream team Becky Carter Nichols and Nicole Andrews Moore over at Stories and Swag Tours, who always hold the best online parties when my books come out and also inspire me in so many, many ways.

To the incredible Kala Ambrose, thank you!

Thank you so much to the dynamic team from Literati Author Services Inc., Rosette Doyle, Michelle Eck, and Karen Everett. When it comes to releasing a novel, no author should be without you! Your hard work and kindness are so appreciated.

Thank you so very, very much to all the reviewers and bloggers who joined our *Enthrall Her* release tour, as well as those of you who continue to share news of the book's release. You dedicate your valuable time to read and review. I, for one, am eternally grateful to you all.

A wave of thanks to my friends and fans on Facebook. Your enthusiasm is contagious!

And thank you, the readers, who have found a place in your heart for my sweet Mia Lauren.

Made in the USA
Charleston, SC
18 May 2016